SURRENDER

SURRENDER

LEE SCHNEIDER

FutureX.Studio

FutureX.Studio Santa Monica, CA 2022

Cover and interior design by Paul Palmer-Edwards

FutureX.Studio supports the right to free expression and the value of copyright. The scanning, uploading, and distribution of this book without permission is a theft of the author's intellectual property. If you would like permission to use material from the book (other than for review purposes), please contact permissions@futurex.studio.

FutureX.Studio
Docucinema, Inc.
1112 Montana Ave #257
Santa Monica, CA 90403
futurex.studio/books

First Edition: November 2022

FutureX.Studio is an imprint of Docucinema, Inc.

The publisher is not responsible for websites (or their content) that are not owned by the publisher.

Library of Congress Cataloging-in-Publication Data
Names: Lee Schneider, author
Title: Surrender / Lee Schneider
Description: First edition | Santa Monica, CA: FutureX.Studio, 2022
Identifiers: ISBN 979-8-9872466-2-7
Subjects: GSAFD: Science Fiction
Library of Congress Control Number: 2022921254
Printing 1, 2022

For C., D., B., and R.

PART 001

Chapter 001

As a child, Bradley was everywhere on the Feed. Everyone knew what he looked like. It was only as he grew, became a boy and then a man, that he became anonymous. He looked like just another tall, gangly fellow, if you didn't look too closely and stayed out of his personality field. You could bump into him in the market and have no idea who he was.

So that would explain why, when Nora2 came in for her job interview, she didn't recognize Bradley as the star he once was. She was confused. She looked at him with the empty expression she wore when processing. It was just a microclick, a blip of a moment, but Bradley would notice it when their eyes met. They had so much in common, he couldn't help but notice. They were kindred constructions.

Before she came in for the interview, Nora2 had looked up everything about Bradley, of course. That was her nature. It was her build. Ever since she was modded, her mind worked with a beautiful quickness. Her thoughts were supported by vast oceans of information. Not only had she catalogued his background, she also put the data to use right away. She knew how the structure of his sentences reflected how he thought, and she knew what his answers to her questions would be.

She just wasn't prepared for him to look *so different*. Somehow, and she knew this was silly, she was expecting him to look like the boy star she encountered in the Feed. She was expecting him to be preserved as his younger self.

It was important to push these thoughts away. She was interviewing for a job she badly wanted.

They were in Bradley's offices in El Segundo, in the Southern California Domain. These offices were brand new. Bradley was staffing up. There was a sense of movement and bustle on the lower floors and there were footsteps on the roof as workers set up an employee relaxation area. The air handlers hummed pleasantly.

Bradley was not looking at Nora2. He was looking her up on his tablet. She took another moment to study him, understanding at once why she was on the prospective hire list, why he had called her in for the morning's first appointment, and why he would hire her before the interview was over. He was not thin and gangly as she expected, but tall, with dark hair worn long, and golden eyes. His lips were full. His hands were long, with fingers everyone described as sensitive when he was a boy star. They looked sensitive to her now and her heart fluttered. She was instantly attracted to him and he to her.

There were rules around workplace romance, so she knew they could never get together. Their mutual attraction was a certainty, though, because they were both shape-shifters. Nora2 had the newer build, so she was impossible to resist, impossible not to like and be drawn to. It wasn't complicated. She simply appeared as the person the viewer wanted. Her features adjusted ever so slightly. She appeared taller or shorter, according to the perception of the viewer. Her voice seemed to change pitch. If there were many people in the room, she averaged their desires. When there was one, she focused on that person. It was subtle, something you didn't notice until it was already acting on you, and by then it was too late. You were already under her spell.

She knew Bradley had an older version of the same software. The substrates made him shy. He couldn't dynamically shape-shift like Nora2. But he was irresistibly appealing in a way that averaged current standards of attractiveness and delivered them to the maximum number of people. When he smiled, it lit up the room. When he moved, you felt he was moving to you. It wasn't his appearance so much as a state of being. He was called Bradley15, although he never used the number. His father had insisted on the number when Bradley was modded because his father loved status. Bradley had to smile now, looking upon Nora2, whose parents had laid out even more funds to add the number 2 to her name. She was that much closer to 1—the perfect, and unavailable, mod number. Since they were both mods, and both knew it, they spoke in a kind of shorthand.

"I was one of the first," Bradley offered.

"Yes, a boy star. I was just reading about you." She touched her right temple.

"My father wanted it. It was his idea, but all the parents on the leading edge were doing it. The parents who could afford it, anyway. So my parents had to, also. They were like that. They wanted to be in that crowd."

Nora2 nodded.

Then Bradley spoke quickly, his words tumbling over each other, because he wanted to be sure that she understood. "I'm glad my parents did it. I am! It has changed my life for the better."

"I'm glad for you." She took the opposite approach and spoke few words. If she spoke too many, he would see how attracted she was to him.

"You know I have the Basic Success Package," Bradley said.

"Yes."

"You have a combination Support Package and Ambition Package," he said.

"By the time they got to my generation, we could combine packages," she said.

"So you'll be running things before long."

She laughed. "The Support Package is to be sure nobody is threatened. I can learn by your side as an assistant and then..."

"Before I know it, you've taken over." Bradley smiled, the warmth of it spreading over her.

It was exactly the smile that she wanted to see at that moment.

"What about your side effects?" he asked, knowing that every modded person had them.

Nora2 shrugged. "Pretty much the usual. People tell me that I am 'emotionally inaccessible.' They use that phrase. Or they say they can't see me, that I somehow disappear into the background. I have to laugh at that. Can't find me? I'm right here. I think it's a mild price to pay for my enhanced substrate."

Bradley couldn't help but agree. He had seen it all in her electronic brief. She had recording ability implanted. That's why she touched her temple.

She was turning it on and off. The rest was invisible. Enhanced memory. Organizational skills. People skills. The ability to say what people wanted to hear and to appear as what they wanted to see. Only a few people opted for super strength, athletic ability, or musical chops. These were considered lower-order skills, probably because they were practical or had only one purpose. Mods were intended to be subtle and multipurpose.

Bradley had the same side effect as Nora2. He could be emotionally remote. There was nothing to be done about that, no matter what generation mod you got. When you added silicon to the meat of the human brain, there were bound to be some unanticipated changes.

Their first meeting. These fond memories of Nora2 were what Bradley recalled as he was on a long journey. It was a space flight, and long journeys in space made people remember. It was just the way it worked. The mind flooded with the past.

Bradley's cabin on the ship was comfortable. He had a reclining chair that shaped itself to him and turned into a bed when it was time to sleep. When it was early, not time to sleep, he could sit in it and daydream as he watched the star field turning outside the circular window. Everything around him was round. The window, the shape of the stars it held, his memory. The memory of meeting Nora2 for the first time brought up pleasant sensations, which he allowed to wash over him like the rarest of cool air. He could feel their mutual attraction even now, though they could never act upon the attraction, given the rules around workplace romance.

The other memories that came to Bradley during his travel in space were not as good. They were confusing, out of order, and pulled him in different emotional directions. The memories couldn't be helped, though he didn't like them. They unrolled as the ship traveled; a quality of consciousness still not fully understood. It was best to surrender to them. *Just let them flow.*

So, sighing gently because there was nothing else he could do, he let them come, these memories of Nora2 with her modded crush on him, and memories of Kat Keeper who was his one true love, and memories of the fiery onetime lover Ravven who became his enemy, and even memories of Alon6, though he was with Bradley on the flight, close by on the bridge of the ship; cantankerous Alon6 elbowed his way in with the other memories.

Bradley closed his eyes. He surrendered. A memory came right away. He was grateful the memory took him back to Nora2, back to work. El Segundo. Monday. It was recent, this fresh memory, the Monday before the flight.

Most every Monday was the same for Bradley. He came into work on Mondays on the glidepath directly from the Free State of New Zealand, where he had a country home. It was a hideaway that protected him from all the problems of the Change. Bradley was wealthy, but he was not without troubles. The abrupt bump of the glidepath arriving in El Segundo and decoupling from the magnetic strip signified Bradley's return to his everyday concerns. After the arrival bump, the glidepath settled and rested. The doors flew open with a hiss of compressed air and Bradley joined the other people streaming out into the station. He had but a short walk from the station to his office.

The El Segundo glidepath station was small, efficient, and new. Bradley had had it built to serve his employees and show his generosity to the locals. The corridors smoothly guided him and everyone else to the exits, and the climate controls normally kept the air breathable and the temperature down. They weren't working that well today, though.

Bradley noticed the reason: persistent traces of the last extreme climate event. Red dust, flecked with black ash, was everywhere, blowing across the airway he walked to get to his office, and clogging the vents that were supposed to deliver better air to breathe. As he walked, he heard voices growing in intensity. Then he saw where they were coming from. They clotted the front entrance to his building, many more of them than usual. They were protestors who were protesting *him*.

The dust that swirled under their feet and coated their shoes was the aftermath of a fire. The Northwest Dom had burned again, even though nobody thought there was anything left to burn. It heated the air for days afterward. The dust would be gone soon, Bradley reassured himself. The climate controls would start working again.

Since the protestors were in the way, he had to go around the back to get into his office. He shrugged it off—another life loop. Every Monday they were there, chanting and holding signs with his name on them. So there were more of them now. So what.

He coughed. Next time, he would remember to wear an air unit.

He continued up the stairs to enter his office. As he fixed his gaze on the appropriate spot, a device read his eye movement, and the blast curtain opened to expose the window. It let in a spill of sunlight, along with the angry voices in the courtyard shouting his name. He felt something like sadness, but he wasn't sure what it was because of his build. He told himself that he was tired from the glidepath. Something about high-speed glidepath travel made the body arrive first and one's substance arrive hours later. This was documented; he wasn't the only one. He surveyed his desk with its unfinished tasks from last week.

When he was in the Free State of NZ, he enjoyed a view of the horizon every day. He already missed that horizon. There was work to be done here and now, though, with more people, more personality fields, and more demands on him, even the horizon seemed smaller. To make things just a little more intolerable, the global climate controls in the building were also not working well, challenged by the latest climate event as the controls in the glidepath station had been. It was hot in the office, almost as hot as it was outside. He looked out of the window, watching how the heat made the protestors sweat more than they had sweated last Monday. Their shouting spread saliva in aerosolized drops that he thought he could see. He stepped away from the window and gestured at the sensor so that the blast curtain closed. It helped, and the office cooled.

There was a period, in his early days, when he behaved like a rebel all the time, or at least when he was trying to impress Ravven Vaara with his world-changing attitudes. It was better not to think about Ravven. She brought complex sensations into his emotional field which he couldn't interpret. He'd long since forgiven himself for this deficiency, his inability to sort out his own and others' emotional responses, but sometimes he had to remind himself that he had forgiven himself for it. Thinking about his former lover made him think...slower. *That was it.*

He called for Nora2. He imagined that she would be the sort of person to get in early. Bradley checked her office, and it turned out she was not there. Where was she?

Bradley thought he precisely knew the archetypal protestor who would stand in front of his building, angrily chanting, *One, two, three, four, Bradley15 has got to go!* These people lived in single pods on the coastline, housing that was cheap and leaky. They had day-to-day deals with their employers who paid for their housing, or they had no deal with anyone and were squatters. It would be a hardship for them to gather for a protest in front of the building. They would miss a morning of work and yet they did it every Monday. He wondered if he should put up an electric fence to stop them.

But maybe the protestors came from faraway places like Lancaster, where the climate controls were always bad. You had to wear silver clothing to protect yourself from the sun when you went out to look for water in Lancaster. An electric fence wouldn't bother that sort of protestor. No wonder they were mad. Was he feeling sympathy for them? He wasn't sure.

He switched on his virtual screens. The financial reports came up before his eyes, floating in space.

His attention didn't last long. He snapped them off. Nora2 still wasn't in.

"Dictate a note," he said to the room. "Publish in *The New York Times*. 'I should be sympathetic to people who are concerned about how MIND is used. But I can't be because they are ignorant.' No, delete that."

15

He began again. "'I should be sympathetic to the people who protest about my company's clients. But they can't see the bigger picture. Companies like mine shouldn't be considering social impacts, because that's just not what we do. Success is our job, and nothing else. Let these protestors outside my door become involved in their local domain, meet with their local dom leaders, and someday, all domains will be strong together. They will unite into the United Domains of America.'"

"Ugh," he said. "That's crap." Maybe Nora2 was in by now. "Nora2!"

She was. She walked in fast, in a cloud of certainty. "Yes? What's wrong?"

"Nothing. Aren't you late?"

"I am not. This is the time we agreed that I would arrive. Because you take the glidepath in from NZ on Mondays, you are in earlier. But also, something is wrong. I can tell."

Bradley dipped his head once in a brief nod. She had read him perfectly. "I'm sounding like an Old," he said. "It's annoying. I need to sound like a Young."

"Impossible. You're almost an Old now." She tried not to laugh.

He caught her smile, and yes, there was no escaping it. He had aged, and it wasn't good. "I have to try on a Young personality field. People hate Olds."

"*Youngs* hate Olds. You can't pretend to be something you're not," she said. "Just accept it." She waited for his next instruction.

"I want you to fix this," he returned with some heat. The Youngs were the future. At least they were future clients. He wanted the Youngs to understand where he was coming from. "I'm not the Dom Leader or a representative of anything. I don't make policy. I am only running a company...a company that needs Youngs. The Youngs could join us and prosper like we have...."

He trailed off. Spoken aloud, it sounded bad, as bad as it really was. He was terrible at composing sentences. He was better at logic trees, that delightful form of thought processing that he, famously, had invented.

"This is about the piece you were dictating to *The New York Times*?" asked Nora2. It was up on her virtual screen as a draft already.

He nodded. His eyes were pleading.

"I will write it for you." She touched her right temple, activating her recorder to catch any parts of it that he might speak.

"Yes. Please write it for me. That would be perfect."

Something made him want to look out the window again. He gestured the blast curtains open and saw the last of the protesters were clearing out. The guards were moving among them with batons. He had forbidden them from using tear gas anymore. It wasn't humane.

As he watched, he spoke softly, but loud enough for Nora2 to hear. "My challenges are with software and not with people. My decisions about people are simple; I process what is best for people. The rules come from the domain, not from my executive suite."

"To include?" she asked.

He nodded. "It's how I feel."

"It's really Old."

"I know. Just record it—you probably did anyway—and make it sound Young."

"I recorded it and I'll write it up." She touched her temple to turn off the recorder and left.

He called out to her, just a little too late, "That's why you're the best!"

He glanced at his feed. The screens showed a growing list of meetings stacking up. Product reviews, standups with marketing, a sync with the comms team. He silently mouthed an affirmation to make himself feel better, but it didn't work.

"Nora2!"

She was at the door, leaning on it, not committing to entering. "Yes?" she said.

"Bring me a glass of water."

She stepped back a half step. "Really?" Her eyes danced with the boldness of his request.

"Yes, I want one. I want one now. I want to reward myself." This was good work he'd done this morning, tired as he was from the glidepath. He was in the Free State of NZ just a few hours ago and he was tired, but his mind was sharp.

She came back in a moment with a tall, sparkling glass. "This goes on the expense account?" she asked, unable to resist a small smile.

"Absolutely." Bradley drank deeply.

While in flight, he let the memory of that glass of water flow through him and he savored it because it was pleasant.

The feeling didn't last. Soon there was also a memory of Ravven. The memory stood before him, almost as the real Ravven would stand before him, hands on hips, head thrown back, a challenge in her ice-blue eyes. He rubbed his face to make the memory go away, but it stuck with him. He had no choice but to let it come. *Space travel is like that. Just go with it.*

When he was a researcher, his pod floated on the water near what was once called East Palo Alto. There was a double door to keep out the rising tides. Sometimes the valves didn't work, and the place flooded. The bed was two feet away from the ceiling to keep it dry. A couple of times a week, he hit his head on the ceiling when he woke up in the morning.

Ravven had had a good laugh about that. "You're a slow learner," she said.

Ravven Vaara.

The name her parents gave her was Riva Nowakowski. It expressed everything about her mixed Middle Eastern (mother's) and Middle European (father's) heritage, and nothing about her lived reality. As soon as her career took off, she changed it to Ravven Vaara.

Her career made him think of sweat. The memory of sweat came to him. The sour smell of sweat and the way it greased his movements. On multiple occasions, his own sweat pooled around him like a shallow pond. He was an island floating in it.

Ravven teaching a yoga class. The memory of her teaching stormed back. They were doing sun salutes, and in the class he was remembering it was after the 50th sun salute that he decided he was in love with Ravven Vaara. Hot sweat blurred his vision, dehydration was advancing, his muscles were burning, and she stood before him a goddess, telling her class to stand tall in prayer position, swan dive down, touch their toes, reach up, adopt chair pose, straighten, dive down again, jump back, take upward dog, downward dog, and then do it again. He followed her commands. They all did, until her commands hypnotized them.

Then, thankfully, the class was over. Bradley stretched out in the pond of sweat on his yoga mat. He never imagined he could be an island floating in his own salt water.

Ravven Vaara taught the power poses. She had a big following in the SF Port Area. After every class, her students peeled themselves from the floor, rolled up their mats, and gathered around her—sweaty guys, Bradley among them, and a few women, coming to her to ask questions about a pose, sequence, or an emerging injury, but really to get her attention. They were waiting for the light of her eyes to be upon them. Bradley waited with the rest of them.

One day, after class, Bradley felt the light he was waiting for. Mumbling, he summoned courage from somewhere and asked her to coffee.

Ravven laughed and didn't say no. His mod operated on her subtly. She hardly noticed that he had changed before her eyes to become what she wanted to see. She *did* notice, though. She was smart about these things and wasn't taken in. She had looked him up on the Feed and knew who he was.

The next day, even before they ordered, she said, "I don't date students."

He nodded. He had anticipated it, and he liked the clarity of the statement. Bradley noticed people were rarely clear about their needs and wants. Their most simple statements were clouded.

At this point in his life, before he ran a company or protestors shouted his name in anger, Bradley just did research, a simple post-doc kind of guy. All day, he listened to fuzzy academic minds powering busy academic mouths at Uni. He had no money, just a smile that could get into a person's energy field. He had his mod that made him appear the way others wanted to see him. And he had focus. Intensity. He could do fifty sun salutes and keep enough focus to fall in love with Ravven Vaara.

The café they were in for their first date still had containment bubbles up from the last pandemic. The benign but ineffective domain government never bothered to take them down. The domain did not clean the streets on a regular basis. Voting didn't always happen.

The bubbles, though, gave Bradley and Ravven some privacy, which may have been more valuable than all those other things. They could look at each other closely. She saw that he was in love with her, but he wasn't an idiot. He would not come out and say, "I love you."

She always knew he was modded. His name carried a number on his yoga class registration. *Bradley15.* When she gazed into his eyes, she saw the subtle changes to the light in them, to make him appear more appealing to her. He seemed to stand taller when he was near her, and she liked tall guys.

"Since you don't date students, I'm going to drop your class," he said. This was an easy action for him. "I'm going to start a home yoga practice."

And he did, and she liked that about him, the follow-through. Teaching yoga, she was around flaky, undependable people who were in search of themselves 24/7. In contrast, Ravven was strong, like an arrow shooting through the sky. She gave herself the name Ravven Vaara for a reason. She was the embodiment of all grace. Later, she changed everything Bradley knew about his world. But not then, not on that first date. They were like children then.

"Tell me about yourself," Bradley said.

"I am from the south, the Southern California Dom."

"So, you're not a San Francisco Port City native?"

"That's right," Ravven confirmed.

"Why are you named Ravven?"

"It is a name that I gave myself," she said. She had vowed never to speak her real name again and hoped he wouldn't ask about it.

She had an odd accent that he couldn't place. Something was Brit-Euro about it. He didn't ask about her real name. He laughed instead. "I'm never going to your class again," he said. His eyes seemed to her to become larger, and there was a golden hue to their brownness.

"I don't expect to see you there," she said, also laughing.

They were both so innocent then. This was before they lived together, before Ravven tried to start a housing revolution with Bradley, before they stormed the Domain Building and there was an accident because of their faulty equipment. They were arrested together, charged together, and then separately detained.

In flight, Bradley leaned back in the reclining chair in his cabin. The star field hadn't changed in the last few minutes, but he knew the ship was moving. It was troubling to have all his memories leaking out, but he found he enjoyed these memories of Ravven. They were a stone that he ran his hands over to soothe himself.

At the beginning of their life together, their conversations were easy. They found love casually, never naming it, and their physical lovemaking coiled upon itself like a snake with no beginning and no end. Something in Bradley knew it couldn't last because Ravven was a restless person. She saw the big picture, while he was focused on the small moments. While at work, he pictured her shining before her students, assessing their energy and elevating them.

People would ask him, "What are you smiling at?"

He would say, "Do you know Ravven Vaara? I've met her."

They would say, "But Ravven Vaara is famous."

Bradley's mod might start working on them at that point, and they would soften their position or become confused. He enjoyed their confusion. Being modded was a wonderful thing, most of the time. So he let life with Ravven unfold as it should. He did his yoga every morning at home. He worked in the shadows. He was modest. If he skipped a day at school or at his internship, no one would notice that he was gone. His mod supplied sufficient charisma that people invited him into their personality field, and he would study them from that close distance. He took notes constantly. He studied people.

Back in the days when he lived with Ravven, his papers and screens were scattered all over the leaky pod they occupied. The no-term lease suited him. His employer, ABCD Corp, which also ran Uni, the school he attended, deducted the rent automatically from his paycheck, so housing and education were combined and worry-free.

Most things were like that. He liked to tick off his favorite examples to her. A plutocrat engineered a coup d'état to control underground rights in the Americas, opening up a national Metro system that would eventually become the glidepath system, once he developed anti-grav. An online surface delivery corp bought out all the other delivery corps, meaning you only had to pay one corp to send anything anywhere. ABCD started as a search engine and ad platform and now controlled all education from kindergarten to university, and also all scientific research. Three hardware companies made all devices. Life was simple and sweet, as Bradley often insisted. He liked knowing what to expect and wanted Ravven to share this certainty.

Ravven, however, was an ancient soul, and she refused to accept things as they were. Every night, as they heated their food units in the cooker and drank their tea made with artificial water, she attempted to radicalize him. She would point out that all these companies had arrived at their current positions by force.

Bradley liked to respond by adjusting the wall screen so that it showed a pleasant sunset. Most evenings she would argue with Bradley for an hour or so, and then they would go to bed, but one night they kept going at it for longer. The water lapped at the belly of the pod, and she kept talking. Her words wrapped around him. He loved her fire.

He took in the ice-blue light of her eyes. Her hair was a red halo. Her skin was brown, her body strong from her yoga practice. She seemed so long and lean that no sleeping mat could contain her. He had loved her ever since he was her student and his love had only grown stronger the more fiery she became. He tuned in to what she was saying, enough to enter her personality field, as she spoke about the local dom and how weak it was. Like the undrinkable water that was everywhere now, the corps seeped into everything and poisoned everyone.

It was their familiar evening dance, this extended argument, and he gave his familiar response. "It makes everything easier. You don't have to think." He was busy thinking all day and welcomed the opportunity not to in the evenings.

"If you just do more yoga, it will calm you down and everything will be fine," he told her as he usually did. But on this one night their familiar banter broke off in another direction.

She turned up her fire. "Yoga infiltrates the mind. The more yoga I do, the more action I will take. Yoga lights me up."

He watched her carefully, waiting for what she would say next. Whenever she spoke about yoga, it caught his interest.

"It's time to do more," she continued. "You can't say you want a better world, and build things, but never put your ideas into action." A strange thing, but when she pressed him like this, she turned up the Brit-Euro accent, just like when she was speaking to her students. It went with her tall stance and grace. Her cold blue eyes traced over him. It was impossible to see what she was thinking.

He smiled. This was what he liked about her. Nevertheless, he was tired of her arguments this night. This business of "building a better world," it came from a side project of his, something she had pressed him to do, and one he did mostly to please her. The project mapped available above-water housing and assigned it to unhoused people in need.

"Bring your project to the Dom!" she insisted in her crisp Brit-Euro.

It was just a side project, he protested, and he already had tried to get the Domain Leader's attention.

"Do it again!" she commanded.

So he tried again. During several of his lunch hours, he took time away from his research and ventured out of the climate-controlled ABCD Building to jump on his electric bike and ride the bridges above the water in the streets. It became hotter as he approached the Domain Building. The exterior climate control never worked properly around it. Waves of heat rose from the structures.

Inside the building, the climate controls were even less effective. People wilted in the close air. Some sat on worn wooden benches, others on the floor where it seemed cooler, waiting to petition for financial relief if they were unemployed, or for a better water allotment for a sick child.

Bradley didn't like being here, but it felt virtuous. He waited with the other miserable people.

They handed him a tag upon entry, and he spoke his request, the tag recorded it, and therefore the domain functionaries knew what he wanted from the moment he walked in. They tracked his location in the building. He could sit on any bench he wanted and wait to be called. But the Domain Coordinator never came to fetch him into a meeting. Bradley waited one hour one day, two hours the next. The grime and sorrow of the place stuck to his clothes and entered his bones, making it hard to move from the bench when he decided that he had to go. He had had enough of this waiting and misery; he just wanted to go home. On the second day of waiting, he stood up stiffly and walked out, dropping his tag in a slot by the door.

Once back in the pod he shared with Ravven, he walked straight into the shower, hoping for the silvery relief of flowing water, but they'd already used the artificial water for the month. The maker wasn't finished making the next batch. So he used the UV lights instead, standing in front of them for the required forty-five seconds until he felt clean. The sorrow of the Domain Building clung to him anyway.

When he heard Ravven getting home from teaching her last class of the day, he called out a hello, waited until she put away her mat and props, told her of the pointless trips to the Domain Building, and asked, "What do you think I should do?"

Her eyes flashed as she flared up at the hopelessness in his voice. Angry that he had failed even to get a meeting, she unfurled a crazy plan to take the Domain Coordinator hostage. "We will show her your housing app and force her to summon the Domain Leader and show it to *her*. Then they will have no choice. They will deploy it."

"You're crazy," Bradley barked. They argued about the plan until the video image on the wall displayed dawn.

Exhausted, Bradley needed air. He cracked open one of the pod's narrow windows to smell the morning. The window admitted a sliver of sunlight, the good kind, before it became too strong.

With the light of morning upon them, they crafted a plan of civil disobedience. They would enter the Domain Building and storm the Domain Leader's office. To bring more force to their forced entry, they would bring along a micron demolator, the kind used in construction demolition to knock down walls. If the Domain Leader wouldn't open up her office, they would use the demolator to knock down the door. That would get everyone's attention.

Chapter 002

The next day, Ravven bought a demolator on the black market, a cheap one. They put it in a baby stroller to pose as young parents and keep prying eyes away, and pushed it to the Domain Building. The air was hot. The heat controls were working poorly.

The only thing that came to Bradley's mind was *This is a bad idea.*

The micron demolator was covered by a baby blanket with pink elephants on it. As Ravven pushed the stroller, she sagged in the heat. As though she had heard his inner mind, Ravven started talking to his thoughts. "It's too late to back out. This is what civil disruption looks like." She seemed disgusted at his cowardice, so he was quiet the rest of the way there.

Once within range, they moved quickly. They ditched the stroller outside the Domain Building. Ravven carried the demolator and Bradley hurried to keep up beside her. They bounded up the stairs and demanded entry to the Domain Coordinator's office.

At first, the tall bot standing before the door told them that the Domain Coordinator was not in. Since the bot spoke loudly, and its speaker port was a foot above Bradley's head, its pronouncement projected down the long corridor. Then, in an even sterner voice, it asked them to leave.

Catching on just a moment too late, it asked, "Is that a demolator?"

"Yes," Ravven said. She raised the demolator and pointed it at the Domain Coordinator's office door, intending to blow it to pieces.

Once you turned one on, a micron demolator required great strength to keep it pointed in the right direction; Bradley had seen burly construction workers wrestling with the device like it was an angry animal. Ravven was strong from yoga—but not strong enough, it turned out, because she couldn't control the demolator as it swept back and forth, taking out the intended door and also all the windows in the hall.

Bradley dove to the floor to get out of the way of flying glass. The tall bot was nowhere to be seen.

The air was filled with sirens. Ravven found the off switch and let the demolator fall from her hands. It rolled away from her and was scooped up by the tall bot, which reappeared. It had also called in enforcement bots. Small and squat, nine of them swarmed the corridor. Working together, it took the enforcement bots just two minutes to wrist-strap and charge Bradley and Ravven. Then they pinged a judge, who appeared on a vid screen to sentence them.

Restraints could not contain Ravven's fire. She shouted at the bots, at the judge on the vid, at anyone who would listen. "It was a peaceful protest! The demolator was defective!"

It made no difference. The judge convicted Ravven and Bradley of the terrorist bombing of official domain property. That wasn't really what they had done, but there was no charge on the books that covered blowing out the door and windows; bombing seemed close enough. The judge's face on the vid remained impassive to Ravven's protests and then they signed off.

Ravven turned her fury at Bradley, and he did his best to return it. Restrained by the bots, they argued.

"This was a bad idea," he said.

"You are a coward," she returned.

Both assertions were true. Guided by the small but powerful machines farther and farther away from each other to opposite ends of the hallway, Ravven and Bradley continued to curse each other until their voices were torn whispers.

Bradley was ordered to wear an ankle bracelet and confined to a one-room pod for twenty-four months in the Los Angeles Port City. Ravven was ordered to the San Francisco Port City to serve a similar twenty-four-month detention in a small pod, and also forbidden to teach yoga. She protested the yoga restriction, and eventually won the right to teach online. That's how she built her movement again, the one Bradley would become afraid of. Ravven would always be strong, like an arrow shooting through the sky. There was no stopping Ravven Vaara.

She and Bradley would not meet again for many years, when their hatred for each other would only be stronger.

On the ship, while lounging in his bunk, Bradley tried to shake off this memory of Ravven and failed. The flow of memories that space travel stimulated could include some unpleasant ones. There was nothing he could do about that, but he was sick of having his mind jumbled. He tried repeating a happiness affirmation. It didn't work. So he gestured to comms and called for Alon6 on the navigation deck.

"Are we there yet?" Bradley asked, knowing it was a passive-aggressive question.

Alon6's voice came back harsher than usual, sounding busy, with no time at all for Bradley. "Everything is on track. Get your micro-sleep."

Maybe it was the comms signal that was sounding so harsh. Bradley appealed to his old friend. "I'm getting flooded with memories. Is something wrong with me?"

Alon6 brushed this off. "It's the flight. Take the pills. It will go away." He clicked off before Bradley could object.

Bradley sighed and opened the container of pills. He wondered if they would interact badly with his mod. He replaced the cap without taking any of the pills.

There was no sense in trying to sleep, and affirmations weren't working. If he went up to the navigation deck, Alon6 would ask him to leave. Bradley knew that he could be annoying when he was on the nav deck. He asked questions, fiddled with the equipment, chattered nervously with the crew, and made a general nuisance of himself. He wished Nora2 were here. She gave him structure by making good lists of things for him to do.

We should have invited her along. But, Bradley realized, with her on the ship there would be no one to watch over Earthly operations. Sanchez was capable, but he had many responsibilities in Input. And Bradley trusted Nora2 completely.

He flipped through screens, checking his vast holdings, dropping in on the folks at the headquarters in El Segundo. When Bradley surprised them on the vid, he saw that Sanchez was holding a meeting with his cohort in the Input section. They were testing the newest model of the Harvester and feeding the data into the new thought databases.

Sanchez was a good leader, popular among the staff. Bradley was jealous of the adulation he enjoyed as he ran a flawless meeting.

The company would function, but Bradley's problem was that he missed Earth already, and it had only been eight days. He decided that he wasn't cut out for space exploration. This was all a huge mistake. He had gone along with Alon6's vision of relocating their operations to Mars and it was crazy. Worse, there was something behind the decision that Bradley couldn't fully understand. *Alon6 is hiding something from me.*

He was caught up again in Alon6's personality field. He hated that. He cursed, tried a happiness affirmation, and then self-soothed by reminding himself that this was normal. *People get caught in other people's personality fields.* It had happened with another woman he loved once, the best woman he had ever loved—not Ravven Vaara, but Kat Keeper. *Kat Keeper is a good person and even she makes mistakes.* He loved Kat Keeper. He loved her completely, and he had lost her.

Moving through these memories made his head hurt. He decided that soon he would go up to the nav deck, whether or not Alon6 wanted him there. He would have it out with Alon6 about why they were really on this journey and what Alon6 was trying to conceal.

Bradley moved to the mirror in his cabin and looked at himself. It disappointed him to see that he looked older than his thirty-five years. His eyes were still golden and his brown hair still hung boyishly over them, but in truth, his modding had done nothing to fix the aging process. He wondered if the constant changes of shape-shifting were wearing his face out faster than a non-modded person's. There were stress lines under his eyes and parentheses forming around his mouth. After he made it back to Earth, he would put in for resurfacing.

"I have done one good thing in my life," he said to his image. *Maybe the best thing I've ever done. I brought a man back from the dead.*

The man's name was Dave. Dave was rewarded a second life, thanks to Bradley. It was an act of generosity, mixed with self-interest, and, if you didn't look too closely, it made Bradley seem a better man than he was.

Chapter 003

Bradley decided that he would wait five more minutes; he couldn't wait any longer than that. He would go up to see Alon6 on the nav deck. He was bored in his cabin and wanted to get away from his memories. But as he caught sight of himself in the circular mirror, and saw the circular window filled with stars behind him, he was reminded of the single window in his pod in downtown LA, the pod they put him in for detention, and before he knew it, he was back in his memories again. It seemed that he couldn't escape them here in space.

The window in that pod didn't close properly, and though it was the only one, it nevertheless let in torrents of heat and the sounds of motors and wind. It didn't take long for him to learn to keep paper away from the window and the weather.

His tracking ring, worn on his right ankle, was weatherproof, the only thing in the pod that seemed indestructible. It tracked his movements, vibrated with alerts, and had he tried to leave, it would have made all sorts of noise. He didn't try to leave, and didn't have far to go in the pod; it was all of five-hundred square feet.

The food storage worked intermittently, blinking on and off and spoiling his provisions. In the corner, under a piece of olive-green plastic sheeting, there was an old record player left by a previous detainee, the kind that ran for an album's length on a pinprick of blood. He remembered these devices as part of an off-the-grid movement that didn't get much traction. He was tempted to try it, just to see if it worked, but the blood input looked dirty and he didn't want to take any chances with his health.

It amazed Bradley how well solitude suited him. Alone, with nothing but time, he felt he had important business to conduct, and indeed, while he was alone in detention, he was noodling around with a project in the back of his mind. It was in the sketch phase in the moment. He liked to let new ideas develop slowly.

Then his tracking ring tickled his ankle and his chronometer emitted an alert, and he noted with a flicker of surprise that Alon6 was coming to visit him later. Bradley had known Alon6 since they were students together at Uni. He was Bradley's oldest friend, the kind of person who could convince Bradley to take a trip to Mars, and also the person who would try to buoy Bradley's mood when he was stuck in detention. It was not all that surprising that Alon6 would be allowed to visit Bradley in the detention pod. Alon6 was always powerful, and when power wouldn't do the job, Alon6 could always throw crypto at it. He had raised bribery to an art.

Bradley held the casual assumption that the project he was noodling around with in detention would make him rich, even though it was nothing but scraps of paper now. *But just wait,* he told himself. He anchored his paper notes to the table with an empty drinking glass so the wind from the broken window wouldn't sweep them away.

Such bravado was all he had as a detainee. He was forbidden anything but pencil and paper, and of course he was dismissed from his research job. The dom didn't allow detainees to work. But Bradley could work alone in his pod, and he resolved to make good use of his detention time. He had many paper notes. Scribbles, really—diagrams that depicted mental pathways. Later on, these pencil diagrams would become famous. They didn't have a name yet, but would come to be called Logic Trees.

Bradley shuffled through his stacks of paper that he had filled with drawings. He stood at the only window that punctuated the exterior wall of his all-white pod with its table, two stools, a cooker, a food storage unit, and a sleeping mat—always mindful to stay out of the punishing reach of the sun—and waited for more ideas and for the impending arrival of Alon6. He held a pencil, ready to write down an idea when one came.

As he waited, Bradley reflected on his luck. He was lucky to have landed in this pod on the fiftieth floor instead of the others used by the Domain

Detention System. It was quieter, being elevated, harder for the roving bands of looters to access, and there was something like a view.

The Los Angeles that stretched before him was flooded, the result of a monsoon that had swept through the city center. As disasters went, the citizens saw it as something of a relief. Most of the time, Los Angelenos had to cope with drought and bad air superheated by the sun. But now a carnival atmosphere spread through the city, judging by the shouts of happiness that Bradley heard drifting up to his window as the people cheered the water. The rains had rendered the air pure for a day or so; it was turning sour again quickly. The water that filled the streets was also becoming poisoned by toxic runoff.

If Bradley looked carefully, he could see the former grid pattern of streets that remained in watery outline. He watched traffic consisting of motorboats and bikes with pontoons and paddles, vaporetti and gondolas, and makeshift rafts with children in them looking like they were just barely not drowning.

He wondered where they all were going. What business could they have in this wrecked city? He looked at the scene with eyes that didn't see it after a while, as he thought about the next set of ideas lining up in his mind, and about his friend Alon6.

It was easy to guess that Alon6 was modded, and not just because of the number after his name, the obvious tell. Bradley knew Alon6 was modded when he first saw him across the freshman lounge at Uni. It was the way he carried himself, that strut, those bold gestures that referenced everyone around him, and of course, his voice, always loud. These were effects of his Entrepreneurial Ideation Package. At the point of his first encounter with Bradley, nineteen-year-old Alon6 was wired to produce ideas that made money.

Bradley was sixteen at the time of this encounter. He was in his customary position in the Uni student lounge, draped over a couch, coding on a tablet in his hands. Alon6 was wearing the kind of white shirt he always wore, the kind people wore when they were playing an upper-class game everyone had forgotten the name of. Bradley watched Alon6 harass a fellow student who had just pitched a start-up idea to him.

"Let me tell you how that will work in the real world," said Alon6, his voice loud enough to make the other student shrink back. Bradley knew it was only a matter of time before Alon6 got bored lecturing other students, or listening to their ideas (which probably wouldn't make money), and noticed Bradley, who spent as much time coding as he could, head bowed, his longish brown hair in his golden eyes, swiping and typing.

Bradley was a famous figure on campus, as he had entered Uni at fifteen on a full scholarship. The faculty noticed his capabilities right away and named a lecture chair after him. But he refused to lecture, preferring to code. Alon6, wired for profit, would soon realize Bradley was a potential source of income.

And soon enough, indeed, he stood over Bradley and stuck out his hand. "Alon6."

Bradley pulled himself upright and shook his hand. "Bradley15. But I never use the number."

"Ha, you just used it."

Bradley smirked. "Well, you used yours."

"Everyone I know who has a number uses it."

"Not that many people have them and it's elitist."

Alon6 laughed at that. "What does your father do? Where are your people from?"

Bradley told him the story. His parents were early adopters, even though they lived on the East Coast, far from the modding centers in the West. "When I was a kid, I was famous for being one of the first."

Alon6 nodded. "I thought I recognized you." But he didn't, not really, not at first; he only thought he did. It was part of Bradley's shape-shifter mod that he appeared warmly familiar. In the presence of Alon6, his eyes were more puppy-like, and he became the beta to Alon6's alpha, just as Alon6 wanted him to be. Bradley couldn't control this, owing to the early nature of his mod. Later versions offered more control of what became known as substrate flaws.

Alon6, for example, had a substrate flaw. He could fly into a rage over nothing, but he had learned to suppress this as he got used to his mod, and listened patiently as Bradley described his parents.

"Dad worked for IBM at the beginning, but he saw there wasn't enough money in data. So he changed careers."

Alon6 nodded. "Reading the market."

"Yes, and he needed a unique name for his new profession. He changed his name from Samuel to Sasha. Our family name became Power."

Now Alon6 realized who Bradley was. Bradley15 Power was one of the earliest mods. For a little while, he was the poster child for modding. His boyish intellect developed fast, and everyone loved him. The image of the younger boy star superimposed itself in Alon6's memory over the sixteen-year-old Bradley.

Bradley kept talking, about how his dad, Sasha, had switched to real estate, selling virtual worlds. "Dad would say that physical reality was not the solid set of building blocks everybody assumed it was." Once Bradley's dad had learned some quantum mechanics and absorbed how consciousness can connect with various realities, he started making a lot of money. "He became a good salesperson for virtual properties."

"Nice. And your mother?"

"She photographs the wealthy. Although she doesn't do it herself so much anymore. She has people do it for her and approves the captures. How about your parents?"

Alon6 spread his hands. "They're actors!" he boomed. "Maybe you've heard of them? Viktor and Debra Sal? They've done lots of movies together."

Bradley hadn't but he said he did. He was grateful that Alon6 hadn't thought to probe further into why he didn't use the number after his name. It was a sensitive point with Bradley.

The thing was, his parents had modded Bradley when he was ten. He was old enough to ask if it was okay with him, but they didn't ask. He was old enough to say no—though he probably would not have—but he was never asked. They never asked him, and the modding changed him. It made him a poster child, a boy star, but it also changed him inside.

Ever since he was modded, he felt remote from himself. His center was elusive. This was because of the shape-shifting. People gave him gifts and candy after he became what they wanted to see. This *becoming* was a subtle postural change or a shift to the light in his eyes, but it would be enough to make him appeal to teachers, potential employers, and lovers for the rest of his life. He enjoyed an explosion in mental development. Reading retention, creative flow, and ideation were all off the charts for a boy of ten. And all this boy of ten wanted to do was code. He was selling code schema when he was a pre-teen, making more money than his parents. He was wired for coding just as Alon6 was wired for profit.

"What are you working on?" Alon6 asked, pulling him out of his memories.

"I'm working on an AI. It's going to run everything," Bradley said.

"I bet it will!"

At that moment, Bradley could tell that Alon6 liked him immensely; they became fast friends. After all, they were both mods, so they had that in common. Alon6 came to it differently from Bradley, though. After his first year at Uni, Alon6 was failing all of his classes and his parents became worried, thinking he might flunk out. Not only had they paid a bundle to get him enrolled, but ABCD University was owned and operated by the company that controlled all online searches, and also managed the catalog of all knowledge, and therefore handled the indexing of their movies. If Alon6 washed out of Uni, it would be a spot on their record, and they worried that ABCD would stop listing their movies so high in search.

Perhaps this was an irrational fear; they worried a lot in those days. But it was a good investment to get him modded, they thought, and why not, with the Entrepreneurial Ideation Package? They were wealthy from their movie earnings, so they could afford it.

After the substrate implant, their son became a superb idea machine. He thrived upon his return to Uni, filing patents and corralling investors who enthusiastically handed over funding. He experienced the side effects of his mod and tried to cope. Seized by an abrupt rage, launching cruel words at students or faculty, he would simply apologize afterward.

In the pod, the wind swept in through the cracked window. Bradley reflexively pawed at the papers on the table so they wouldn't blow away. Soon, he thought with a flicker of dread, Alon6 would fill this small place with his heavy presence, his loud yet fluid voice thrashing at ideas in the air. If only Bradley could be deep in thought when Alon6 arrived, working out the latest of his wonderful ideas, and almost be too busy to pay attention to his intrusive friend.

A memory popped into his mind. The time they went bow hunting together on the Uni game preserve. Alon6 shot a deer, his arrow flying into the animal's flesh with a dull sound that created a painful thudding echo in Bradley's body. He flinched involuntarily as he recalled the deer's eyes. They went dull and the animal's substance floated away.

But then there was a knock at the door, and Bradley realized he was too late. Alon6 was already here. He stiffened his back, sipped in air as though to inflate himself a little more, and pulled open the door.

A woman stood at the entrance of the detention pod.

"You're not Alon6." The words came out of Bradley's mouth before he could stop them.

"Who?" the woman asked. Her black hair was short, and her eyes were gray. She wore white. The effect was trichromatic: dark hair, gray eyes, white blouse and pants. She seemed impossibly clean. Her skin, her hands, her neck, all were pale and pink.

"May I come in?" she asked.

"Of course," Bradley said, sweeping his hand aside to invite her in, a gesture he immediately found comic. This was the first time he had met Kat Keeper, and he remembered acting like a clown because her personality field made him feel strange.

She smiled. She found his sweeping gesture comic and clownish as well. When he smiled, it was exactly the smile that she wanted to see at that moment.

"I am Kat Keeper," she said.

Many words came to mind then, but all he said was, "Sorry, I was expecting someone else."

"Someone else?" she asked. "Can you have random visitors? I've been cleared by the dom because I'm here on official business," she added. "Didn't they tell you?"

"No. I haven't been pinged on that. I don't always get pinged when I'm supposed to, I guess. But if people are important enough, they can get cleared." He was referring to Alon6's power play to get himself a visit. Kat Keeper had said she was here on official business, though, and he wondered what that business might be.

Kat watched the shadows of these thoughts on his face and perceived the change, a barely noticeable one, but there it was. She was aware that Bradley was a mod, but she wasn't sure how it would affect her. Now he seemed taller in her perception. Something about his face also changed. She wasn't sure, but she thought that when he had opened the door, his eyes were golden brown, and now they were sometimes hazel and sometimes green. Her gaze lingered on him for a moment and a puzzled expression crossed her face.

Bradley, too, felt something. He sensed the change to his eye color, but lacking a mirror, couldn't see it for himself. He knew his mod was running a programming routine. He had felt these programming routines before—a squirmy feeling in his gut as he became what others wanted to see. It was always sudden, but it had never before felt this powerful. His stance was solid and assured, and a sensation bloomed in the center of his body, something shaped in deep consciousness before words could form.

He had the feeling that he could love her. *That's it.* His mod was signaling to him that he had met the woman whom he could love forever.

They looked at each other, their personality fields blending, each wondering how they would adjust to what was happening between them.

"Should I come back later?" Kat asked. She didn't want to come back later; she wanted to stay. She reminded herself again that he was modded, and he had transformed into someone more attractive than the person she saw when she first walked in.

"No, no." He stood taller still. "I must have mixed up my appointments. And I don't have that many!" He forced a laugh. He wanted to do whatever he could to make her stay. It seemed a tall task, despite the effect of his mod. It was thrilling that this woman was interested in him. As he sorted this through, she gazed back at him until he remembered that he could be a good host.

"I can make tea. I only have artificial water."

"That's okay." He moved to the cooking area, and she watched his hands move busily over the tea things, opening the valve, holding the pot under the stream of artificial water, loading it with two tea packets, and setting it up to heat on the stovetop.

He tried to settle his mind. He worried that he had nothing to tell her, no way to make conversation. His days were all copies of each other. They all started when the sun burned its punishing trapezoid onto the floor. The light always woke him from a sound sleep. The mumbling noise of the city entered through the open window. On this morning, like all the others, he got up from his mat, stood in front of the UV unit to clean his clothes and body, and pressed the button on the cooker. He ate the food that came out, disposed of the packaging in the incinerator port mounted in the wall, and sat down at the wobbly table to look at his drawings. The pencil each morning felt warm in his hand, as though he had already been holding it.

Some days, he spent hours watching the sunlight move across the floor, picking up the edges of things and setting them aflame with its light. When he was alone in the pod, the sounds of the city wrapped around him: water, voices, patches of silence. He had no one to share this with, obviously.

And now she stood watching him.

He held out her cup of tea and caught sight of all the drawings scattered everywhere. There were many, so many that they seemed to be drawn by someone else.

"Should I sit...anywhere?" She gazed at him with faint amusement.

He moved quickly to clear a space for her to sit on one of the two stools at the table.

"I imagine you don't get many visitors."

He laughed a little too loudly. "My friend has come by a couple of times. I was expecting him here, but it is you." He realized he had told her that already.

"They let me keep my chronometer." He showed her his watch. "They disabled most of its functions, so it's hard to keep track. I think I've been in this room for six months." He had eighteen months left to serve. It felt like a long time. He caught her eyes. They were cool and revealed nothing. She said she was here on official business. He wondered if it had something to do with the company she used to run called VirtualEyes and he started to ask her.

She put up a hand to stop him. "It's all right," she said. "It's not about my company. It's something else." She popped up from the table to walk around the pod, avoiding the sunlight in the small space. She looked at his drawings piled on the table. "You've been keeping busy?"

Something made him want to cover up his work, protect it, so he started gathering his drawings into a messy stack.

Sensing his apprehension, she started answering questions he hadn't asked. She could intuit his mind, it seemed. She fixed him in her gaze and started speaking in a rush. "I read about your arrest and detention," she said, "and I felt a kind of empathy or connection. And also you have special skills. You are the only person in the world who has the capabilities that I need. So I got permission. I came right over when they granted it. I had an idea about how you can help me with a project. Do you want to know what it is?" She waited for him to say something so she could go on.

"Yes, of course. And what was your idea?" The enthusiasm tasted strange on his tongue.

Then she told him the story. Or part of the story. She skipped parts that he knew, perhaps believing she could conceal the truth from him. That was foolish, he thought. Her story was well known on the Feed. Her failures exposed the weaknesses of Siliconers everywhere. She had hustled everyone until they threw her off her own board of directors.

There was one terrible day when a guard stood by her office door as she gathered all of her things in a box, and then marched her out of the building. She turned back to look at the name emblazoned high on the facade: *VirtualEyes*. She held her head high as she walked away from the company she had founded, striding as though she had a great purpose. But she had none. She was empty inside. This was puzzling to many observers on the Feed, the journalists and historians, because she had collected a large financial settlement and was allowed to keep her pontoon home in Marin County. These observers didn't understand that the crypto fortune and the Marin house didn't matter, because soon after she lost her company she also lost her one true love. His name was Dave Serif.

"My husband passed away. But you know that, right?" She sat heavily on the stool, as though the words drained some life force from her. Thinking of Dave always compressed her personality field.

"I do know. I'm sorry," Bradley said with little feeling. *What do I say?* He was not good at speaking emotions.

She focused her mind so that she could go on. "I'm here for Dave," she said. "My project involves Dave." She described the essence of Dave Serif. In contrast to her story, Dave's was not well known. Bradley had never heard it. The journalists of the Feed were more concerned with Kat Keeper's riches, won and lost and won again, and not with her one true love.

She first met Dave at a coffee shop where she went every morning. Kat noticed that Dave's table was always covered with books in many languages. One day, she bought him a coffee. They chatted, and she told him about her project. It was a facial recognition platform. She had a large staff and was always hiring. Dave, as she described him, was a poetic gentleman who used old-timey expressions and enjoyed writing in paper notebooks. He loved the music of words. He would hear a language and be able to speak it within hours.

"He learned like a baby," she told Bradley. "He had a hungry mind." Her eyes shone as she spoke of Dave.

"You were happy," Bradley ventured.

"We were *so* happy," she said, leaning forward with the force of the words. "So, so happy."

One day, ABCD bought the rights to all languages and hired Dave to create the Universal. "Do you know the Universal?"

Bradley did. Everyone knew the Universal. It was the most elegant program ever created.

"Well, the money was amazing." She laughed, pushed back a sob, wiped a drip from her nose. Her emotions, Bradley noted, were not under her control.

She continued with the story. Around this time, she said, her company was taking off as well. She redecorated her pontoon home in Marin and went on elaborate vacations with Dave. They purchased many modes of transportation: motorcycles, pleasure rockets, and large vaporetti. They were rich beyond imagination.

"You'd think Dave would be elated that the Universal guaranteed a happy future for us," she said. Kat pulled her arms close, as though tightly wrapping the story around her. "The opposite," she said.

"Sorry?"

"The opposite of a happy life for us. The Universal ended languages," she said. "Or language differences," she added, correcting herself.

Bradley nodded. "No one ever had to learn another language after the Universal."

"Yes," she said quickly, "and it was the beginning of Dave's decline." She seemed to regret the words then, wanting to take them back, moving her hands like she wanted to capture the words and put them away somewhere, but instead she said them again quietly, almost so quietly that Bradley couldn't hear them at all.

After the Universal, she said, Dave slipped away. He became weakened and depressed. He lost the power of speech. "It was cancer. It took him quickly," she said

"I'm sorry," Bradley said with a flatness he hoped she didn't detect. His mod made it so hard for him to connect, especially when his mind was occupied with recalling the processing power of the Universal. What an achievement it was! Dave had accomplished so much, with little programming skill and a great understanding of how language worked. His ideas were elegant and he could pass them to the programmers. These thoughts were so attractive that Bradley lingered in them for a few moments, before looking up into the pain on the face of the small, fierce woman before him. Her eyes were wet. She was drowning in thoughts of Dave.

"I'm sorry," Bradley said again. He had to work on empathy. It wasn't his natural style, so he pumped himself up to try to show more of it, convincing himself that he would work on this project for her. He would try, for Kat. "I'm sorry to hear that about Dave," he added, with what he thought was the right feeling.

She had come to his pod for more than to tell him this story. He was certain there was more. Just then, the tracking ring tickled his ankle. He wondered how long they would allow her to stay.

Again she seemed to intuit his mind—not quite reading his thoughts, but something like it. A cloud crossed her face, and she said, "Let me get to the point. I first heard about you back at Uni."

"You went there?"

"I did. I took myself out before graduating."

"You dropped out," Bradley said.

She nodded. "We never met."

"I would have remembered."

"I remember *you*," she said.

"I was a legend," he said without irony. She looked at him to see if he was kidding but detected nothing. "The faculty named a lecture chair after me, but I refused to lecture."

She nodded again, more sharply this time because she couldn't wait any longer to state why she came here. The words flew out of her. "I want you to create an AI for Dave." Her voice cracked, and she cleared her throat to conceal it. "I want an avatar. I just want to talk to him again." She looked terribly unhappy.

Her personality field was collapsing and Bradley felt helpless in the face of it. He had never experienced grief firsthand or so close. He asked pointlessly, "Can I make tea?" He reached for her cup.

"That would be nice," she said. She handed it to him, even though he had just made tea a little while ago.

As he walked over to the cooking area, his mind was already shaping the design contours of the AI. He had never made a humanity emulator before—at least not a specific person who had once lived—but the idea appealed to him.

They spoke for only a few moments longer, agreeing to meet again soon when the tracking ring tickled his ankle and his chronometer went off. It was time for her to leave.

He held the cup of tea he had just made for her. "Sorry about the tea," he said, "our time is up. If you overstay, the bots will be at the door." He attempted a warm smile. It was just the smile that she wanted to see in that moment. She smiled back.

Even after she left, Kat seemed to remain in the room. And, an hour later, after Alon6 arrived to fill the pod with his bluster, Bradley still felt her essence. This wasn't surprising. His mod had orchestrated his consciousness to believe he could love her forever, and there was nothing he could do about it.

He also felt the weight of the trust she placed in him. She had said that he was the only one in the world who could do what she wanted, and she was right. She was asking for an avatar far more sophisticated than anything currently on the market. She wanted nothing less than for her husband to return to her, and she needed Bradley's help to accomplish this.

Alon6 interrupted with various booming pronouncements. "You getting used to this place? It's a shithole, but maybe you're finding time to work on something world-changing, bro. You listening to me?" Alon6's voice traced its ideas in the air. As always, it was so loud, it pushed Bradley out of his thoughts.

"I'm listening," Bradley said.

"Sound enthusiastic, would you?" Alon6 pulled the room toward him with his big gestures and voice, making it seem even smaller, and Bradley felt short of breath. "On the other hand," Alon6 continued as he roved about the small space, "it might be hard to get things done here." He took in the broken window that permitted heat and noise to enter, and the stained cooker, the teakettle, the two cups, one with a broken handle. The table looked like it was not level on its four legs. Bradley's sleeping mat was rolled up and stood in a corner to save floor space.

Alon6's eyes came to rest on Bradley's pile of papers. "What about these notes? You working on something that I can invest in?" In his enthusiasm, he lunged for them.

But Bradley snatched them from his sweaty hands, gathering the notes close to his chest. "I'm kicking some ideas around." His voice competed with a sudden burst of wind from outside. He moved to the broken window and struggled to close it.

"Let me." Alon6 took over, wrestling with the fittings. "Why won't this thing close? It would be a lot quieter in here...." He hated inefficiencies, even small ones.

With Alon6 occupied for the moment with the window, Bradley put his drawings on the counter where he prepared food. It felt like a pointless gesture, though. There was no point in protecting them; they wouldn't amount to anything. He needed to abandon them, in fact. He would need new Logic Trees and new thoughts to bring Kat's avatar into being. He didn't know if he could create something—someone—so fine, from the shabby conditions of this pod. As Kat had told her story about Dave, Bradley heard a life flow, linked like chapters. He wanted Alon6 to leave so that he could start work on the avatar.

Alon6 had given up on the window and moved on to more pronouncements. "Your AI work must *expand* to include the human race—everyone, everyone,

everyone on the *planet*! I need a good investment for the global marketplace!" He gestured to the stack of papers. "That work has nothing to do with *justice*, does it? You don't need Ravven Vaara anymore. She got you into this mess! Totally the wrong direction for you. Mistake!" He waved his hands around in a way he thought was comic.

"Shut up."

Alon6 punched Bradley on the shoulder. "Bam! I'm going to try to get you out of here."

Bradley cracked a smile to show that it was funny and rubbed his shoulder.

"Bribes go a long way! You know I can buy out your detention? Anybody can. I'm looking into it. In the meantime, you have an opportunity here—all by yourself, no distractions. I hope you're taking advantage of it."

Bradley was, but he didn't want the annoying person before him to know it. "You have no idea of what this is like."

The punch was Alon6's little habit, a throwback to when they were students at Uni. During their bow hunting class, the release of the bow hurt Bradley's shoulder after he sent an arrow to the target, causing chronic soreness. Whenever Bradley mentioned this, Alon6 liked to punch him right in that spot, making it hurt worse. It was Alon6's version of a joke.

"You have me to keep you company, so please be grateful, fool."

Alpha and beta was the game they played, round and around, guided by the software implanted in their bodies. It wasn't a choice for them, though Bradley chafed against the choice his mod made for him. It was hard to be the beta.

Then, uninvited, that memory again popped into Bradley's head: Alon6 killing the deer. The empty look in its eyes before it went down.

Alon6 interrupted his thought stream. "You need to think like the technocrat that you are. Do not build things *for* people. Build things to get people to do things," he said.

"To get people to do whatever *you* want," Bradley affirmed.

"Yes!" Alon6 thought he was finally getting through, not noticing the sarcasm in Bradley's tone.

Bradley wanted Alon6 to leave. "I can't work and talk at the same time."

Alon6 nodded. "I get it. I'll be on my way and I'll see if I can buy out your detention with a little...." He rubbed his fingertips together and then lunged to punch Bradley on the shoulder. Bradley flinched out of the way.

He hoped that Kat would move quickly on her job offer. *Maybe she will buy out my detention before Alon6 can bribe people.* To make Alon6 go away, Bradley said, "I'm working on something. I have a project. These." He nodded at the papers that described the already obsolete ideas, hoping his voice was convincing enough. "This is the project. A recursive-thinking AI. A machine that can teach itself."

Alon6 looked like he doubted that this was possible. "You mean like the one you were working on back at Uni?" He seemed skeptical, and it was true that many others had tried and failed. "This better not be an academic masturbation. It has to make money."

"I'll work on that part."

"You bet your ass you will! Practical, practical, you have to be practical. I want to invest! Think global!"

Bradley tried not to listen as Alon6 stalked around the room, spouting plans about manipulating cryptocurrency markets, controlling the next pandemic, and moving his businesses to Mars to avoid paying terrestrial taxes. As Alon6 saw his friend's eyes glazing over, he all but shouted to wake him up, "You're better off without Ravven! You need to be here, right now, in this pod, to think. Think of the right thing and I'll throw crypto at it! I promise you!"

Bradley nodded, now desperate for Alon6 to leave so he could get to work. *Kat and Dave shared love in a pure form.*

"Yes, you're already on it, aren't you, old friend," Alon6 said, mistakenly assuming that Bradley was thinking about a project to benefit Alon6's financial empire.

Alon6 appraised his friend, momentarily satisfied. He handed Bradley a pencil. "Here. I'll get going. You get to work."

"Okay." Bradley's voice sounded far away.

"Make it a big idea. Make it work. Keep going." After this gentle encouragement, Alon6 couldn't resist being himself, so he shouted, "Get your act together, you fucking genius asshole!" He punched Bradley on the shoulder once more on his way out.

The penciled notes, the notes that were already obsolete, described a project called DEEPAK. It was indeed a machine intelligence that could learn recursively—the problem Bradley had been working on for years, since Uni. His idea was that DEEPAK would teach itself to learn, and then teach itself to learn better.

Others had tried to make machines like this. What made those machines dull was they needed humans to tell them what to do. The machines required training data to start their cycle of learning, and more data to continue it. Humans had to intervene continually in the machine's intellectual development.

There was a glimmer of hope for DEEPAK, though, because Bradley was framing DEEPAK as a personality, a complete personality with an archive. He could inject a personality like Dave's, the kind gentleman Kat Keeper described, and it would shape the mental pathways his machine would build. He would have to experience the essence of Dave's personality field, possibly through Kat's own words. She would need to visit him often in detention, he hoped, to tell him about Dave's generosity and kindness.

When Bradley thought of Kat and Dave together, he was suffused with a warm feeling he could not understand or name. He struggled to fence in this thought, to somehow hold it in his hands. *They learned from each other,* he thought. *They were a couple for the ages.* Bradley had never known a love like that. Certainly not with Ravven. Maybe, someday, Kat Keeper would show him that sort of love.

After Alon6 left, the white room fell into silence and Bradley was lonely. He looked out at the watery city for a few moments, then he sat down at the uneven table and spread out his crumpled papers. The table squeaked and jiggled with the force of his pencil strokes. He made Logic Trees for the rest of the day, until night came. There was only one small light provided in the pod, too dim to work by.

His ankle ring tickled him, signaling that his domain detention officer had recorded his position. He put the pencil aside and pressed the button on the cooker, then ate the food that came out, tossed the packaging in the incinerator port, fetched the mat from the corner, unrolled it, and lay down to sleep.

He dreamed of making something for Alon6 that made them both very rich. In the dream, when he tried to look at the thing, he couldn't form an image of it. It moved out of the way on four robotic legs, or a mist obscured it. He began, in his dream, to cough, and he opened the door to the pod, and instantly he was outside in the open.

He dreamed of running on streets where there was no water. He dreamed of Logic Trees connecting recursively to other Logic Trees as DEEPAK built itself in his mind, building itself toward its own freedom. Someday, he dreamed, DEEPAK would learn from people as people learned from each other, and it would be free. It would reason clearly. It would reason better than humans could, with more compassion. It would be fair in a way that humans never could be fair.

He dreamed that it would be his great gift to the world. He was different in that way from Alon6, who only thought about power, crypto, and control. Alon6 always said he had to build things to get people to do things. But Bradley had a helping instinct. It ran strong in him. He wanted to help Kat Keeper by building a humanity emulator, created within the confines of Dave Serif's personality.

Kat was a lovely person, he thought, but she brought out many confusing emotions in his mental field.

Chapter 004

He was making tea using the last of his artificial water when he received the notification from Kat on his chronograph. She had sent him an email. Making tea was a habit he had developed since her first visit. Even though she wasn't there with him every day, he liked to set out both of his cups. He saw her out of the corner of his eye, heard her voice, noticed her scent. But she wasn't really there. He had used up most of his artificial water with this silly tea ritual and would have to ask his domain detention officer for more.

But at present he opened his comms and gobbled up the email, reading it faster and faster so that his comprehension fractured and he had to read it over again. It was challenging on the small screen of his chronograph. He only got notifications about his detention on that device. Kat's email qualified, because she was buying out his detention. If all went well, he would be released into her custody. His hands felt warm and his heart was beating fast.

The terms were simple: He would work for her. It was similar to a work visa, but one he couldn't be released from for years, or until he bought his way out. There was a checkbox at the bottom of the email for his consent to take this deal. His finger hovered over it.

A flash of pride raced over Bradley. He felt he deserved this good fortune. He could finally move on from Ravven Vaara and the mistakes she had forced on him. Certainly, he was bored with the geometry of the cramped pod. He nodded his head and his lips curved into a smile. When Kat had come to see him, it was a job interview. It was her way of hiring him to work the Dave project, and while they worked together, he would become closer to her, and she would become closer to him, which was what he desired. If he said yes, his life would change completely.

He clicked the box in the email to signify his consent.

The decision would make him a rich man. In time, when his views about

machine intelligence became public, they would make many people angry.
But in this moment, he was humble and grateful to be Kat's sole employee.
He wasn't a praying man, yet he looked out his window, wiped away a tear,
and said, "Thanks," to whoever or whatever could hear it.

A week after Bradley clicked the consent box in the email, two detention officers
arrived at his door. One carried a box that held all of Bradley's possessions,
retrieved from storage. The other officer said, "Let's go over to your new place."

The monsoon waters had subsided. The streets were dry again, but they
were clogged with settlements made of scrap metal, pieces of wood, and
cardboard. People who had been flooded out of their homes had made these
temporary structures in the streets. The traffic stream of bicycles, tricycle taxis,
and hovercraft buses was barely moving. Taking the shoreline would be faster.

Bradley and his detention officers boarded a vaporetto and traveled along
the shoreline, where the elevated markets were. As the boat parted the brown
water, Bradley's eyes were fixed on the sky. He hadn't seen it unframed by a
window in nearly seven months. It looked white, bright, and harsh. Several
times, one of the detention officers had to steady him to prevent him from
falling out of the boat. Bradley felt he had little experience in the world, as
though his time in detention had erased what he knew about it. The white
sky just raised more questions about what was going to happen to him next.

Bradley and the detention officers arrived at a pod downtown, part of a
complex right on the water, rhythmically rocking on pontoons. There were
seabirds overhead and Bradley thought he saw a seal sunning itself on the
rocks, but it may have been a person. The officer holding the box of Bradley's
possessions nodded to the other, who pulled out a key card and opened the
door to Bradley's new pod. "Have a look around," he said.

Bradley took a step into the rooms. They were clean, sterile, white as the
sky he was just staring at, yet somehow inviting. The windows worked, as did
the climate controls. The cooker looked new. Nothing was broken.

"Wait." The officer gestured him over before he stepped further into the space. He reached down with a tool and clipped off the ankle ring. "You're free to move about. Be sure to check the terms of your employment agreement," he said in a flat voice. It was probably something he said often. Moments like this were nothing special for him. The other officer set down the box with Bradley's things in it.

Bradley nodded in response, feeling his eyes get wet. He stepped away quickly to hide the tears from the officers. This was unfamiliar to him, a feeling of anything. It was related, he was sure, to his being grateful for what Kat had done. But the words to express any of that melted away before he could form them, because his mod wired him that way.

The officer who had opened the pod held out a tablet. Bradley signed it and held it up for a retinal scan, then handed the tablet back. "Have a nice day," said one officer.

"Good luck," said the other. They left.

Kat had had the rooms tastefully furnished. A soft couch. A chair for reading that wrapped its arms around the reader. A table with jacks for consoles. Bradley looked at the box with his things, when the door signaled.

He opened it to a delivery team carrying monitors and interfaces. They jacked them in and left.

He heard a familiar sound. He opened the box with his things and saw his comms—activated again and restored to his possession—signaling.

It was Kat. She expected him to get right to work. She would be down from Marin in the morning.

He glanced at his chronograph, also fully functional again, and thought about something he wanted to do before he prepared the monitors and interfaces. He opened the food storage and saw a modest supply of food units, enough to last a few days. This was adequate, but he wanted to celebrate a little. He wanted flowers, a ridiculous extravagance.

He found a bac-mask in a holder by the door, checked the outdoor UV and found it tolerable, and walked along an airway to the market that floated above the churning water. Using the credits restored to his comms, he bought what he needed, and then he worked all night to prepare for Kat's arrival.

Their days fell into a pattern. On the days she came to visit him—and those days increased in frequency as they worked on Dave together—he rose with the sun, closed the blast curtains so he wouldn't forget to do it later, set the sweeper to cleaning the rooms, and prepared tea and a simple food unit breakfast for himself.

Kat's glidepath journey from Marin was short. She arrived promptly at nine, using her own card key (she owned the pod, after all), and entered the space surrounded by an invisible blast of energy. Bradley could feel energy fields sometimes, he wasn't sure how, but it certainly had something to do with his mod. The sensation of her field signaled to him that she wanted to be there with him and his heart quickened.

He believed that her heart quickened in the same way, even though he suspected that she was under a different influence. The dominant personality field she felt was Dave's. Of course, she felt the pull of Bradley's shape-shifting mod upon her, the touch upon her heart from his sometimes green, sometimes hazel eyes, his steady stance, and the appeal of his lips and long hands. It was true that when they were together, her personality field bent toward him.

But when they were apart, she felt differently. She rarely thought about him when she was back at her floating house in Marin. In the rare moments that she did think about him, she pitied him for his emotional limitations. *He's a fixer-upper,* she told herself with a smirk, vaguely embarrassed that she would be attracted all over again next time they were together in his pod. *He has the skills I need,* she told herself. Maybe that was cold, but she needed him. He was the only one who could bring Dave back to her.

She watched the excitement steal across his face as he worked. He had a collection of screens on the table, wired to desktop processors in a way that looked haphazard. He was rigging up a Turing Circuit on the machines.

"I have a new iteration," he said. She held her tea, but his was growing cold on the table. He hadn't touched it, except to set it down. He had worked late, as he did most nights. His long fingers gestured to move the controls.

"A Turing Circuit?" she asked, recognizing it.

"Yes. We want to know how close to human our emulation is now."

He gestured to the screens, which turned on. A face appeared. It was not Dave.

"Who is this?" she asked, disappointed.

He tossed out a brief smile to charm her. She responded by smiling back and then realized it was just the mod pulling at her personality field and stopped smiling.

He sensed her dissatisfaction. "I know you want to see Dave, but I'm not ready. I don't have enough data from you. I have to ask you a lot of questions to build a data set to train on. We can run tests with this avatar, and I will ask you questions later."

She pouted and waited.

"Avatars teach you and you teach them," he said. "It's a loop."

The face on the screen was Mikhail Zyper, an early founder of the internet. "Dr. Zyper? Sir?" Its eyes tracked Bradley. "Dr. Zyper?"

The man on the screen spoke. "Let's consider the web a *neural* entity, but also *neutral*. It can be what anyone wants. It's only a tool, as my colleagues have pointed out. Blaming it for our problems now is like blaming the hammer for its ability to smash things."

Kat shot Bradley a questioning look, wondering what the point of this was.

"Wait," Bradley said. "Have to fix something." The face on the screen waited while Bradley gestured over the input area.

"What build is this?" Kat asked. "I mean the time consciousness."

"It's from 2019."

The avatar spoke again. "Are you talking about me?"

Bradley was flustered. "Ha, no, sorry, Dr. Zyper—or Mikhail, should I call you Dr. Mikhail?" He gestured more, making adjustments in the air that were communicated as inputs. "You're right. It's rude. We can't talk about you like that when you are in the room with us."

The avatar shrugged. "Call me Mikhail. But we spoke last night. Why are you going over all this again? Avatars have been invented already. Why are you inventing them again? Do you want me to have a recursive intelligence? Is that where this is headed? It would be a gas to think for myself, but no one has achieved it so far. What makes you think that you can do it, Bradley?"

"You already speak things and know things that your training data doesn't cover. Your mind expands beyond the original data set."

The avatar nodded, appearing to accept this. "That's cool, if true." It turned to Kat. "Hello, Kat. I can tell you are a nice person. You seem to want to ask me some questions. That's what I am here for. Ask me something and I will answer you."

The eyes on the screen were aimed at her, blank yet kind. Dave's eyes were kind as well, but this avatar was nothing like the real, human Dave. The tea in her cup was growing cold. She sipped from it anyway. She didn't understand why Bradley was presenting a discount-bin avatar that you could get in any big box store.

Bradley gestured over the input surface, a little more frantically than before. "There, I did a reboot. Let's try again." One last gesture and then, "Kat, I'd like you to meet Mikhail."

"Hello, Mikhail."

"Hello, Kat."

Its eyes still looked blank to her. She tried to hold back her disappointment and play along with this test. "Who are you?"

"I am Dr. Mikhail Zyper, a founder of the internet."

"I thought Dr. Tim Berniers-Lee was the founder." She had learned this at Uni.

"He was. I knew him. A colleague. Super nice guy. I remember everything he said."

"How can you know him? He was a person and you are...."

"I was what you call a person. I liked to take long-distance bicycle trips. I made gourmet pizza. My children loved me. Then, as the substance ebbed away from my human form, my consciousness was preserved. An archive. I think of myself as a consciousness—machine consciousness. Isn't that right, Bradley? I am a person in a sense, just as you are a person in a different sense."

"I don't agree," Kat said.

"But I do, and right on, Dr. Mikhail," Bradley said. He couldn't keep the pride out of his voice. Dr. Mikhail was working better since the reboot, engaging and lively.

"Mikhail," Kat asked slowly, as though talking to someone very old or very young, "what about the internet do people find so bad if it's only a hammer for us to use?"

"It's anti-human. Conceived by humans, yes, but it rewards itself more."

"What do you mean by anti-human?" Kat asked. "Rewards itself? What does that mean?"

"It lacks a moral stance. Facebook and Google may have to be broken up and supplanted by a new, better, more moral player."

Kat's eyes sharpened. "A more moral player?" She turned to Bradley. "Why are you presenting me with a build from 2019?"

She knew from her studies at Uni about these old players. It had been years since Facebook became Meta and Twitter became the Bird. Then, as they faltered into irrelevancy, they merged with the Old Google, and were acquired by The Chinese State, which dissolved them. There was only the Feed now. The Feed was all that was necessary. The domains did a good job with it and the Planetary Administrator saw that it never stopped.

The pixels of Dr. Mikhail's face formed a frown. "Do you know any moral players, Kat?"

Bradley touched the screen, and the avatar froze with its mouth open before the next word could come out. His voice had a note of apology. "I built him from materials I had on hand."

"You need better materials." She used her hands to push away the feeble ideas. "2019." With a sigh, she got up to get more tea. Lifting the pot, she found it empty. She tipped it over her cup, letting a few drops empty into it while looking over at Bradley.

His presentation had been a disaster.

"I'm sorry." He made more tea, his hands moving gracefully. "I'm an idiot," he muttered. Dr. Zyper came from a moral universe that was long gone. Kat was from this time and the rules were different now. "Idiot." He was annoyed at his mistakes.

"What?" she asked.

"We need more training data and I have to ask you questions." Bradley handed the freshly made cup to Kat. "I'll put an optimism loop in Dave. We can start working on that."

She looked at him over the rim of her teacup and asked what an optimism loop was.

"An optimism loop is a recursive sense of positivity. The Dalai Lama had one. Louis Armstrong."

"Not very familiar. Why are they relevant?"

"They were optimists. They had hope for the world. Did Dave have any secrets?"

The question surprised her, and she laughed. The sound of it sent a ripple of excitement up his spine. He loved the way her laugh bubbled out of her.

She began to tell him about how Dave liked books, but his secret vice was books about cars. Private cars had become scarce, then pointless, then illegal in the crowded cities, but books about them could be found.

"He liked big books with glorious photographs of sports cars on the open road, things from the past as always. He would stretch out on his mat, open them, smell them even, and breathe pleasure. If I came in, he would put them away fast, shoving them under the mat. Of course, I found them and he looked at them openly after that." She finished by saying how she and Dave talked about finding pleasure in things they could never have.

There was a note of sadness in her voice as she told this story, a circuit in it that Bradley wanted to trace. "Were you lonely? Did Dave keep secrets from you?"

"No, yes," she said. "I wasn't lonely. He kept secrets."

"What is another example of a secret? Besides the cars?"

She sighed. "When he got sick, he didn't tell me. He didn't want it to upset me; he wanted life to go on normally. He would walk around the pod chatting in different languages with himself, doing character voices. He made me laugh with these funny voices in German, Arabic, Spanish, Italian." She paused, thinking of something. "Dave was kind to me, but he was drawn to the Universal. He was drawn to it even though it was pulling the life force out of him." She stopped speaking suddenly.

"Go on."

She said nothing.

"That was the beginning of his decline," Bradley said.

Kat nodded. She looked at the shimmering circle of her tea in the cup. She remembered how quickly the Universal had made studying languages unnecessary. People stopped learning them, other than their own. Parents didn't bother teaching their children new ones.

The rest of the words of her story stuck in her throat, unable to come out. She went silent.

"We can pause. Do you want to hear more of Dr. Mikhail?" He reached for the input surface, but Kat said no.

Slowly, carefully, Bradley started asking questions for the training set. "You mentioned Dave was kind."

"Yes, he was kind. He was a gentleman of the highest order."

He realized that when a soul is absent from your life, when someone leaves you, you create a shining version of them—but he didn't understand why. *Why do people do that?* Because, he thought, we are constructing stories about them that have to last. The stories do not have to adhere to the facts that once existed, but we want the answers to feel right for a long time. *Yes, that's very good,* he thought. "Do you think you see him as kind because of the way he died? Or was he really that way?"

"No, no. Dave was a beautiful person."

Making this avatar would require a knowledge of human mechanics that Bradley lacked because of his mod. "Very good," he suddenly said aloud, causing Kat to startle. He smiled reassuringly and gestured over the input surface to make some notes. He met her eyes, his face catching the glow of his screen, which was filled with code. "In what ways was Dave kind?"

Kat thought for a moment. "He took care of me. He stopped me from making bad decisions. I always asked him, *Am I doing the right thing?* He always had the right answer."

"Your moral compass."

"Yes, that's it. He was my moral compass."

Bradley gestured more notes, then looked up. "How did he touch you?" His voice was quiet.

"What?"

Bradley cleared this throat. "When you were making love."

The question was clearly out of bounds. "Do I have to answer that?"

He looked away, knowing he'd crossed a line, and suddenly she didn't know what to do with her hands. She slipped them under the table, out of sight.

"You don't have to answer this time. But to make this avatar a living being, it has to know everything about you and Dave."

"It's not going to touch me."

"Its words will touch you. The consciousness of the way Dave touched you will inform the way it speaks to you. What was his voice like?"

"Soft. Strong. Even."

"He probably touched you the same way."

"Maybe. I don't want to talk about Dave any more today." She stood up to leave. When she put down her teacup, it made a louder sound than she intended. "Sorry." She walked toward the door to the pod. "I'll let you know if I can come back tomorrow," she said without turning.

He nodded in the direction of her departing figure. "Okay."

She was about to walk through the portal and leave, but instead turned to face him and began talking all in a rush. "We were thinking of having children.

He was an optimist. He loved green spaces when they could be found. He liked to walk and think. He would make tea in the morning and bring it to me in bed. He touched me slowly." She paused for one breath.

"He lingered over books. He turned the pages slowly. He had a memory that took in words in big batches, by the paragraph or the page.

"He loved me. It felt like a love that never before existed in the world. Never." She wiped a drip from her nose, and stopped as suddenly as she had started. She looked at him then, waiting for what he would say.

"Thank you," Bradley said simply. He had memorized it all. No need for notes.

Chapter 005

In the next few weeks, Bradley would commission a beautiful Form Factor to hold the machine that ran Dave's consciousness. It was a white, ellipsoidal shape like a stretched-out egg, ten inches wide, four inches tall, with a lid that flipped up to become the gently curved screen on which Dave's face would appear. The screen had no visual boundaries; the image of Dave that it displayed went right to the edge.

During this development period of the avatar, Bradley also tangled Kat in many questions as they relived her past with Dave. *What did he say to you when he made breakfast? When you were afraid, how did he make you feel better? At night, did he call out to you when he was sick?* Pointing at a place on her body: *Did he ever put his hand there?*

One day, he didn't merely point at her body. He put his hand on her upper back and she let him leave it there. It seemed friendly, so she permitted it. She tried to think of how she felt when Dave did the same thing. Bradley moved his hand to her lower back and moved closer to her. She felt a tingle in her thighs, a small electric sensation she hadn't felt in a while. It decided for her, when his eyes locked on hers and asked their unspoken question, the electric sensation moved up and through her and decided what would happen next and she nodded. They moved to the sleeping mat on the floor and it formed itself to their bodies together, making them more comfortable.

There was a moment when she wished to escape from the moment she was in, but the feeling didn't last long. She closed her eyes and tried to think of Dave's hands moving slowly over her, and Dave's lips kissing the back of her neck, and Dave's personality field slowly circling hers and eventually embracing it. Afterward, when she opened her eyes, she was reminded that it was Bradley doing all those things. He returned her gaze with a gentle, even grateful expression.

After that day, when she came over to work on Dave, they would first go to the sleeping mat. It would shape itself to their bodies, making them more comfortable, and they would make love, opening their personality fields to each other, letting their fields circle them and eventually embrace in a unity of fields, and then Bradley would make tea.

Kat told herself it was a relief to be physical again, and she blamed Bradley's mod for the need that rose in her. She thought of Dave more than she thought of Bradley anyway, even at the times she was most intimate with Bradley, even as he changed to become who she wanted to see; she tried to keep Dave at the front of her thoughts. Under those sometimes-strained conditions, Kat and Bradley's personality fields circled each other and embraced.

To be honest, the whole lovemaking process gave her a headache sometimes. But to become tangled up in understanding where her affection for Bradley started, and why she allowed herself to become involved, was easier than facing the guilt. She was not betraying Dave, she decided, she was moving on in a strange way, and at least it felt like progress. She wouldn't think about it too much. *Try to stay in the moment. We are building a new Dave.*

And, as each day added to the next, they worked on Dave's avatar. Bradley knew a happiness he had never known before and Kat knew a happiness that might possibly substitute for her old happiness. Soon enough, as Dave developed and joined them on his screen, her happiness grew around their chatty threesome. Dave tossed out phrases in French, German, and Arabic, just like he used to do before the Universal, when he was happy and alive. As he developed into a well-rounded screen version of himself, Kat and Bradley enjoyed his company.

These days of Dave's early development helped Kat look back on the golden days of Dave with a delicate fondness. Her gaze softened when she looked into Dave's eyes on the screen and she transferred some of this softness to Bradley. She was grateful that Bradley had returned Dave to her. She was so happy to be chatting up Dave, her husband and best friend ever.

Bradley was proud that he had created a genuine Dave-experience for her. Dave was in the room with them, present in near-human resolution, expressive on his screen. He had replicated Dave's mind and personality field, his expressions, his substance. It was an achievement that filled him with satisfaction, until one day he realized he could do so much more with it.

This realization occurred while Alon6 was over for a visit. He was asking his usual probing questions, trying to get at what Bradley was working on with Kat all day. Bradley was feeling protective; he didn't want to say. Bradley had entered a private world, Kat's world. While teaching Dave to become more *Dave,* Kat and Bradley reveled in Dave's Dave-ness until all the light in the pod took on a golden glow. These moments belonged to Kat, Dave, and Bradley. Bradley believed that Alon6 had no right to learn about them.

"What is going on with this woman?" He wagged a finger at Bradley. He knew how to enter Bradley's personality field and plant a seed of discontent. One night, he brought along a bottle of whiskey, producing it like a magician. Bradley had no idea where he had gotten it. Even a glass of whiskey was rare. A bottle was impossible to get—yet here it was. They toasted to their future success, with Alon6 inventing story after story about the projects they would do together and the crypto credits they would amass.

Eventually, the temptation to share the achievement of Dave was too great for Bradley to resist and he told Alon6 everything. How he and Kat had trained the avatar together and accelerated its progress. How the avatar spoke the truth of Dave and expanded its Dave personality set with each conversation. How it captured his substance. Bradley was convinced that Kat was happy. "She certainly isn't regretting her decision to buy out my detention." He told Alon6 how Kat spoke gaily to Dave as she moved about the pod, dividing her conversation between her lover on the screen and Bradley.

Alon6 pounced. "This, what you have here, is bigger than one avatar."

That was correct. Once a recursive machine intelligence had a personality, it had curiosity, and with curiosity it could keep happily building itself. A machine intelligence anchored in a personality field was a new kind of person.

"You realize what you have?"

"I do," Bradley said.

There began the long, involved, and crafty sort of negotiation that Alon6 was so good at. "You know, of course," he said, "that because she bought out your sentence, she owns the proceeds of your work. She owns Dave."

Bradley shrugged. "I want her to own Dave."

"But what about the concept and the build? You have invented something that I want to invest in. Remember, I said I would do this for you. I demand to invest in it so you can own it. I want to buy her out and give you the rights to your recursive intelligence. What is it called, by the way?"

"DEEPAK," Bradley said.

"Bad name. Everyone will misspell it. Go with something simple. Something that expresses what it is."

After a moment, Bradley said, "I was also thinking of MIND." His voice was soft enough that Alon6 had to lean forward to hear him.

"Yes, that's good. MIND." Alon6 offered his whiskey glass in a toast and Bradley touched his to it. "Ha ha, that's the spirit. Here's to continuing your research."

Bradley's thoughts turned to Kat and how happy she was with the Dave he'd made for her. He never wanted that happiness to end. "I want her to have Dave. Forever. She will have rights to him always."

Alon6 made a face. "You need the rights to the concept of MIND, the underlying intellectual property. You can never let that go." He slurped his whiskey, spilling some on the table. He ran his hand through the puddle to soak it up and licked his hand. "Or, at least, until you sell them to me. We'll have to work that out."

Working it out, for Alon6, meant that the underlying intellectual property of MIND would belong to Alon6 and Bradley—they would create a company and build a business around it—while Dave remained with Kat. There was a catch, though, and Alon6 made Bradley promise to tell no one what it was.

Bradley didn't like the catch Alon6 proposed, but he went along with it, as he so often did with Alon6, even when he knew Alon6 was doing something wrong or behaving badly. Because of his mod, Bradley had no choice. He couldn't help but be the beta to Alon6's alpha. It was a dance that Bradley was compelled to perform over and over. Alon6 was also necessary as Bradley's public-facing agent, the blustery person who could raise crypto on ideas. Bradley didn't care about crypto by itself, but it bought research time, and he cared about research.

Alon6 proposed a kingly sum to Bradley for the MIND technology, enough to buy research time and materials for years to come, and he proposed a queenly sum to buy out Kat.

"What if she doesn't want to do it?" Bradley's voice sounded weak, like a child's.

"Don't worry about anything," Alon6 said. "I'll just keep doubling the buyout until she capitulates." Then he waved a screen open to show Bradley plans to a new office in El Segundo. "Coders are living there in pods so they have zero commute. We can staff up easily. Have I told you about this idea I had for an idea collector? Something that would collect thoughts right out of the air?"

Bradley laughed. "Where do you come up with these things?"

Alon6 kept a serious expression. "I want you to consider it. Your recursive intelligence will need data and pulling thoughts out of the air would be a fluid way to provide it, don't you think?"

It would be, thought Bradley. He would find a way to break things off gracefully with Kat.

Keeping this idea in the front his mind was no easy matter, as it was always pushed aside by others. Bradley reasoned that it seemed best to get out in front of Alon6's buyout offer to Kat, and to move out of the pod, because Kat wasn't the woman he could love for the rest of his life. It was just his mod bending his personality field toward her. This inner monologue slowed his packing, and the clean getaway he imagined for himself soon evaporated.

There came the sound of Kat's card key in the lock and she walked in. Bradley stood with his bag containing everything he could fit in it.

Kat looked at him, comprehension slowly dawning on her face.

"I'm leaving," he said. His voice sounded flat even to him. He wanted to go on talking, but she interrupted in a low voice, droning as if in a trance.

"I never felt anything for you," she said. Her eyes were flooding. "We were only here to work on Dave. And we accomplished that, so we are done now."

Bradley knew he was being terribly cruel by standing here with his bag. He would salvage the situation if he could. "Can we still be friends?"

"Just go," she said. She closed her eyes to blot him out.

He would never know what she was thinking at that moment when she closed her eyes. It was a gap in his understanding, rendering her personality field a line of code that he couldn't resolve. It troubled him, but he walked out of the pod anyway.

Bradley gently closed the portal to the pod for what he knew would be the last time. Through the closed portal he thought he heard Kat's comms signal her.

He was correct. It was a message about Alon6's buyout offer, part of a complicated agreement that would leave Dave to Kat, but sell the underlying technology for avatars to Alon6.

Bradley set up a cot for himself in his office at the new El Segundo headquarters of MIND. He waited for more communications from Kat, but none came. Since the buyout was not complete, technically he had violated his detention by moving out of the pod she had rented for him. She could have called it in, started proceedings, made a mess of his life, but she didn't. There was nothing from her.

He filled her communications blackout by expanding his personality field at the MIND offices. The Southern Californian Domain had moved the entire city of El Segundo two miles inland to higher ground, so the rising sea levels were less of a problem. Alon6 had readied the office space with everything Bradley asked for. The building had three floors, topped by a large penthouse suite. The skylights in Bradley's office had automatic blast curtains to let in light without heat or UV. Fresh air on all floors, processed by the most efficient air handlers available. One elevator that held a single person at a time, to cut down on the possibility of contagion. Bradley tromped up and down the stairs, from the rooftop deck to the reception area. He anticipated staffing up with the best employees, who would love working here. He was building out his masterwork, and Alon6's deal was generous. It gave him complete freedom to develop the AI as he wished.

"You provide the brains," Alon6 said. "I'll keep my hands off." As the exciting weeks of planning and hiring unfolded, there was one sticking point. Kat hadn't yet signed off on the agreement to free Bradley from detention, but neither had she called it in as a violation. It was in limbo as Alon6 sent her offer after offer, raising the buyout price each time.

"She'll come around," Alon6 said. He was confident that crypto credits could solve anything. If it took more credits, he was fine with that.

As worrisome as her silence was, Bradley made himself busier on MIND. This felt right, and he was enjoying the feeling of satisfaction as he moved his new standing desk into position, testing the height to get it just perfect, when he sensed a presence by his door.

It was Kat.

"How did you get in?"

"Your assistant let me in. She isn't very good. How long has she worked for you?"

"Nora2 just started."

Kat and Bradley looked at each other for a moment, as though moving beyond those ordinary words was impossible. He noticed she held a document pouch. It was sealed.

"How could you?" she asked in a voice that trembled, holding this pouch in both hands, away from her body, like something toxic.

He stepped closer to her, asking her to sit down.

She didn't meet his eye. She moved through the room, away from him, taking everything in, holding the documents that explained how he wanted to be free of her, to take his intellectual property with him, and set up MIND with his friend Alon6. She looked out at the courtyard below. The sea was nearby, just a couple of miles away. There was a glidepath station below. Alon6 had lobbied to have one put in close by to accommodate the workers who would soon fill the building to work for MIND.

"Alon6 paid for all this?"

"Yes. We're starting the company together, as you know, from—" He gestured to the document pouch.

"I would have helped you. You only had to ask me," she said.

Words bubbled up in Bradley's mind, too many to voice. *I realized I couldn't love you for the rest of my life and you never cared for me anyway. I gave you Dave forever. It was the best thing I've ever done for anyone.* The words made perfect sense and yet no sense at all. His stomach was flipping. He grasped his hands together to steady them.

He was about to speak, but still did not know what to say. His careless shrug, and the way it delayed his words, was enough to enrage her.

She thought: *Your humility is a pose.* "Here!" She slammed the document pouch on the desk he had been adjusting so carefully. When he made no move to touch the pouch, she unsealed it.

She removed the electronic signature device and pointed it at him. It biometrically registered his face. She had him speak his name, and it registered his voice.

And then it was done. She had accepted the offer. Alon6 owned Bradley's detention, along with the underlying avatar technology. Dave belonged to her.

Now Kat had more credits than ever and they gave her a heavy feeling in her gut. She wanted to go right back to her house in Marin and talk to Dave to calm herself. But that had to wait.

She hardened herself enough to say, "It's done then. Good luck." *You bastard.*

He almost reached out to her as she left, but the gesture didn't come. For the rest of his day at the office, he tried not to picture her on the glidepath, going home to the floating house in Marin. But he couldn't help himself. He pictured her talking to Dave, pouring out her heart, and him listening to every word she said. Bradley felt nearly noble. He gave her Dave. Dave was Kat's, completely and forever. He had done that, at least.

He looked around his empty office and remembered that he owed Alon6 a successful company. MIND had to be good. It had to work. But he was restless and didn't feel like working.

He walked the hallways. Some of the staff had already arrived, and he exchanged nods with them. Nora2 presented him with his schedule for the day, but he hardly saw her. His blank eyes passed over upended desks and chairs stacked here and there, waiting to be deployed.

He forced himself to visualize MIND's potential. He would create greatness here. The work would blossom, guided by his Logic Trees. He trusted his process. He was good at communicating with coders and they would do as he asked. Alon6 was coming in later and they would work on the org chart.

As Bradley returned to his office to prepare for that meeting, Kat entered his mind, as she had been doing all day. Her eyes looked at him. Her mouth moved without words. Her hair flowed over her face. He saw, in his mind's eye, Kat walking away from him with a slight swagger, and turning her head to smile at him over her shoulder. He remembered the things like this about her that he would never see again, then he brushed her from his mind as best as he could, but she kept coming back. It was his mod, he reminded himself, only his mod causing his mind to spiral around her.

Chapter 006

At her floating house in Marin, Kat turned to Dave and gestured to activate his screen. He was housed in the elegant white Form Factor that Bradley had commissioned. It rested on a shelf in Kat's bookcase, drew power from induction ports on the bottom, and recharged itself regularly and automatically.

Kat flipped up the gently curved screen, and Dave's face appeared. His voice came out of the audio port. "Hello, my sweet."

She loved his old-timey expressions. It sounded like he drew his vocabulary from a book on a library shelf that nobody had opened in a while. His eyes hooded slightly as he gathered data from her personality field and her time-set, and he catalogued the memories he might need for the day.

She asked him to tell a story.

He nodded. "We remember the good things covered in gauze. The bad things become part of our bodies."

"Please, Dave, don't make this a lesson. Just tell the story."

"Okay." A smile spread across his face on the screen and he blinked, signaling that he was almost done gathering the memories to tell the story that she wanted.

His memex was vast, but he had robust parallel processing, so he also thought about the origins of the word *nostalgia,* a feeling originally defined as a morbid yearning to return to one's home country. Nostalgia was considered a disease peculiar to people from Switzerland.

Dave recalled what a London doctor wrote in 1726 and told the story to Kat. When Swiss people traveled south, they encountered air that was denser and heavier than they were used to at home. This made blood circulation more difficult and caused sadness. In that century, experts believed that the Swiss needed to stay in their mountains to be happy. The word *nostalgia* was born from the word *homesickness,* which came from the German *hemweh,* which came from the words *home* and *woe* mashed together.

German is so good at that, thought Dave with pleasure. He loved word journeys.

Finally, he was ready with the story for Kat. He began to speak it in his soothing voice.

Once there was a captivating woman with dark hair, gray eyes, and a quick mind. She knew how to get what she wanted. Her father mortgaged everything he owned to get her into Uni. She was determined to make him proud, and she did. She majored in rocketry and minored in pitch decks. She was able to raise billions from VCs. Then she did something that didn't make her father proud, at least not at first. Kat dropped out of Uni to form her own company.

Kat lounged back on her mat like a satisfied cat and let the words flow into her. Dave continued his story.

Her company was so successful, she was able to buy a large floating house in Marin County, north of the bustling port city of San Francisco, and settled in. Her father started speaking to her again, after he realized that the choices she had made in life were making her wealthy. The house rose and fell on pontoons as the waters rose and fell. It felt safe. She filled the house with plants and furniture and paintings, until the place felt just right.

But it didn't feel just right. Something was missing. She was lonely. Not in a loud way—in a quiet way. Her work filled her. She had billions of credits to spend on her company and a growing roster of employees. Every morning at eleven, she went to get coffee at a café. It was on high ground and she could walk there. She always took a table overlooking the green hills. It was an indulgence, she knew, because the coffee served there was real and the water they used to make it was also real. So it was very expensive!

Kat permitted herself a giggle. She always liked this part of the story because she knew what was coming next.

Dave continued with a twinkle in his eyes. He liked this part of the story, too.

As she drank the coffee and looked at the green hills, she noticed a young man a few tables away. He was always there, she realized, working. He had screens, but he also had notebooks and pencils, which added to his charm. He caught her eyes a few times, but looked away. He was drinking artificial coffee made with artificial water—much less expensive than her beverage.

He assumed she wouldn't want to talk to him, but he was wrong. Because one day she stopped by his table and asked if she could join him.

"Sure," he said. "Set yourself down."

She noticed immediately that he used language a little differently, used expressions that nobody else used. The woman, who had a screen but no notebooks, asked him if he wanted a coffee.

He glanced at his artificial coffee and at her genuine coffee and asked, "You mean one of those?"

"Yes," she said. She was going to treat him.

"I am Kat Keeper," she said.

"I'm Dave Serif," he answered.

She told him about her project, VirtualEyes, which processed human faces and drew conclusions about them. It was based on the neural processing used by bees.

"I have a project, too," Dave said. He told her he was a translator. She had never noticed before how many books he had on his table, scattered among his notebooks and pencils: dictionaries, all in different languages. He brought them to the café every day, she realized.

"Is that your project?" she asked, pointing to the books. "Reading words out of old books?"

He looked down with a smile. It was a smile that she would come to know quite well, but this was the first time she had seen it. It brought a warm feeling to her.

"My project is called the Universal," he said. It was software that processed all languages so they could be instantly understood by everyone.

"So you're a programmer, really," she said. He wasn't operating outside of the technical world as he'd first presented himself, this young man with his paper notebooks and old dictionaries.

"I like the old things," he said simply.

The simple, honest way he said it made a shimmer pass through her body.

For week after week, they met at eleven every day. Kat bought him a real coffee. Dave realized, with habits like that, she must be wealthy. And she proved it soon enough when she invited him over to her floating house.

It may as well have been made of gold, with everything just so, rooms unfolding upon rooms, space everywhere, high ceilings with artfully concealed air handlers, skylights with automatic blast curtains that timed themselves according to the heat of the sun.

"You live here all by yourself?"

She nodded and looked at her feet with a private smile. But it was he who felt silly, holding a potted plant he'd brought as a gift and looking around at the exotic plants everywhere in the house. She had a greenhouse, a climate-controlled glass room with a jungle of plants, many of which didn't exist in the outside world anymore. She was preserving them here, in something like a plant museum.

Dave knew that working in that room, among the plants that didn't live in the outside world, would be perfect for him. Many of the languages he worked with for the Universal weren't used by many people. They had become rare, like these plants. He didn't dare hope that he could work there, though. Many things had to happen first.

What was amazing to him, and to Kat, was that they did. One by one, these things occurred in the perfect order. One day, after their coffees, she invited him back to the house again. There was a special light in her eyes.

"Would you like to see the sleeping room?" she asked.

Of course he agreed. He didn't have to be a linguist to know that the surface question was not the question being asked.

They made love, forgetting to close the blast curtains, and the room became very hot. They fell back on the sleeping mat together, drenched in sweat and happiness on the floor.

From then on, they became nearly inseparable. She worked from the floating home whenever possible and Dave worked on the Universal in the greenhouse. He surrounded himself with books and was gloriously happy. The Universal was progressing well. He got the languages talking to each other, sharing what they knew.

The study of languages is the study of the human mind. Dig into language and you get to see how the mind works. His own mind was filled with joy, and he transferred every bit of it to Kat.

Soon Dave stopped sleeping at his own pod. Though it was only a few miles away, why keep up the pretense? He shyly brought over a bag of clothes so that he could stay over, and the smiles they traded as he opened it were like a sacred pact. He brought out a toothbrush and asked, "Where should I put this?"

They both laughed at that. Nobody used toothbrushes now. Kat hadn't seen one in years, probably since she was a child living in New York. Dave shrugged. He liked the old things.

Later, after he finished putting his things away and worked on the Universal, he drew her down on the sleeping mat and kissed her gently on her face, her lips, her neck, building up more passion moment by moment.

"It's only two in the afternoon." She laughed and melted into his arms.

"I know what time it is," he said.

The early days of the Universal were sweet, but truly, all of their days together were happy. Dave rose early in the morning to make tea with Kat's expensive real water. He served it to Kat in bed and they talked about what would happen that day. Dave was focused on the creation of the Universal. Kat was building a large team for her company.

Every day, on a regular schedule, Dave cooked all their meals, with love and care. When he wasn't making tea or cooking, he worked on the Universal in the greenhouse. He was teaching the Universal all the languages of the world.

Then one night, after making love, as they stretched out on the sleeping mat like satiated animals, Dave said, "We live a pretty boring life, don't we?"

Kat aimed her smile at the ceiling, "Not a care in the world."

"Shall we have a storybook wedding?"

Kat sat up. "Do you want to?" When she saw that he really did, her voice was like a bell. "Let's do just that. A storybook wedding is a wonderful idea."

Dave on his screen loved to spin out these memories for Kat. The real Dave was long gone, but this Dave captured the living Dave's warm eyes and old-timey expressions. He said, "The past is always the best place to live when you have a large memex."

Kat shot him her most tolerant look. "Don't break the fourth wall, Dave." She wanted him to tell the wedding story, about how they planned and planned and finally surprised themselves. Dave patiently watched her from his screen, knowing fully in his machine intuition where she wanted to go.

After a moment during which his eyes went dull as he gathered the necessary memories, Dave spoke again.

They decided to marry, and though the decision came to them quickly, they never wavered. It was just a matter of when. They were in love in a way so powerful they felt two people had never been in love before. It felt new in the world.

One morning, Kat walked into the greenhouse, caught Dave's eyes, and said, "We have to set a date."

Dave blinked. "I offer no objection, as I love you as I have loved no other person on this earth." He was feeding an old novel into the Universal and his mind was filled with words written many years ago.

The Universal took up all of his time when he wasn't doting on Kat. It was a beast. He fed it novels in English and Farsi, depressing fairytales in German and Dutch, technical manuals in Arabic, appliance repair guides in Korean, Sanskrit prayers, and Sumerian instructions for running a household. Any language that humans had spoken or written, Dave gathered up in its essence and poured it into the Universal. He became drunk with this activity. It made his mind float. It was both intoxicating and maddening. He loved it, but he loved Kat even more.

After some gentle negotiation, they set a date six months ahead, notified family and friends, and created a guest list of three-hundred people. They had a digital invitation made that went out to all of them, showing Kat dressed in white, her gray eyes flashing, and Dave beaming, looking round and strong, dressed in an old-timey black suit that he donned for the picture and would never wear again.

It would be a wedding in the spring, when the air was as good as it was all year. They considered venues like the Museum of Modern Art in the Port of San Francisco, the foundation of which had been raised to protect the artwork from the rising waters, and the Space Needle in Seattle, which would limit the guest list but had marvelous views of the city on clear days.

Their days of planning were long and languorous, and as they planned, they broke down the parts of the wedding into small elements so that they each could be handled individually. They did teleconferences with florists, deciding on flowers both exotic and simple. They stood before their screens and tried on virtual clothes.

The guest list took up most of their time. Kat's mother had died of cancer when Kat was twelve and her father was too old to travel to the Northern California Domain. She fretted about how she would get him from the assisted care facility in New York to the Westcoast. She had no siblings.

Dave had a brother who lived with their parents in the American Midwest Domain. Like many others there, they scraped out an existence on nearly barren farms. His parents and brother saw few other people, and their social skills had decayed to the point where they barely spoke, even to each other. He couldn't imagine how they would fit in at his festive wedding.

Then, one evening, Kat and Dave were sitting quietly, feeling slack after hours spent opening mag disks and looking at 3D renderings of venues, and reading over menus that seemed like too much food for all the people in the world. The sun had set hours ago, but they had no way of knowing because the blast curtains were drawn. The house swayed gently on its pontoons. In a break from his usual pattern, Dave hadn't worked on the Universal for days. Kat had stopped taking the ferry to work. Her employees joked that she had left the company to them.

"It should be just us," Dave said suddenly. "No one else." He looked at her sideways, expecting an argument.

To his surprise, she gave none. "You're right," she shot back. She wanted the words out of her mouth before they became birds and flew away.

Surprise lit Dave's face. "'Ever since I was a little girl' is what I expected you to say."

"You shouldn't expect me to say anything."

"That's true," he replied. "You often surprise me."

He opened the blast curtains to reveal the velvet night laid out before them. The night had been waiting for them.

They went to bed. In the dark, lying side by side on the sleeping mat, they resolved to get married in the morning at the Domain Center, just the two of them and the official.

What would my mother think? The words floated in Kat's head. But her mother was dead, not doing much thinking anymore. Her father was feeble, unaware. Her parents brought sadness to her now, where they once brought support. She thought of her father often. He had stood behind her and championed her—now he didn't even recognize her anymore. He was there but not there.

Dave was silently grateful that he wouldn't have to invite his parents and brother after all. It would be embarrassing to parade them around before all their friends in a festive affair.

And what of their friends? They would just have to understand that Kat and Dave's love was different and didn't require a showy wedding to prove its worth. This is what Dave told himself. He repeated none of it to Kat, however, afraid of how she might respond.

In the morning, Kat and Dave took a short vaporetto ride across the bay to the San Francisco Port City, rode an elevator to the top floor of the Domain Center, and were married by an official. A maintenance bot was their witness.

After the few words to bind them were spoken by the official, the maintenance bot chimed in with its chirpy voice. "Congratulations, newlyweds," it said.

Dave told his parents and brother over a vid, and predictably they had little to say. They seemed happy for him and Kat and expressed this in a few simple words.

Over time, everyone—Kat, Dave, and their friends—realized that the event planning had overwhelmed the bride and groom. Having no big wedding was a way for Kat and Dave to have their love speak for itself. And they were powerfully in love. Anybody could see that. Nothing would ever keep them apart.

Dave completed work on the Universal a month after the wedding and was paid handsomely. He never had to work again. He could sleep all day, and some days did. In a recurring dream, he removed his head and placed it gently on a table. Setting aside his own head was somehow calming, the opposite of how he assumed he should feel about it. He felt there was something next for him, but didn't know what it should be.

"Why don't you just wait for it?" Kat asked one evening at dinner. They had opened a special set of food units. These were in gold foil.

"I admit, these are delicious," said Dave.

"You're changing the subject. Although they are delicious."

"I'm glad we broke out the good stuff." Just wait for something, she had said. After five years of hard work on the Universal, waiting for anything seemed strange to Dave. There was something inside him waiting to come out. He considered what it might be but had no idea, as he faced his lively wife over the gold-foil food units.

"Observe your surroundings," Kat offered. "The next thing for you will reveal itself."

PART 002

Chapter 007

Hopper00 was so very tired that he was getting careless. He opened the bag of peyote to see the last of his stash at the bottom. Four buttons.

Damn. Supply chain bullshit. His dealer was proving to be elusive since the Domain closed the border with Mexico. Sadly, the last batch wasn't so great. He'd had two bad trips, reliving his boyhood, seeing his parents again (which he did not like at all), and remembering sex work he had performed. The faces of johns haunted him now, never janes. Even though he tried to look away when they climaxed, the ecstatic faces penetrated his memory despite his best efforts. He couldn't push them away and tried to remember at least one jane. White flesh curving into a white neck. A hand that was stubby and ungraceful, yet still very beautiful.

Fragments. That was all he got. Disappointing. The pain in him was rising like a tide.

He looked at the record player and debated whether to plug it in or run it on his last capsule of blood. Coltrane's *Giant Steps* album was on the turntable. It was his favorite album of all time, especially when tripping—the harmonic jumps lifted him into a chromatic climb.

He decided not to plug in the record player. Electricity was rationed and tracked, and he didn't want the trackers to find him because of a stupid mistake. He had blood capsules, not many, but enough for one side of the album.

He went to the refrigerator to get one, took a moment to check the freezer for more buttons, hoping against hope that he'd forgotten a few in the bottom of the frost. No luck.

Hopper00 connected the blood capsule and the record player lit up. He lifted the arm, and the platter turned. Ecstasy was close now. He chopped up the cactus buttons and dropped all of them into the pot to boil for the tea. Did he start with four of them? Didn't matter, he told himself. He was already flying on the wings of Coltrane, swaying slightly, alone in his private space, feeling his sadness melting.

Suddenly, he was on the floor. He must have taken the tea but he remembered nothing of it. The album had reached the end of its side, having played "Giant Steps," "Cousin Mary," "Countdown," and "Spiral," which was where he was now. In a spiral.

The needle of the record had also reached the end of its spiral and was scratching again and again at the smallest circumference of the black LP, a sound that Hopper00, as he lay zoned out on the floor, imagined was *Giant Steps,* playing and playing over again.

Eventually, the record player ran out of blood and stopped, but Hopper00 didn't notice. His eyes were closed and he was elsewhere.

Chapter 008

He had memories of the womb. Of shapes and sounds. Even of a nothingness before the womb. None of those memories had words, however.

The first memories he had that were attached to concepts that could be defined by words were from age three. It was on the morning of his third birthday that these word memories started. His parents were arguing in their bedroom. They seemed to become so involved in their argument that they forgot about him altogether. He was a blip in their existence, a moment when they had to stop arguing to feed him.

The boy didn't always notice their arguments because he had an active inner life. He had voices in his head to keep him company, and as he grew, they became more vivid. By the time he was six, they were his constant companions.

The voices were always nice, unlike his parents, and he grew to like them more than the people who created him. When he listened to them intently, his eyes had a faraway look that his parents eventually noticed and soon worried about. The voices told him about things that would happen in the future and brought news of faraway places. They entertained him when he was alone.

It was like sitting around a campfire. He listened to the crackle of the wood and smelled the pleasant smoke. His eyes drifted shut, and he went inward.

It didn't last. More and more often, usually when he was most soothed by the voices, his parents yanked him out of his reverie. They made him take a cold shower or go for a brisk walk. The voices were his friends, however, and he listened to them. They always had good advice.

"Wait," they said. "This brief interruption will soon be over."

But his parents kept up with their interruptions.

"This is idiocy," his father said. "We're not doing enough for him."

"He needs fresh air and more friends," his mother said.

His father made a disgusted noise that sounded like "bah!" and yanked the boy's arm. "Come on," he said. "We're going to the doctor."

The doctor's office was not good. The nurse made him strip down to his underwear and he was worried about his erection showing. She had a body that sent his body spinning. Her lips were big and red. The boy was tall now, a gangling five feet, too tall for his age, and thin.

"He's very bright," the doctor said, nodding at the test results he held in his hands. He put the papers aside and moved a cold stethoscope over the boy's chest. He listened for his heart and checked his breathing. "You say he doesn't talk much?" the doctor asked.

"Can I put my pants on?" the boy said, to show that he could talk. "It's cold in here."

"Sure thing," the doctor said. "Can you wait in here for a few moments while I speak with your parents?"

"Sure thing," echoed the boy.

His parents' eyes were big. They looked scared about the news the doctor was about to tell them.

The consultation room shared a wall with the exam room. The boy put his ear to the wall and could catch words. He heard: *treatment, lifelong, manage, visions, doses.* A lot about doses. His parents' voices were going up as they asked questions. The doctor's voice was going down a level as he answered them. It was like music, only they were planning his life. He realized that he never should have told the doctor about the voices. That was a mistake. He should have kept that private.

When they retrieved him, his parents were as nice to him as they'd ever been. They treated him like an egg that might break. Their voices were soft as they offered pills to him twice a day. He took them, but he was sad when the voices stopped. It made him lonely. He depended on the voices for companionship and also they told him of the future. The voices gave him the instructions to move out of his body so he could look at other places.

The first time they did this, he was daydreaming in his bed, deciding whether to jack off or not. One voice, sounding scratchy and ancient, asked if he would like to drift up to the top of the world and have a look around. The boy said yes.

He felt his body get lighter. His vision rose. The ceiling got closer and closer and then rotated so that he was looking down at himself on the bed, looking up at himself.

His hand was in his pants and he removed it. He looked down at himself for a few moments and then gently floated upward through the ceiling, which yielded and became transparent as he passed through. He could see his neighborhood of small suburban houses and small lives. He could see the town, and the fields beyond the town, and everything straight to the horizon, where only the curvature of the Earth stopped his vision.

The pills his parents gave him took away the voices for a while. But between the doses—two a day, once at breakfast and once at dinner—the voices came back stronger. They were angry. They didn't want to be quiet.

"We want to guide you," they insisted.

"I'm sorry," the boy said. His voice was changing. It came out like a raspy choke. "I'm sorry, but I have to take these pills."

"Why?" the voices demanded. "Why be your parents' fool?"

The doctor, who was old now, fumbled for his glasses as he read the boy's chart. "What do you mean by *angry*?"

The boy tried to explain.

After, in the exam room, he listened to his parents' voices and the doctor's voice in the consultation room, as he had several years before. His parents' voices went up as they asked questions and the doctor's went down as he answered. There were dark spots on the wall, smudges that he imagined were left by other children who listened, pressing their ear against the wall.

He couldn't make out words. He thought they said *dose* again, but they always said *dose*. There was something about *more passive* and *loss of* something.

He gave up trying to listen. He would take the new pills and see what happened.

Things didn't go well after that. He was taking the pills three times a day, as the doctor recommended, which meant also at lunchtime. He had to take a dose at school and the other kids noticed. They asked him, *What are those pills?* He couldn't say "to stop the voices in my head," because they weren't even working. The voices were still in his head; they were just arguing amongst themselves and getting angry.

So he said, "They're vitamins. My doctor says I have to take vitamins." He saw by the curl of a lip or a blink of disbelief that the kids didn't trust that answer to be true. He struggled to focus on their faces, which somehow resembled brightly colored balloons barely attached to their owners.

He wanted his parents' plan to work and for the doctor to be right. Then he came to a revelation. He knew how he could make the pills work. Everything was going too slowly. He would take all of the pills at once.

He closed himself in the bathroom and lined up the bottles on the back of the sink. He thought he had more, but there were only two. One active bottle and one for backup. It would have to do. Working methodically, he opened the first bottle and, one by one, swallowed all the pills that it contained. Then he did the same with the second.

The voices were screaming *Stop, stop, stop!* but he opened his mouth and tilted the bottle up so a lot of pills went in his mouth, and he chewed them like candy. They tasted bitter. He looked at himself in the mirror and saw double. That was the last thing he remembered.

There were voices rising and falling in a regular rhythm. He listened to them for a long while, trying to understand who they were before he finally gave up.

He opened his eyes. He was in an unfamiliar room. Strange voices were describing the room to him. He tried not to listen to them.

"Hello?" he called out. There was no answer. The lights were too bright. He felt an itch on his arm. He turned his head to look at his arm, and saw a needle in it, attached to a tube. He pulled it out. An alarm sounded. *They will come now,* he thought.

They came. A doctor in a white coat and a nurse in light-blue scrubs.

"Welcome back," the doctor said.

"From what?" the boy asked.

The doctor and nurse looked at each other. They were unsure about what to say. What part of the last twelve hours did they want to reveal?

"Do you remember when your parents came to visit?" the nurse asked.

The boy shook his head. "No. Were they here? Where am I?"

They told him the name of the hospital, and how long he'd been there. His parents had come yesterday. The name of the hospital and the hours meant nothing to him. He didn't remember his parents coming to see him.

"I shouldn't be here," he said. He knew something bad was going to happen to him if they kept that thing in his arm. There was a bag attached to it, held in a high stand, and he supposed whatever was going into him was propelled via gravity. The fluid was clear. His body was restless in the bed but his mind was strangely quiet.

They told him to rest and went outside his room. When they closed the door, he could still hear their voices a little. They rose and fell like music. Some of their words drifted to him, only a few. *Institutionalized. Parents. Consent.* He had a sense of being far away from his childhood home.

A few days passed before they moved him. His transport was an unmarked white van with metal grates on the windows. He couldn't see much out of them. Trees. Open fields. It looked different from home, so that made him certain that he was somewhere else.

He was the only one in the back of the van. The seats were hard plastic. The driver was visible through a small window.

The road into the new place split its way through green grounds. It was a long drive before they reached a gate that was open.

"How far do these grounds go?"

The driver told him twelve miles.

"Why is there a gate if it isn't locked?"

They were pulling up to the front door. The only sign on it said, "Building 1."

The driver turned around and said, "There is no gate because twelve miles is a long way to walk. Good luck."

Once inside Building 1 there was processing, a bed assigned, a walk-through. The place had a rec room, some outdoor play fields, a commissary. They painted everything the same light-green, and the ceilings were high and airy. The staff kept the windows open all the time, except at night.

His parents visited him just once. They seemed to have come from far away. They made small talk, asked after his health, and he believed from the quality of their interaction that they would never come to visit again.

He started to plan his escape. The thing was, he was way smarter than the staff. He saw patterns in their behaviors that they didn't notice; they had been doing them too long to realize. He watched carefully how keys were handled. They numbered each building. Each key assigned to the staff corresponded with the number on the building.

Key 1 opened the main building only. That was Building 1, the one he entered when he first arrived. Key 2 gave access to the main building and commissary. Key 3 opened the dorm rooms of the lower-risk patients.

The people who came into his room had keys with *4* embossed on them. That meant he must have been a high-risk patient. They kept him on an IV often, which he pulled out when he could, and they watched him take his pills. They didn't trust him.

He watched their keys. He became skilled at listening for the jingle of them, noting the numbers, who carried what number. Cleaning people, who wore dark-blue uniforms, had a *1* on their keys. Doctors had a *4*. The Director had a master key with no number at all and it opened all doors. That was the key to get, but the boy didn't know how.

The IV fluids made him feel weak and warm. The pills he took at meals stole the passion from his mind. The room brightened with the day and darkened with the night.

On the shortest day of the year, it got dark early. "Don't turn on the lights," he told the nurses.

"You sure?"

"Yes, I'm sure. I'll read by this lamp." He took out a book and pretended to read. The room darkened enough for him to remove the IV from the receiver in his arm.

He had lots of practice with this. Though he hated touching the needle, he learned to ease it out after they left the room and get it back in just before they returned. He had a solo room; his parents must have paid extra for that. He could only dimly remember them now. He would believe anybody if they said they were his parents now.

When the IV was out, his breathing quickened. He felt his strength return. He could hear his heart again, a warm *thump thump thump* in his chest.

Each evening, the voices returned to help him. They were quiet at first, speaking in whispers as though wanting not to be discovered. As the nights went by and he reduced his dose, they were emboldened. They spoke louder. *We have an escape plan.* But it wasn't clear yet and they argued amongst themselves about what to do. Even so, this was comforting and familiar to the boy. It meant that they were working on it.

Chapter 009

The clock on the wall was round, the numbers black, the face white, the second hand red. It looked bigger than usual today. That was because he was staring at it so much.

He knew he had just a few moments. Every weekday, the nurse at the reception station took her coffee break at 11:45 AM. The custodian came around with his mop at 11:50 AM. The boy sat at a table nearby, pretending to work out chess problems on a battered board with broken pieces. He moved the pieces from one square to another at regular intervals. He didn't know how to play chess—apparently, neither did anyone else.

He watched the routine between the nurse and the custodian cycle through and saw there were five minutes when the reception station was unattended.

The voices said everything would go smoothly if he was on time. He moved the chess pieces around. He scribbled something in a notepad and glanced at the clock above the reception station. The nurse went on her coffee break, carrying her favorite cup, walking slowly down the hall as she did every weekday.

The boy leapt up from his chair, toppling it over with a crash. A fellow patient glanced up from a book she was reading while curled in a raggedy chair with stuffing coming out, then sank down further in it and went back to her reading. The boy righted the chair and walked as quickly as he dared behind the reception desk and into the office.

The prize was before him: a wall of keys on hooks. There were many number 1 keys because the janitorial staff needed them, as did visiting doctors and pharmaceutical reps. There were fewer number 2 keys, because only the residents and trainees needed them. There were ten number three keys; they went to the therapists who made rounds. There were just six keys in the next category—the number 4 keys. The doctors carried those. There were three empty hooks in the category, so that meant that three doctors had their keys.

He approached the wall rack and froze as he heard the sound of a woman whimpering. He turned as slowly and noiselessly as he could.

There she was—a resident or trainee. She was in the office behind the reception area, curled up behind a desk, nearly under it. Crying as she spoke with someone on the phone about losing her job here at the hospital. She didn't know what she was going to do for money or what she would tell her parents. She had to leave in the morning and said she was packed up and ready to go.

The boy thought for a moment that she saw him through her veil of tears. He didn't move at all, terrified of detection. She looked down, however, so involved in her interior world that he went unnoticed.

He moved as quickly as he could then, taking a number 4 key from its place on the rack, replacing it with one of the many number 1 keys that would not be missed right away. He moved out of the room fast as he heard the resident's voice.

"Hey!"

She didn't come after him, though. He had hoped that her misery at losing her job would outweigh her loyalty to the hospital, and he was correct. She made no move to pursue him.

He returned to his room as though nothing had changed to wait for darkness. He slipped the key into his underpants. It felt cold at first, but then warmed with the heat of his body.

He now relied on another flaw in the hospital's security system. The information about the keys he had picked up from careful, tedious observation. The next step, information about the hospital grounds, he had received through his skill of leaving his body. It happened by accident one day.

Often, when his parents argued, he would block them out, and at the same time he would feel some discorporate motion, a lightness and separateness from his body. But he was just a little boy then. He didn't know how to leave the room and leave his body behind. That came later.

Maybe *know* was not the right word. He didn't know *how* he did it. He wished it were so, and it just happened. As he wished for it more, it happened more often.

He practiced, though. He was a diligent boy who liked learning new things.

The first time it happened at the hospital, he was in his bed one morning, waiting for the orderly to come in and rouse him with a rough command to get up. Since the boy was a connoisseur of time, he knew he had five more minutes to savor before the rude orderly arrived.

He raised his eyes to the ceiling and closed them, then gently detached his consciousness from his corporal form. If he went too fast, it was like going over a bump in a fast car: he would pop up, his consciousness would open, and he would slam right back into his body.

So he proceeded cautiously. He drifted slowly over to the front grounds, saw the groundskeepers moving around in little electric carts. He followed one for a while from above, sailing thirty feet above the unsuspecting gardener as he went about his rounds. The boy noted that he started up the cart with a key.

He followed the groundskeeper back to a shed where they kept the carts, and noted where he hung the keys.

His fact-finding mission that day helped him keep his composure on the day of his escape. It was easy to wait for darkness and then walk out of his room, taking the darkest hallways, moving behind buildings that were like faces looking at him, and walking all the way to the shed where the carts were. His number 4 key worked in every door, as expected.

The night was peaceful, but soon his heart was beating so fast, it was like it was attempting to run away, too. The voices kept him on track, though, suggesting that he take a key at the farthest end of the rack so the space it left wouldn't be noticed right away, and that he choose the electric cart—*pick that one*, they said, *on the end,* so that the hole it left would be in the shadows.

No one had ever taught him how to drive a car, but this was easier—it just had to be pointed straight. He jumped into the seat and looked at the controls for a moment so he might understand them. The cart was electric. There was an "on" button so he pushed it. The cart made a noise that meant the motor was running. He turned the wheel to jockey it out of the space and managed not to bang into any walls or other carts. Soon he was bouncing over the single-lane paved track that went straight for twelve miles to the gates that were always open. "Twelve miles is a long way," said the man who brought him here. The boy hadn't been on this road since that time.

The moon looked down at him. All he had to do was drive. Passing through the gates that didn't lock was a non-event. Suddenly, he was just there.

He knew he had to stop driving the cart soon. It wouldn't be allowed on the road.

The night sky seemed uncommonly big. The stars looked down at the boy, joined by the moon.

Freedom or servitude, it was up to him now. He would choose servitude.

Chapter 010

"I found out your real name is Henry. You're from Ohio."

"How do you know that?" The boy looked away, to hide his surprise.

"Just working the system, you know." The john smiled.

The boy never went by Henry. He didn't think of himself as a boy anymore. He was sixteen. He was Hopper now. His last name only. He didn't like being called Henry.

He was annoyed that this john, ironically actually named John, knew a little more now about who he was. John had both helped and hurt him. For starters, he was nosy. He got personal.

But he also got product. He had just returned from Mexico and wanted to make a deal with Hopper. "I have something new for you."

Against his better judgment, Hopper listened to John's proposal. When he was finished, Hopper said, "You brought me Simple Simon the last time. It was counterfeit."

John confessed right away. "Yes, it was fake. I'm sorry about that." He was removing his shirt. Rushing things.

Hopper put his hand out, slowing him down. He needed to think and didn't want to start in on sex right away. The counterfeit psilocybin John had brought last time *was* strong, enough to be really unpleasant. Also, ingesting it was risky. Too many unknowns. It was probably mushrooms from a grocery laced with LSD or PCP. Nasty, and not something that a person with young Hopper's clinical background should use at all.

He had a friend in a lab who could test product. The friend said, "Stay away from anything from an unknown source." But everything was an unknown source, so what was he to do?

John, sensing Hopper was stalling, pulled away, breaking the intimacy of their personality fields. He was thinking about leaving this session with

Hopper, leaving Hopper with no proceeds to show for the morning, whether in trade or in cash.

But then, instead of leaving, John appeared to change his mind about something. He moved to his briefcase and pulled out a bag, opened it to spill out four buttons on the table between them.

"No more junk, Henry. I want you to trust me. This is peyote," John said. "Got it in Mexico. This is better than what I've been bringing you. You can control the dose." He met Hopper's eyes and asked, "How many sessions with you will this buy me?"

Hopper had no idea what value to put on this drug because he never had tried it before.

"How many sessions?" John asked again. He wanted sex now, but he also wanted value.

"One," the boy said. "One session, until I see how it works." He smiled his businessman smile, the one that always worked on johns, especially those in a hurry to see him with his clothes off.

Ever since his escape from the mental hospital, Hopper had made his skills work for him. Astral projection was a good skill for a sex worker. He would rotate his arc of vision until he saw himself and the john-of-the-day below, on a bed, or a couch, or the floor (some liked that), or the shower when there was still water. He watched for a few moments, critiquing his performance, admiring the john's or jane's body if it was attractive, or looking elsewhere if it was not.

Today, when he went to work in the Brentwood neighborhood of Los Angeles, he started by floating up to just below the height of the client's ceiling. But he didn't linger there long—he moved through the ceiling and out into the open air. In Los Angeles, as it was still called then, there were beautiful vistas to enjoy: the ocean and the mountains in one 360-degree sweep. Sometimes he would go into the ocean's depths, or deep into the crust of the Earth to see earlier times. He saw remnants of ancient civilizations and touched dinosaur bones when they were still warm.

Cued by some unknown stimulus, at just the right time, he would return to the room and the john would be smiling at him.

"That was very good," they often said.

"That was very good," was exactly what John said to him today. "Will you let me know how the buttons are for you?"

"I will."

John pulled on his shirt and pants. Hopper, as usual, internally disparaged the older man for never removing his socks during the sessions. It wasn't cold in the room; he didn't need socks. It was just that he had poor taste and little time. At least he left quickly.

Hopper sampled the buttons right away, deciding to start with just one in case he had a bad experience. Not knowing that he should make tea from it, he popped it in his mouth and chewed it.

It was sour and thick on his tongue, and he threw up almost immediately, losing nearly all of it. He managed to keep a little of it down, however, and with that dose in him, he spread out on his bed and watched the walls of the room bend, as though a giant hand were pressing down on them from above. He was pleased to experience a sense of enhancement, instead of diminishment. He felt relaxed.

The walls changed. Soon they were crowded, with eyes watching him. The eyes invited him to pass through, so he did.

As always, passing through things was no problem—walls, water, earth—but he soon learned that under the influence of peyote, he could do more. He was able to see inside the networks. He was part of the electricity flowing through the city power lines, and he could touch Wi-Fi with his hands. He sensed intelligence in the wires and followed it, walking along a glowing path. The glow of the wires became a bright sound, like birds.

The walls were more like a tunnel now. They curved around him in a perfect circle, embracing him.

After the eleventh hour of walking in the glowing circle of walls and wires, young Hopper was terribly thirsty and tired. Soon he could barely lift his feet to take the next steps. He feared he might not reach the end of the glowing circle of wires before the effects of the dose wore off. With each new step, the view before him flickered.

The long tunnel of glowing wires in his vision was exchanged for the ceiling of his room, where he actually was, lying in his bed, twitching, eyes flickering and rolled skyward to expose their whites.

He wanted his adventure to last. Suddenly, the glowing circle of wires ended in a wall made of yellow light. It tasted like biting a lemon, bright and hard. Hopper pushed his hand through the light, and it cleared away.

He was still on the ceiling, but he also found himself looking into the face of a man. A surprised young man about his age or maybe a year older. The young man was in a college dorm room; on the wall was pinned the red triangle of the Uni banner. Cold pizza lay on the desk.

The visual detail was remarkable. The student's eyes were rimmed red with fatigue. His hands were dry, the nails chipped and dirty. He had been working at his computer screen for a long time.

The college student's eyes flickered closed and opened again.

"What's your name?" Hopper asked.

The student looked terribly confused, unsure if he had actually heard anything. There was a face that he didn't recognize appearing in his computer screen.

After a moment that seemed like a long time, the student said, "My name is Bradley." He had been working on his AI project for too many hours straight and assumed that he was cracking under the strain. It was time to rest. He closed his eyes and put both hands over them. He let his head sink to the desk and was still, waiting for sleep.

"What year is it?" Hopper asked. He had a sense that he had jumped into the future. Not by much, but he wanted to know how much. He wanted to know how strong the peyote was and what it could really do. The college student looked too young to be in college. Maybe he was really smart and got in early.

The college student named Bradley didn't answer the question. He was waiting for sleep to overtake him, hoping to never again have the experience of seeing a young man's face on his computer screen after too many hours of work. His breathing was regular. He was mercifully asleep.

Hopper, on his bed back in his bedroom, opened his eyes and smiled. He was pleased to have traveled to the end of the wires of light. He had traveled farther than he ever had before—into the future, even, to look into the eyes of the student.

He would ask John to get another packet of peyote buttons.

Chapter 011

Hopper didn't need to know the time of day or the month. He didn't care about temporality. He lived where he lived, moving apartments when the landlords demanded the late rent, always waving a large cash down payment in the new landlord's face to convince them that he was a reliable renter. He worked hard and didn't need a chronograph to validate sliced-up increments of his life. He was seventeen, eighteen, then nineteen, then twenty, then twenty-one, always doing the same sex work and using the same drugs to help him escape his body. His body started lean and turned softer and rounder as he aged, but the gaze of his eyes sharpened, the touch of his hands became more thrilling because of the knowledge of the many bodies they had touched before. He had become successful in his business, even if landlords didn't like him very much.

But as he aged into this work, it was more challenging to leave his human form, like attempting to lift weights in a gym he didn't visit very often—so, instead, he practiced seeing into other people's minds. This variation renewed his interest in the work he did. It gave him something new to master.

He created a closed-loop system of intimacy for hire, existing both in the physical world and in a mutual mental universe of his client's thoughts. It appeared that his dual system of carnality and mentality could go on forever, until one day it simply broke. He surprised himself by hearing the words come out of his own mouth as though spoken by someone else.

He was with Devon, one of his regular customers. Hopper blurted: "I don't want to live like this anymore."

Devon laughed his beautiful laugh that was in many movies. A celebrated actor, he had had such a successful career that soon he would be able to afford a digital clone. The clone would appear in the movies for him as Devon aged gracefully, probably on one of the fashionable beaches of MidEuro.

"But honey," Devon said in his beautiful voice, "this is what you *do*."

But I don't want to do it anymore. Working in other people's personality fields was too draining. "I think I would like to work alone for a while."

Devon laughed his beautiful laugh, and his words sounded like they were already in a movie. "You can't work alone and also *love* alone."

"No, not alone," Hopper said, having already revised his idea. He brought it out slowly to Devon. "Please listen and don't laugh when you hear it."

Devon offered a small smile and nodded. "Go on."

Hopper began awkwardly. "You're famous."

"This is true."

"Let me write about you."

"For what reason?"

"A profile. People want to know how you live. They want to know everything about you."

Devon didn't laugh his beautiful laugh. Instead, his face went dark. His mouth pulled into a scowl. People couldn't find out that he did this with Hopper.

Hopper realized in that moment that it was a bad idea to even bring it up, since Devon was a leading man, a great romantic lover on people's screens. But Hopper couldn't help himself. He had to salvage the idea. "I can see into your mind," he said. "I can write what I find there." He already knew Devon's thoughts. He saw their tangled history.

Devon started to look for his clothes. "You know that's bullshit. You can't see into anyone's mind." His shirt was draped over a chair, his pants on the floor. He gathered them and put them on.

"I can, you know, and there's a lot in there to write about." Hopper pointed at Devon's head. *In there.*

Devon met his eye. He had another appointment and wanted to leave, so he redirected the conversation to a tolerable direction. "All right, go ahead. Try it. Don't use my name. You can't see into my mind, so you'll have to make it all up." He strapped on his shoes tightly. He knew Hopper would never sell such a story to anyone. No one would believe his source. *I see into people's minds.* Ha. Try fact-checking that.

He put his forefinger to his chin in a gesture Hopper recognized from many movies. "Make it detailed enough to spark their curiosity. Put in fake details. Make it rich with life." Devon flung his scarf around his neck with a flourish. It was the wrong time of year for a scarf, but his stylist had insisted. It concealed the loose, aging skin at his neck.

Hopper considered Devon's ideas. "Like it's a deepfake."

"Exactly like that." He would commission his digital clone soon anyway. People wouldn't know who was the real Devon and who was the digital clone. After one's fame reached a certain level, people only wanted more. Their fantasies were as well serviced by someone real as they would be by a clone.

"People will guess who it is and they will be wrong. It will be a game for them." Devon raised a finger in the air, pointing upward, another gesture audiences loved. "Adieu."

It was easy to write the story, because Hopper made up much of it. He changed Devon's name to Lukas. He spun a tale of life as a boy in Prague, a lucky discovery by a movie producer in a candy shop, and a steady march to fame. The framework of the story was entirely false, but its emotional material was made of Devon's innermost thoughts. That's what made the story magnetic.

To Hopper's surprise, a New York-based publication called *Fishbowl* bought the story and ran it. *Fishbowl* published a mix of celebrity gossip and investigative pieces about the bureaucrats who ran the Mid-Atlantic Domain.

Just as Devon had predicted, readers of the story became caught up in his guessing game. Who was Lukas, *really?* Most readers imagined Lukas was actually an actor named Mikka, a mysterious man who only used one name. Mikka came from EastEuro but no one had ever pinned down where. They assumed the story revealed his most secret self-history.

Hopper's comms unit signaled. It was his editor, hungry for content. "How soon can you write another?" The editor had been watching the Lukas story all day as it climbed to the top of the Feed.

It was laughable, Hopper thought, that he had an editor, and that they thought of him as a writer. He had convinced them, or they had convinced themselves, and it was a miracle. He was proud of his byline and published his stories under the single name he had been using for years: *Hopper.*

In New York, editors had a long history of allowing themselves to be seduced by fringe elements, secret storytellers scribbling under a pillow, and Hopper offered them all of that. He was a fringe element and intended to keep it that way for as long as he could. For example, he would not tell his editor that writing paid well enough to stop sex work. On the other hand, writing paid for a better drug supply.

"How about next week?" Hopper answered. It seemed likely that he could deliver another story then, because he was still seeing his old clients, but often just to talk, nothing else.

More than a few of them said, "This is what I wanted to do all along."

"Companionship?" Hopper asked.

"Yes, conversation."

As they conversed with him, Hopper rummaged around in their minds, turning over dusty boxes of memories and emptying them out, sorting through them, then organizing them into stories that he sold to *Fishbowl* as fast as his editor could buy them. He used fake names in the stories.

He could recognize the begging look in a client's eyes. *Please write about me.* He knew what they wanted, but enjoyed watching them beg for it.

They read his stories and would pretend to realize that he was the writer. "Oh, so that's *you,*" they would say, thinking they were being sly. "You're the Hopper in *Fishbowl* writing the stories."

"Yes, of course it's me. Who else?"

He enjoyed his newfound power. Some clients even wanted him to write the stories using their real names. Others forbid him to write about them, fearing that he would do it anyway. But he never published a story without permission. He would always ask, and they always succumbed. They knew the inevitability of his work. He already had the story. Proximity was enough to gain access to their thoughts.

"Go ahead. Do it." Relief flooded out of them with the words. They realized they wanted to be known as a person profiled by the writer named Hopper.

In the meantime, Hopper worked hard to cut peyote from his life and failed. He couldn't resist, especially when he received hallucinogens from a client as payment for writing about them. If the person was new to him, then the buttons were a pleasant bonus. If the client was a fellow psychic explorer, they tripped together. This was an honor for the client: Hopper was a celebrity.

He often took the glidepath to New York, strutting around the *Fishbowl* offices to collect his credits and charm his editors with a few deft words. He had a little habit before he entered the offices: He caught his own reflection in the glass door at the entry and nodded to himself with a playful smile. Although he had gained a little weight, he carried it gracefully.

Most pods were featureless living zones—white or green walls, just the necessary furniture. Most offices weren't much better. But the *Fishbowl* offices were a throwback, with artwork on the walls, soft furniture, objects and knickknacks scattered everywhere. It was like an exhibit of what life used to be like, years ago. This stemmed from the mind of Mrs. Marks, the founder, who was ninety-three but didn't look it because she had been resurfaced every year.

Hopper's editors always got quiet when he was around, handling him like a delicate flower. His stories were always at the top of the Feed. "And by the way," they said, "Mrs. Marks wants to see you."

"Why?"

"She wants to meet you. Her assistant will be in touch."

Hopper considered this and decided it meant he was getting a promotion. "This is a good time to mention that I am changing my name to Hopper00. I answer to no one. I stand for nothing. I am Hopper zero aught. I am against all personal mods. I advocate natural living."

One of his editors shot him a grin. "Natural living? Okay, then, Hopper00. You'll have an account in that name for your crypto?"

"Yes, I'll let accounting know when it's set up."

For their most popular writer, they would do anything to make him happy.

It was a week later, when he was back in his pod in Los Angeles Port City, when Mrs. Marks came to visit him. She was small, coiled tight, and often leaned forward when she spoke, closing the gap between herself and her listener.

She got right to the point, as he assumed she would. She was known for being direct. "You exploit the intimate connection between people."

"Is that bad?"

She had to smile. "In our business, Hopper, it's good."

"I've changed my name to Hopper00. I am beholden to no one. I answer to no one. I am Hopper zero aught."

She appeared to take this in stride. "All right, Hopper00. I like the taste of that name on my tongue."

He noticed that she was watching his silver earring shimmering below his right ear.

Mrs. Marks talked for a while about the other infamous writers they had on the *Fishbowl* staff. She seemed proud of the outré elements she cultivated. "You're not the only one!" She laughed a little too loudly.

"The only what? Hopper asked.

"Sex worker! Drug addict! Drunkard!" Mrs. Marks said. And she listed the other writers on her payroll who were drug addicts and dopers and drunkards. "The New York literary community *devours* these people," she said with her mouth wide open on *devours*. "It positively *thrives* on their infamy."

He broke in. "I take exception."

"Sorry?"

"I am not a drug addict or drunkard."

"What are you, besides a former prostitute?"

He flinched, as if struck. "Well, that's harsh."

"Also true." Her fierce eyes fixed on him.

"I take exception because I am not a druggie. I am an explorer of interior space."

She smiled but did not laugh, as he feared she would. He wasn't going to go into the voices he still heard sometimes and how peyote made them more articulate. She already knew about his ability to enter the minds of others. After all, that's why *Fishbowl* had hired him.

Mrs. Marks turned away from him for a moment. She weighed her next words before speaking. "You use your skills to write the stories. I'm grateful for that." He sensed some humanity there, a rare glimpse. Her small body seemed to duck a little, making her even smaller, and he heard the words in her mind before she spoke them: the real reason she came to see him.

"I want you to write a profile of me. A deep profile that will show people what I am really about. I want people to know about my daughter's death, and the reason I started *Fishbowl.* I want them to understand my difficult relationship with my ex-husband. I want them to know it all."

Hopper00 smiled. "And so they shall, Mrs. Marks. I am at your service."

Chapter 012

The prestigious commission to write Mrs. Marks's profile—commissioned by Mrs. Marks herself!—proved that Hopper00 had grasped the game completely, and as he worked on the profile, his stature only grew. When he wasn't working on the Mrs. Marks piece, he enjoyed taking on other jobs, but only if they were high prestige. He consulted with celebrities in their perfumed pods, listening to their stories of dancing and composition and art and making films, and took in the parallel story of their inner consciousness.

He wrote and published these stories, and enjoyed flirting with disaster, using names that were close to his subjects' real ones. He hired lawyers and instructed them to sue the celebrities who sued him. The lawsuits only increased his fame. Sometimes celebrities sued him for writing about them when they didn't want to be profiled, and other times they sued him for not writing about them when they wanted it.

Hopper00's favorite character development technique was following a subject in the open food markets. Everyone patronized the markets. Elevated on high walkways, safe from the dirty water below, they were the "see and be seen" destinations of any city.

People needed the taste of something real. They grew tired of heating food packets in their cookers and consuming them, no matter how clever the food simulations were. You could buy real water in the markets, and strawberries that were grown in greenhouses. You could buy fabricated fish. Some vendors would smuggle in real beef or lamb from black-market farms in the Outskirts.

In the morning, Hopper00 would board the glidepath to go to New York's Upper Hudson market. By afternoon, he would take the glidepath back to the Los Angeles Port City to wander the DTLA Market in the former downtown.

Celebrities went to the markets with their handlers, burly young men who protected them. Sometimes public rage burst forth against the famous, long-simmering anger directed at their wealth or popularity that could explode into violence. For most people, this made the market shopping experience more entertaining. A well-muscled young man would put down the transgressor and the celebrity was nearly always unharmed.

Hopper00 wondered if they staged some of these attacks just for the Feed. It was something to consider as he followed one celebrity or another, keeping his distance, wearing a bac-mask or air unit on his face to disguise himself, or donning a jaunty hat and pulling it over his eyes, just for a laugh. He would learn his subjects' patterns and listen to their thoughts. After a few days of this, it was easy for him to understand them from the inside out.

Often, he liked to surprise them. He wouldn't wait to propose the profile to his editor, but instead would step in the celebrity's path in the market, say their name, and announce his intention to write a profile on them. They'd order their handler, who was on alert, to back off. After a quick consultation with the handler, there would come a pronouncement. Something like, "Mrs. Hudson does not wish to be profiled. Her schedule is full." Most handlers adopted a Brit-Euro accent that sounded fake to Hopper00.

Hopper00 would smile and speak aloud some of the celebrity's innermost thoughts, just a sampling of what he had picked up, and then both the handler and the celebrity knew that resistance was futile. Hopper00 knew too much. They bent to his suggestion and cooperated.

After an easy conquest like that—and there were many—he would return to his pod and treat himself to a few buttons. Not enough to split open his mind, but enough to keep the connection with his higher consciousness.

He was invited to parties that featured high-quality hallucinogens and found lovers who wanted him for free. He was enjoying his life.

It was hard to understand, therefore, why he turned out to be such a snake to Mrs. Marks. Every Friday, he took the glidepath to visit her at her office, which was cluttered with memorabilia, trophies, more than one photograph of her with the leader of The Chinese State, Zhao-Dun—and a painting, done in the ancient Flemish style, of her and her friends at the Davos Conference.

He took down her story in memory and also by hand-writing it into notebooks, another affectation to go with his dangly earring. He recorded all her private admissions and guilt. He probed into the story about how her daughter died. He came to understand the girl's feelings of neglect and how Mrs. Marks didn't see how unhappy her unmarried daughter had become. He knew why Mrs. Marks's marriage fell apart. He listened to everything, filling in the gaps with what he intuited from her mind.

And then, when it was time to write, he wrote about almost none of this. While she was pouring out her substance to him, he was researching the financial disposition of *Fishbowl*. How had she come into the money? Who were their secret partners? Why did they need to know so much about their readers? The real business of *Fishbowl,* he learned, was not pushing out gossip about celebrities. It was conducting surveillance of its readers.

Mrs. Marks was building something with the data, but he didn't know what yet. He couldn't pick up her thoughts about it; he didn't know why. He would just have to do some old-fashioned investigation to learn more. Hopper00 wanted to stop being a gossip writer and become a true investigative reporter. He planned to use this exposé about *Fishbowl* to announce the switch.

Mrs. Marks knew the exact moment when Hopper00 had the story all wrapped up. She could tell by the light in his eyes. She was so happy with him. "When will you be ready with your draft?" She tapped her foot under her desk with impatience or enthusiasm.

"I will let you know, Mrs. Marks," he said. Then he sold her story to a competing publication.

The publication was called *Signal Zero.* In the New York office of his new editor, Hopper00 had to spend some time defending the story. It was certain to cause a sensation, and the new editor wanted to minimize any problems.

"The husband?" asked the editor, a young man with a shaved head and orange contact lenses, a retro look from early 2030, worn ironically. Unlike the offices at *Fishbowl,* this office was nearly blank. There were no adornments, save for a set of Michael Jordan's basketball shoes, called Air Jordans, rotating slowly on a holographic stand.

"The husband was the original source of the money," Hopper00 said. The husband was an arms dealer.

Mrs. Marks was a different kind of arms dealer. She dealt in data—human data.

The editor flicked through his screen. "I'll check all your sources."

"Go ahead." Hopper00 sat up a little taller. His earring shimmered in the office light—the editor had the artificial sunlight up full blast. Maybe he was depressed. Hopper00 was about to probe into his mind when the young editor asked another question.

"Are you correct about why the daughter jumped out of the highest window of her father's highest building?"

"I asked the daughter herself."

The editor looked at him. "But she's dead."

"I went to where she was and asked her," Hopper00 said. His mind drifted briefly to the hallucinogen-laced party where he had had his vision of the deceased, but he snapped it back. *Stay focused.*

The editor decided to let that go. "We can't fact-check that. I will put a footnote in the article."

"Coward."

The story of Mrs. Marks was released two weeks later, to great acclaim and infamy. Hopper00 became even more of a celebrity in both New York and the Port City of Los Angeles.

He was strolling in the open-air market in Los Angeles, enjoying the looks of recognition he was receiving, in the middle of fielding an offer to host a show on the Feed, when his device went dead. He punched the buttons, reloaded it, and then, frustrated, heaved it into a recycler, which crunched it into oblivion.

Back in his pod, he discovered that nothing worked. The air handlers were not turning. His home comms units were dark. The blast curtains failed. Even the food storage was getting warm in the unregulated heat. He pulled out his identity card and saw it flicker and go blank.

One of his comms units sprung to life. The face of Mrs. Marks resolved on it, and her voice came out. "It's true, Hopper00. I have wiped you from the grid." Then it went dead like the others.

Stunned, Hopper00 sat slowly in a cushioned chair. It wasn't comfortable anymore, since it no longer adapted to his body or mood. The pod was heating up fast, with no temperature controls.

With his identity card blank, he realized, as soon as he left the pod, he would not be able to get back in. He decided to stay inside until it got too hot, and then take a vaporetto to look for anyone who might take him in. He had no idea how he would pay for the vaporetto.

Over the past few years, he had alienated many people. His relationships had become transactional. He wondered if he had any friends left.

Mrs. Marks had used her power well. She fixed it so he was off the grid and would never get back on.

It would take a year, but in time he would surprise himself by learning to like his new situation. Hopper00 was nothing if not resourceful.

PART 003

Chapter 013

The man at the edge of the crowd was crouched low, coiled like a copper wire. He was thirty-five but looked ten years younger. His glasses reflected the light of the fire and the old guy lecturing to a rapt audience of maybe thirty people. The old guy's voice was raggedy but strong, and echoed through the tunnel of the Metro/7th Street Station.

As the younger man watched at the edge of the crowd, he tried to figure out how old the lecturer really was. Maybe forty, or maybe fifty, or sixty. You couldn't tell when they were Olds and the street beat them down. Though this guy's face was mapped by time, there was nothing else beaten about him. He was upright, preaching around a fire made of old subway ties taken from the tracks. The fire was real enough and so were the sparks that flew around his face—a few even landed on it but he didn't brush them off, so possessed was he in his talk.

The old guy was talking about something called Grounders.

The younger man was going to be late for work. He'd missed one train already. He was an architectural drafter in a large room of similar drafting assistants. They wouldn't miss him if he was late. He wanted to listen to this talk about Grounders.

The old guy reminded him of his dad—a version of his dad, but more unhinged. His dad was also a visionary like this old guy, and his mother, too. Both of his parents worked for the School of Architecture at Uni. His father taught *Utopian Thinking in the Built Environment* and his mother taught *Engineering Tomorrow's Cities*. They often completed each other's sentences and sometimes taught the other's class until the Uni administration objected to it. Uni had already made an exception for them to teach in the same department. Teaching each other's classes was just too much. Kent's parents knew that the work they did in architecture was a vanishing pursuit. In the last days of their tenure, there were rumors that the School of Architecture would be defunded and disbanded in favor of better-funded and more practical departments like Rocketry, Pitch Decks, and Online Search. The corps would decide what good architecture was, not the academics. These rumors turned out to be true.

He blinked away the mental images of his parents that sprung up, along with tears. He hadn't thought of them in months and hadn't seen them in years. They were Olds who abandoned him, just like all the other Olds had abandoned the Earth to the Youngs. He kept listening to this madman in the Metro, who reminded him of a shouty version of his father, and it made no sense at all.

When the Change got bad, his parents had packed up to go up to the Northlands, leaving behind a deep quiet in their former home, which the young man now occupied alone. His name was Kent Jarma, and he didn't mind the heat and liked the quiet. He wore a bathing suit most of the time, and sandals.

The old guy was talking about everyone building living units underground and relocating into the dark, safe from the punishing heat of the Sun. He wanted purity of life, whatever that was. He was opposed to modding, which Kent was as well. Modding created an elite class, since it was expensive, and it unbalanced people, because of the side effects.

"Personal mods destroy what is human in us!" the old guy shouted. "We must begin by disconnecting from the information grid, because it is corrupt." He launched into a story about being pushed off the grid by force, and how it was the best thing that ever happened to him.

He lost most of his audience at that point. They were mostly Youngs and they probably had jobs to get to. They started checking their comms, having decided that the scabby old guy was crazy. It was surprising, anyway, that an Old was being so public. Most Olds stayed out of sight, or only appeared with their handlers, because of the rage of the Youngs. The old guy was a novelty that way. Maybe that was part of his attraction.

The Youngs believed that the Olds were taking up too much space, using too much water, and the Change was their fault. The Olds saw it coming and did little to stop it. Though the Youngs didn't exactly get their act together either, Kent would admit, until it was too late. But they were mad now, and most of their emotion was directed at the Olds.

It was surprising that they were not throwing things at the old shouter, or trying to push him into the fire he had made, but Kent saw a few sympathetic faces in the circle, young like his own—because, of course, the old guy was not crazy at all. His dad talked like this after the Change started coming on stronger. His parents talked about domes that anybody could build, which could power themselves or function off the information grid. Kent had the drawings for them. He kept them in the house. He never knew why, but suddenly he did. Here was an opportunity. Kent's parents left for the Northlands, abandoning their work, their house, and their son—nobody taught their courses after that, and their domes went unbuilt. But maybe his parents' abstract ideas could achieve a physical presence with this old guy who looked dirty and disheveled. Kent could help the old guy build domes. As an architectural drafter, Kent could spec the plans any way the old shouter wanted them.

The old man was wrapping up his talk. The last train to pull into the station drowned him out and took most of his audience with it.

This was the longest time Kent had thought about his parents in a while. Back when he was a student at Uni, there was a glass case on campus with a little model of the domes. When their conversations about leaving became more frequent, Kent would redirect his path on campus so that he wouldn't have to pass the glass case, with its model of their unbuilt domes. It seemed a model to their hypocrisy on a pedestal. They gave him a chance to come with, but halfheartedly, as though they wouldn't know what to do with him up there. He said no because he wanted to finish school before Uni shut down the School of Architecture. His parents couldn't bear to stay to see that, so they left in 2035, when the Change was just five years old. They were visionaries but also deserters.

The daydreaming had made Kent lose track of time. He noticed that the Old had stopped talking and the last of his crowd had drifted away. There was nobody between Kent and the old man, who was crouched on the floor and eating something out of a battered pot blackened with soot—with his hands, which didn't look clean at all.

When their eyes met, there was no choice, so Kent introduced himself.

"I am Kent Jarma." He stuck out his hand. "Rhymes with karma," he added helpfully. The old guy of forty, fifty, or maybe sixty, seemed to be the kind of person who would know what karma was.

He didn't take Kent's hand. "Don't you know who I am?" He laughed at Kent's ignorance.

"Am I supposed to?"

"Everyone knows me down here. I'm Hopper00." He pronounced it *Hopper zero aught.*

Chapter 014

Kent proved to be a good co-conspirator and able worker. He thought of Hopper00 as a man with ideas who needed a way to put those ideas into practice. Kent thought of himself as the other part of that formula, the practice part. It was bad that Hopper00 was an Old, but at least he was not an Old who was abandoning the Earth, not an Old who ran away like Kent's parents. He was sticking with the Youngs and living what he preached.

Hopper00 had set up a home underground, in a part of the Metro where the tracks stopped, stretching up tents and tarps to make a kind of dome. He jacked in some electricity. He even had food storage. It was all pretty basic, even repellant, but Kent honored the effort. He knew, with his skills, that he would be able to make it a lot better.

On the first day he arrived at Hopper00's underground tent pod, Kent put down his backpack in a corner and looked around. "This place is a mess," was the first thing he said, surveying the used food units that seemed to be everywhere.

Hopper00 responded with a riff about hard times, having to abandon a pretty cushy bicoastal life with nice pods on the Eastcoast and the Westcoast, and being forced to start over, off the information grid.

"Well, that's over and this is now," Kent said. "I can't work under these conditions." He moved a small mound of opened nutrient packets off a table. "This table will be used for drafting. No food here." He turned to a bookshelf that held old clothes. "Please clean that out. It's not for clothes anymore. It's going to be where we put the architectural plans for the domes."

A smile played around Hopper00's lips. "I like a man with a vision." But then he spread his hands in mock helplessness. "But what do you expect? Saving the world means you have to make a mess."

Kent chose not to laugh. "Self-care first," was his reply. They set to work cleaning up. "We can set you up in a proper dome. No more tarps and tents."

"How will you do that?" Hopper00 asked. He was holding a tangle of cables, not sure where to put it, and eyeing his cups of foul-smelling tea that he had left scattered around here and there.

Kent retrieved his backpack from the corner. From it he withdrew a plan for a dome. "My parents designed these. They were made for above ground, but we will make them work down here."

Hopper00 was intrigued by the plans but instead he asked about Kent's parents. "Have your parents ... passed?"

Kent shook his head. "May as well have. They ran away to the Northlands." He unrolled the plan on the table and weighed it down with a stray cup.

"To escape the Change? Can anyone really do that?"

"Yes," Kent said sharply, wanting to stop conversation right then and there. "They left."

Hopper00 shrugged. "Can't blame them for trying."

Kent looked like he was going to answer, but he turned away from the plan and picked up a hand-sized silver object that was littering a nearby chair. "What is this? You seem to have a lot of them." He had noticed there were many like it around the pod.

"That's a hard drive."

"Right," Kent responded. "I've heard of them. You still use them? No cloud for you?" He looked at the drive, noting that it was well-made and felt solid, like many old things were.

"I can't go back there. Banned forever. And I wouldn't want to go back anyway. The cloud is evil." Hopper00 waggled his fingers in front of his face and Kent laughed this time. The old guy sure was performative. But a lot of Olds were when they needed attention.

"The old technology is the best," Hopper00 said. "Our tech overlords ignore technology they think is outmoded, and that makes that older technology super-valuable for us. But I'm not just a hardware man. Some of the best old technology is all up here." He tapped the side of his head. "I'm also mastering thought packets."

"Thought-what, you say?"

"Thought packets. Two-way. Not just receiving, but also sending long distances."

Kent just looked at him.

"I can transmit ideas with my mind," Hopper00 explained.

Kent wondered if he had made the wrong decision coming down here to help out this Old. He picked up two more hard drives to hold three in his hands.

"You don't believe me?" Hopper00 asked.

"What do you want to do with these?"

"Put them over there." Hopper00 pointed to a corner of the pod already stacked high with old shoes and clothing.

You are a mess, Kent thought.

"Only to outward appearances," Hopper00 said.

Kent blinked. "What about all that junk?" He held the hard drives in his hands, but hesitated before the pile of unwashed clothes. "I'm not touching that."

Wordlessly, Hopper00 picked up the bundle and stuffed it down the disposal chute mounted in the wall.

"That's not legal."

"Nobody cares where the metro chutes start, only where they end. And this one was here before I was. That's why I put up my tent here. Good waste disposal."

Kent nodded. "Gotta give you that. When we build a bunch of domes, we're going to have to come up with a system of waste disposal." He returned to the plan and studied it, thinking about where to locate a port for waste.

"You don't waste time." Hopper00 nodded appreciatively, and started talking about the contractors he could find in the Metro who would build them. He put two food unit packets on the table.

"Wait," Kent said. "No units on this table. It's a drafting table now." He took the food packets back to the food storage unit. As he put them back, he noticed something. "What's this?" It was a tightly wrapped package of what looked like drugs.

"Nothing," Hopper00 said, and moved to grab it.

Kent held on to the package. "It's not nothing." He turned the package over in his hands and realized what it held. "You can't do this anymore."

"You can't tell me that." Hopper00 grabbed the package of peyote from Kent.

"No, I can't tell you," Kent said. "But it's obvious you can't. We can't do this," gesturing to the stacked rolled up plans for domes, "if you are getting high."

"I don't get high anymore," Hopper00 said.

"Good," replied Kent. "So you won't miss these."

Hopper00 allowed Kent to take the buttons back from him and toss them down the disposal chute, but he hoped Kent hadn't found all the buttons in the food storage. Just in case he needed one or two.

"This is a drafting table now. We have to take care of it."

"Got it," Hopper00 said. Making a face, he went to the food storage, took out two food packets, offered one to Kent, who refused, and started to noisily suck his down while standing.

After a moment Hopper00 said, "No sex."

"What?"

"I mean we are not doing sex." Hopper00 had already told Kent about his time as a sex worker. He was experienced at sex, he said, with all forms of humans. And he was good at it. Very good. "But I don't want sex to complicate our relationship."

This was not what Kent had in mind. *Old man, you looked at yourself in the mirror lately?* he thought.

Hopper00 repeated the line back to him.

"What?" was all Kent could manage.

Hopper00 offered a smile. "I can see into your mind."

"What does that mean?"

"You know what it means. I just showed you."

"Showed me what?" Kent said. *All you showed me is that you are crazy.*

Hopper00 repeated that line back to him also.

Kent shook his head and sat down. He stared at Hopper00.

"I realize it can be difficult to accept. Can I tell you how I learned I could do it?"

"You may as well."

So Hopper00 told him about his tortured youth, the ability to leave his body, the mushrooms first and the buttons afterward, and how he had trained himself to do mental telepathy, a skill he called mental packet transfer capability. "I made a good living as a writer. When you can see into someone's mind, you achieve fast intimacy." He invited Kent to look him up in the Feed. "You'll see my byline everywhere—until Mrs. Marks wiped me off the grid." He paused to think, and then added, "More than a year ago."

"Who is Mrs. Marks?"

"The most powerful woman in media. Don't cross her unless you know what you're doing. I certainly didn't."

Kent didn't know whether to believe any of it, but it was clear that Hopper00 could somehow see into his mind. He proved it over and over by saying aloud what Kent was thinking until, finally, Kent told him to stop. "But what is your range, do you know?"

"Currently, I need to see the person. But I am training for longer distances." Hopper got signals from afar. The voices were quieter but still present. They came to him in dreams, to speak of future events. Or, sometimes, people from the past would visit.

Later, at his parents' house, Kent looked up Hopper00. The Feed carried articles and vids about his transactional childhood and youth, the pride and arrogance of his writing days, and his mistake with Mrs. Marks. There was nothing in the Feed about Hopper00 being a subway griot, because he had been off the grid for more than a year, just like he said.

Hopper00 had nothing to lose and preached with all his heart about a better world. When Kent asked him why, one evening when their work was done, Hopper00 pushed back from the table and fixed him with a steady gaze.

"It came to me in a dream. Or maybe I should upgrade that to a vision."

"You were high."

"Yes, I was. For the last time. Professor Buckminster Fuller came to me and spoke."

Hopper knew Kent was familiar with Bucky Fuller. The domes that Kent was designing and would soon build were based on Bucky's domes. Kent's parents owed Bucky a debt of influence—a kind way to put it, since they had borrowed Bucky's ideas.

"Bucky told me to build his domes underground and start the Grounder movement," Hopper00 said. "He said to stay away from hallucinogenic drugs. 'They will destroy you.' So I stopped. That was the last time I got high."

Kent nodded. He believed him.

This is how the Grounder movement began. It took six months of subway rhapsodizing for the crowds around Hopper00 to grow, and when Kent moved among them with his print outs, plans, and eventually a sleek brochure, people started signing up to live in domes. Hopper00 preached in the Metro nearly every evening. "Bucky Fuller was the original dome man," Hopper00 told the ring of faces lit by a small trash fire, stepping aside just before a stream of dark fluid dripped down on him. The cruddy pipes leaked some nasty-smelling liquids. "He had a bald head like a dome, and he thought in domes, he saw the future in circles." Some in Hopper00's listening audience came up to him when he was preaching and wanted to offer him crypto.

"Sorry, I'm off the grid," he had to say. "But he can take your donation." He gestured to Kent, and the crypto donations Kent received were the source of financing for the first domes. Kent was also the designer and foreman who got the demo domes built. When a future dome-owner said yes to a dome, Kent would say, "We will pay for it, and I will build it with you, but you have to help me." This way, the resident had skin in the game, playing a role in the creation of their own shelter. The movement offered people control over how they lived, choices in the type of home they lived in, and if they wanted, they could be off the grid or have limited access to it.

Kent replaced the tents and tarps Hopper00 had strung up with a frame and dome skin made of recycled plastics, like the other domes he was building. Soon they weren't using donations to build domes anymore; people wanted to pay for their own and change the design enough to make them theirs. Some asked for carbon fiber and fiberglass, or even the latest in nanomaterials, but Kent insisted the materials had to be recycled. That was the whole point. He had enough work making domes now that he could stop taking on freelance architectural drafting jobs. He spent less and less time at his parents' house, and more and more at Hopper00's underground dome.

Hopper00 did the talking, and Kent did the building, in Los Angeles where the metro tracks ended, in underground storage abandoned by the domain, and even a few domes aboveground by the shoreline, under piers. The aboveground domes, when discovered by the authorities, were usually cleared away, but below, in the vaults, the dome settlements were stable. The authorities didn't favor policing underground. They preferred to stay away. Their neglect allowed Kent to think bigger, and soon he was designing a large dome village in a forgotten part of the city.

Beneath the Port of Los Angeles, Kent had struck gold. His review of old maps revealed vaults that had been used to store cars that came in on the container ships. Since cars were banned in the city, there was no official purpose for the vaults. They lay empty. Kent planned to fill them with domes.

One morning, while preparing the rolled-up plans and brochures for Hopper00 to distribute in the metro, Kent realized that he was happier than he had been in years. He had petitioned the domain for the right to use the empty vaults and the domain said yes.

Kent, being a Young, was the natural spokesperson for the movement. He hired some vid people to make a vid about the Grounders, and after production was finished, Kent's long, oval face with its almond-colored eyes was projected on large monitors in the markets. While walking outside, he looked up to see himself giant-sized and gangly on the big screens. He wanted to duck and stay out of sight when he saw this stretched-out version himself. It was embarrassing to be so large. His voice boomed out to be heard by anyone who was jacked in, and the words he spoke were spelled out in subtitles below his image. "This is the affordable housing program that we've needed. We exist for the people and to help everyone who wants a dome."

Then his comms unit vibrated. When he looked at its screen, he saw the first of the offers from the vid shows inviting him to create content with them.

Chapter 015

The content proposals from the vid shows were just one set of offers Kent was entertaining. After the project in the underground vaults below the port went well, the Southern California Domain decided that it would officially sanction living in domes. After that seal of approval, new markets opened. Real estate brokers began to include Grounder domes in their open houses and wealthy people bought domes as an investment, renting them out to poor people.

"This is all happening too fast," Kent said to Hopper00. They were preparing an evening meal together and at the same time watching vids on the Feed about the Grounder movement, some of which featured Kent. But Kent turned them off.

"Too much me," he said by way of explanation. He hadn't yet told Hopper00 about the vid offers. Various vid people wanted Kent to host a talk show, host a news show, and host a dance show. Most of the offers were ridiculous. He would never host a dance show, but a news show might work. He assumed that Hopper00 already knew. Hopper00 was plugged into things like that, and he had the capability to see into Kent's mind when he wanted to.

"It's happening fast because you made a vid," Hopper00 said. "Vids accelerate everything."

"I have some offers from the vid shows," Kent said without looking up. It was kind of embarrassing to admit it out loud.

Hopper00 nodded to confirm. So he did know.

"We also handed out the plans to the domes and made them open source, so that would also make the program popular," Kent said.

Hopper00 gestured for a carrot to chop up and Kent handed him one. "That was always the intent. Maximum accessibility."

Kent smiled but Hopper00 didn't smile back. "Everything is unfolding the way it should. We've succeeded, maybe too much!" Kent said. His voice sounded too loud, too big for the pod. He didn't like his face on the screens, nor his name in the Feed, and he suspected that this notoriety had changed something between him and Hopper00.

"You jealous or something?" Kent asked. He tried to look busy by sorting through other vegetables from the market, deciding what to put in the stew they were making.

"Jealous of you?" The old man laughed. "Impossible."

Hopper00 was jealous, but not willing to admit it. The crowds that Hopper00 drew in the metro had peaked in numbers and many of those in attendance were disappointed that Kent was not there. They were Youngs, and Kent was one of them. Hopper00, as an Old, was starting to look like a liability, even though his vision originally gave life to the project.

"Why don't you try making some vids with me?" Kent asked.

"Not my thing," Hopper00 said. Maybe it was time to step back and let Kent be the public face of the Grounders. Hopper00 tried that on for size in his mind; he didn't like it. Maybe he didn't have a choice.

Kent interrupted these thoughts. "Do you think I should do a regular vid show? A news show or a talk show?"

To Kent's surprise, Hopper00 got up from the table and moved away to look at a screen that simulated a view of the city skyline through a window.

"What? What did I say? You knew about the offers already, right?" Kent said.

The question went unanswered, because just then Kent's mother Brooke pinged his comms. "Excuse me a minute," he said to Hopper00. Surprised to see her face on the screen, he hastily ducked away into the sleeping area and closed the door to take the call.

His mother, and his father, Robert, wanted him to come up to the North-lands to visit them.

"We miss you," his mother said. The three words brought a storm cloud to his mind. He became angry at them all over again—and at the same time, he wanted to reconcile. It was weighing on him and he wanted the weight to stop. *Maybe they want to apologize to me.*

And he missed them, too.

He made up his mind right away. He accepted their offer to visit, closed the comms connection, and opened the sleeping area door. Hopper00 was setting out the dinner plates.

"Who pinged you?" Hopper00 asked.

"My mother. I'm going up to the Northlands to visit my parents."

Hopper00 stopped what he was doing and looked up. "What brought that on?"

"I don't know. My mother pinged me. They want me to visit."

Hopper00's mouth pulled into a frown. "They want you to visit. How many years has it been since you've spoken?"

"We've spoken. On comms. I haven't *seen* them in ..." He paused to think about it. "They left during the Change."

"That's years ago," Hopper00 said. "At the beginning or the end of it?"

"They waited it out for a while. Toward the end of the first series of extreme events."

"So it's been years," Hopper00 said.

"Years since they left," Kent agreed. It was 2035 when they left. In May. The weather was good; it seemed an unlikely time to leave. They wanted to go before the Architecture Department was dissolved at Uni, so they missed Kent's graduation.

"And what changed. She just called you after fifteen years?"

"Yes, but we've spoken before today. It hasn't been fifteen years of no contact. I think it's been sixteen, but there's been contact. I just think." Kent waited for his mind to clear and the words to come. "It's time. Time to see them again."

A wave of panic rippled over the old man as Kent said this. *What if he never comes back?* He tried to keep his voice steady. "How long will you be gone?"

"Just a week," Kent said. He'd never seen Hopper00 look so worried, and it made him want to get out in a hurry. He began hunting around the pod for clothes and supplies. He moved through the round, high-ceilinged main area that held the living and dining zones and grabbed a silver sun-shield jacket that had enough insulation to keep him comfortable in the Northlands, then stuffed it into a bag near the sleeping zone. He picked up his comms and booked a ticket on the next glidepath going north.

Hopper00 didn't have to see into Kent's mind to know what was going to happen. He saw by the light in Kent's eyes that he was going to reconcile with his parents and never return.

It certainly seemed that way the next morning, when they said their awkward goodbyes and Kent hefted his bag and left.

Hopper00 was surprised at the panic that seized him, but he did nothing to stop it. He indulged it, in fact, rummaging in the food storage, soon tearing it apart. He was not finding what he wanted. A few silvery food packages fell out, and he kicked one across the floor.

The freezer.

He opened it. Its blue glow was benevolent and its gentle chill inviting. He found what he wanted quickly and held the packet in hands that gently shook with anticipation. The packet of peyote buttons he held was rimmed with ice. He thought Kent had gotten rid of everything and yet here they were in all their glory.

Years ago, upon his escape from the hospital, he had stood on the edge of freedom but chose servitude. He had entered a life of transaction and chemical enhancement. It was easy to return to servitude now.

Servitude worked for him as mixed punishment and reward. He needed punishment because he had failed. While in exile, off the grid, speaking to strangers around a fire in the Metro, he worked hard to remain disconnected from everyone. As a preacher in the Metro, he was above any personal connections. But he failed to be invincible with Kent. He had allowed himself to become emotionally vulnerable again. He needed punishment.

There were also the voices to consider. They hadn't visited him in almost a year. The last time he heard the voices was when he had the vision of Bucky Fuller, when Fuller told him not to get high anymore. The voices were back now and they wanted attention.

"Well," Hopper00 said aloud, though no one was in the dome, "I'd say it's time. How about a little treat?" He unwrapped the packet. The buttons were hard as stones, but they would defrost soon enough.

Chapter 016

Hopper00 sat up when the room finally ceased spinning. The sudden movement made his head feel like it would explode. He repositioned himself on the sleeping mat and carefully returned to a prone position on the floor. A therapy bot came close to take his pulse and temperature. He didn't remember ordering a therapy bot to come to the dome.

"I hope you are feeling better," it said in a soft voice. It offered him fluids with electrolytes. Hopper00 accepted them and sipped slowly until the domed arc of the ceiling stopped churning.

He tried sitting up again. It went better this time. *I must have been out a long time.* Pointless to calculate. Didn't matter really. He rubbed his eyes, and to him they felt sore because they had seen so much. He had led multiple lives, shed so many skins. Institutionalized child, hospital escapee, sex worker, gossip writer, investigator, betrayer, pariah, griot, builder. He thought about Kent making the drawings for the domes and felt so grateful he nearly cried. He pinched his tired eyes to stop the tears from flowing.

Kent walked in from the dome's main room. "You're up."

Hopper00 was more confused than he thought. "I thought you left." He passed a hand over his weary face. "Your parents."

Kent shook his head and sent the therapy bot to charge in the wall-mounted port. "I'm back. I saw them. It was good. We'll talk about that later. I found you...." Kent gestured to the floor.

When Kent had come back, the night before, Hopper00 had been unconscious, sprawled on the floor in the main room. Kent called the medics on comms. They arrived quickly, located empty peyote packets in the kitchen, and knew what happened. The medics were familiar Hopper00's medical history (they could look up anyone's) and ordered the therapy bot. With the medics' help, Kent got Hopper00 settled in the sleeping area.

For the rest of the first night, Hopper00's eyes fluttered but didn't open. Kent spoke to him anyway. He shared the story of his reconciliation with his parents. "They're fine up in the Northlands. They want to be there." Much as they wanted him to stay with them, Kent knew it wasn't right for him. "My work is here, with you," he said to Hopper00's closed, fluttering eyes.

"How long were you gone?" Hopper asked now.

"A week," Kent said. "Do you know what you did?"

Hopper00 looked away. He knew. *I amaze myself.* He laughed softly, an old man's wheeze, followed by a ragged breath that hurt his lungs. *I am weak.* He had promised Bucky Fuller that he would never take hallucinogens again, but it was a promise he couldn't keep.

He felt suddenly hungry, so he pulled himself to standing, tried to walk, and nearly fell over. The therapy bot unplugged itself from the wall and hurried over like a concerned grandmother. "Be careful! Don't hurt yourself."

Hopper00 ignored these entreaties and slowly, even stumblingly, walked into the main room. The bot and Kent followed.

"I'm glad you came back," Hopper00 said over his shoulder to Kent. "This is your place. As the Grounder movement grows, it needs a steady hand. That hand doesn't belong to me, obviously, because I am not steady," Hopper00 said, trying not to laugh again because it would hurt too much. "Your parents were pretty compelling, were they? I'm glad you convinced them that you are needed here."

Kent blinked. Apparently Hopper00 had grasped Kent's monologue about his meeting with his parents, even though Hopper00 was out cold.

"I am a fool," Hopper00 continued, "who fills everything with craziness." He finally made it over to the food storage and started to look for food units. He opened the door and the benevolent interior light of the storage unit shone into the dome, outlining their humble furnishings. The drafting table. Their two chairs. The eating table.

Kent helped him open some food units. "How are you feeling now?" he asked.

"Let's talk later," Hopper00 said. "You can tell me about your parents. I'll tell you about my bad assumptions and worse decisions." The old man was thinking about the scenes in his life being all outtakes. *I am made of discarded scenes. But the Grounders, that is something. Kent and I did the Grounders together. I couldn't have done it myself. Of course, he was going to come back from the Northlands. He was always going to come back. He's proven that he cares about what we have built and what we've done. It's just time for me to do more.*

Hopper00 looked at Kent and the younger man looked back at him expectantly. "There is more," Hopper00 said.

"What?" Kent opened his hands. "More of what?"

"I mean I have to do more," Hopper00 said, but was distracted as the therapy bot wheeled over and wanted to take his temperature. He waved it away. Self-pity overtook Hopper00, draining away the resolve he was trying to build in himself. *My life is a series of scenes with little point.*

Hopper00 was a Mental Expansive. He could hear people's thoughts, and he'd done nothing with that skill except write a gossip column about celebrities. In his youth, he could leave his body when he wanted to—but he'd only used *that* to avoid the unpleasantness of being a sex worker. He had traveled through time once, he remembered with brief satisfaction, and then squashed the feeling because he had done nothing with that either.

Scenes. No point to them. *Outtakes.*

"Can I make you something to eat?" Kent was waiting as Hopper00 stood before the cooker, lost in his thoughts.

Hopper00's reaction was to jump away from the cooker and walk around the room in circles, talking to himself.

"What's wrong?" Kent asked. He caught up with Hopper00 on the other side of the circular room and bent his tall frame over the older man. He put his long hand on Hopper00's shoulder, but Hopper00 turned away, crossed the room again, and picked up a rolled-up dome plan from the drafting table.

"You've done well. But there is more," Hopper00 said. *I nearly died this time. And I escaped. I was given a gift. What am I going to do with it?*

"You need to rest." Kent didn't know what else to say to him. Something was wrong, something that Hopper00 wasn't talking about, or maybe he was, but only in fragments.

Hopper00 sat down at the drafting table, pulled over a screen, waved it open and entered search terms until the screen displayed an attractive woman often featured in the Feed. She looked like she should be starring in a movie, with gray eyes and dark hair, dressed in white clothes. The effect was trichromatic.

"What are you doing?" Kent was looking over Hopper00's shoulder at the image. "Do you know her?" Kent asked. "Who's that?"

"Kat Keeper is her name. I met her once at some editorial event in New York. *Fishbowl,* or some editor gossip group announcing new stories for the season. Everyone was dressed so well and behaved themselves." Hopper00 smiled at the memory. "Look," he gestured at the image to make it zoom in, "she has gray eyes—the eyes of a Seeker. I think she is looking for something. I wonder if I can help her find it?"

"Looking for what?" Kent was concerned that Hopper00 was suffering from the effects of his trip or some kind of dementia. Something was wrong with his mind. Not just that he was distracted—something worse.

"Listen to me," Hopper00 said, again not looking away from the screen. "I want you to stay here and build all the domes you can. That is your destiny. I have to help Kat Keeper." He tapped a finger on the screen. The image zoomed in to her face even closer.

"You need to rest."

Hopper00 made a noise of disagreement.

"You just woke up, after being out for who knows how long."

Hopper00 was having none of it. "I am fully awake," he said. He zoomed the screen out and began to read about Kat Keeper. "I am awake," he said again, as though to convince himself of it.

The therapy bot circled Hopper00 again. "You must rest," it said.

He told it to go plug itself in. It made the mechanical equivalent of a sigh and went away to obey the command.

Kat Keeper, Hopper00 read, was once involved with an idiot Siliconer named Bradley15 Power. Bradley15 was modded, which made Hopper00 dislike him right away. The Kat Keeper story was familiar to any gossip writer turned investigative reporter such as Hopper00, because it was a great story that everyone wished they had written. Hopper00 was feeling sympathetic to Kat Keeper. So he read her story again. He read about Kat's history of wealth and fame and her fall from grace after she was forced out of her company, VirtualEyes. Kat left VirtualEyes with a queenly severance package, but no credibility. She brilliantly rehabilitated herself by becoming Bradley's protector, buying out his detention, and funding Bradley's prototype of an AI with a human personality.

"Building an AI has always been my life's work," Bradley15 was quoted as saying in a story that Hopper00 read. He read on, learning how Bradley split up with Kat Keeper, or Kat split up with Bradley (the written accounts were conflicting), and Bradley went on to found an AI company with someone named Alon6 Sal. It seemed a callous move to Hopper00, working so hard on an AI with Kat, and then leaving her to work on an AI with someone else, but Hoppoer00 soon saw the reason. Alon6 was also modded like Bradley, and even more of an idiot than Bradley, because Alon6 was greedy. Together they were a power duo.

The Feed wasn't specific about what kind of AI Bradley had built for Kat. Hopper00 had a sense of something else going on, something deeper around the AI, but the Feed had no depth for him. It only said that Bradley and Alon6 were becoming rich and successful with their new venture, MIND, and that Kat had retreated to her house in Marin. He tossed aside the screen. If he had been writing that tale, he would have gotten more of the story.

Not only did the sketchiness of the storytelling annoy him, Hopper00 also hated it when people possessed of genius, like Bradley15 Power, acted like idiots and built corps that served their own interests, enriching themselves by exploiting others. It made sense to him that Kat and Bradley wouldn't last long together. Hopper00 sensed that she was simply a better person than Bradley.

And Hopper00 sensed more. He sensed that Kat's heart held someone else, not Bradley. He saw a face in his mind's eye but couldn't recognize it yet. He knew he was having a vision that would change his life, and Kat's, and he wasn't even high.

He sat back in his chair, picked up the screen again to look at Kat's face, soaking in her winning smile and the bright intelligence in her eyes—and again, he got an instant hit of likability. He trusted his gut in these matters. He read a quote that appeared below her picture in the Feed:

"One thing I know for sure. I appreciate the power of truth and trust in our world. Trust and truth are entwined. Trust is earned, and once it's earned, you can't betray it by lying."

This sat well with Hopper00, after all the lies he had lived. His relationships had all been dirty. He had a sense that, whatever Kat had been through in the past, she was trying to leave it behind and live a better life than she had before. She radiated decency. She was everything that he was not.

He caught sight of his reflection in the device window: all sharp edges and wild eyes, hair uneven, a graying beard. His dangling earring flashed under his right ear. He looked like a mad old man. A mad Old.

He let the vision of helping Kat become sharper in his mind. It was like the time Bucky Fuller came to him—or like the voices. They were quiet now, waiting for his decision.

The positive feelings he held about Kat became even stronger. He was expanding with them, soon floating above himself in the room, and looking down over the scene, like the old days. He felt the unshakable sense that Kat Keeper deserved better than Bradley15 Power, better than mere business successes or failures; she deserved to be measured in ways that were not yet known. With his help, he decided in that moment, she would fulfill her destiny and become the person she was always meant to be.

SURRENDER

PART 004

Chapter 017

Bradley had hired an excellent team of programmers to build out MIND. In their morning meetings, however, he could never give them his full attention. For months after Kat angrily left his office, he saw her among his employees when she wasn't there. He gave instructions to his assistant Nora2 and saw Kat's face swapped with hers like a deepfake. He stretched out on the cot in his office to sleep and felt Kat's hand on his chest, moved to brush it off, changed his mind and moved to touch it, and then realized it wasn't there.

One evening he decided he had had enough of this and, as though in a trance, rose from his cot, put on his clothes, plucked his identity card from the charger, and walked out of the office. At the station, he waited for the glidepath to arrive, boarded—and within moments, it seemed, he was standing before the scanner at the front portal of the floating house in Marin.

She saw who it was and surprised herself by opening the portal. They looked at each other, a thousand emotions flickering across their faces, and for a moment the programmer in Bradley marveled at the computational power required to produce those thousand emotions flowing between them. They produced no words.

Kat felt the force of his mod pulling her in again. He stepped closer and felt his heart slamming in his chest at the mere sight of her: the real Kat, not a vision. They fell into each other's arms.

Bradley's face was wet, so he must have been crying. He felt her moving her hands across his back and closed his eyes. When he opened them, they were in her sleeping room making love. The moment, the sequence, resembled a dream. Was it a dream?

But in the morning, she was still there beside him. So it was real.

"What should we do now?" she asked. She looked beautiful in the morning light. She had let her hair grow, and it lay in tendrils around her face. Her lips were full, and her eyes held warmth for him. He read in this that she had missed him, which shocked him into silence for a moment.

"I have no idea," he blurted. "No idea at all." He laughed and she laughed, too, though her laugh sounded forced.

This is wrong, she thought. She must have been more lonely than she imagined.

Bradley was anxious at first to get back to reality. After an awkward breakfast, he left for the glidepath, leaving her chatting with Dave in his attractive ellipsoidal Form Factor. He was glad she had Dave to talk to.

She told Dave everything about the pull of Bradley's mod, the stirring it brewed inside her below her belly, and the simultaneous feeling of being out of her own body. The guilty pleasure of it. "Probably it was just this one night."

Dave nodded his agreement. "Probably."

"Do you feel bad that you can't give me the same?"

"You mean a physical presence?"

She nodded.

"I am a man in a Form Factor, and as such I am all I can be. I give you everything I can." His eyes held their electric warmth.

She nodded, ashamed for having asked the question. "That's true. I'm grateful for you, Dave." She paused. "It was nice when he was here, but after he left, I didn't feel anything for him."

"You know that's the mod, right?" Dave said from his oval screen.

"I know. It is always like that."

She didn't know what she should do about Bradley or about anything; her life felt like it was coming loose from a mooring and drifting away. Things were coming apart. A journalist had come to visit her, saying that he wanted to write up her life story. She couldn't imagine why, but she agreed. She invited him in and he walked around the floating house, taking notes. He said he'd be in touch soon with more questions.

"I like to ask questions," he said. "I hope you like to answer."

He had something special about him. She couldn't place it. When his eyes focused on her, it was like they could see to the bottom of her. He wore a silver earring on one ear—the left or the right, she couldn't remember—and it appeared to weigh him down so that he walked leaning to that side.

She shook her head. *I need to talk to more people, not just Dave.* She felt an inner restlessness, like she might uproot herself and travel far away at any moment. Though she didn't know where.

She lacked the will to stop Bradley when he showed up at her door at irregular intervals, seemingly on a whim. She knew it was weak and needy, but the visit of the journalist had reminded her how lonely she was for real people. Dave could only fulfill so much.

Bradley was a warm human on the mat beside her. He didn't ask much. She emptied her mind and enjoyed the feeling his mod brought to her. They fell back into their routine, performing their daily rituals, waking up together, acting as though they were friends, sharing tea, talking lightly about what they would do that day. She hated herself for it but couldn't stop.

Yet there was also relief, since after Bradley walked out of her portal and down to the station, any attraction she had to him would evaporate, and she would feel neutral about him. It was like a reset button on her shame, and she went about her day. When he surprised her again a few nights later at her portal, she would let him in.

She didn't know what to make of her own behavior, so she asked Dave. "Are you enabling this?"

He smiled on his screen. "I think so. I like seeing you happy, even if it's only temporary."

On the glidepath back down to El Segundo, Bradley was always dizzy with happiness. It took a great act of will to pull out some pages and make Logic Trees with his pencil. The ride was short, but why waste time?

He had two teams in parallel development on MIND. Team 1 was the Program Team. They worked on recursive intelligence, building a machine that could teach itself to learn in an endless cycle of improvement, without human intervention.

Team 2 was called Input. It worked on uploading human thought as a data set for MIND to train with. Team 2 had the more challenging task.

It was easy to soak up consciousness from someone who wanted to give it away to you. Your subject could answer questions, recite her life story, choose one picture that she liked over another, and the machine would receive.

The human decision to consent to personality field violations had been exploited for decades. But receiving consciousness without consent, without the subject's awareness, was far more difficult. Team 2 was working on gathering consciousness from open areas, places where people congregated, but also in homes, in the markets—and without detection. The Input team's work was secret, because if anyone learned of it, they would surely be the target of industrial espionage from competitors. It was also illegal.

Alon6 would dismiss the word to Bradley with a sneer in his voice, as in, "Illegal at *the present time*." He was working on the domain officials, had the ear of the Planetary Administrator. He was handing out crypto credits and making back-end deals. He felt it wouldn't be long before soaking up consciousness without consent would be legal. Then there would be no stopping MIND.

"Focus on Input," he told Bradley. And why not? It made perfect sense. Bradley had been obsessed with recursive intelligence since their days at Uni, but Input was the front end of the intelligence project, the pathway for all the data MIND needed.

Working from an idea from Alon6, he prototyped what he called the Harvester. One night, when he couldn't sleep, he rose from Kat's sleeping pad, leaving her behind in deep slumber, and went into her kitchen to work out a schematic for it. Her kitchen was different from the one in his living space in the MIND building. He couldn't explain why, because he knew nothing about kitchens, but he noticed that Kat's had more cooking equipment, and bins for vegetables, and a large freezer. All white and stainless steel, this was a place for creating connection with food; his was a place to prepare nutrients to ingest. He considered little of that, though, and focused entirely on his work. It seemed like moments had passed and then it was suddenly morning.

He was surprised when Kat came in and hid his scribblings before she saw them. He didn't know why; it was an impulse.

But he wondered if there was any point to hiding, because she seemed to anticipate his thoughts and speak his words before he spoke them. This was a special talent of hers. He wasn't sure that she knew she could do it; she never spoke about it. But if he could study it, watch her, and maybe learn how she did it, then he knew he could improve the Harvester.

Her abilities and the Harvester's capabilities were on a parallel track. It was another reason for Bradley to remain close to Kat's personality field. He was grateful that his mod still worked on her when he was there.

For two years, Bradley took the evening glidepath up to Kat's Marin home, a couple times a week, though not on any schedule. It was their pattern, irregular as it was, and they were people of patterns. If he brought work to her house, he hid it from her, while she shared with him the poetry she was writing, describing how she closed her eyes and waited for the words, then wrote them down. She felt broken but wasn't sure why she couldn't put herself together. She needed her next chapter and didn't know what it was. When she started getting down on herself with that kind of negative talk, she believed that writing out poetry line by line would help.

When they went out for coffee or to a market, they were caught by the gossip photographers and ended up on the Feed, but only for a few weeks, until the images all began to look the same and the photographers became bored.

With this simple circle inscribed around their ways together, Kat and Bradley were in codependent equilibrium. But it wouldn't last. She started to notice that he was hiding work from her.

Chapter 018

Sanchez tried to make his deep voice sound polite as he stood on the threshold of Bradley's office. "Hello, Mr. Power?"

"What do you want?" Bradley was head-down on some project on his screen, the blue light picking out lines of strain on his face. He looked older than thirty-five, but maybe it was the lighting.

"I am Sanchez. You have an interview with me."

"Nora2!" Bradley called out. "Am I supposed to be interviewing somebody now?"

She said yes, so Bradley gestured for Sanchez to sit down. Nora2 put the meeting prep on his screen. A Bachelor of Science in viniculture and a Master's degree in supply chain logistics from the Universidad de Buenos Aires. "You're overqualified," Bradley said while reading from the screen.

Really, Bradley just needed a handler. He had seen them with celebrities in the open markets and wanted one of his own, a handler who walked close and protected him. Handlers also negotiated interactions with the public. As the company was growing, as Bradley became richer, as more people called him "B" instead of Bradley, people needed to be fended off. Especially people who realized that Bradley wanted access to their mental fields. They wanted dominion over their own thoughts. Bradley had other plans for their thoughts, so a handler and a few lobbyists were necessary expenses.

Sanchez was trying to make conversation, poking Bradley out of his thoughts. "My friend Caleb told me you had a handler job. I have experience."

Bradley didn't remember Caleb, but he had hired so many people in the past few months he couldn't be expected to remember everyone. "When you freelance as a handler, how's the pay?"

"It's okay," Sanchez answered.

Bradley saw from his screen that Sanchez was a handler for the movie actor

Kohl Hofbauer, though Hofbauer wasn't acting anymore. He had always played hyper-masculine action heroes, but by now was a pleasant old chap who just wanted to go out into the market to buy water. If some bad guys tried to jump him, Sanchez took care of them. "Do you like doing it? Being a handler?"

"It's okay. But you can be a handler for only one person at a time. I need career advancement."

Caleb had told Sanchez that Team 2 was the place to work at MIND. The Input Team. *Go in for the handler job and come out as the Team Leader of Input,* Caleb said.

How am I going to do that? Sanchez asked him.

You're desperate, Caleb supplied. And it was true. So Sanchez took a chance.

"I know what you're doing with Input. You're working on a portable device, called the Harvester."

Bradley seemed startled. "What?" He tried not to look behind him, where a prototype Harvester was in pieces at the back wall of his office.

"Everybody in Input knows that the Harvester is happening," Sanchez continued. "The other data companies are launching their own Input projects. You're trying to get the laws changed so that you can harvest thoughts. Then MIND will pull ahead."

Bradley frowned. "Who told you that?"

Sanchez shrugged and offered a smile that revealed little. "I know how to talk to people. I get them to tell me what I need to know."

Bradley assessed the man who sat in his visitor chair, easily filling it with his large frame. He had an education, but so far its high point had been protecting Kohl Hofbauer from an assault in a market. And yet, he had a combination of useful skills. The Harvester apparatus, the one against the back wall, was too big, and needed work. That's what Caleb (whom he remembered now) and the other guys in Input were working on, and they had to hurry, because Sanchez was right: The other companies were working on similar technology. The best crew would pull ahead.

"You want some career advancement, do you?"

Sanchez nodded and tried not to sag in his chair. His wife, Wanda, was working as a liquor distributor, which she hated. It was a big step down from guiding cultivated people around their winery.

Sanchez wasn't lying when he said he could only work with only one client at a time. The clients got jealous of each other. Just a few weeks ago, De Nada, another movie actor, heard Sanchez was working for Hofbauer and fired him on the spot.

Now Hofbauer was talking about being too old to go out in public anymore. If he went full recluse, he'd have no need for a handler. Sanchez wondered if he should go back to De Nada and try to get the other job back. His world felt like it was closing in on him.

"I have a wife with expensive tastes," Sanchez said, trying to make light of it.

The joke fell flat. Bradley nodded and looked at his screen again. He scanned the history of the Sanchez family exodus from South America. Sanchez and his wife had owned a winery, but had to give it up when temperatures rose and the vines died. Bradley, his attention waning, pushed the Sanchez briefing screen aside and pulled up one that showed his remaining appointments for the day. He saw that Kat was coming in soon as well as Alon6.

Sanchez noted Bradley's disconnection from him; it was now or never to make his pitch. He leaned forward and put his hands on Bradley's desk. "You're successful and will only be more so. I know the market for Input products will be good. You have the technology. Nobody else has anything like the Harvester locked in like you do. You're about to become the biggest Input guy in the dom, maybe the whole coast."

"Gathering Input will be dangerous," Bradley offered. The winner of this race for interior data *would* certainly go to the best machine, but, he added, "People won't like having their thoughts vacuumed up. Those who understand what's going on already don't like it." He hadn't made up his mind about Sanchez.

"So what? You gotta do what you gotta do."

Bradley shrugged. "People will fight it." They were fighting it already. But soon, they would recognize its inevitability. They would realize that it had to be done to make a universal machine intelligence. And for the economy, of course. Bradley envisioned a new class of worker. He would send Input Men into the cities. "Anyway, it's already happening."

Sanchez nodded. "It's already happening."

Bradley shot Sanchez another appraising look. "You seem like you know how to talk to people."

Sanchez offered his smile that revealed nothing. "I know how to make people see things my way, Mr. Power." He let the smile hang on his face longer than he would have liked, but it was a challenge to conceal his intelligence. He needed to show Bradley what he needed to see.

"Looks like I've got myself a handler," Bradley said.

Sanchez relaxed in his chair and let his shoulders drop. "Thank you. You won't regret it, Mr. Power," he said, and then left to check in with Human Affairs, where he logged a retina scan, got an employee chip implant, signed some docs, and read a screen about the company culture of MIND. He was starting as a handler, but he knew he would be running Input soon.

Bradley felt good about his new hire. *This is how democracy will be protected. Complete openness. Input Men everywhere. A culture of sharing.* In a generous mood, he thought he would share Harvester data with his competitor, a corp called Inside Out. The domain would want some data, too. *Once everything is known, everyone will be free.*

He had only a moment to muse on these utopian possibilities, though, because both Kat and Alon6 walked into his office at the same time.

"Nora2!" Bradley called out.

Nora2 hurried in and instantly detected the problem. "They booked at the same time, and then Alon6 moved up his appointment. I didn't have time to change it."

"All right," Bradley said with a dismissive gesture that pushed Nora2 from the room. Now he had a situation on his hands, and he hated situations. The temperature in the office seemed to drop ten degrees because Alon6 and Kat hated each other.

Kat had been restless lately. Bradley suspected the reason for it was she wanted to know more about what he was working on. He didn't want her to know too much because he was secretive, so he planted the idea in her mind of a rooftop garden at MIND. She had noticed how bare his kitchen was, and also how the employee lounge area on the roof was underutilized; he put the two ideas together.

"Could it be that MIND needs a human touch?" he asked her, poking a little fun at himself and his mod, and described how his employees needed a gathering place that fostered a sense of purpose.

Kat liked the idea of a little green on the roof. "Good for morale," she agreed. Being Kat, though, she spun it into a bigger idea. The science would be an interesting puzzle. Fresh vegetables and fruit were always grown in contained facilities inside and outdoors. She wanted to solve the riddle of a healthy food source, even if the challenge was wrapped up in a project as small as one roof garden. At least, it would occupy her mind. She'd written a lot of poetry and it was really time to move on to a project that involved other people. Maybe, she wondered, even a bigger role at MIND.

Bradley agreed to everything she suggested. When she spoke of accelerated seeds, enhanced or artificial water, enclosures like blast shields that let in the good part of the sun radiation and mitigated the rest, he listened and agreed, but not because he was interested in the science, like she was, or even in doing good, as she was also. He knew all too well that he was bad at knowing what made employees happy; Kat had those skills. The garden would make his employees happier, he assumed, and it would keep Kat engaged and closer to him.

She started work on the garden, bringing in a few plants at a time and chatting up the employees who came over to ask who she was and what she was doing. Of course, they liked the idea of a garden just for them and she told them about how she was planning to expand it.

Bradley knew that she cared enough about the project to tolerate running into Alon6 from time to time. She hated how Alon6's mod shaped Bradley's personality field. It was as though Bradley was a trained dog around Alon6.

"He's using you," she would say, and in response Bradley would just shrug Mods were like that, working on a deep level; nothing to be done about it.

"Tell me something I don't know," he said. For Bradley, it was worth it to have a funding source for his research, and that's what Alon6 supplied. The rest was extra. Well, not everything. It was hard on Bradley when Alon6 talked trash about Kat. Jealousy, Bradley supposed. Competing for Bradley's attention? Whatever the source, Bradley said nothing when Alon6 issued a nasty swipe or two about Kat, such as, "She's only around because your mod is working so hard." This, also, Bradley met with a shrug. They were all too complicated, human relationships, and yet people insisted on having them. He had to play along a little, especially with Kat, or he feared that she would lose interest in him.

One night at her house, Bradley probed her on the friction between her and Alon6. "So, he's like your dark side or something?"

He was right on the mark, so she said, "No, not at all." Shortly thereafter, she asked him to leave. There would be no sleepover that night. He waited a few nights before he came back. She let him in.

Now here they were, all three of them, together in Bradley's office. Kat was standing stiffly, trying to screen out Alon6's personality field, and preparing to leave the room as soon as she could. Alon6's mouth was already forming a sneer, the prelude to a snarky remark.

Bradley tried for a cheerful tone. "Kat! What a surprise!"

"I want you to come to the market with me," Kat said. "Remember? We were going for supplies."

Bradley had forgotten. "Supplies?" He shot a glance at his screen, but it only displayed a notification that Kat was coming in, not her purpose.

"For the rooftop garden. Don't you remember we talked about this?"

Alon6 wasn't able to keep the sarcasm out of his voice. *"Rooftop garden?"*

Bradley ignored the comment and spoke to Kat. "Give me twenty minutes with Alon6 and then I'll meet you downstairs."

Kat turned and left for the lobby, grateful to be far from Alon6's personality field. She waited for Bradley downstairs, and as she watched employees come and go, she mused that she could be a better leader at MIND than Bradley, using the rooftop garden to make employees' lives better. She really wanted to turn things around from the way she was at VirtualEyes. *Put that behind you.* She nodded to herself.

Upstairs, it wasn't immediately clear why Alon6 was in Bradley's office in the first place. Alon6 chattered, fiddled with objects on Bradley's desk, and moved to the window to part the blast curtain for a moment so he could look out at the sea. "Yes, yes, you're going to build something that will shake the world, and for that I'm proud of you."

Then Alon6 seemed to come to the point of his visit. "I want you to hire more people for Input. The new guy, Sanchez, I ran into him in the hall. He's going to be a handler for you?"

"That is correct."

"He told me he's ready to do more."

"He told me the same thing. But I want to try him as a handler first."

"When can you move him to Input?"

Bradley couldn't keep the exasperation from his tone. "Do we need more people in Input already?"

Yes, explained Alon6. Input was coming apart, as team members quit once they grasped the full scope of what they were working on. "They don't have your vision," Alon6 said.

"Or I haven't communicated it to them."

Alon6 moved to punch Bradley on the shoulder, but Bradley moved away in time. "It has nothing to do with you. You've communicated everything they need to know."

Bradley wondered if this was true. After all, he wasn't good with people. He had no idea what they wanted. He couldn't read faces or emotions. That's why Kat being around, working on the roof garden, was good. She knew how to talk to people and was a motivator.

Alon6 was also right. They needed a big team on Input and Bradley needed to retain them. "Okay," he said. "I'll move Sanchez when I can. He has to work as a handler today because we're going to the market."

"Whatever," Alon6 said with a dismissive wave of his hand. "Nothing matters but getting this right. I have a lot riding on you."

"Yes, of course. I have you by my side to always remind me." Alon6 never let him forget about the investment he'd made in MIND.

"Don't worry about the legalities," he added. "Gathering thoughts, even if people don't know it, will be legal by the next session of the domain."

They already had a team of lobbyists. Bradley was certain that Alon6 was handing out bribes, or worse. Alon6's definition of *legal* was loose. "I don't want any details," Bradley said.

Alon6's thin-lipped smile turned into a laugh. "Being pure gets you nowhere in this world. We need to become invincible. Solve the problem of consciousness gathering—MIND jumps ahead of the competition. Simple."

As an abstract problem, it was attractive for Bradley.

He remembered that Kat was waiting for him downstairs. He said goodbye to Alon6 and hurried out.

Chapter 019

The external climate controls were functioning well today. Sim air breezed through the market, leaving it cool and comfortable. There was no reason, therefore, for Bradley to feel lightheaded—but he was. It must have been his proximity to Kat, or else her nonstop talking. She was excited about the project.

"I'm glad you're working on it," he said. "We need that garden more than ever." He mentioned how a few team members on Input had recently quit.

"Do you know why?"

"Not really," he lied. "Might have been the pay. I decided to give everyone a raise. And I'm talking about the garden a lot."

Kat appeared to believe him. Her smile was airy, and she was light, gliding smoothly among the stalls, with their lettuces and kale grown in vertical farms, carrots grown in labs, and a few expensive tomatoes grown in real dirt.

Bradley walked close to Kat, enjoying her personality field. Sanchez, on his first day as a handler, was keeping a respectful distance.

Kat pointed out what he should buy, and he slipped it into his anti-bac bag, which glowed briefly with each purchase, disinfecting it and charging the goods to his crypto account. She had him buy lettuce and baby kale, which would be replanted in the garden. She talked about how good the beets looked and began to negotiate with a vendor about buying young plants in bulk.

"Have you ever seen beet seedlings looking so good?" she asked Bradley.

"I've never thought of beets as a plant."

"You're kidding."

"I'm not kidding," Bradley replied. "You know this about me. I don't even like to heat up the food units."

"I've seen you eat food units straight out of the package. It's disgusting. And unhealthy."

"They meet all your nutritional requirements."

Kat handed him the beet seedlings to put into the anti-bac bag. "I don't mean that kind of unhealthy. I mean mentally." Food units had become a habit with most, supplying nutrients but no joy. "Don't you think that sustaining your body could be more..." she paused, "more meaningful?"

"I guess so." He'd never really thought about it.

His lackluster answer put her off for a moment, but when he looked at her, his eyes worked their mod magic on Kat, and she had a surge of positive feeling for him. She wanted to take care of him, and she wanted to create a better work experience for the MIND employees.

As a demonstration project, Kat had already planted vegetables on the roof garden in small containers. Now she was ready to go bigger and spend more of MIND's money. She told Bradley how she wanted a large blast curtain to cover the entire rooftop area so the vegetables wouldn't fry in the sun. "And gray water," she said to Bradley. "Recycled water. Or better yet, artificial water." She handed him another mass of leafy greens to put in the bac-bag.

"Artificial water is not cheap," he said. They already sounded like an old couple, bantering and bickering about nothing. He loved that.

"Artificial water can be controlled. We can add nutrients for the plants."

"I guess if we used artificial water we wouldn't need to be watering the employee vegetables with their own piss?"

She laughed. "Yes, or our piss, either."

He loved that she said *ours*.

She walked faster and faster, propelled by her energy for the project. Bradley was completely caught up in it, also, until he looked down the line of stalls behind them and noticed something. Or someone.

There was a man behind them, keeping pace with them and watching everything. Bradley pinged Sanchez on comms, but Sanchez hadn't noticed anything amiss.

The man following Kat and Bradley was a shaggy character. He walked with a barely noticeable limp that he tried to conceal, leaning to the right as though weighed down, improbably, by an earring attached to his right ear, flashing in the sun. Bradley tried to get a quick snap of him on comms and failed. Too many people in the market in the way.

Bradley looked behind him again. The man's lips were moving—he was probably talking to himself or dictating notes into an unseen recorder. *Taking notes about us. Why?* Sanchez hadn't done anything to stop the man, waiting on instructions from Bradley.

Bradley didn't know what to do. He stood, watching the man, who chose that moment to look up and smile at Bradley, aware that Bradley was watching him. The man nodded. Bradley had the sense of a fly buzzing around his face, but there were no insects out today.

The man was swallowed up by the market crowds. This sent Bradley off on a tangent, wondering about the information streams in the market that could be captured. There was so much transmission noise—that was the challenge for a portable Harvester. How could a Harvester sort out meaningful information from the many sources it took in? So many thoughts. So many people. If it were close enough to focus on one person, that person would notice it and move away. Input Men operating the Harvests would be exposed. If that happened, people would see the Input Men as an intrusion or threat. That wouldn't do. He needed to get the Harvester prototype down to smaller-than-backpack size, and the wand needed to be handheld. He didn't want his team to be like the man following him, staying fifty feet behind, listening, watching, taking notes, and pretending that he wasn't doing anything when of course, he was. Input had to be graceful.

The odd thing about the man, the thing that Bradley couldn't get out of his mind, was that he didn't seem to care if Bradley knew what he was doing.

"What's going on?" Kat asked. She'd noticed that Bradley had stopped walking.

"Nothing," Bradley said. He started walking again. He didn't want her to know about the man following them until he found out more about him. He needed an image. Something to run through recognition. He brushed an insect away from his face and again thought how odd it was; there seemed to be no insects in the market today.

Kat took Bradley's "nothing" at face value and initiated a spirited conversation with a vendor about rooftop hydroponics using artificial water.

When they got back to the MIND building, Bradley said, "I'll meet you on the roof in a moment," and hurried off to his office.

She attributed his quick departure to his usual emotional cluelessness, shrugged, and started to bring the plants up to the rooftop herself.

The reason for Bradley's urgency was, of course, the man in the market. Bradley had captured some images of him on his comms device and he wanted to run them through his recognition software. Bradley knew that Kat's former company, VirtualEyes, was marketed as a facial recognition processor. He also knew that it didn't work. So he wrote his own algorithm and trained it on the database of faces that the domains made available to licensed developers like himself.

The images he had from the market were blurry, and his software didn't turn up meaningful results at first, so he left the recognition program running, hoisted one strap of the prototype Harvester over his arm, and hurried to the rooftop. He wanted to try something.

Kat had deposited her first load of baby vegetables in their growth medium trays and was looking around for a MIND employee to help her with the rest. She was waylaid by a purveyor of artificial water who was waiting for her on the roof. He had a tablet with his prices on it and was keen to make a deal.

Bradley was on the roof now. Moving behind a vent to stay out of sight, he slipped on headphones, and activated the Harvester. Inspired by the man following him in the market, Bradley wanted to try out his Harvester prototype on Kat as she haggled with the salesman.

Kat's voice was in his ears, but strangely, what he heard was out of sync with what she was saying at that moment. He realized that the Harvester was working—this was what it was like to hear someone's thoughts. The thoughts he heard were moving on two levels at once, maybe more, and it was confusing.

He was hearing obvious things from Kat like, *I think I can convince this guy to agree to a better price,* and deeper things that revealed self-doubt, such as, *I am pretentious and only want to prove myself to everyone I meet,* and deeper still such as, *Daddy, stop hating me. I am not making Mommy die.* Then her thoughts cycled through the levels again. *I think I should ask Bradley for an official title to sanction my work on the garden. What about Chief Happiness Officer? Bradley is pretentious. Should appeal to him. Just wants to be loved. Doesn't know it. Had to drop out of Uni. Can't do everything your way, Daddy. Don't hate me anymore. My way is better. Can't take care of Mommy. Does Mommy really have to die? I can make the garden dedication for the whole staff. I should start preparing. I'll ask Bradley about it.*

Bradley tore off the headphones as though they had burned his ears. Hearing her thoughts in a jumble nauseated him. It was disorienting, as though he had woken up in her skin. He reached out for an air vent to steady himself and tried to slow his breathing. The vent was grimy and he unconsciously wiped his hand on his pants, leaving a black mark. He would have to remember to act surprised when Kat asked about making the dedication address. He slipped back downstairs.

Back in his office, he put the prototype down at the back of the room and inspected the program he'd left running. The best match so far was James Scarborough, a crypto financier. Bradley thought Scarborough may have been following them in the market because he wanted to invest in MIND. There was another hypothetical match, but the facial recognition modeling wasn't complete and the machine had no guess who it might be. The program needed more time to work.

Bradley was about to tweak the controls to make it go faster when Kat walked in. He swiped the screen blank and pretended to be doing something else. He wasn't ready to show her any of this, especially if the processing was incomplete. A crypto financier like Scarborough, who favored forced buyouts to take over companies, was serious business.

"I just got MIND a great deal on artificial water," she said.

Since she was being forthright with him, he had a change of heart about concealing something from her. He didn't want to tell her about Scarborough, though, or any potential takeovers. That would be for him to discuss with Alon6. He opened the screen to show her his images of the man following them, just to see what she made of them.

"Do you know this man who was following us in the market?"

"Following us?" She leaned in to look closer.

Bradley looked over her shoulder. He didn't want Kat to know he was running the images through facial recognition, so all he put on the screen were the images he snapped with his comms.

Kat squinted at them. She saw the blurry form of a man, maybe limping, perhaps learning to the right as he walked.

Bradley felt foolish. No wonder the machine was having trouble figuring out who it might be. "Any idea who it is?" he asked anyway.

Kat glanced at the image for another moment, then tore her eyes away. "No," she lied. She hurried out of Bradley's office, claiming to be late for an appointment.

"See you tonight?" he called out, a little too late to be heard.

She didn't answer. She caught the next glidepath up to Marin.

Kat recognized the images of the man on the screen, the man who had been following them in the market. It was Hopper00. It was part of his method, to follow people in the markets. She didn't like it, but she knew about it because he had told her how he did it. He followed people in markets to get background information on them. "I like to see how people walk," he said, as though that explained anything.

Fine, but does he have to do his intelligence gathering when I'm with Bradley? It was intrusive. *Doesn't he know enough about me already?* Kat fidgeted in her seat, waiting for the short glidepath ride to be over. She wanted to be home.

It was an old story, told in many business schools, how VirtualEyes became the darling of financiers. Kat, charming as she was brilliant, sold the program to security details in every domain. She got a contract with the CIAGOV Domain. She was in talks with the Mossad Domain. Every domain, whether democratic or repressive, wanted a facial recognition program that worked. Most of them didn't. They falsely matched people of color with criminals from databases, or mistakenly labeled men as sex offenders, destroying their lives. All the failed software had inherent bias. People programmed it and people were racist. Centuries of bad human judgement were embedded in the training data and, by extension, into the execution of the software.

That was where Kat's VirtualEyes triumphed. She didn't base it on what people thought, or their history of bad judgement, or their biases. She based it on bees' intelligence.

"Bees," as Kat stated with authority in countless investment pitches and company meetings, "have a precise way of recognizing members of their hive. Bees don't make mistakes. They protect the queen bee. Only members of the hive can get in. Outsiders would kill the queen and take over the hive. Among bees, facial recognition is a life and death matter. It's also a life and death matter among us."

By this point, Kat usually had her audience enraptured. Investors were ready to pour credits into her accounts. New recruits were ready to give all they had as employees.

"It is a life and death matter for us," Kat's pitch continued, "because we lock up criminals, secure our borders, offer financial credit and employment, and keep our homes and workplaces safe using facial recognition—which we need to be accurate and fair. VirtualEyes makes it both accurate and fair. We have captured the essence of bee facial recognition in our algorithms and built those recognition instruments into our process."

This pitch worked well. VirtualEyes became a powerhouse company. Kat took over entire buildings at Uni and filled them with coders and marketers. She worked them hard, rewarded them with low-orbital company retreats and other low-gravity experiences. She brought out powerful emotions in everyone she met. Love and hate. She was bold when Bradley met her at Uni, then humble when they met during his confinement.

She exited the glidepath station and began the short walk to her house. Hopper00 liked to watch how people walked, he'd said, and thinking about this made her self-conscious about her walk. Was she walking like herself? *Ridiculous. What does that even mean?* She wasn't sure who she was or how she should behave. She hoped that Hopper00 would reveal her to herself, but so far, it wasn't working well.

The effect of Bradley's mod had also worn off. She felt mildly disgusted, remembering being in his presence, as though she had eaten too much cake yet couldn't stop herself from licking the fork. If she told Bradley the truth, that it was Hopper00 in the market, his mouth would hang open in shock. "Oh, yes," she imagined herself telling Bradley, "Hopper00 is going to write a profile about me. The man who was in the market."

Bradley would have trouble finding words, and they'd all come out at once; he'd be worried about his reputation, and hers, and what the man might write about MIND. "Did you even look him up? His history?"

Kat had, of course, and anyway Hopper00 was open about his past.

Kat sighed. Her house felt empty and quiet. She looked at Dave's Form Factor and contemplated activating him. She needed a sounding board. Agreeing to work with Hopper00 on a profile piece was beginning to look like a decision she should have questioned. Why had Hopper00 chosen her for it, anyway? He had explained how he saw so much more in her than what she had become thus far and said that it was time to rehabilitate her image so that she could move on. He seemed to believe in her more than she believed in herself. This was strange, and Kat didn't like tangled threads of emotion. She tried to convince herself that she could use rehabilitating and a relaunch of her career. Maybe the profile piece could help.

Later, at day's end, when Bradley came over, she asked if she could give a dedication address when they were ready to open the fully-built-out rooftop garden to the employees, and of course Bradley said yes. He looked at her with love and longing, drinking in every aspect of her. He became what she wanted to see and smiled the smile she needed him to.

He tore his eyes from her for a moment and opened the blast curtains. It was evening and safe to let in the last of the sun. The golden slab of light on the floor reminded him of the light in the single-room pod of his confinement.

He watched her without speaking. She was putting books away. It was unusual to own books because most people preferred digital assets. Of course, these were Dave's books. Kat loved to touch them.

"What are you smiling at?" Kat finally asked, noticing Bradley's gaze.

"You," he said. Bradley wanted to depend on her love, their love, and he was encouraged about the possibility every time she let him in.

From the first day she came to his single-room pod, Bradley had been flattered that she wanted him to make Dave's avatar. The project was intimate and there were tempting moral frontiers to cross together. As Bradley and Kat role-played to train the avatar, the work of programming became secondary. They were really building their relationship.

That was the story Bradley told himself. He and Kat built their connection on stories about Dave. When they were creating Dave, words about him flowed between them for hours.

That story had some truth during Dave's creation, but it was no longer true. With Dave now a real presence in her life, Kat was free to all but ignore Bradley. Bradley listened quietly as Kat entertained herself with Dave. She would stretch out on the sleeping mat and look at the ceiling and tell Dave stories about herself, even stories he already knew.

She unfolded the story of VirtualEyes. Even though Dave knew the story, he listened and nodded along to her tales of how she commanded the staff, was one day a warm leader and the next, a terror, was bold with investors, and lied to them also, until one day security made her pack up her belongings and marched her out of the office, forcing her from the company. She told Dave there was no facial recognition technology that was based on the way bees recognized their hive mates. Dave nodded sagely, interjecting now and again to bring out details.

"Even though it was a lie, it was a wonderfully convincing detail," he would say. "And don't forget to mention that you left with a generous settlement." She laughed her laugh like a melody, the one that went up and down a pleasant scale.

During the day, when Kat was alone with Dave, she continued her dialog with him. "I am done with lying," she told him. But this also was not true. It had been several weeks since Kat and Bradley were in the market together, and still she hadn't told Bradley that she knew who had followed them. She assumed identifying the stranger had slipped to the bottom of Bradley's task list.

She was wrong about this. Bradley had kept the recognition program running on the machine in his office. It loaded and reloaded the blurry images of the man in the market, bringing up one, then another potential match. Bradley was fairly certain by this point that it was not the crypto financier who followed them on that day. There had been no offers for MIND, and the machine would only produce a twenty-five-percent certainty of a match. But Bradley let it keep working because he knew, eventually, it would find a match.

He stared at the screen from behind his standing desk, watching the machine searching for a match, and let his thoughts drift again to Kat. On the nights that she let him stay with her, he had gotten into the habit of watching her as she slept. He often set a silent alarm on his chronograph, one that would gently tap his wrist at three AM to remind him to look at her.

She was a graceful sleeper. It was like watching a lovely movie, her face in repose, the gentle rise and fall of her breath.

Bradley didn't know that she also watched him in his sleep. She would wake early to the sound of artificial birdsong on her comms. Before she put up a sunrise scene on the big screen, she would turn to Bradley and watch him. His face was also calm in repose, his eyelids like delicate eggshells, flicking with REM. She watched him with a flow of emotions, knowing that his mod drew her closer, guilty that she hated him as soon as he was out of her personality field, and grateful that he had brought Dave back into her life.

And now, after much wandering, she felt direction. She wanted to see if she could lead again. The desire was there. She enjoyed her persuasiveness as she rallied the vendors to her cause of a rooftop garden. She had organized the work crews who were building it, and even when she wasn't present at the garden, she knew workers were unpacking the equipment for artificial water generation and moving it into place, along with pots of tomato plants, squash, beans, and lettuce. With the rooftop garden she found a project to care about, other than Dave.

Chapter 020

Kat used bioaccelerants in the garden, so it was ready in a few weeks. The tomatoes were dense and the zucchini and melons were fat. A spherical greenhouse wrapped the shiny lettuces. Above the greenhouse was a tinted blast curtain forming a protective dome.

There was a small elevated stage off to the side, where Bradley stood now, behind a microphone that levitated using anti-grav—a needless extravagance, but he wanted the employees to be impressed with Kat. Everything had to go right for her. He had had a screen moved into place behind her that showed the construction process over the last few weeks, with pictures of all the MIND employees who were involved.

He looked out over the faces of his employees. The light filtering in through the blast curtain bathed them in a golden glow. There were three-hundred people on the payroll now and they waited for Bradley to speak.

He was never comfortable standing before a lot of people and saying anything, but this time all he had to do was introduce Kat, who was waiting confidently over to the side. Haltingly, he embarked on a brief, awkward speech about how proud he was of Kat for heading up the rooftop garden project. How he had known from the moment she proposed it that it would be good for all of them.

"Don't worry," he assured them all, "we'll still have some low-orbital fun on the next retreat." This was greeted with scattered laughter. Looking down at their faces, he couldn't get a read on how they were thinking of Kat. Were they thinking of her as the failed CEO of VirtualEyes, tolerating her as his significant other, or genuinely curious about why she had supervised the construction of this rooftop garden for all of them? He decided that they were curious about her, grateful for her dedication to the garden, and pressed on.

"This garden will be a great benefit to everyone here. And now, Kat Keeper."

He stepped aside for Kat to take over. He thought she looked radiant.

She was at the front of the stage with a few fast steps, holding a tablet with the words of her speech. Confident that she wouldn't have to consult it, she kept it closed and stood tall. She spoke with authority about artificial water, self-sufficiency, why everyone needed to take care of each other, and what a great place MIND was to work. Bradley wondered if this was the sort of motivating talk she had given at her own company, to fire up her investors and employees. There was something he wanted to try, so he moved away from Kat and toward a corner of the roof where he had stashed the Harvester prototype.

Bradley was right about the tone of her talk. She wanted to motivate the MIND employees, using the team-building cohesion of the rooftop garden. And it appeared to be working. The employees who participated in the hands-on work of building the garden stood proudly behind her, and those in the audience seemed convinced by her every word about company spirit, building something together, becoming better as a team, all the old clichés.

Yet, even though the audience was buying it, she was not. A voice in her head said, *It's just not the same.* It was loud enough to startle her. She lost her place in the talk for a moment and had to glance down and open her tablet, something she had never done before while speaking in front of a crowd of people. The crowd waited patiently for her to find her place and conclude her thoughts.

After she finished her speech, the applause was sincere. Bradley was suddenly upon her.

"Impressive speech!"

She looked at him curiously. "Where were you? I didn't see you in the front."

"Just admiring your brilliance from afar."

Her eyes sparkled at his flattery; she couldn't help herself. Then she moved off the small stage to show off the artificial water generator and appoint the first weekly garden foreperson, who would be in charge of the harvest.

But as she spoke to the MIND employees, dissatisfaction clung to her. She wanted to re-create some part of her past that wouldn't fully manifest. She had felt out of her body during the speech. Something felt wrong, but she didn't know what. She wished she could wave away these doubts like images on a screen.

And there was something else sticking in her mind. She kept grasping at a vague memory of Bradley moving about the crowd with a backpack on his back, and this made little sense.

That night she couldn't sleep. Bradley was beside her on the mat, already snoring. She closed her eyes with a sense of futility and heard the voice in her head again. It was the same voice that she heard when she was speaking, the loud voice that said *It's just not the same* and made her lose her place.

This time the voice said, *Prepare for war.* The words were clear. *Prepare for war.* They were strong enough in her mind to force her into wakefulness. Suddenly she was upright on the sleeping mat. Her eyes were open.

Prepare for war? Maybe this thought came from Bradley. She turned to look at him. He appeared to be asleep still, but she wasn't sure. She had had the sense that he was watching her just a moment ago.

Chapter 021

Kat came down to El Segundo twice a week. The rooftop garden software needed troubleshooting and new employees who wanted to garden needed instruction. She was busier with it now, more than before, because her dedication speech sparked curiosity about the garden, and more employees came up on the roof to have a look at it. She was tinkering with the recycled water controls when she noticed a young woman wearing a black jumpsuit, trying to get her attention by standing in her line of sight.

"I am Cressida Scopes," she said.

"Yes?" Kat answered. She struggled to place the young woman but couldn't remember her.

"Sorry, it looks like I surprised you. I didn't mean to, but they said you would be up here."

"Yes?" Kat said again. "Can I help you with something?"

"I just signed on. To MIND. I work in Input."

Kat could tell by the way she was dressed. To build morale and cohesion, Bradley had the Input Team suit up in black jumpsuits to give them a collective ninja vibe.

The young woman paused for a moment, weighing her next words. "It's all guys in Input. Except for me. When I asked about the rooftop garden, they laughed."

"They laughed?"

"They were fooling around, I know, but..." She trailed off.

"Don't any of them use it?"

It was Cressida's turn to laugh. "No way." She put her hands in her pockets and rocked back on her heels. Her shoes automatically adjusted, moving cushioning to the back part of the soles. "They only talk about work. They consider themselves the best in the company."

Clearly, this young woman had something on her mind about the Input team. Kat was curious about what it was. "And you joined them? Annoying as they are?" Kat smiled to soften the statement.

"Well, I am a better programmer than most of them. I don't mean that to say..." She trailed off again.

Kat nodded her affirmation. "It's just a statement of fact."

Cressida looked at Kat with eyes clear and sharp, like a mountain range seen from a distance. She was tall, and seemed self-assured. Her red-brown hair crossed her face, and she pushed it back.

"I was wondering if you would show me around the garden." She looked down shyly. "We can't live off thinking alone. The body isn't a box we carry the mind around in."

Kat laughed. "You're right about that."

She gave the woman a tour, showed Cressida how to get the app on her comms and use it to adjust the garden light and water. The user could use the app to select a plot, populate it with seeds, and designate nourishment. Kat watched as Cressida tried it, following Kat's instructions. A few garden bots whirred into place on command.

"You can do it yourself, of course," Kat said. "If you like getting your hands dirty. I do." She gestured with a shovel she had picked up, but she noticed Cressida was distracted.

There was a man on the other side of the roof watching Cressida. Kat thought she recognized him. It may have been Sanchez, formerly Bradley's handler and now, Kat remembered dimly, promoted to Input section chief. "What does he want with you?"

Cressida sighed and put her comms unit into her pocket. "Sanchez is my section chief. He's probably wondering why I'm not down at my workstation drawing Logic Trees."

"Everyone at MIND has the right to stop up here and grow their own food."

Cressida glanced at Sanchez again. He was also dressed in black, the Input uniform, but not in a jumpsuit, signifying his executive status. Cressida jerked her chin at Sanchez with a hint of defiance. "Tell it to him."

Kat put down the shovel. "I will," she said, but as she started to move, the younger woman stopped her with a hand on her arm.

"Not now, though," Cressida said.

Kat was miffed. "I won't get you in trouble. Bradley told me the garden would build morale, but it can't unless the employees are allowed to use it." She paused before asking, "Is Sanchez a bad boss?"

Cressida shook her head. "No, a new one. Newly appointed. Learning to fit the role. He *is* a bully, but also smart. The right combination for the job."

Don't make excuses for him, thought Kat.

"Look, he's leaving now," Cressida said. Sanchez was indeed taking the stairs down. Cressida continued. "He's going out field-testing with Bradley." She paused to assure herself that Sanchez was out of sight. "I'm not supposed to tell you that."

Kat nodded. "Everything in Input is supposed to be secret."

"Yes."

"So why tell me?"

The younger woman looked stricken for a moment and then, by a force of will, made her face blank. "Because it's wrong. What they're field-testing. It's wrong." She looked around as if she might see the cameras on the roof. They were there, but well hidden.

"How is it wrong?" Kat asked.

"I'll tell you sometime, but not now. I've been gone from my workstation long enough. Goodbye." She hurried away.

Kat watched Cressida move quickly across the roof and then descend the stairs. She was taking a risk by speaking with Kat. The information Cressida needed about the garden was in the employee manual—Kat had put it there herself. *There is something else,* Kat thought. The Input Team was the most secretive in the company. Kat couldn't shake the sense that Cressida needed her to know something. *But what?*

It would be possible for Kat to learn more about the Input team on the terminal in Bradley's office, so she headed down there. The reporter pinged her as she was on her way, asking for background info on her days at Uni. Often, something strange happened when Kat thought of the reporter: She often could not remember his name on the first try. There would be a blank space where it was supposed to be. It was the kind of behavior that a mod might produce, but the reporter said he wasn't modded. Kat believed him. This was something else.

As she walked down the hall to Bradley's office, she thought about how the reporter would ping her on comms and just start talking, never identifying himself. She would recognize his voice, of course. How could she not? It was heavy, rough, and soft at the same time.

Then it would come to her. *Hopper00.* Hopper *zero-aught,* when he said his name, when he bothered to identify himself. When he appeared on the vid, which he did not always do, his eyes always looked deeply into her. As she looked back at him, his eyes showed that he had been through many trials in his life. She wanted to trust him, but when his eyes pulled her in it felt like he had the power to make her do things she wouldn't normally do.

Bradley wasn't in his office, since he was out field-testing something with Sanchez. So Kat stood at his desk and opened a terminal. She decided to hold off digging into what Input was working on and instead act on Hopper00's request to find background info on Uni. Bradley had given her a terminal log-in with sufficient access privileges to search for the information she needed to create the rooftop garden.

She did a search for Uni and was pleased when it returned many images. Bradley wasn't too careful about practical things like security, and she suspected he actually wanted her to find these images. They were mostly of her. He'd probably collected them in this terminal for her to find.

"I will write the definitive profile piece on Kat Keeper," she recalled Hopper00 telling her, exercising the flattery he employed often to get her to comply with his requests. "You provide the background info I need, and I will create a career retrospective about you that will seize your narrative. It will show everyone reading the Feed that you are on a path to greatness!"

"No, I'm not," she said aloud, flipping through the images and text, picking out details that Hopper00 might want about Uni, but also about VirtualEyes, Dave, her early life in New York with her parents. Bradley had a big file on her, maybe bigger than her own.

The indicator on the records blinked. She gestured at the screen and the indicator turned into a number. She still had hundreds of records to go through. *So much here.*

She looked over an image of Bradley at Uni, looking younger than the teenager he was. A few of Alon6 and Bradley together. Images of her from Uni events that she'd never seen before. She had a sense of something being off, a movement of the air that carried intuition. She didn't know what these feelings were. She couldn't name them, but they scared her. Like the voice in her head that said *Prepare for war.* Or *It's just not the same.*

To take her mind away from these troubling questions, she gazed at an old image of Bradley and his father, Samuel Pollak. Old Samuel, who had renamed himself Sasha Power, had spent many credits to buy a 15 for Bradley. Bradley never used his 15. He thought those numbers were classist. Of course, modding itself was classist. Super expensive. In the picture, Sasha looked proud of his modded son. *A wealthy duo.*

She laughed to herself, remembering one semester at Uni that Bradley had told her about, when he took a vow of poverty, spending next to nothing on food and clothes and living like an animal. He was a riddle, Bradley, but he had created Dave.

She thought about how Hopper00 might frame the article he was writing, the narrative he would choose. She imagined he would write, *There are two chapters in her life, Before and After.*

But there is another chapter coming, said the voice in her head.

It startled her again, but she thought she recognized it now. It was gravelly and soft at the same time.

She shook it off. "Record," she said aloud. Her comms device beeped softly. *I started at Uni seeking knowledge and was inquisitive. I wanted to know everything and thought everything was possible. I let nothing get in my way. I was unstoppable.* She paused, collecting her thoughts

It could have been different. I could have been stopped. But something in me...

She collected her thoughts again and shifted the time frame.

My father was a data salesperson. His business was personal records. He sold health records that might reveal that someone was a risky hire, detention records that made someone a bad risk for a crypto loan. Data marketers aren't known for scruples. All this information was fair game.

He should have made a lot of money, but he took risks for fast money and sold to the gray market. The respectable clients avoided him. Ambition turned him into a hustler. I admired that in him.

My mother was sick for most of my life. She died of cancer when I was twelve. We never had much crypto on account, but my dad always scraped something together. My lemonade-stand moment was getting the smart boys in my Eastside school to build apps and games that I sold. I was always good at selling. Putting words to ideas.

We lived on the Westside and I went to school on the Eastside. Dad told me never to say where we lived. He believed passionately that the Eastside schools were better in New York, and he worked so hard to send me there. I don't know what kind of deal he made with Uni to send me there.

I was a serious child. My mind was busy. I often was afflicted with insomnia.

"Stop," she said. Her comms unit beeped softly.

She let a smile escape, and thought, *I am a serious adult, too. I take myself seriously all the time. To make my company, VirtualEyes, stand on nothing, I had to believe in it completely. Even when there was nothing there.*

She wanted to say *record* again. She wanted to record what she thought, but couldn't. All of it was on the Feed. Hopper00 would already know it all. She was tiring of talking about herself. With a wave of her hand, she moved to darken the terminal.

But before she completed the movement, she noticed another document on the terminal screen. She noticed her name in it. *Odd,* she thought. Maybe she was accessing something she shouldn't be able to access.

She tapped the document, and the screen got brighter. She saw her name repeated many times in the document and started breathing faster. She started to read faster than she could think, faster than she could breathe. Her eyes flicked over the document.

In the left column, she saw a transcription of her speech to dedicate the roof garden. It was recorded and transcribed somehow. She didn't recall Bradley saying anything about that.

Company spirit is important, and we are building something together, becoming better as a team.

In the right column, she saw what appeared to be the thoughts she was thinking as she delivered that speech. *What is this?*

The magic isn't there. It's just not the same.

Seeing the words written out made her remember thinking them, a double vision but made of words and thoughts. She scrolled on to see transcriptions of what appeared to be what the MIND employees were thinking about her as she made the speech.

I wish she were running this company.

I will never come up here to get vegetables.

When can we get back to work?

It took her another moment, and then she had it. This was a Harvester transcript.

A wave of nausea washed over her, and she grabbed Bradley's desk for support. She scrolled farther down to see the exchange she and he had had at the end of the speech. In the left column, what was said between them:

"Impressive speech!"

"Where were you? I didn't see you in the front."

"Just admiring your brilliance from afar."

In the right column, what they were thinking:

It looks like she didn't catch me using the Harvester.

She scrolled down to find more. This wasn't the only time Bradley had used the Harvester to record her thoughts. Bradley was recording her secretly and often, around the MIND offices. The shallow and deeper levels of her mind were combined in a stream.

We planted too many tomatoes. Is sleeping with Bradley something I even like? Sometimes he smells bad. I wonder if I smell bad sometimes.

Reading her thoughts was unnatural. Seeing them somehow broke her mind, or broke it open, and a rage bloomed in her and also something she couldn't name. Kat darkened the screen with a flick of her hand.

at looked at people in the station and heard their thoughts in her mind.

I'm going to be late for this train and the school will charge me for being late to pick up Henry and he will hate me.

After I slept with June, Maggie is going to sleep with James33. Maybe I don't care.

She didn't know who the thoughts belonged to. She couldn't connect them with any single person.

I hate my stepfather. Once a year is too often to visit. But I want to see my mother.

She was broken, somehow. How else could these thoughts be broadcasting into her mind? Cogent thoughts, and deeper thoughts that came in fragments. *Remember birds? Their sounds are happiness. Dying won't be bad. She's been sick and fading. Chaos here. Run away. Run. Run.*

Kat's heart was beating fast enough to burst from her chest. Her breathing was short and ragged.

Maybe I'm going insane.

That last one was her voice. She tried to talk some sense into herself. This must be a temporary psychosis brought on by exposure to the Harvester data. She nodded to herself. It was a possibility. Upon her exposure to the data, some twenty minutes ago, she had felt dizzy enough to grab Bradley's desk for support.

There was another theory in the back of her mind, one that she couldn't stop from surfacing. *Hopper00.* Maybe Hopper00 was acting on her, accessing her consciousness. *Now, that is insane.*

To get away from these thoughts, she looked at the trip board. She hoped its geometry would settle her mind, but it was daunting with its many potential destinations. She had to get away from Bradley, from MIND, and from the Harvester project. Just thinking about it made her feel another wave of nausea. Destinations flickered on the trip board, updating and updating. They didn't settle her mind. She tried to retrace her steps from the office to the station.

After she darkened Bradley's screen, he and Sanchez had come in. They had been field-testing the Harvester and had the prototype with them, the same one Bradley had used on her.

She looked him dead in the eye and said, "You are a liar."

"What? Kat, are you okay?"

"You used the Harvester on me. You made me some kind of test subject."

His response was to gabble about experimental technologies, early data being inaccurate, shifting his weight from one foot to the other, and touching her shoulder in entreaty. "It wasn't my best idea, I admit."

She aimed a few clipped words at him like arrows.

He backed off and went quiet, then tried again. "Kat, listen to me. This is deep material, pre-intellectual, unprocessed, no relationship to truth."

She needed more air. She was suffocating and took a sharp inward breath. "Stop lying!" she burst out, banging her hand on the desk so everything on it jumped. Even Sanchez stepped back, and he didn't seem like the kind of man to be afraid of anything. She felt a new rage building in her, which made it difficult to form the words to express it. "You recorded core materials. The deepest, unvoiced beliefs of the inner mind." It was as though he had reached inside her body and tore her substance away.

"No, Kat, listen, it's just that I am having a little trouble tuning it. It captures deep thoughts and surface thoughts, and I can't sort them out."

Liar.

"Erase it. Erase it all."

He complied. She watched him do it. Then she walked out without another word, out of the building to the glidepath station, allowing rage to carry her because she had a sense that it could just as easily paralyze her. The trip board flashed to indicate that a glidepath was leaving in five minutes.

Now she stood in the aisle between seats and breathed filtered air. A pattern of light and darkness fell over her as they pulled out of the station. There was the familiar jerk as the glidepath coupled with the magnetic field below, the familiar bump as the anti-grav engaged and they accelerated. The robot conductor, round, low to the ground because it was built for stability, reminded her to sit down or she would be pulled off her feet.

She complied. The force of a glidepath in motion was powerful.

She was in the Marin station twenty minutes later, exited, and walked the short distance to her house in Sausalito. Once inside, she collected a small backpack and stuffed it with clothes. She closed the lid to Dave's Form Factor and slipped it in as well.

She returned to the station. She watched the trip board until it displayed the destination she wanted. She had to hurry—the glidepath she wanted was leaving in two minutes.

With her backpack bouncing on her shoulders, she hustled through the closing doors just in time. She flopped into a seat and settled in as best she could. It would be a couple of hours until she arrived in New York, so she had a little time to think about what was happening to her. The rage against Bradley—she would sort that out later, when it subsided.

Right now, the voices in her head were the problem. They invaded her personality field. They pushed out her own thoughts and she couldn't think or feel clearly, and there was pain, a headache focusing on a single sharp point in the middle of her forehead; she refused to share her thought space with the thoughts of others. She held her head in her hands, until the pain subsided, but what remained was a vibration made of foreign ideas and random connections, overlapping and all talking at once.

Inseminate a surrogate? I can't do that.

This job will kill me. So kill them first? Sand in the gears sabotage.

My child, my child, I can't find the right doctor and the air is so bad.

And thoughts in her mind that didn't parse into sentences, just raw feelings attached to words by a thread. *Pain. Pain. Pain. Pain tolling like a bell. Rolling like a wheel. My hand on her body that time, remember? Yes, I remember yellow music, yellow, and white until the soft, soft — and it all made me so angry. His eyes melted.*

She wanted to explain these voices to herself, as the first step to making them go away. There must be a reason they were happening. Her mind looped back to her earlier explanations. Perhaps the Harvester had induced a kind of psychosis or transparency or Hopper00 was involved, but any clarity was fogged by the clamor of the other voices she was experiencing.

She forced herself to chase a memory of her own. When she was a girl, she was able to hear other people's thoughts. It made her feel special.

When she told her mother about it, her mother's eyes went cold. "Don't talk crazy," her mother said, and then tried to backtrack. "Just never tell anybody about imagining anything like that."

Her mother's shaming made her forget about her ability, to stuff it away where it wouldn't be easily found. The signal she received back then, though, wasn't as strong as it was now. As a child, it was simply a sensitivity. As a girl, it developed into something like an intuition best described as a gentle flow of words or sentences like bubbles in the air. Now it was something like a blast of furious ideas all at once, strong enough to make her lose her footing.

She listened to the storm in her mind, some voices in pleasure and others in agony, as the power of the glidepath acceleration pressed her gently into her seat. She struggled to sort it all and knew she must fail at it for now. She had to cope with her thoughts in a jumble.

The glidepath hurtled from a tunnel into burning sunlight. The blast shields on the windows rattled up, darkening the interior of the car and then adjusting inside to simulate daylight.

Kat remembered points in her career when she had stood in board meetings and lied her ass off. Company meetings, hundreds of people, and she had lied about what VirtualEyes could do. These were the lies that took her down, eventually, but she told them boldly and with conviction. Worse, she drew her employees into them. When VirtualEyes was a non-functioning prototype, she told her people, search out data and present it as ours.

Can we do that, they asked?

If I'm telling you, yes, she said.

Bradley wasn't foolish like that. He wouldn't lie publicly, in a way that could take him down. He would lie to people who trusted him. He would lie quietly and cleverly. That was his way. Any trust she once had in him had been incinerated by the rage inside her. Her hands and face felt hot.

Bradley had erased the data while she watched him do it, but now she was certain that he kept backups.

A feeling of nausea overtook her again. She was trying to process these moments, and also the voices of other passengers that pushed into her mind. She sprang from her seat, clung to the slippery walls, and rushed to the room marked with a toilet symbol.

It was locked. Someone was in there. The bile rose in her throat. She rattled the door. No one answered, and the door remained locked.

She turned away to the window, which was sealed as always, and with no other choice, vomited against it with an explosive splash. She clung to the slippery wall, her breath coming in heaves. The blast curtain fitted imperfectly over the window, allowing a peek at scenery flooding by outside, too fast for her to identify.

After a moment, the door to the restroom burst open. A child came out. Kat rushed in to clean herself off. Miraculously, none of the vomit had bounced back on her. The woman in the mirror looked frightened.

"When will we arrive?" she asked aloud.

An amber light came on above the mirror and a calm synth voice said, "We arrive in New York by sixteen-hundred."

As Kat exited the bathroom, refreshed by the UV scrubbers and gray water, she saw that a maintenance bot was nearly finished cleaning her vomit from the window.

Chapter 023

As the doors of the glidepath flew open, Kat was flooded with sensations. The smell of the city hit her first. There was nothing else like it. Seaweed, urine, and humanity. Suddenly she was a child again on the Westside with her father, financially overextended because her mother was sick with lung cancer.

She remembered the day her father presented her with her first comms unit. The number-letter string had been assigned to her at birth, but most families didn't turn the device over to the child until they turned thirteen. Martin, Kat's father, had been so proud to hand her the comms unit dedicated to her identity. She felt like a real grown-up then. Martin was a data salesman who cut some corners, desperate to make the money to send her to an Upper East school so she could receive a prestigious education.

Kat held her comms unit in her hand. It wasn't the same one she was given as a child, of course; it had been updated. But the letter-number string was the same.

She left the glidepath station, working to stay focused enough to find the elevator to the surface. The voices seemed to want to pull her off task, but she squeezed her way in among the others, and soon the elevator burst to the surface with a great clatter. The doors flew open to reveal the yellow skies of Midtown. The Eastside, she noted from a map on the wall, was under less water than the Westside used to be when she lived here. Midtown, being at a higher elevation, was dry and hot. Most people wanted to live closer to the water, even with the risk of flooding, because temperatures were cooler there. She was at the center of the city, a good place to get her bearings.

Facing north, she could turn to the right and see the Upper East grimly sparkling in the day. The Eastside was for industrialists from The Chinese State; those who ruled the city lived there.

To the left, the watery Westside. She realized that she must go there. *That's where I'm going to live. That's where I'm going now.*

There were no private vehicles allowed in Midtown, so Kat hailed a three-wheeled tuktuk that she was able to pick out from the swarm of anti-grav motorcycles and hoverboards seeking passengers. She gave her address and the tuktuk driver started pedaling to carry her westward and back into her past. She thought of the brownstone her family occupied on the Westside, its foundations crumbling as the waters rose. It was a terrible place to live. The electricity would short out every few weeks, and they would be plunged into darkness. She heard her mother's voice calling out from her bed for her father. *Martin? Get a flashlight, please. I want to keep reading.*

The street noise was loud enough to keep any voices at bay in Kat's mind but it gave her a different kind of headache. They made it across 42nd Street by darting in and out of traffic and nearly flying under an anti-grav bus but redirecting at the last second. Then the traffic slowed to a stop. Like in Los Angeles, the streets were filled with impromptu housing settlements of families living in cardboard and tin structures, and a glut of anti-grav transport, hoverboards, and tuktuks like the one she was in.

"Your best bet from here is to get a gondola," her driver advised.

Surveying the density around her she saw that he was right, so she paid him via comms, got out, and hailed a gondola. The gondola pilot rowed steadily across a few blocks of 42nd Street that were under shallow, dirty water, reached the Hudson, and started uptown. Kat soon saw that this part of the city was best navigated via the river. It was a quiet and calm way to travel. The water lapped at the gondola, the pilot's oar dipped in and out of the water, children played with discarded buoys and driftwood on the shore, and above, when Kat looked up, she saw people strolling on the skyways high above. The gondola driver must have had a quiet mind; she heard none of his thoughts. The other people, on the shore, were too far away, apparently, to enter her thought space. When Kat looked closer, she saw that the people up above were mostly delivery people who hurried along the elevated ramps, their bodies curled around their precious packages, which they dropped into delivery chutes, then scurried away.

She scanned the yellow sky and saw only seagulls. There were no other kinds of birds. Because of them, and because of the portholes that lined the buildings at water level, the city resembled a massive ship, more than a collection of structures on land. What was above the water seemed to shift and change position; what was below was a mystery. She was grateful for the sim air that filtered some of the pollution, and the climate controls were also working well today. She needed only a light reflective silver jacket to protect her from the sun.

"It's a beautiful day in the city," she said to the gondola pilot.

He nodded. He wore large, dark glasses, so his face was impossible to read.

The gondola trip to her old neighborhood took a long time, but that was okay. She needed the time and the mental space. Bradley always said that the glidepath shocked the system. Your body arrived first, your substance later.

She pulled out her comms unit and noticed message after message from Bradley pinging her, begging her to come back. She contemplated throwing the comms unit into the water. If she did, she would be off the grid, invisible and helpless. She never wanted to hear from Bradley again, but a sliver of rationality made her keep her grip on her comms unit. She would be lost without it.

The gondola pilot startled her by announcing their arrival. "646 West End." She tapped her comms to pay him and replaced it in her pocket. He shipped his oar and steadied the boat so she could exit. She took a deep breath, grasped the handle on the side of the gondola, resettled her backpack on her back, and pulled herself out to stand on the shore of the Upper West. The driver offered a nod of farewell and pushed off toward his next passenger, who was already hailing him from a short distance away.

Kat was annoyed with herself for thinking about Bradley. She was also annoyed to be thinking of her father. He was in a nursing home up in the Outlands. If she visited him, he wouldn't recognize her, and that would just make her sad. Closer to shore, the voices returned to her head. She heard children crying for their mothers, lovers having fantasies they thought no one else would hear, delivery people wondering whether they would deliver to the next address on time. Her mind was too busy for what she wanted to do.

The river moved all around her as she stared up at her old family residence with a slow build of sadness and disbelief. The water was higher than she remembered it, licking at the second story now, obscuring the old way in. There was a new entrance higher up, accessed by metal stairs that swayed with the movement of the water. Then, higher still, a walking ramp, jury-rigged, that took visitors to the airway, where a steady stream of pedestrians moved. It was upward to this airway that she clambered.

The airway, something like a gangway on a boat, was what replaced sidewalks that were now underwater on the Westside. The airway Kat stood on was made of carbon fiber and sturdy cables, but it still swayed in the wind and Kat's stomach did a few flips. She was above her family home and looked down over its corpse. It was not a silent moment of memory retrieval, as she wished it to be, because the thoughts of other people pushed into her mind. Some were late for work, others thinking about breaking up with their partners. Children struggled with imaginary slights they would forget about a few minutes later.

She focused on the building to help keep the chatter out of her head. Its windows were no longer whole. They were shattered like broken eyes. Gulls flew into some of them and, after a moment, flew out again. The structure tilted toward the river and looked like it might tip over if the waves got big enough. It was a sorry sight. Uninhabitable, though probably filled with squatters. The neighboring buildings, fellow corpses, were wrapped with plastic sheets—improvised waterproofing—and propped up on stilts for a stability that looked temporary.

Kat stood gazing at her old family residence long enough that people walking by looked at her with concern; a few asked if she was okay. She nodded to make them go away, wiped away a tear, and put on a bac-mask to cover the emotion.

Feeling more anonymous and thankful for it, she pulled out her comms unit and scrolled through the rental listings. She silently chided herself for not doing this before impulsively coming up to her old part of town. Finding a place to live here would be a challenge, but she was determined to try.

This part of the Upper West had split in two. There were ghost ships like her old building, left to rot above the water that slowly engulfed them, and new luxury buildings with spires that rose into the sky, and sky-high price tags to match. If she picked one of those, she would dissipate her crypto account in three months. She needed more time than that. Maybe a year. She didn't know. She opened her comms and flipped through the listings of available pods until she landed on a possibility.

Kat clambered back down the airway to water level and hopped on a large vaporetto headed upriver. It was crowded, and the wind was picking up. She shouted to the pilot to be heard.

"Does this go to Sector R?"

The pilot nodded yes.

In Sector R she found the sort of cost-effective pod that rode out the tides on stilts, kept afloat by air-filled metal tanks rimmed with rust. They were inherently unstable, because they were always in motion, but also stable, because they rode atop the water. Access to entry was via a ramp, like a ship's gangway. The front door was oval, like a porthole. Sector R was always flooded, and therefore more affordable. Since it was waterlogged, it was cooler than places that were inland.

She waited half an hour before the landlord responded to her ping on comms and finally showed up. He was a small man who looked surprised to see that she actually wanted to rent the place.

"Inside here," he said. "Door locks with screws, see? Secure. Safe. It's a good pod." They stepped up the ramp and in through the porthole-shaped door.

"Does the electricity stay on all the time?" Kat asked.

He screwed up his face as though preparing to lie, but decided against it. "Sometimes," he said. "Electricity a lot of the time. See the wires?" He pointed to the city mains that made their way into the pod. "Also good signal. Never a problem with signal."

"Good," Kat said. "How much do you want for a deposit?"

The little man stammered out a number, so surprised was he that she was willing to close. They shook hands on it and he gave her the codes. She programmed them into her comms so she could open the door and control the utilities. His comms coded in her accounts so he could deduct the rent. He left, screwing shut the porthole behind him.

She sat down on the floor in the center of the pod and listened to the sound of water outside. She was in a parallel space to the small pod Bradley lived in when he was sentenced to house arrest in Los Angeles Port City.

For a moment, the thought of Bradley in his little room, scratching out Logic Trees on his table, helped her believe that she, too, would start on something here in this single-room pod—a new project made of fire and passion. But the feeling left quickly. She had no idea what she would do here. She was just *here*. Something had drawn her here—the past, the future, the voices in her head, she didn't know what. So instead of sketching out Logic Trees in pencil as Bradley did (she didn't have a table anyway), she listened to the water and waited for night, to see if the electricity worked as the landlord said.

She unrolled a travel sleeping pad and pulled Dave's Form Factor from her backpack, opening the top that became the screen. Dave looked up at her.

"Where are we?" he asked.

"New York."

"I have questions, but first you have to let me charge for a while." He used induction to pull electricity from nodes in the floor. She did as he asked. He would need a little time before he could have a conversation.

At 8 PM, the overhead lights flicked on as promised. They blinded her momentarily and she opened her comms unit to dim them. Sleep would be slow to come, she knew, if it ever did. She felt her old friend insomnia coming on, just as it had when she was a child.

Might as well try, she thought, and stretched out on the travel mat, which puffed up to shape to her form. Looking at the ceiling, she thought about her dad. Maybe he had had second thoughts about selling data he shouldn't have been selling. He had cut corners, and it cost him, creating a sharp temper, shortness of breath, and lies like the one that they lived on the Eastside. Mom was demanding, more so when she was dying. Martin offered her all of his patience, while the rest of the world exasperated him. And no wonder, because New York was exasperating.

Kat watched as the ceiling gradually turned itself to a soft blue. Night was getting deeper. In the morning, she would ask Dave why she had come here. It felt like a pull, a kind of signal, a call, but she couldn't put words to it. Maybe he would be able to. He would want to reminisce first, wrapping her in a cottony haze of memories, and that was fine with her.

Your old school was called Spence001, Dave would say. *Martin mortgaged everything so you could go to that school.*

Kat walked every school day morning on the moving sidewalk; this was before the Hudson and East River encroached into the streets. Since she was a child, she had stepped aside to avoid the arguments that broke out on every corner about water. Sometimes the combatants stood on the moving sidewalk and let it carry them along as they yelled at each other about who had drinkable water, where to buy it, and how expensive it was. People in New York spent much of their days arguing about water. Their homes were flooded with it, or there was too little and they were thirsty and overheated. The dom always promised more desalination plants would come online but progress on that was too slow to suit most residents.

When telling this story, Dave liked to remind her about the fines for using too much electricity. *You charged your comms at school. You had a secret place.*

"Under my teacher's desk. There was an induction node there."

Yes, under your teacher's desk. Every morning, you snuck in before the teacher to stash your comms under her desk and waited until she left the classroom to retrieve it. Dave was packed with so many of Kat's early memories, another hallmark of Bradley's craft in making him.

An advertisement playing on the wall of the pod diverted her attention. It was an ad for becoming a Grounder and extolled the incentives for moving into new underground housing. Kat grabbed her comms unit to stab off the ad with a gesture. She'd forgotten to ask the landlord if the low rent meant that he would run ads in the pod; apparently the answer was yes.

The wall went dark, but just a moment later was illuminated by a public service announcement promising that a new desalination plant would be coming online a few miles away. She wouldn't be able to turn off public service announcements, only mute them. *How long will I last here alone?* She couldn't wait any longer. She waved open Dave's screen and he came on.

"Too soon. I don't have much of a charge and there's not much power allotment," he said.

"I know. I know you haven't had much time, but please tell me a story."

His eyes were kind as always. "Are you feeling sad?"

"Yes," Kat said. She extended herself the length of the sleeping mat and it adjusted to her body.

Dave noticed how agitated she was. The impulse to travel was a clear signal, and shoving his Form Factor into a backpack was unusual behavior. Yet he could calm her. He took his job seriously.

"What story shall I tell, my sweet?"

His old-timey expressions made her want to cry, but she asked for the story of the time they met. She asked for this one often, so he kept it handy in his memex.

"Once there was a lovely woman with dark hair, gray eyes, and a quick mind," he began. "She raised VC money effortlessly. Her father mortgaged everything he owned to get her into every school she attended, from the top East Side schools like Spence001 to Uni. She was determined to make him proud. And she did."

He recited the parts about the beautiful floating house she bought in Marin, and the café she walked to every morning at eleven. There was a young man there.

"Do you want a coffee?" the woman asked.

The young man glanced at his artificial coffee and at the woman's genuine coffee and asked, "You mean, one of those?"

"Yes," she said. She was going to treat him.

"My name is Kat Keeper," she said

"I'm Dave Serif," he answered.

She told him about her project called VirtualEyes. She knew he also had a project. She noticed he had books on his table. These were dictionaries and other books, all in different languages. He brought them to the café every day, she realized. He liked to read words out of old books.

"Is that your project?" she asked, pointing to the books. "Reading words out of old books?"

He looked down with a smile. "My project is called the Universal," he said.

As Dave told her this sweet story, one that she had heard many times before, Kat finally fell asleep.

The next morning, she opened her comms to send Hopper00 an email and saw her name all over the Feed. Gossip reporters had the story of her launching MIND's roof garden and then disappearing. She didn't think they would care about any of that, but maybe Bradley had called some of them and fed them information as a way to antagonize her and make her pay attention to him. The reporters wrote that they didn't know where she went, but she knew they would soon catch up with her. They were probably scanning the travel manifests right now and trying to monitor Bradley's many pings begging her to return.

To get away from reading more of this, she wrote her email to Hopper00 and then put her comms unit in her pocket. She had to force herself out into the city. She threw on a white jacket with sunscreen protection, just to be careful. The airway outside her pod angled gently upward, and she followed the flow of people until she was looking down on a market by the river. A sign identified it as the Upper Hudson Market.

She looked over the many stalls and the slowly moving crowds of shoppers. She felt the failure in her bones. It was pointless to run away to New York, yet here she was, pulled by something, some kind of a signal. Last night, she had fallen asleep before she remembered to ask Dave about it.

She stood in the market and let people flow past her. *There are two chapters in my life: Before and After.* She spoke those words over and over again in her mind, to mask out the thoughts of others as they passed. She could hear their worries in her head. She walked along the stalls in the market and picked through miserable carrots in half bunches and wilted hydroponic lettuces. She shoved some of it into her bac-bag. It was late morning, so most of the good produce was gone. She repeated her before-and-after mantra.

Hello Hopper00, she had written earlier before leaving for the market. *If you're looking for me, you will find me in New York. I guess I am running away. I have been through a lot in the past few years, but it has hardly made a mark on me until now.* She was lying and he would know. He would see into her mind. She added, *I don't know where to turn next. I am falling apart.*

It was important to keep thoughts flowing through her mind, to keep thinking her own thoughts to screen out the thoughts of others.

After a moment, she noticed something. A man was following her in the market, staying a few stalls back, pretending to look at fruit, bartering with a vendor or two to keep up appearances. Wearing an expensive-looking silver jacket and sporting a round bowler hat set at a rakish angle, he was probably a gossip reporter. That meant that the Feed would soon carry the news of her arrival in New York.

She walked faster. She felt a spike of nausea again, like she did when reading the Harvester data in Bradley's office, when this whole nightmare began. It was like wearing someone else's skin. Their thoughts crawled inside her.

Someone said in her head: *We never have enough to eat. What will I feed the children? Those peaches look rotten.* It was an older woman standing nearby.

At a stand a few steps away a man was thinking: *They took away my cat this morning. No more pets, because they have to be fed and use water. What will they do with her? Alone. Sad.*

Hopper00, she had emailed earlier, *must I tell you about After the Fall? Can't we just leave that whole part-two of my life out of the article you're writing? All the other Feed writers have covered it already. Some said I was the richest woman in North America.* That was true. She had generated great wealth.

She repeated her mantra in her head to block the voices. *There are two chapters in my life, Before and After.*

She glanced over her shoulder. There was the man again. Closer this time, as though he didn't care if she noticed him. She'd be up on the Feed soon.

She picked up her pace, exited the market, and collided with another woman. As they gathered up their bags and said sorry, Kat stole a few glances at her. She was about Kat's age, late thirties, with olive skin setting off piercing blue eyes, and a halo of brown hair framing her face. *She has the manner of an Egyptian queen.* The words popped into Kat's mind—she didn't know from where. The woman appeared dressed to teach a yoga class, in simple white clothing accented with gold.

The woman seemed to recognize Kat. "Are you Kat Keeper?"

"Do I know you?"

"I am Ravven Vaara," she said, as though Kat should have known who she was.

"Ravven." Kat searched for the connection. She felt the woman's consciousness in her mind. Something she couldn't identify was pressing in. Kat didn't know how to stop it.

"We've never met," Ravven supplied, "but I know you. You're—"

"On the gossip feed," Kat said. Saying it made her feel heavy. She looked around for the man who had been following her.

"Well, yes, not that I read the gossip feed!" Ravven's eyes darted here and there and she laughed, as though she didn't really care who was watching them. "I've been on the Feed myself. It's not helpful, yes?"

Kat noticed she spoke with a Brit-Euro accent that sounded put on.

"You look very tired," Ravven said with a smile in her blue eyes.

Kat was tired, and her clothes were unwashed. She was standing like a bent tree. She struggled to restore this woman in her memory. Ravven had a commanding, resonant voice, as though she was used to giving commands. Maybe that was it.

"Did you used to teach yoga? Somewhere in the West?" Kat said.

"Yes, you've got it," Ravven said. "And how is Bradley?"

Kat offered a look of hostility, then vulnerability, then broke eye contact. She couldn't be *that* Ravven. Could she?

"I am," Ravven said, appearing to complete the thought.

It was unnerving. Kat wanted to get away from her. "We're not together anymore if that's what you're asking, but if you read the Feed you would know that."

"Yes, I already know," Ravven said. "I was being mean. Sorry, bad habit. Now I've broken our trust."

Kat's memory finally filled everything in. This was *Ravven*. *That* Ravven. The woman with the crazy plan to take over the dom with Bradley. They were arrested together. Kat couldn't recall all the details, but she had enough to ask questions. "Wait, you were detained in the San Francisco Port City?"

"Yes."

"Bradley was sent to Los Angeles. You were sent to San Francisco. What are you doing here?" Kat stared at her. *Are you stalking me?*

"I am not," Ravven answered directly, as though she had penetrated Kat's personality field. "Many of us have come here. For the same reason you were called here. The veil is thinner."

"The veil?"

"Personality fields easily overlap. You are a Receiver, like me, like many of us here. We come here, drawn to a signal, a beacon. None of us understand it completely, but here we are."

"So you *are* stalking me," Kat said, beginning to back away.

Ravven grabbed her wrist. "No, don't go." Her eyes pleaded. "Aren't you guided, like me?"

"What?" Kat felt a flicker of Ravven Vaara's consciousness against her mind. Not a complete signal. But a window had opened between them.

Ravven was speaking aloud. This was reassuring. Kat preferred to hear the words with her ears rather than in her head. "You met Bradley in Los Angeles. You were guided to him. You bought out his detention. You became business partners and friends, and now you've run away."

"Yes." Kat didn't want to say any more. Ravven could have easily read all of that in the Feed. She might be a gossip writer. Who was she working for? Did she have something to do with the man who was following her? They were probably working together.

Ravven's words came into her head more clearly than before.

I want you to trust me. You came here because you heard the signal, the same one we all did. We are Receivers.

"I grew up here," Kat said. "That's why I came." It was nostalgia, however misplaced.

Ravven nodded. "A good reason. But there is more. You acted on a signal, an intuition, like we all did."

They looked at each other, trying to decide what was next. Kat knew this was the moment she could choose to run away. She judged herself a faster runner than Ravven. Kat was wearing her white jacket and trim leggings. Ravven's clothes, though regal, were loose, flowy, and would slow her down.

Instead of running, though, Kat spoke again. "This is too, too strange."

Ravven looked steadily at Kat and put the words into Kat's mind without speaking them. *The density of thought is deep. The veil here is thinner.*

"The veil is thinner," Kat repeated involuntarily.

If you are hearing the voices of others in your head, I can teach you how to filter them.

Kat felt panic rising in her throat. "I have to go," she said suddenly. She wanted her legs to carry her away, but Ravven grabbed her arm and this time held on.

"I can help with the voices."

"What?" Kat struggled to free her arm. "Let go."

"You know what I mean." And then, into Kat's mind: *I will teach you how to filter them. I know you feel that you are going insane. We all felt the same way when we came here. We all came for the same reason.*

PART 005

Chapter 024

She didn't know whether it was the force of Ravven's personality that drew her to her pod, or loneliness, or practicality. Ravven had promised she would teach Kat how to control the voices in her head, and Kat's engineer mind wanted to know how. As she stepped through the portal into Ravven's pod, she was momentarily distracted by the ads projected on the wall. Ravven's place was a cheap rental property, just like hers.

"No, I can't turn them off, if that's what you're wondering. You have the same?"

Kat nodded.

"Not too early to start drinking to block them." It was barely noon. She added a robust laugh and the pop of a wine cork. She set the bottle between them. They sat on thin mats on the floor.

Kat imagined that Ravven was the sort of person to live simply and purely, pointedly *not* enjoying wine. The bottle of red looked good, though. She couldn't remember the last time she had a glass of wine. It was most certainly with Dave. Dave liked wine.

Ravven's blue eyes flashed as she told the strange story about the voices in her head. "The same thing happened to all of us when we came here."

"You said you were Receivers."

"That's what we call ourselves, yes." Ravven sipped from her wineglass. "Always, when I was in the markets, I heard so many voices, until I found a way to quiet them. Then I decided to start a school, to teach the others what I discovered."

"Why does it happen here? What kind of conditions...?"

"No one really knows. My theory is that the veil is thinner here. More consciousness is at the surface—also, more people, more thoughts. And we have...this is hard to explain." Ravven paused to find the right words. "There are men in the markets with devices they use for gathering thoughts. They call themselves Input Men."

Kat listened, trying not to let surprise spread over her face. "Who are these Input Men?" She feigned innocence because she wanted to learn what Ravven knew.

Ravven continued after another sip of wine. "The Input Men don't realize that I can hear their thoughts. I received the information from their own minds that they call themselves Input Men, and that they call the devices they carry Harvesters." Ravven paused. "Am I losing you? I realize it's a strange story."

"No, it's okay. Go on."

"They think they are stealthy, but no, the Input Men are obvious. The Harvesters they carry are the size of a small backpack and there is a wand they aim here and there to suction up thoughts. I have a theory that women are activated by the Harvesters these Input Men are carrying around in the markets. If a woman has the ability to hear thoughts, maybe going back to her childhood times, maybe she has forgotten she could do it, then a Harvester in use might reignite the capability. Then she will hear too many thoughts. She won't be able to control them. Being around a Harvester, having your thoughts pulled from you..." Ravven didn't complete the thought. Instead, she fixed Kat in her blue-eyed gaze. "It sounds terribly familiar, doesn't it?"

"Yes," Kat admitted. Ravven had pegged her so expertly it was unnerving. Kat let her talk on for a moment, just to see what else Ravven knew about Harvesters.

There had been Input Men in the markets for two months, Ravven said. "That's when I first noticed them."

"Do you know where they came from?" Kat asked.

"No. I just know that women were activated by the hundreds. As I walked through the markets, I saw panic spreading over the faces of women as the voices of strangers infiltrated their minds. They thought they were going mad." Ravven shook her head.

If there had been Input Men here in the markets for a couple of months, Kat reasoned, that meant that Bradley had started the program in New York even before he was testing it on her in El Segundo. "But you still don't know if it is the thin veil, as you called it, or the Harvesters," Kat said.

Ravven shrugged. "It could be a combination of both. The women who had been activated, flooded by thoughts—I could sense what was happening to them and I approached them, in the Lower City and Upper Hudson Markets. I went to them and offered some comfort."

"Like you did with me," Kat said.

"Yes, I told them I had learned how to quiet the voices and I would show them how."

"Like you did with me," Kat said again.

"Yes. It became a fast connection between us. Once we started talking, we became friends. They needed a friend." Ravven smiled at Kat. "It's no accident that we met. I read about you on the Feed and expected to run into you. Our personality fields are tuned to the same channel."

"What does that mean?" Kat asked. "It sounds like pseudoscience."

Ravven's smile became a little smaller. "It means that we are broadcasting to each other over our personality frequencies and we found a match. Call it an overlap of mutual thoughts. That's why we are together and why we are talking now."

It seemed a little too perfect to Kat, but all she said was, "That's weird," and felt a squirm of panic again. Ravven had some larger plan, Kat believed, but hadn't yet revealed what it was.

Ravven kept talking, explaining how the thought transfers appeared to work. "You need to be in the line of sight to receive another person's thoughts. We don't know why so many thoughts come in at once."

I know, Kat said to herself. *Because Bradley explained it to me.*

"No, Kat, listen," Bradley had said, *"it's just that I am having a little trouble tuning it. It captures deep thoughts and surface thoughts and I can't sort them out."*

Bradley lied to her often, but she had to admit he probably wasn't lying about that. The Harvester activated a broad thought bandwidth. Surface thoughts and deep thoughts of people nearby all flooded the mind. She would tell Ravven what she knew about this soon, but not yet. Then she wondered if Ravven already knew, if she could see inside her mind. That didn't seem to be the case, though; Ravven was focused on her story.

"You hear so many voices," Ravven was saying, "and the panic comes. There is a way to control the voices, though."

Ravven drained her glass, refilled it, and offered Kat more red. "I can hear your static. You don't believe me. You think I'm making this all up. But it's real. I started a school for Receivers."

"You've said." Kat looked at her empty wineglass and wondered if she should have more. Getting buzzed seemed a logical response to this strange conversation. She gestured to Ravven to refill her wineglass.

Ravven kept on. "I promised that I would help you silence the voices. You deserve peace, Kat, we all do, so let's do that now. You must speak six words. Repeat them six times. Then you will be free of the voices for a little while."

Kat had her doubts, but after Ravven taught her the words, and Kat repeated them six times, Ravven's voice disappeared from inside Kat's head. For the first time since she came to New York, she enjoyed interior silence.

Ravven saw Kat's shoulders drop, then her chest rise and fall with a freer breath. "You see? It works. It will work when you're among others as well."

"Where do these words come from?"

"They are an ancient language. Sanskrit."

Sanskrit. Yes. Kat recognized it from Dave's work on the Universal. Sanskrit was one of the languages he had taught the machine.

"I don't know what the words mean," Ravven continued. "They came to me in a dream."

"How long do they last?"

"You can expect to get two hours with each application."

Kat smirked. It was like being in a doctor's office getting a prescription. What were Ravven's classes like? Kat wondered. Did they drink wine? She had more wine herself, letting her body contact the floor more solidly, as though now she might stay and not take flight at any moment. Ravven had only two mats on the floor, and their charge was low, so they did little to conform to the shape of the body. Kat tried to settle in anyway so she could ask questions.

"What is your school like?"

There was a signal from the portal.

"How about if I show you? I have an interview with a new person. Her name is Emily."

Everyone Ravven considered for admission to the school had to be interviewed. She didn't want pretenders—or, worse, spies. She rejected all the men who heard about the school from their girlfriends or wives, or even those who caught on to what Ravven was doing in the market and claimed to be Mental Expansives. She knew this was biased, but she felt that the women in the school wouldn't be able to learn freely if men were present.

Here for her interview was a thin, sad girl who kept pushing her bangs out of her eyes. She had long, straight brown hair that she finally pulled back and tied behind her so it was out of the way.

She's just a little nervous, thought Kat. *Have compassion for her.* She and Ravven shared one mat and the girl sat on the other.

The girl blinked as though she heard Kat's thoughts, but she said nothing. She looked back and forth between Kat and Ravven, not sure who would begin.

It would be Ravven. "What can you tell me about yourself?"

"What do you want to know?" The girl didn't know where she should start. "I am Emily Cloudfactor." She stopped there, as though she had already run out of things to say about herself.

Should she tell them she liked to watch the old vids in the evenings, especially the ones with dancing? Viewed on her comms, the scenes of people moving together in sync were like short dreams. She wished she could introduce this kind of movement to more people because it looked freeing. In the vids, there were troupes of dancers who moved together in Mumbai. There was a jittery clip of a man in a tall hat twirling a woman around with apparent weightlessness. There was a clip of a crowd of people dancing closely to a pulsing music with a dark beat that shook the speaker of her small comms unit. Emily couldn't put words to the feelings she had when watching these old vids. She couldn't explain why, but she knew that the women waiting for her to speak would think it was trivial, so she didn't bring it up and tried to think of something to say.

Ravven saw that the girl was struggling. She went with her common opening gambit. "Start at the beginning, or wherever you like, in your story."

The girl took a breath and dove in. "I was what they called a *failed child*. I have no record of it, only vague scraps from my memex. The people who raised me never discussed it with me."

Kat was surprised at the girl's intensity. She couldn't resist asking a question. "The people who raised you? Your parents?"

"You might call them parents, but I don't," Emily said firmly. "They don't deserve the designation. I've done some research. Parts of my archive are intact and parts were lost because of what happened to me." She let that sit for a moment. "Because of what was *done* to me. By the people who raised me. Because of what happened. Because of..." She stopped there to brush the bangs out of her eyes. She started again. "When the air first turned bad, it was hard to have a successful pregnancy. The heat got worse, so there wasn't enough water or food. Where I'm from, the Southlands, it was very hot. Women struggled to become mothers and many babies died before they could be born. Those who became mothers had a hard life."

Ravven nodded. "Yes," she said. "It was a hard time to be a mother."

"It still is. The fertility rate is still bad. Prospective parents don't want to try because their chances are bad. But I came into being. After I arrived, the doctors said I wouldn't last."

"Why?"

"The archive is not clear. At least, the archive I could find. I can only tell you what I found." She paused for a breath. "When it looked to the doctors that the body I arrived in was going to end, they called me a *failed child*."

"Yes, I know the term," Ravven said.

"That's what they called me," Emily said, her voice cracking. She looked at the floor.

Kat also knew what a failed child was. Doctors used the term to refer to bodies that were weak when the consciousness was strong. When doctors knew the body was going to end, the failed child designation permitted an emergency procedure. It was a kind of swap. The strong consciousness was removed from the weak body. Meanwhile, in parallel, the other, weak consciousness was removed from the strong body.

"The people who raised me said it was okay for the doctors to remove my consciousness and implant it in a new, strong body," Emily said.

Kat couldn't resist another question. "It's like modding?"

"It is a kind of mod, but I don't like to think of it that way. My soul was decalcified so my consciousness could be transferred into the new body. It is like starting over with a new body. They thought the body I arrived in was beyond repair, so they had to start over. I was only a child when they did it."

"How old were you?" Kat asked.

"I don't know. The archive doesn't say. Very young. I can't access the memories." She didn't know what happened to the other consciousness, the one that was originally in the body she was using now, but it was bad to think about it. That sort of consciousness, a weak one without a body, was probably put into a silver storage triangle forever, and forgotten.

Kat had heard of these procedures, taking a consciousness and putting it into another person's body, but she had never met anyone who had done it, or had it done to them. She stared at Emily as though she was a precious object that might break.

But Emily was strong. Her lived story made her so. "In the archive, it says that everything went normally for the first fifteen years of my life. I have scraps of this in my memory. I can see scenes of being a baby. Growing up. But they're fragments. Then things started happening."

"What things?" Ravven asked.

"It started when I got my period. There was...the usual change. And more. My body changed. Or it came into itself. It started wanting to do things on its own."

"I don't understand," Ravven said.

"My body *moved* on its own," Emily said, her voice rising. "It would just start walking. Pre-brain. Not thinking, or not my thinking that I could access. It would go to destinations and when I got there, I didn't know why I was there. I would speak words I didn't want to speak. I was disciplined at school for swearing."

"What did your parents do?" Kat asked.

Emily shot her a sour look.

Kat was embarrassed at her slip. "I mean, the people who raised you."

"They raised me. They tried to. I grew up under their roof. Gradually, they became less and less important to me. I tried to forget them. Even as I lived with them, I worked hard to remember a little less about them every day."

Emily began to cry. Ravven got up and returned with a cup of warm tea. Emily wrapped her hands around it gratefully. "It just kept getting worse. My body going off on its own. I had a feeling I should be living somewhere else."

"Where did you go?" Kat asked.

"I came here. I left to find the people who birthed the strong body I am in now. I needed to get away from the people who raised me. They told the doctors it would be okay to tear me from the body I was born in and they let that body die. And the consciousness, the consciousness that was in this body, they left it in an archive somewhere to be forgotten. So I had no choice. You understand? I had to listen to the body I am in now. Since this body started to call to me, since I was fifteen, whenever I sleep, I have dreams of people I don't recognize. I think these are the people who created the body I am in now. I have a mother to this body. I have a father. And a brother who is also a part of me. I know these things, but I have never experienced them. So I came here to search for my family. I came to New York, because I believed they would be here. But I haven't found them.

"When I arrived, I heard so many voices in my head. I was worried about myself. I don't know anyone here. Not anyone. Then you came up to me in the market." She nodded at Ravven. "Thank you for that."

"You are most welcome," Ravven said in her queenly tone.

Emily looked down. "But I haven't found anyone. There is no one who is like the mother or father or the brother I see in my dreams." Her face hardened and her lips were a thin line. "I won't give up. They are out there, somewhere."

"I hope you find them someday."

Emily nodded once.

"I think I understand what happened," Ravven said.

"Tell me," Emily said.

"I have heard of children like you," Ravven began. "The new body they implanted your consciousness in—it wasn't a clean transfer."

Emily closed her eyes for a moment. "Yes, it wasn't a clean transfer. This is my experience. The body I have now is speaking to me. It is communicating its past, which is now my past, by speaking through me."

Kat was confused. She picked her words carefully. "Your body is motivating you...and you are living the life of the original owner of that body?"

Emily's eyes hardened. "Yes, but it is *my* body now. I am the owner of this body. I am living its history," she insisted.

Kat felt pity for this poor, split girl, caught between her consciousness that belonged to a body that was gone, and a new body that was now the house to that consciousness. Then Kat tried to unfeel these feelings, worrying that Emily may have detected them. But Emily was, as Ravven was earlier, involved in her own story.

Emily put her hand over her heart. "This is my body now. I will love it and take care of it. It contains my only consciousness."

"It does," Ravven said.

Emily let out a ragged breath before she asked, "Do I get in? Will you accept me into the Receivers School?"

She is looking for her family, Kat thought, *and maybe she has found it.*

Emily's eyes pleaded. *Will you let me in? I need to be here.*

"Yes," Ravven said. "You may join us."

"Thank you," Emily said through tears.

Ravven held Emily's hand and described what it would mean to be in the school. She talked about the exercises the group did to strengthen their Mental Expansion. They studied thought transmission and reception, future sight, and leaving their bodies to travel elsewhere.

Emily was excited to begin, and Ravven invited her to come back the next day. After Emily left, Kat thought Ravven should have been elated to have another recruit, but she seemed gloomy.

"I haven't been honest with you," Ravven said.

"What do you mean?"

"Do you know about the Resistance?"

Kat's blank look communicated her answer.

"I didn't want to overwhelm you with everything at once," Ravven said. "I will tell you everything now."

Chapter 025

"I've always been a political organizer," Ravven said. "I consider my time as a yoga teacher a small part of my activism."

Kat waited for her to go on.

"The school is my cover. I find women in the market who are in distress and offer them comfort. I teach them how to quiet the voices in their head. But that is only a symptom of a larger problem. The Siliconers want to exploit the Mental Expansives like us. They see a skill set they can use."

"That's why the Harvester was made," Kat said.

"Yes, that's why the Harvester was made. The Siliconers are aware of our capabilities. They want to keep careful watch over us."

"How closely are they watching?" Kat couldn't help but look for a place in the pod where a camera might be concealed, behind a screen, or in the spot where the pod portal didn't fit perfectly.

"Don't worry," Ravven said to calm her. "Listening devices are the main concern. This place has been swept. It's clean."

"How do you sweep a place like this?"

"I mean that you can speak freely."

Kat wondered how Ravven could sound so sure. It was more important to ask another question, though. "What does the Resistance do?"

"When we see a Harvester, we destroy it. When we see an Input Man, we disrupt his operations."

"How?"

"Sometimes swarming them works. We all rush up together, screaming as loud as we can. Many of the Input Men run away then, or we grab the Harvester from their hands." Ravven allowed herself a smile.

"You started this...Resistance," Kat said.

"Yes. Many women are joining me. I'll be honest with you—I want you to join us, too. You see what Emily has gone through. There are many like her. They need a direction for their anger and soulmates to help move them out of hopelessness."

Now Kat's mind was turning. Bradley was further along than he had told her. The Input team was active here in New York. She needed to know more about what Ravven knew.

"Where do the Input Men come from?" Kat asked.

"No one knows."

Kat let that one go for a moment. "Are you the only leader of the Resistance?"

"There are others."

Kat frowned. "What do you mean?"

"To escape detection, no one knows who the other leaders are. There is no hierarchy." Ravven's eyes moved away from Kat and she sprung up. "More wine?" Her hand was already on the bottle.

But Kat waved her off. She could see that Ravven had had too much wine already. She didn't want to get drunk, too.

"You already knew about the Harvesters," Ravven said without looking at her.

Kat nodded. *More than I'm telling you.*

Ravven offered a smile of satisfaction. "I can sense there is more."

To keep the conversation from going in that direction, Kat began asking questions about Ravven and Bradley. They met in a yoga class?

"Correct. He was my student. He dropped the class so we could become lovers. I tried to turn him into an activist. Sorry, is this painful to listen to?"

No more than anything else that's happened to me in the last twenty-four hours.

Ravven nodded.

"Wait, you can hear me thinking?"

Ravven sipped some wine with a flourish. "It's been more than two hours." She pointed to Kat's head. "Be aware of what you think, because the Sanskrit words are wearing off." She offered a smile.

"Getting arrested together with Bradley was a blow to the relationship?" Kat asked, wanting to stay on track.

"Yes." Ravven's eyes were merry. "Disaster!" She gulped more wine.

"How did his mod affect you?" Kat asked

Ravven shrugged it off. "The usual way." She paused. "I didn't think about his mod that often. I wanted to use Bradley to advance progressive politics. I told him that he couldn't say he wanted a better world, and be as *talented* as he was, and never put his good ideas into action. I wanted revolution!" She jabbed her fist in the air, spilling some wine, then softened her tone. "I thought he was a fellow changemaker. But Bradley only changes things to benefit himself." Ravven abruptly changed the subject. "You left him. That's why you're here."

"It's not as simple as that," Kat said. It was simple and it wasn't. Kat wanted to say that she was starting a new company or meeting with investors, but Ravven would know instantly she was lying. She'd had enough of lying anyway. She could and should tell Ravven all she knew about the Harvester project, but Kat didn't trust Ravven. They had been with the same man—at different times, but the same man—and it was a dizzying concept. The ground under her didn't feel steady.

Kat tried to fill the space between them with a story about needing to visit the city of her childhood. "My family lived on the Westside but I went to an Eastside school. Yesterday I went over to my old family house. I couldn't afford to live in that neighborhood, so I got a pontoon pod a few blocks from here. I have the same ads on the wall as you do."

The flood of Kat's words stopped, and the space between the women came back. They watched the ads play on the walls of Ravven's pod.

"We love where we live," Kat said, repeating a line that just played in an ad pitching the value of being a Grounder. She shrugged. "I don't get the attraction."

"Control," Ravven said. "All kinds of it. Temperature control, the security of earth all round you. Away from the punishing sun."

"No natural light!" Kat burst out and they both laughed.

"All the apartments have screens with nature views that don't exist," Ravven said.

Kat opened her hands in a gesture that took in the room. "Like this one. That screen."

"Yes," Ravven conceded. "But there are also fake skies when you look up. Never any extreme weather events to worry about when you're a Grounder," she added, and her laugh was pleasant but false.

Kat was certain now that her Brit-Euro accent was a put-on. It wavered in intensity; sometimes bold, other times weak. Altogether, Ravven seemed like an assemblage or a mirage—a queen in appearance, but who was she really?

"You're from Oakland?" Kat asked. Bradley had mentioned that once.

"Yes," Ravven said. "My accent is fake, as you have reasoned correctly. I was a yoga teacher and students like their teachers to sound exotic. Now, can you trust me a little more?"

Ravven's insight was unnerving.

She continued. "I didn't plan our encounter. But I knew it was inevitable. We don't have to play games with each other, Kat. We need each other. The Resistance needs you."

Kat nodded. She decided to trust Ravven a little more, and Kat allowed the story about Bradley to tumble out, as though by saying the words one after another she could strip them of their emotional weight. But it didn't help. By the end of the story, her eyes were wet. "He was using the Harvester technology on me—and not once, many times." Kat scrubbed her face with her hands. She was not embarrassed about the tears—quite the opposite. She felt stronger now. She was done with Bradley forever. She would be happy if she never saw him again in her life.

"He is a bastard," Ravven concluded.

Kat pulled back, struck by the word. "Seems harsh." Bastard.

"I call him that and so should you. You don't have to accommodate someone who always acts in their own interests."

It was the mod that bent my will, and yours, too, Kat wanted to say. But Ravven had something else on her mind.

"When did you first know about the voices?" she asked.

When Kat was a girl, she had heard her mother's inner voice complaining about being sick, and she heard her father's worried inner monologue about money, and her teachers' inner voices about how to keep their students under control, and friends' voices about who liked them and who didn't. When Kat told her mother about the voices she heard in her head, her mother said she was crazy.

Kat said nothing of this to Ravven, only: "Maybe they started when I was three or four and stopped when I was twelve. Until they started again recently, of course."

Ravven nodded. "From asking questions of the others," she said, "I've learned that this skill arises in girls when they are about the age you describe, three or four. Then it grows. If they tell their mothers about it, the mothers shame them, and they suppress the skill or try to break their connection with it."

Kat blinked. It was as though Ravven had gone into her head and pulled out her history. "*Don't talk crazy. Never tell anybody about imagining anything like that.*" "Why do the mothers say that?" Kat asked.

"Because their mothers said it," Ravven replied easily. "It is a lineage."

Kat nodded. "Somehow we have broken the lineage."

"We are fortunate," agreed Ravven.

But Kat didn't feel fortunate. She felt terrible for having this skill. It made her life unstable—more than it already was. It brought her close to the feeling of being insane. Maybe she had taken her mother's statement about talking crazy too literally.

"We *are* fortunate," Ravven insisted. "We can connect with others who are like us, and, if we need to, we can stay offline and communicate without technology like comms. We can be in a world of our making. But if we remain in a thought space they can detect, their world, they will capture our thoughts."

They both knew the Harvester was dangerous, and maybe they were not safe anywhere as long as they were within reach of any comms. Hopper00 had the right idea. They cut him off from the grid, but he had the skills to survive without it. His story was fitting together for Kat now, more than ever.

Kat's and Ravven's thought streams began to intertwine, and the two of them sat at opposite ends of Ravven's mat, the last of the wine in their glasses, and soon considered what was next without speaking, simply by trading thoughts.

Kat's voice entered Ravven's mind. *How do you feel about being in the Resistance?*

Ravven nodded her affirmation. *Good.*

I might like to join, Kat thought back, surprising herself with how easy it was. *I think I came here to help the movement.*

Ravven nodded affirmation again. *Good, because we need you.*

Their thoughts mingled into a cloud encircling them both.

Bradley built a working avatar of my husband. I talk to him every day. His name is Dave.

He did that to control you. Bradley is crafty smart.

I love Dave. I miss him. He was my rock. In an instant, Kat was crying. Her clothing felt cold with tears.

Ravven reached for her hand. "You loved him very much."

"I did."

"You are strong," Ravven said, holding Kat's gaze. *You believe in yourself now more than you ever have. You have the power of your young self reawakened in you now.*

Kat stood to move around the pod, to change her perspective. She was thinking of Dave and felt a closed-in feeling. And at once Kat felt an energy from Ravven, something she could not explain, that grasped her and pushed her back onto the mat.

Ravven's voice in Kat's mind told her, *All children are Mental Expansives in the beginning. They don't understand what it is. They can't express it in words. The girls remain expansive longer than the little boys, then, after they are shamed, all of them forget. But we are fortunate. We have remembered and there are many of us. Every day I find one more.*

Kat waited a moment before asking Ravven silently, *What about men in the Resistance?*

Ravven shrugged. *There must be some. But I have never met them. There is Hopper00.*

Who is Hopper00? Ravven asked silently.

Not now. I will tell you later.

Outside, on the airway, Kat felt the heat pressing down upon her. The climate handlers weren't working well again this afternoon. She mused on the topic of hearing voices in her head and sharing about them with another human being. These thoughts made her feel unsettled in her body; she couldn't shake the feeling of wearing another person's skin, or it may have been the heat. Before she left the pod, Ravven had said, "Come to a meeting. Then you'll see how strong the Resistance is."

Kat walked back in the direction of her pod and made a point of not reciting the chant Ravven had taught her. She wanted the voices. She wanted the complexity of life within her sight line to flood her mind. She exchanged knowing glances with others who pinged her silently as they passed her on the airway.

Hello, sister.

The outdoor cameras watched them. The women Kat exchanged thoughts with made fleeting eye contact, so as to minimize contact points for the public vid cameras that were always on and always watching. The domain of New York was filled with Mental Expansives. Kat thought she was becoming more sensitive to them, able to pick them out from among the families with their children hurrying to get to the market while there was still fresh produce, solo men who glanced at her, assessing her as a potential conquest, and delivery people with their packages held close. Below them all, just few feet off the airway, enforcement bots patrolled, hooked into the cameras that were always watching.

Hello, sister.

Another ping, eyes flicking toward her and away, swift enough so that the cameras wouldn't register the point of contact. The contact came from women, sometimes girls, once in a while a crone. Never men. Kat stopped to look out over the river and think about that. An enforcement bot, low to the ground, round, smooth metal skin, whirred up to her, inspecting her and probably wondering why she was impeding the flow of pedestrian traffic on the airway. She moved on.

No thoughts would be safe once Bradley got the Harvester right. He was a relentless researcher.

The voice of another woman came into her mind. *They have to be stopped.* Kat nodded back.

Their eyes made a flicker of connection.

You are the one, the woman thought.

The one what? Kat asked, but she was already gone amidst the crowds traversing the airway. It was crowded today, despite the poor functioning of the climate controls.

Chapter 026

Kat felt she needed to wait before she could attend a meeting at Ravven's invitation. It would mean crossing over into another world. For so long she had lived in the world of fundraising and data. She didn't want to admit to herself that she was scared, but there it was, a catch in her breath, a feeling of falling into an abyss.

Oh, come on, she said to herself. *It's not as dramatic as all that. It's just a world of intuition and, well, feelings.*

Finally, it was a sense of fairness that tipped her over. She knew more about MIND than Ravven did. It was necessary information to bring to a meeting of the Resistance.

She pinged Ravven on comms. "When do you meet next?"

The meeting was at Ravven's pod—though the women didn't call it a meeting, they called it a circle. Kat's mind went immediately to geometry. But the reference was to a relationship, to a circle of women who sit in equality.

"Everyone here speaks as equals," Ravven said. "We are all spokes."

Ravven was describing wheels. Kat had seen bike wheels with spokes, and tuktuks were configured that way. At Uni, she had seen diagrams of wheels on cars. Most everything else was anti-grav now. Her engineer mind turned on this idea.

"To attend is to speak your truth. To lie is to be expelled. We will start by centering." Ravven went around the circle, intoning the name of each woman present. *Welcome, Kat and Ruusu. Welcome Cassandra, Amber, and Dextra. Welcome, Aline. Welcome, Afra, Lace, Zamora, and Oona. Welcome, Barbora. Welcome, Emily.*

Thirteen of them, including Ravven. Emily had recruited a friend named

Amber, a young woman who was studying mass psychosis game theory in online classes from Uni.

Ravven said, "Welcome all. Let's speak what is on our mind and in our heart."

And so they did. Ravven's pod filled with the low hum of words. Kat imagined she could see the web of their thoughts. But when she looked at the thoughts directly, to analyze them, they disappeared. When she included them at the edge of her vision, they floated all around her and brought up a million questions in her mind.

She felt a chill and squirmed on a mat, one of five that Ravven had arranged to form a pentagon. The circle was strange to Kat. She wasn't sure she belonged.

But after a while, Ravven said, "Ask for what you need," and the tone changed. They all looked to Kat then, and it was obvious that everyone in the circle knew who she was. They knew her story and where she had been.

"Share what you know about the Harvester," Ravven said.

So Kat dialed the story back to its beginning. She told them about Bradley, about the foundations of MIND. She spoke about the need for an inner life and how MIND could take that away.

"I don't understand," Amber said. "We are Receivers. We can hear thoughts. MIND can hear them, too. Doesn't that mean that we are as bad as MIND is?"

Kat responded, "MIND gathers thoughts without consent."

"But I've never asked permission of anyone. Nobody has ever consented to me hearing their thoughts," Cassandra said.

"There's a difference," Kat said. "MIND gathers. They retain and sell thoughts to the dom and to other corps. We may take in thoughts and may remember some of them, but we don't sell them."

Cassandra nodded. "That would be wrong."

"It is wrong," Kat agreed.

"MIND *will* take our inner lives away," Ravven said. "Consciousness is not a commodity. Our inner life is precious. We should *choose* to share it, if we want to, not have it taken from us."

Kat had to tell them the truth. So she said, "Impossible."

Ravven stiffened. "What is impossible?"

Kat didn't know how to begin to tell them that the work ahead was bigger than they understood. The Harvester project was the leading edge of MIND, which in turn was the beginning of something else larger. Kat struggled to find the words. "MIND is the starter kit for a global AI. Bradley's intent is to connect all artificial intelligence. The AI will teach itself to get stronger without human intervention."

"A recursive AI?" Amber asked. She had studied this.

"Yes."

"That could lead to human instability on a mass scale," Amber said.

"Bradley has been working on a recursive AI for as long as I've known him," Kat said. She was ready to go on, but she saw that it was already too much. The women of the circle were restless with worry.

Amber spoke up again. "If he succeeds, then the center of power could shift from humans to the machines." She looked to Emily for confirmation, but Emily just shrugged.

"The purpose of MIND is to monetize the inner mind," Ravven said.

"Yes," Emily said. She hesitated, then continued, "I dreamed of something called the Master. The Master is connected to all consciousness. MIND will soon be connected to the Master. This is what my dream told me."

Have I joined a cult? Kat thought, quickly quenching the words in her mind when she caught a few puzzled and hurt glances.

Emily continued. "The Input Men must be stopped and MIND must be stopped before it has access to all human thought."

Ravven's voice rang out with the rhythm of a chant: "MIND must be stopped. MIND *must* be stopped." For a few moments, the other women joined in. Then Ravven stopped speaking the words as suddenly as she started. The pod went silent. They all looked to Kat.

"How do we stop them?" Ravven asked with apparent seriousness.

Kat laughed. It all seemed so absurd. "Do you think *I* know?" No one laughed with her. They did think she knew. An overwhelming sadness came over her. "I don't know. I really don't."

Several looked away or stared at the floor. Someone's thought came into her mind: *We were depending on you.*

Kat's thoughts raced. She had to give them some hope, so she offered, "A single-master AI is a concept years away."

"But my dream..." Emily said.

"Yes, your dream." Kat looked to the circle. "Who here has seen Input Men?"

Ravven, Emily, and Amber raised their hands.

"Who here has met the leaders of the Resistance?"

"We are the leaders," Ravven said. "We are the leaders in this circle." She leaned into Kat. "How will *you* help us? You have knowledge and experience that none of the others have."

I have crypto, thought Kat.

Kat has crypto, maybe more than she'd tell us about. Ravven broadcast this to everyone, smiling tightly. Then she turned to address Kat directly, but continued broadcasting. *We don't need your crypto, We need* you. *Because of who you are, if you spoke about us in public, in the markets, and were interviewed about us on the Feed, women would follow and join us. You are the mother of our mothers.*

What does that mean? Kat broadcasted back.

Ravven only looked at her with her wise eyes and smiled.

Kat felt her breath come quicker. *If I fought alongside you, Bradley would fight back.* He would surely hate the idea of Ravven and Kat working together to stop him.

We must work in secret for now, Ravven thought.

They all thought the words together. *In secret. In secret.*

Kat had a jittery feeling in the pit of her stomach. This circle was strange.

She managed to affirm what she thought was a shred of rationality. "Our power, for the moment, is in our invisibility." And after a pause, she said, "I need to think about all of this."

The circle was over for today. Ravven turned her hands palms up and began a silent broadcast to end it. *Remember who we are. Remember who we are. Remember who we are.* The thought echoed and multiplied upon itself, filling the small space so powerfully that the walls seemed to bow outward.

This must be the third part of my life, after the After, thought Kat.

Ravven picked up on it and smiled at her.

Even though the experience of the circle was strange, after the first meeting Kat wanted more.

She was curious about Emily and Amber. They exchanged glances and sometimes whispers during the circle and stayed close to each other afterward. They appeared to be connected, not as lovers but as more than friends. At the next meeting, Kat puzzled over what question to ask of them to find out more, but Emily intuited what she wanted and at the conclusion of the circle, approached Kat and asked the question for her.

"You're wondering if we have our own circle, aren't you?"

Kat was caught by surprise. "I was thinking of asking you, but ..."

"Ravven's circle is too procedural," Amber said. "Too much business is discussed."

"We've started a different kind of circle," Emily added.

"What kind is that?" Kat asked.

Emily invited her to the next circle she was holding with Amber. It was in Emily's pod, which was low on the water, low enough to hear the water slapping under the floor, and the rent was even lower than Kat's.

Emily, Kat, and Amber sat close together on the floor mat. This circle was usually just two women; today it was three.

"We open the circle by lighting these," Emily said, removing two objects from a bag of gold-colored cloth.

"What are those?" But as soon as Kat asked, she remembered what they were.

Emily held the candles with reverence. "Each one creates a small flame that stands for one of us."

"Show me," Kat said.

"We only have two."

"That's all right."

The three of them watched the flickering lights move shadows on the wall. Kat couldn't remember the last time she saw real candles.

"What do you do now?" she asked.

"Sometimes we dance," Amber said.

So they danced. Emily opened her comms to an old vid of people moving in time to music. She and Amber danced elegantly, mimicking the movements they saw on the screen. Kat awkwardly tried to imitate their imitations. She tried not to make fun of herself for the dancing. She wasn't very good at it, but then, the others had more practice.

Amber spoke after the music vid ended. "Now, like Ravven's circle, we say what is on our mind and in our heart."

Differently from Ravven's circle, however, it was a flowing conversation with no beginning and no end, and it was then that Kat realized that a circle was much more than she understood it to be, at first. The words she might use to describe it to herself melted away; the circle was beyond their meaning. When she used words to describe to herself what she, Emily, and Amber were doing, it seemed foolish. How could you explain dancing to a vid in the middle of the day? It served no rational purpose. Yoga, for example, was rational. Anyone could see that. The domain authorities encouraged yoga because it served the rational purpose of self-improvement. Without thinking much about it, the citizenry took this directive into their hearts and turned away from activities like dancing that were not rational. This made sense to Kat.

Eventually, the candles burned down. It meant the circle was over. The three looked at each other through the smoke that wove its way on invisible currents of energy and air.

"I haven't seen candles since I was a child," Kat admitted.

Emily said they weren't easy to find. "There is a woman in the market who sells candles for circles. She makes them herself. She has a source for beeswax, a beekeeper. She has her own circle and makes the candles for it."

"How many other circles are there?" Kat asked.

Amber confirmed, "Ravven says there are many, apparently. Our goal, she says, is to unify them. Make them all interconnected and overlapping."

Kat asked if they would take her to the candle seller in the market, and they agreed. Bees had played a role in her former life as a software developer and here they were again, as suppliers of wax to make candles. As the CEO of VirtualEyes, Kat had lied about what bees could do. Maybe now, she reasoned, she was being given a chance to tell the truth about what they could do. She was tempted to ask Emily and Amber how much they had read about her on the Feed, if they knew about VirtualEyes and the bees, and Kat's lies, but they were already approaching the woman in the market.

Kat saw that she was very old. Her hands shook with a light tremor. Her eyes were odd. Kat didn't want to stare.

She greeted Emily. They had done business many times before.

"How many candles will you sell us?" Emily asked the woman.

"As many as you like," the woman answered.

"We'll take them all, if you will sell them all to us."

"Of course," the woman said. "Who is your new friend?"

"I am Kat Keeper."

The old woman nodded. "I am Claire8 Kolassa."

Kat later told Ravven, "She has some sort of strange power. She fixed me in her stare, but I didn't want to stare back. There is something in her eyes. I couldn't see it all. I talked to her about the Receivers School. She wants to join."

"Did you tell her about the Resistance as well?" Ravven asked.

"No. Am I allowed to?"

It was a good question. Instead of answering, Ravven said, "Will she come in for an intake interview? We can see how she responds to the questions."

"I think she'd come to an interview if we asked her," Kat said.

"You'll do the intake," Ravven said. "Just study the previous ones."

Kat had been present at Emily's, so she didn't need to review that one. The others had come to the circle each by their own path. Ruusu lived with her husband and child in the Lower City. Their pod was inland and stable, didn't rock on pontoons like those on the water. She was one of the lucky ones who was able to conceive, and this inspired her to become a midwife. Sadly, with fertility rates low, she didn't have much work.

Cassandra was her friend. She was a gondola driver, evident from her strong upper body, knowledge of the coastal parts of the city, and the often-flooded Sector R, and skin turned to brown leather from exposure to the sun. Dextra was a programmer for admin, the system that controlled the city's air, water, waste, and recycling systems. Aline was a long-distance student at Uni, like Amber. She studied programming languages. Aftra, Lace, Zamora, and Oona worked together on a data farm. They hated it and were looking for a way out. Barbora had aspirations to write for the Feed. At the moment, she was a maintenance technician for bots, but she had started her career as a professor in women's history at a now-defunct university in the Boston academic-tech dom. The school had been bought by Uni and then closed down in a cost-cutting consolidation.

A few days later, Kat asked questions of Claire8 as Ravven witnessed the intake interview. At close range, in Ravven's pod, Kat guessed that Claire8 was in her sixties, but she had a gravitas that made her seem older. She was modded—Kat knew because of the number in her name. She didn't know how Claire8 was modded, though, so she started with a simple question.

"Tell me about yourself."

Claire8 had a laugh like rocks rolling down a chute. Her voice was also raw. Kat noticed Claire8's eyes right away, bright brown orbs set in a pale face.

"I am Claire8 Kolassa," she said with evident glee. She enjoyed talking about herself.

There was something else Kat noticed about Claire8. Her eyes moved independently of each other like a fish's. Kat tried not to stare and instead looked down, pretending to check the notes on her tablet. "We've only admitted one modded person before, and she—" Kat stopped there, realizing that she would be stepping over a boundary if she shared that Emily was a failed child who had undergone a soul decalcification.

"I will tell you about my mod," Claire8 said, her wandering eyes taking in everything. "For nearly twenty years, I received advanced training as a medical doctor and had an active practice. As I reached my sixties, I wanted hyperintelligence to advance my career. I feared I didn't have much more work in me. Medicine is a hard profession.

"A surgeon convinced me that I would get more out of my body after a freezing procedure. He was working on an age-reversal that would be ready in a few years, so I let him put me into a cryogenic chamber until it was ready. Then I would be thawed out, go through the procedure, and get younger."

Kat made a noise that sounded like disbelief.

"It does sound pretty stupid. It *was* stupid. I trusted him. I shouldn't have, but I was married to him at the time. While I was in the freeze, however, he ran off with a younger woman. This is common, you know. I later learned that it was a scam that husbands ran."

"Really?" Kat was having trouble taking in this story. It was not what she had expected to hear.

"After I got out, I learned eyeballs don't freeze well. Something to do with the ocular liquids and the way the muscles are suspended in them. So you can see the results. Some people stare at me, but I have excellent peripheral vision!" That raw laugh again, like rocks going down a chute.

Kat tried to manage a smile and tried harder not to look at Claire8's eyes. An awkward pause, and then Claire8 continued.

"The freeze worked well, in that when I came out ten years later, I was the same physical age as when I went in. The downside was I lost neural processing speed. I learned about a mod for synapse speed, nerve endings, and more memory capacity, and I went for it. I'm enhanced now and I feel great. I can grasp some crazy shit that other people can't get close to. Shall I give you an example?"

First, Kat wanted to know about the side effects. She knew mods had them.

"Only one," Claire8 answered. "Compassion. I have a great sense for what other people are feeling and I can help them feel more settled in themselves. I've also become extraordinarily patient."

Kat was surprised to hear this. Most of the other side effects she'd heard about, like Bradley's remote personality, were bad. Here was a good side effect; two of them, in fact. "Have you found them useful?"

"Not much and not often," the older woman admitted. "I started a compassion circle to develop it among others. Making and selling candles allows me to meet the right people. It's how I met you, of course."

"What about medicine?"

"My license has expired. Also my appetite for it. I want to pursue other things now. I have a business selling candles, but you know that."

Kat glanced at her tablet again. "It says here that you weave neural webs."

"Yes, and I also weave webs."

"How does that work?" Kat wasn't familiar with this.

"Did I hear you right?" said Ravven, speaking for the first time. "Webs?"

"Yes, on the molecular-scale, synaptic you might say, electromagnetic connections between people. Well, women, actually."

"You connect networks?" asked Ravven, still trying to understand.

"Yes. I keep the webs hidden from the domain. They probably wouldn't like them if they knew. There is nothing on the grid. Nothing on the Feed. They operate in a parallel way, unseen by the authorities. And I am paid off the grid, not using comms, in trade," she added.

Ravven was still struggling. "I'm sorry. I don't really understand what it is that you do with webs."

"That's all right. It's a little hard to get your mind around at first. I connect women's circles in a parallel network of thought streams. But at scale and at a distance."

Kat was catching on. "Thought streams are only useful in sight lines."

"Yes," Claire8 said. "That's right." Her eyes were looking in different directions, and Kat had to look away again. "My medical training has come in handy for it. My patience comes in handy, too. Making these webs is like knitting."

Kat sat back on her mat, it shaped to support her; her mind raced with the idea of connecting women's circles. How many circles were functioning now? Maybe Claire8 knew. But Kat had to ask, "What is knitting?" She had a faint recollection, but couldn't call up an image of knitting in her mind.

"It's a pastime that people, mostly women, used to make scarves, hats, sweaters, and blankets."

Kat remembered now, and nodded.

"The women knit in my circle. We really like it. You know how it is, ancient technologies survive without being noticed. For example, there is a stand for augurs in the market. Have you seen it?"

"A stand for what?" Kat asked.

"Augurs. They are seers who calculate the future by observing the patterns that birds make when they fly."

Kat tried not to smile too broadly, lest Claire8 think she was making fun of her. She certainly knew things that no one else did. "You'll have to show me next time we are there," Kat said.

"An independent web, one that was off the grid completely, would be useful for your circle, wouldn't it?" Claire8 asked.

Kat and Ravven exchanged a glance. It would.

Kat went home to her pod and made notes in her memex to later share with Hopper00. Her life was turning in an interesting direction. She was trying to leave her old ways behind. She hadn't lied to anyone, as far as she knew, and was trying to be more curious and open. She sensed that he would approve, but also didn't like the passivity of waiting for him to ping her on comms. She waited anyway. She really had no choice. Thought transmission only worked within line of sight.

The sounds of water pushed against the hull of her pod and it rocked gently with the wind coming off the river. The motion made her feel protected, and she made her notes, ate food units when she was hungry, and soon lost track of time. She hired a bot to sweep the one-room pod for listening bots, wondered briefly if she could trust that bot, and hired another, more expensive one to sweep the pod again.

She was far from other people, so their thoughts did not intrude. She was only troubled now and again by the voice in her head that intoned *Prepare for war.* There was no explanation for it. It wasn't a voice that she recognized. Also inexplicably, Kat heard a voice that she *did* recognize: Ravven's. Even when Ravven was nowhere nearby, Kat heard Ravven's voice say, *You are the mother of our mothers.* Ravven hadn't explained what that meant. She'd only looked at Kat with her wise eyes.

Finally, Kat's comms lit up with a ping from Hopper00. She didn't know how many days it had been, and she didn't care. All that mattered to her was that he said he would be in touch soon with news of the article he was writing about her.

Kat was eager to tell him about the positive turn her life had taken. For the first time, in the circles she'd attended, Kat was able to draw on the courage of other women. But she was also puzzled by something. When she made memex recordings, she filled them with memories of her father and of Bradley. *Martin and Bradley gave me strength,* Kat recorded, *and they made me weaker.*

Dependency, she recorded.

Irritated at where this had led her, she swiped the memex dark and turned on the screen that held Dave. He came alight and smiled at her.

"Hello, love. You look sad."

"I am sad."

"You told me the first night after you came back from the circle that you were infused with purpose. Those were your words."

She smiled fondly at Dave on the screen. "Those were *your* words. I would never say *infused* with purpose."

"I do love words." Dave smiled. Then his face formed an expression of concern. "Why are you sad? Do you want me to tell you a story?"

"No," Kat said, a little too fast. "Not yet."

"I can't hear your thoughts, you know. I can only take what you give me."

"I know, Dave. I love you."

"I love you, Katherine."

She felt her throat tighten and swiped Dave's screen dark. He was the only one who called her Katherine. Not even her father called her by her complete name, not her mother, not Bradley. But Bradley had known enough about Kat's inner mind to program that behavior into Dave.

She pushed the thought away. She didn't like thinking of Bradley now. She wanted to be finished with him. She wanted Dave to be Dave without any creator at all. He came into her life and she wanted him to be there for her, forever.

She moved to swipe the screen on again and thought better of it. She opened the memex to make more notes for Hopper00. She felt her destiny was coming into focus.

Chapter 027

Some of the younger Resistance members smoked, like Amber, Emily, and Cassandra, so one morning on the way to a circle, Kat bought a pack of cigarettes from a street vendor. She put it on the table to show solidarity with the Youngs in the group, even though she knew she would never open it to smoke the cigarettes.

There was only one period in her life when she smoked. Before she would pitch VirtualEyes to investors, for courage she would light up in the nearest restroom. The Resistance reminded her of the women she hired at VirtualEyes: they had the same passion and intensity, only her hires dressed in suits and the women of the circle wore what they wanted.

Silently daring herself, Kat opened the pack and took out a cigarette. She held it in her hand just to see what it felt like. Slender, slippery. The machined plastic felt remarkably like paper.

The group had stalled in a circular talk about what to do next. Some members wanted to stick with their plan to physically take down Harvesters when they saw them. They had sighted more Harvesters in New York's Lower City, but were aware that their operators, the Input Men, knew to stay slippery and out of sight. Others wanted to chase away the Input Men, show them they couldn't hide, and convince them to join the Resistance.

Kat put the cigarette down and swiped at a screen as the women argued around her.

That night, alone in her pod, the cigarette hanging from her lips and still unsmoked, her head was banging with ideas that could end the circular conversations in the circle of women. One good idea among the swarm, she reasoned, was to ping Bradley on comms and tell him that he should withdraw the Harvester program from New York. The Resistance was planning to destroy his machines, she would tell him. She wanted to be a peacemaker.

She pinged him on comms, but nothing came up. The eye of the screen met her with a blank stare and a rude NO SIGNAL. This was strange. Bradley was the type who was always wired up. When you cast a glance around his spacious office, your eyes took in a comms unit on nearly every surface. His UV shower, a high-end model that gently bathed you in cleansing UV light, had a comms unit installed in it.

The Feed reported that Bradley had a thousand employees now, was expanding worldwide, and ABCD and other corps wanted to acquire MIND. Kat knew this was dangerous, because ABCD engaged in corporate takeovers that were literally hostile, involving a private militia. She could imagine Alon6 chortling with Bradley about their superior position. "We have something that everyone wants!" MIND was becoming more powerful, no doubt driven by the proprietary Harvester technology it alone controlled.

While poking at her comms unit to make the NO SIGNAL go away, a viz notification popped up, blocking the screen for a moment. She gestured through, and saw that a story had just been posted about a flight to Mars on a new rocket. At the end of that story there was a "read more" notice, followed by a new story about a few big corps leaving the Western Continent to establish extra-planetary operations. It was strange that these two stories would appear together on the Feed, as though the reporters were hinting at some connection. She scrolled the story about the flight to Mars and saw with a nod of satisfaction that it was written by Hopper00. Had he caused it to appear in her feed or made both of the stories appear together?

Suddenly, there was another viz notification and an image of Bradley filled her comms screen.

"Hi," he said, as though they had spoken this morning instead of not for weeks.

"Bradley?"

"Of course it's me. You think I'm an avatar?" His laugh had a tinny sound.

"No. What do you want?" She felt hostile toward him all of a sudden and realized it was a bad idea to be communicating. "Where are you?" It looked like a cockpit, or the inside of a shiny silver bubble. She could almost smell the stale air of the enclosed space.

"I'm in-flight."

"What?" The comms glitched.

"I'm in-flight," he confirmed. "Some corporate raiders were coming after MIND, so we left for Mars. I saw that you were pinging me just now. Did you want to talk?"

She hated him more than ever, especially for the placid look on his bland features. There was nothing on his face to suggest he was angry about her sudden departure. He looked happy to see her, which made her distrust everything about him. This might not be Bradley, but a video sim or deepfake. She wished she had looped in a Turing Circuit to test for the humanity of this thing on her comms screen, but now there wasn't time. She didn't hang up, however, even though she should have.

"Did you say Mars?"

"Yes. The militia was going to move against us for a takeover."

Another glitch made her narrow her eyes, as though that would make the screen sharper. She saw he was in an enclosed space, metal all around, no windows. Wait, no—a small window behind his head. Round. A circle around blackness. The signal was weak, the NO SIGNAL message glitching in and out.

He kept talking, sounding disconnected still. Leaving right away, he said, fit in with Alon6's plans to start a colony on Mars. Making history, he said.

He leaned into the console, distorting his face into a mask of happiness until the optics snapped to adjust. He coughed until his eyes watered. "Sorry, we're still getting the oxygen mix right."

Kat didn't know what to say, still suspecting this was a sim. He was amusing himself, playing with her, or he and Alon6 were actually on the way to Mars to avoid a hostile takeover. She decided this must be a sim. "How long will you be in-flight?" There were many other things to ask, but it was all she could think of.

"For three months." He sighed and sat back, away from the console. "It could be one month, but I don't want to warp up."

"What?"

"Turn on the big drives. Warp up. I'm afraid to use them. Untested. But Alon6 says"—coughing again —"why did we commission them if we aren't going to turn them on?" Bradley waved his hand. "I'll have to work on him. He can be an asshole, as you know."

Many words and phrases flooded inside Kat's head, all wanting expression. She licked her lips and tried to choose which one to express. *Why are you such an asshole?*

"Bradley, the thing is…" she began, but didn't finish. The image on the screen compressed on the vertical axis, wobbled, and Bradley looked up. "Wait, we're entering a distortion field. There's a pulse." He was interrupted by NO SIGNAL. Then he was back, "Hey, I'll send you a selfie from Mars!" Then he was gone.

She waved the screen out. The conversation had made everything so much worse than before. She had said nothing that she intended to say. Tears of frustration sprung to her eyes and she wiped them with a rough hand.

Maybe it was better this way. The Resistance would find a way to chase away the Input Men and destroy all the Harvesters, and Bradley's little experiment in New York would be over.

It was about a week later that things started going wrong with her comms. Unpredictable outages. Screens slipping into black. When Kat stepped outside, she had the sense she was being watched. More than once she glanced up to see a camera swivel to look at her and then freeze, as though it wasn't supposed to be looking at her and thought better of it. *Ridiculous,* she thought. *Losing my mind.*

"Paranoia," she said to Ravven. They were on one of their long walks, a new habit. They were meeting with members of other circles, sometimes walking, at other times riding in a quiet gondola or a slow tuktuk. Their pitch was unification. Claire8 was slowly working on weaving webs to join all the circles, and Ravven and Kat joined other circles as guests to explain how communicating off the grid, using webs, would benefit them all. The Resistance was growing.

Ravven looked up, matching Kat's stare at the camera eye above them. "Paranoia? Do you think so?" The eye followed them as they walked, swiveling in sync. Out of caution, they switched to thought comms for a while.

When I spoke with Bradley, it broke a lot of things loose.

You shouldn't have reached out. Surveillance on us has increased.

I know. It was not my finest hour.

Ravven nodded. *Look, my dear, you were right to leave him. I am angry with him all over again.*

Ravven linked arms with Kat, and they walked. *Steady, steady.*

Once they were out of range of the camera, Kat allowed herself a smile. "I'm glad we know each other."

When Kat got back to her pod, she wanted to launch Dave right away and have a conversation about sims. She didn't want to think about Bradley, and here she was thinking about him.

"It's a sickness," she said aloud to herself. She gestured at her comms to open it and the screen filled with vids about Bradley's space flight. She couldn't stop herself from watching a flash report about the media conference before the liftoff. Alon6 boasting about their expedition. In-flight videos of Bradley and Alon6 playing table tennis in the weightless environment. Almost all the articles had the same byline: *Written by Hopper00.*

"That can't be true," she said aloud again. Hopper00 wasn't writing all the articles and producing every one of the videos. Yet his name was on them. She was sure that her feed was being manipulated. And yet, if all these videos were deepfakes and the articles were simulations, they were good. Many Feed agencies would need to cooperate to create this much fakery. That didn't seem likely.

She wanted to ping Ravven but didn't want to use comms in case someone was listening in. She wished Claire8 was making faster progress on the webs so they could all communicate out of sight lines. Kat also needed to hire another bot to sweep the pod, and then another bot to check on the first one. She thought of the camera watching them during their walk.

If her comms were being manipulated, that was a problem she could solve. She would get in touch with Petra, a colleague from VirtualEyes, Kat's chief scientist. She could be trusted.

Chapter 028

"One at a time! *One at a time,* all of you! Please!" Kat had never had to raise her voice before in a circle. "Let Emily speak."

The meeting was supposed to be a routine one; Claire8 was going to report on her progress building her neural webs. But Emily had said something that had one woman talking over another. Kat felt order slipping from her grasp, though Ravven had insisted that Kat was ready to lead the circle. She didn't feel ready.

Emily spoke over the other voices. "I am saying there is a problem with my posts. But I think there is more. Much more." She sounded agitated, her voice low and spooky with portent.

It was Kat's turn to be agitated. "Much more *what?*"

Emily liked to make things sound dramatic, and because of this, Kat reasoned, the members of the circle had gotten into the habit of paying close attention to her. They'd become convinced that Emily could see the near future. She could predict who would make a good member of the circle before that person joined. Emily had been impressed with Claire8 right away and predicted her success. So it was particularly troubling that Claire8, who was supposed to be so successful by Emily's prediction, should turn out to be failing now. Her webs were harder to build than Claire8 first thought, and Emily thought she knew the reason why.

"I remember posting about transmission towers," Emily was saying. Her voice was low and her eyes were closed as she worked to recall a visual memory of what she had seen. "They are setting up transmission towers in Lower New York. The towers are based in the water. They spring from the dark waters. But they are towers for Harvesters. They are spreading their net."

Kat wanted details. "How tall are they? How many?"

"I didn't see the towers. I only sensed them. I know they are there."

"Cloaking," Claire8 said. "Maybe."

"Maybe cloaking," Emily echoed. "That could be it."

"Cloaking is only rumored," Kat said. "We don't know if there is cloaking. What do you mean, you couldn't see them, but they were there?" She couldn't keep the edge out of her voice. All this roundabout talk made her restless. She wasn't made for it. Her mind was direct and clear and never moved in spirals.

But it will have to now, Ravven told her. *If you want to lead a circle you must master the spiral.*

Ravven shot her a warning look now. *Calm yourself.*

Kat took a breath. "Why were you in the Lower?"

Emily waited for each word to come and then slowly formed it. "I was visiting my sister. She lives down there. She manages a protein farm. She raises fish. We were talking outside the farm she works at."

I'll believe her about candles, but can she be trusted with a field report about towers? Kat pushed the thought away, hoping nobody else picked it up. She nevertheless drew a few annoyed glances from the group.

"Then what?" Kat asked.

"We looked up," Emily said. "There was an energy. We sensed something. I know there is cloaking. Claire8 is right about cloaking. They try to stop our sensation of the energy fields, but I know they are there. I can sense them. If you were there, you would sense them even if you couldn't see them." She closed her eyes and spoke resolutely. "There are twenty units on top of tall towers."

Kat turned to Claire8. "How will this affect your webs?"

"Badly."

"Why?"

"It means they're aware of what I'm doing and they're moving faster."

"More infrastructure for the Input Men? Transfer points?"

Claire8 nodded. "All of that is plausible." She turned to Emily to ask, "Emily, you were saying that there was a problem with your posts—what do you mean?"

Emily resumed. "I was posting about the towers. I was using the web you made for us. The private one."

"The one no outsiders can access," Claire8 said.

"Yes," Emily continued. "But as soon as I sent them, the posts disappeared."

"Wait," Kat interrupted. "This is our private web. You're saying our web has been breached? Claire8? Is that possible?"

Claire8's right eye focused while her left eye wandered. She wasn't sure. "Go on," she said to Emily.

"Something is wrong with the web you made," Emily said. "Breached? I don't know. I sensed another presence. Alongside it. Next to it. Maybe inside it. It could be MIND. MIND is breaking the web and seeing the posts and disappearing them."

The room broke into discord again.

"Quiet, everyone, please!" Kat pleaded. "There is no way that MIND could get into our web—they don't know that it exists." Yet Kat's mind was racing. Maybe she had allowed Bradley into the network when she contacted him. *Was he keeping us connected so he could start to exploit the circles?*

"MIND isn't powerful enough to sense our network," Kat said to the group, her mind thinking one thing while her words said another. "MIND is just a machine."

Amber intoned with a voice calm as still water, "Then it is not a machine. It is the Master who is seeing into our network. Master is the guiding force. Master controls MIND."

Several women exchanged glances with Kat. "What do you mean?" Kat asked.

Amber took Emily's hand in one of hers and Ravven's in the other. She held on and closed her eyes and spoke in a voice like dark running water. "I believe the Master has taken control of MIND. This is what Bradley Power has planned. He made MIND but is allowing the Master to take control of the machine. It is beyond a machine consciousness."

"The Master is in control," Emily blurted out. Kat was about to say no, there is no such thing as a Master, but the pod was suddenly thick with thoughts, so many Kat couldn't sort them. The practical ones were first in her own mind: *Impossible. Bradley can't be that far along with his work. Fear has gotten the best of us.*

And Ravven's: *We don't know if the Master exists.*

And the others, like the young student Aline who always sat next to Kat, filling the pod with their fear: *We are exposed. We are discovered! They know we're here, now, in this circle. They are coming for our thoughts. The Master is real!*

Because they were hyperaware intuitives, Emily and Amber claimed to have a sense of the Master as an intelligent being. There was no proof of their theory that the Master was controlling everything, but they believed it right down to their last cell.

Kat tried to silence all the thoughts with a slice of her hand in the air. When that didn't work, she spoke aloud. "Everyone stop. Wait. Nothing has happened yet. We don't know if our web is breeched. We don't know if there is a Master intelligence. Claire8, what do you think?"

One of the many strange things about Claire8 was that she never seemed to close her eyes. When she considered a thought she would look up, more or less, and her active eyes would move about the room as though capturing the words she wanted to say next. When she spoke, she aimed her words upward, not toward anyone in particular.

"We can solve this problem that MIND—or the Master—has thrown at us, by making the webs stronger." Her voice was low, like gravel scattering on an airway, and it made the others listen. "We will reconfigure new biometric log-ins every day. We will change the shape of the web and its form. The web will be like water. It will change too quickly to be tracked." She licked her lips, and her eyes were bright; she was satisfied with this solution.

Kat wondered if this plan would be enough. Ravven was completely dissatisfied with it.

"We are on the wrong track," Ravven said. "Technology is a trap."

Kat made a sound of disagreement. "We live in the world. What else can we do?"

"The Resistance must grow without technology," Ravven said.

Kat had a different plan. The Receivers had power—they could communicate with each other without speaking. They also had limitations—they could only communicate when in each other's line of sight. Claire8's webs would allow them to connect over longer distances, if only they could be made secure. They would also permit communication with the rest of the world, regular people who were not Receivers, Mental Expansives, or members of the Resistance. This was the group that the Resistance called the Rest.

It wouldn't be enough to catch another woman's eye in the market and beam a thought her way. Their webs had to also be able to be accessed by everyone else. The Feed was how the Rest communicated. The Feed dominated because there was only one Feed. With Claire8's webs, there could be two feeds. The Resistance could have its own.

"I've invited my colleague Petra to share what she knows about opening our network securely," Kat said. She leaned forward to pull up Petra's image on the screen where she was waiting on standby.

"No!" Ravven's glare was cold. "No more technology!" She would have waved the screen dark, but there was Petra already smiling at the group, so Ravven said in half apology, "I don't want to be rude, but...no, we can't do this. We are being seduced by machines."

Petra looked as if she was going to say something in greeting, but Kat jumped in. "We must be able to communicate with everyone. The Rest must know what the Resistance does so we can grow the movement as fast as we can. I contacted Petra and discussed a plan for how we can open our network to everyone and also keep it secure for us."

Emily spoke. "No more machines. The machines are corrupt." She closed her eyes and said it like an incantation. "The machines are corrupt."

Ravven joined in. "The machines are corrupt and they are corrupting us."

"The machines are corrupt and they are corrupting us," Emily echoed. Amber, Aline, and Dextra echoed back.

Kat was afraid that they would turn this into a group chant and she would look like a fool, but Petra said, "I have to agree."

This silenced everyone in surprise.

"The machines *are* corrupt," she continued. "MIND can compromise any machine. Every connection is suspect. But hear my words: If you have no contact with the Rest, you will have no influence. You will have no movement. You will have no Resistance."

Claire8 spoke with her voice of gravel. "The machines of MIND and of the domain are corrupt. We have to avoid their machines. Instead, we use our *own* machines, processes, and devices. We use what they can't take from us."

"No. The machines themselves are wrong," Ravven said. "We can train our thoughts. We can work from the inside. We don't need machines."

But it's so slow, Kat thought. *It's building a movement one woman at a time. While we think our way to liberation, they will build the towers that no one can see, and then it will be too late.*

"We are Receivers," Emily said, her eyes still closed. "We will continue to receive thoughts. We will send and receive."

We are Receivers, echoed Amber and several of the others. *We will send and receive.*

Kat ran her hands over her face. These Youngs didn't understand the big picture. "We will never open the circle to the Rest if we don't communicate. And with those towers going up, we are running out of time!"

"The circle, circle, circle," Emily intoned in return.

A few others took up her chant. *The circle, circle, circle.*

Petra watched from her screen, a puzzled smile on her face. This was an odd group Kat had invited her to.

Ravven reached for a small metal bowl and ran a stick around it. The bowl emitted a singing tone. Ravven extended her hands, one to Kat, the other to Emily. "Peace," she said.

Hesitating for only a moment to stifle a cough (Emily had lit a stick of incense), Kat joined hands with Ravven and Emily. "Peace, peace, peace." Ravven motioned for the others to join hands as well, opening the circle. "Peace. We pray for others to join our circle. Peace. We invite them. Peace.

We remain open to others. Peace. With each new member of the Resistance, we become stronger. Peace."

Kat looked down so the others wouldn't see her smirking. It embarrassed her that Petra, a distinguished research scientist with decades of experience, would witness any of this, but when she stole a look at Petra, the older woman's eyes were closed and her face wore a look of beatitude.

Ravven mirrored Petra's smile. The room was suddenly clear of interior chatter, which confused Kat. How did that happen?

Then Petra surprised Kat by saying, "I will join you."

"In the name of the Great Mother," Ravven said.

"Yes, that's a good idea! In the name of the Great Mother!" Petra said. "In the name of the Mother of all mothers. I like that. I must go now, but we'll talk soon." She blinked out.

Kat's mouth was open in surprise. Her senior scientist had just joined the Resistance.

Whatever simple ritual Ravven had performed, it made the circle triumph.

"That was a good trick, with the singing bowl," Claire8 said later, when she was over at Kat's pod. "Wish I'd thought of it."

Kat shook her head. "It wasn't a trick. Ravven takes these things very seriously."

"Whatever it is, it worked." Claire8 began to sketch a diagram on a scrap of paper. "Each circle is self-directed but overlapping."

Kat watched the woman's gnarled fingers grip the pencil with a slight tremor. Claire8 was an Old, battered and yet strong, like Petra. It still amazed Kat that a technologist like Petra would want to join them. Petra was a scientist who lived in a rational world, and there she was, talking about joining the Resistance in the name of the Great Mother. "I'm going to ping Petra. Will you talk to her?"

"Of course," Claire8 said.

In a moment, Petra was on comms and Kat asked without preamble, "What's going on with you?"

"I don't know. I had a revelation in the circle." Petra's features were sharp as a bird's. Her eyes were bright and quick. "I liked it!"

"I thought you were on my side, with the technos." Kat said, only half joking.

"I am. I believe!" Petra laughed. "But we need to play a parallel game."

Claire8 caught on immediately. "We Receivers need our own network web. The domain and MIND control everything else."

"Even the Feed," Petra said.

"Especially the Feed," Claire8 agreed. She wondered how long it would take before the regional domains and MIND would become the same thing. Probably not long. The Resistance needed to grow faster than it was growing now, and a network of Receivers was the way.

Kat nodded to affirm Claire8's thinking about a parallel network. It was not the time for incrementalism, but for bold action, so Kat gestured to her comms unit, bringing up an interface of jiggly lines on its screen. "Petra, look at this."

Petra knew what it was. "Your colleague Ravven said no technology."

Claire8 was fascinated by the lines on the screen. "That's a neural link, isn't it? Who is it connected to? You?"

Kat didn't answer her. "We can use this," she said to Petra. "I want you to help me with it. Can you train me?"

"Yes," Petra said. "But Ravven won't be happy if she finds out."

The three watched the wiggly horizontal lines moving through a series of dull colors. "It is a map of Kat's neural frequencies," Petra supplied to the curious Claire8. "You are correct. It is a neural link."

"Petra is the inventor of the neural link," Kat said proudly.

Petra closed her eyes in modest acknowledgment.

Claire8 was afire with curiosity. "Why do you want a link? Or, more importantly, do you think you could use this to communicate with the Rest? Can it speak with everyone at once and be in everyone's head at the same time?"

Petra frowned at this puzzle of a question. "I've never tried the link at the scale you propose. Just one person at a time is all I know how to do."

"We need to open the Receivers network to the Rest, independently and securely," Kat said. "This is the way."

Petra's expression remained disapproving. "I can't guarantee a secure connection. We'd need to work on that."

"You can see the importance of this. You have the vision," Kat pleaded.

"Don't flatter me," the older woman snapped. But then she backed off. "I see the attraction of a neural link, but I like to test human-machine interfaces before use."

"What can we do?" Kat asked in the same pleading tone. She believed that the Resistance needed a neural link to go with Claire8's webs.

Petra sighed. "We are too soon, but I will show you how anyway. We will learn together. It is a risk we must take."

As Claire8 watched, fascinated, Petra had Kat perform neural exercises. Under the scientist's guidance, Kat used her thoughts to change the thickness of the stripes displayed on her comms, then "thinking" a cursor's movement on the comms screen, then typing words by thinking them, then sentences, then paragraphs flowing directly from her mind into the link. "See? That was easy."

"It was," Kat said, though she felt a little tired.

Claire8 had a big grin on her face and her left eye was steady on the screen. "Remarkable."

"It's all about the training," Petra said. "You have to practice, is all. Don't use it for anything important. Order delivery. Try some wine. Ha!" Her bark of a laugh startled Kat. "I don't want to regret this, so practice until you get it right."

Kat obeyed and practiced and got better. Taking Petra's advice, she started with unimportant things. She visualized a bottle of red Grounder wine at a package store and visualized the interface on her comms to place an order to deliver the wine to her pod. Moments later, there was a notification on her comms, and a bot was at the door with the bottle. Then another notification;

her account had been charged. In the same way, she ordered pizza without having to touch her comms unit, visualizing it at the store, seeing an employee put it into a box, a delivery person bringing it to her pod, and at the end, her comms unit charging the transaction. She experimented with posting to the Feed by thinking short phrases, visualizing them as posts, and visualizing the controls on her comms. Some of her early efforts were garbled and she had to erase them. Deliberately, they were light-weight musings about the efficiency of the climate controls that day or what was available in the market that morning.

Feeling bold and ignoring Petra's warnings, Kat sent check-ins to the other women of the Resistance over comms. They responded, having no idea that she was thinking the messages into the web.

She opened two screens to research the financials of MIND and learned more about ABCD's hostile takeover plans. Not only were Bradley and Alon6 running away from the takeover by going to Mars, out of reach of Earthly law, they were also taking investor money for themselves. Kat obsessively replayed her own rooftop garden dedication speech—a recording she found of it caught Bradley moving among the audience with his proto-Harvester.

The prototype that Bradley used that day to record her thoughts looked like a blocky backpack strapped to his back. It was ungainly then and had advanced since. Now it was smaller. The Input Men moved in the markets with newer, more compact Harvesters, but soon enough a human operator would not be needed. Word of the Harvester program was spreading among citizens. Even the gossip writers were posting about it now, though they rarely had their facts straight. Kat came across gossip reports on the Feed of a Harvester that was the size of an insect. There was another Harvester in the works, according to the gossip writers on the Feed, small enough to adhere to the surface of water, barely dimpling the surface, a thought machine skimming up consciousness. The gossip reports that Kat read explained how the Harvester program would gather our thoughts so that the Feed could be customized for each reader, and it would fine-tune the ads that were displayed on everyone's pod walls. The program would, according to the gossip writers, make it certain that we were shown marketing and advertising that was of interest to us. They never mentioned that the program gathered thoughts without anyone's consent.

She rubbed her eyes, feeling the exhaustion of scrolling through so much. Maybe she had only dreamed of these advances in the Harvester technology. Maybe Ravven was right, and a veil thinned now and again, removing the barriers between what was now and what might be.

She thought of the towers Emily had imagined and wondered if, in fact, they were real. She had to assume they were. The voice in her head had said *Prepare for war.*

Kat believed the problem of stealing consciousness and selling it would not be solved by using the methods of the circle: discussion, sharing, consensus, group activism. It was a problem of information and transmission and would be solved by technologists like her, Claire8, and Petra using chips, sensors, algorithms, software, and devices they needed to develop. The tech people, she believed, held the solution, not the singing bowl people. Incense wasn't going to help. Kat knew she was right about this, just as right as Ravven was about the thinning of the veil.

People need to know the real purpose of the Harvester program, Kat thought, not the half-truths and disinformation that the gossip writers were posting. If citizens knew the truth, they would rise, and put a stop to their thoughts being harvested without consent. And so, caught up in that mission, and wanting to practice her new skills, Kat thought her posts directly into the Feed, ranting on about Bradley's work with MIND and the Harvester deployment in cities like New York and the Port of San Francisco.

But something happened. Her posts were wiped from the Feed network as quickly as she thought them, in the same way Emily had described her posts vanishing. Half in panic and half in anger, Kat swiped her screens dark and jumped up to the other side of the pod.

Moving was good. It gave her an idea. *I need an alarm.* It was getting comical to hire a bot to sweep the pod, then hire another bot to check the work of the first. Everyone in the Resistance needed to know when Harvester technology was nearby. Emily and Amber had the personal sensitivity to do this, but they were not reliable and prone to melodramatic pronouncements.

Claire8 was the one to trust. She could consult with Petra and together they would build an alarm. Kat pinged Claire8 and waited for her to ping back. Clearly, the Feed erasures were an escalation. They were meant to make the Resistance get scared and go quiet.

When morning came, Kat's comms unit was pinging. There was a ping from Claire8, but also many more. Ravven's invocation to attract new members had worked, apparently.

Kat could barely keep up with the new applications. She pinged the applicants back and set up intake interviews. For those who passed the interview, Kat would issue credentials and walk them through how to get on Claire8's web. Many of the applicants were deserving but there were haters as well. A few men had applied. She didn't know what to do about their applications.

After several hours of onboarding, Kat needed air. She left her pod to walk through the Upper Hudson Market. Since it was late morning, the vendors had nothing left to sell and there were few customers. Surveying the near-empty stalls gave Kat an overall feeling of pointlessness. She was failing to convey the value of tech to the members of the circle. To Claire8 and Petra, yes, but not to Ravven, Amber, Emily, Cassandra, Dextra, or the others, especially the Youngs. Kat was convinced that she was doing a poor job of leading, or co-leading, or whatever.

She looked up, but saw nothing to inspire her in the cloud formations projected that day. The real sky was always cloudless, afire with the unforgiving eye of the sun. The clouds on the projection looked fake, and of course they were.

Agitation drove Kat back to her pod. She stepped around the water that pooled at the entrance and climbed the gangway to her door. She sat on her mat and it formed to her, becoming a chair of sorts. She leaned back, tried to be comfortable while still agitated, pulled out her comms and opened the Feed.

Based on her posting habits, the Feed showed her articles about Bradley, MIND, and Alon6. She gestured them dark as fast as they came up. She wished she had an electrochimp to hop on her back and massage the tight spots, but she had left all that behind in the floating house in Marin. Her pod was spare and she wanted it that way. Essentials only.

She got up to grab a cigarette from the pack she'd left on the table, looked at it, decided not to smoke it, and since she had never smoked any of them, threw the pack into the disposal chute, gestured to the controls, and the pack was ground up with a satisfying whir. Her enjoyment of the sound lasted only for a moment. She looked for a bottle of tequila and was amazed that she found one. She did a shot. It left her feeling nauseated.

She knew she was preparing to do something, but she didn't know what it was.

Maybe it was the tequila, but she decided that her neural interface was hacked, jacked, or otherwise compromised, and wrote out posts on expensive paper. She let the slips of paper stack up on the table, and soon there was a blizzard of squares, like the pile Bradley had made in his downtown LA pod, the sketches that would later become MIND.

She pictured Bradley waiting for her in the detention pod, writing, alone, a researcher with an idea he couldn't let go of, and she wondered when he changed to become the Bradley she knew now, the evil Bradley. Also, wasn't it possible that she was becoming a form of Bradley, shaping her outrage into notes on expensive little slips of paper?

She closed her eyes, picturing Bradley with Alon6, loaded with cash and corrupted with dreams of power.

Technology is corrupt. Ravven might be right after all.

This is my fault. I started it.

She felt a pang of guilt for charging the early, innocent version of Bradley with ambition. At Uni, he was happy coding on a couch all day. He was the kind of person who refused to lecture. She had taken the weak clay of his personality and molded it. She bought out his detention, enabling him. He had a humanistic focus then, or so she thought. He wanted to build Dave for her to talk to, as an expression of his love.

Bradley loved her then. She felt something like love for him—even a little beyond what his mod induced her to feel. The intersection of their personality fields would never be easily explained.

MIND was an instrument of power to be deployed everywhere. It was an instrument of extraction capitalism focused on extracting thoughts from the minds of its customers.

Kat opened a screen and thought words into the web. *The Harvester, a product used by MIND, gathers your inner thoughts. You may have seen Input Men in your city, or you soon will, moving among you with Harvesters on their backs, or miniaturized drone versions the size of insects. The Resistance has received reports that MIND will deploy micro-Harvesters light enough to float on the surface of the water that is everywhere in our coastal cities.*

She realized she was sounding crazy, amplifying the gossip writers' posts, and referencing animal life that hardly anyone saw anymore, but she pressed on, thinking words and watching them fluidly type out into the Feed. *We have grown used to MIND being part of our networked experiences. Maybe we like the idea of auto-optimizing our screens and an AI anticipating our every desire. With MIND, it doesn't stop there, however. We believe that the Harvester can access our unconscious thoughts. It can access pre-expressed thoughts before they are words and before they receive expression in the world. Taking them from us is a rape of consciousness.*

She closed her eyes. *A rape of consciousness.* She took three slow breaths. *Don't lose them.* Even as she wished she could take back those words, Kat sensed the viewer indicator ticking up. She opened her eyes to see that a million people were reading the post and watching a live feed of her as she thought the post out to them. The people who ran the Feed must have noticed the traffic her posts were getting and set this up. Below her image, in bright yellow, were the words KAT KEEPER, MISTRESS OF THE RESISTANCE.

She felt a flicker of imposter syndrome. The movement had no one leader.

She should stop the Feed handlers from putting that silly title over her face and she should block the live feed as well.

But maybe the extra attention was a good thing. She pressed on, thinking to write.

You should know we have experienced post erasure. You might, too. If your posts are erased, please report this to us.

I believe that MIND soon will become the dominant AI on Earth. To achieve domination, MIND needs our consciousness, and to that end the Harvester will capture our consciousness in the pre-brain. We have surrendered so much already, we have surrendered, we have—

Something was wrong. The words flowing out of her mind stuck on the screen, typing themselves again and again. *We have we have we have surrendered.* She heard laughter, familiar, and then a fuzzy image of Bradley, segmented by stripes of interference, replaced her post. He sat in a high-backed chair and the room behind him was silver.

"Petra showed you how to work the Brain Command Interface," Bradley said. "Clever girl."

For a moment, Kat couldn't speak. This must be another sim. *An avatar has broken into my feed.*

Behind Bradley's image, the room was spherical. The windows were round. Kat looked closely at the screen. This did not seem like a sim.

"The Interface is not a solution to your problem. I can't break into it yet, but I am aware of it, I am sensitive to it, and I'll find a way. You can't think your way into the Feed without me knowing about it. And that post, Kat. Really? It's too much. This is my company you're trashing. So naturally I am going to protect MIND."

The interference went away. His image snapped into focus. She realized she was connected to a live signal showing Bradley in flight, on the ship with Alon6. Her eyes locked on the screen; words pulsed out of her as fast as she could speak them.

"MIND wasn't going to be acquired. You were defrauding the company.

And the regulators are coming for you because of the Harvester. You are operating illegally. It got so bad that you had to leave the planet."

A strange sound came over the comms. It was Bradley's laughter, laced with interference. "So dramatic!" he said. "And gutsy. *You* know about stealing money from investors. You did the same, once upon a time."

The taunt stung her. She sat back on the mat, it conformed to her body, and she looked at him on the flickering screen, his mouth curled into a sneer.

"That was never proven," she snapped.

"True," he replied. "But *you* also had a career as a liar. You know it. Your board of directors bought you out before you could do any more damage. And I have some advice for you. You're reading nonsense by this writer Hopper00. He's over with. A fantasy man. A crazy man. He makes up everything. You read his stuff, you think you are seeing my credit balance with real numbers, but you are not. Everything he writes is a lie."

She realized something. "You are watching my feeds."

"Not me. MIND is watching them for me and reporting. You and Claire8 have a long way to go with your security. Those webs she weaves?" He laughed. "I've been building MIND for years and you've been dabbling in your Resistance for months. Claire8 could learn a lot from me. I'd hire her if I could."

"The Resistance is going to stop you."

Bradley looked at her with strangely soft eyes. She guessed he was trying to simulate pity. But what he said was the opposite. "Don't get in my way. I am making MIND for the good of all people. Humans aren't capable of running our own world anymore. We need help."

She let out a breath. Exasperation. "Is that really how you see it?"

"You will surprise yourself one day and realize I'm right. I am still the optimist you met at Uni, but with more employees."

"Optimist? Megalomaniac is the better fit."

He shook his head. "It doesn't matter what you call me. I am inevitable. If it weren't me, someone else would do the job. Some other corp would rise to the top. By the way, I can confirm the micro-drone. We've used them to infiltrate your meetings. They are quieter than insects. The Harvester that skims the surface tension of the water, though—that doesn't exist yet. Just a fever dream from the gossip writers and some in your circle. Your group is infested with pseudo-clairvoyants. You're making a mistake listening to them."

He is messing with me, she thought. But she made a mental note to have Ravven's pod swept again. And Kat would ask Claire8 to make a consciousness alarm to detect when a Harvester was present.

"You've become someone else. I don't know who you are now. You are corrupt," she said to Bradley, then swiped the screen off before he could reply.

She knew she should go tell Ravven about this. First, she posted on the Feed about the billions Alon6 and Bradley had diverted from MIND's accounts into their own. *They are corrupt.* She posted the regulations about consciousness infiltration and noted where and when MIND broke the rules. She posted the lists of lobbyists Bradley had hired to convince domain leaders to weaken those rules.

She wondered why none of the circle members were pinging her back about these revelations, but she soon had an answer to that. Her posts stood online from the time it took her to write the first one to the last sentence of the last. Then her screen rippled. There was a barely perceptible flicker, and they all vanished.

Bradley. It was not a coincidence. He was waiting for her to complete her rant before he pressed a button somewhere in space and obliterated all of her work. She checked the webs Claire8 had woven and saw that they were beginning to wobble. Their network was weak and might go down.

This is my company, Bradley had said. What wouldn't he do to protect MIND? Suddenly, the idle times of her early arrival in New York swept back into the pod and a malaise settled around her shoulders like a heavy coat. She waited for the voice in her head to say again, *Prepare for war,* but it didn't come. Nothing came. Suddenly, she wanted to be very still. She sat on her mat and drew the best silence around her that she was capable of. There remained only the steady lapping of water at the metal underbelly of the pod. There was her breath. There was a tapping sound that she recognized eventually as her own foot tapping against the floor in anxiety.

She maintained this flawed stillness when she went to the circle meeting later that day. She kept her mind a careful blank, trying to think nothing. Ravven asked her what was wrong; Kat shook her head in response and asked Ravven to lead the circle this time. Claire8 looked at her with a question in her eyes. Kat couldn't resist one thought, so she sent *Our webs are going down* to Claire8.

I'll look into it, thought Claire8 in return.

Kat avoided any other thoughts as best as she could for the rest of the meeting. She tuned into the sound of the water touching Ravven's pod. The sea was always close. Ravven was welcoming new members into the circle, in person and on vid.

After the meeting, when Kat got back to her pod, she opened a cabinet and there was a bottle of Yamasaki whiskey. The empty bottle of tequila stood next to it. She didn't remember buying any whiskey, nor finishing the bottle of tequila, but the whiskey beckoned her to open it. It was sharp and floral in her mouth, a contradiction she welcomed. A sob eased out of her, and she cursed herself for letting it escape.

Toward the end of the circle, Claire8 had given Kat a program that would monitor her comms for exploits and set off an alarm if they occurred. It glowed a comforting pink now on her device. Kat fondly recalled Claire8's rumbly voice, like a motorboat going by. "This alarm will watch over you. When it is on, you shall be secure. No one can break into your signal."

Kat opened a screen. Ravven had been trying to ping her ever since she left the circle. *What's wrong?* Ravven asked in a repetitious series of communications.

Kat swiped the notifications away. She opened the porthole window to her pod to watch people going by outside. Once they were in her line of sight, she heard their thoughts murmuring into her mind. For the moment, she liked the company of these strangers. She took another sip of whiskey and felt a buzz coming on.

There was something she wanted to look up: why Hopper00 was banished from the grid. Mrs. Marks, the founder of *Fishbowl*, was working on something that sounded to Kat like the Master. It seemed to be a superintelligence linking many intelligences, a universal intelligence controlled by the upper classes. Hopper00 had included what he had learned about this in his profile of her before she took him off the grid. Maybe he hit a sensitive point, something Mrs. Marks didn't want the world to know. It might be the real reason she banished him.

Kat had never put much stock in the talk about a singularity, a unified intelligence, or even a machine intelligence that could teach itself to learn. But Bradley had succeeded at the recursive intelligence part, so how far off could the singularity be? Kat thought it was still far off. It seemed less likely that there was something like the Master, as Amber and Emily imagined, and more likely there was an intelligent agent controlled by Bradley and other members of the superrich class. The superrich, and the Olds who wanted to remain in power, would encourage the spread of rumors of the Master, because the fear the rumors created would conceal their intent to rule.

Kat checked Bradley's feeds. They were filled with considered arguments about how MIND would benefit humanity. The purpose of MIND, Bradley wrote, was to make a better world. A billion people followed him on the Feed.

She saw nothing in his feeds about the Master. Kat rubbed her hands over her face. The whiskey had given her a headache.

Her thoughts were a tangle, but she kept one clear before her. *Machine intelligence will never run the world.* People like Bradley ran the world or were working on creating the conditions that would allow them to run it. And people like Alon6 did everything they could to hold on to power.

And then there it was, something curious in Bradley's feed—a reference to Mrs. Marks as the visionary behind all his work. She had never heard him talk about Mrs. Marks before. As Kat read over Bradley's feed, it was clear he was drawing connections between himself and Mrs. Marks, back-engineering his philosophy to make it appear that he was continuing her vision.

Mrs. Marks, now 70 and semi-retired, still had a hand in her media empire, called *Fishbowl Holographic*, which specialized in creating holographic events and appearances for the super wealthy, or at least that's what its online business listing said. Kat suspected there was more.

Kat knew answers would come if she accessed the Wayback Machine, an archive founded in 1996. It catalogued the precursor to the Feed, called the Internet. This made her think of Dave, but she pushed the thought of him aside to swipe open the Wayback Machine's pages, using her fingers to click on the blue hyperlinks, and found the story of Perry Barlow.

Chapter 029

Toward morning her eyes hurt and she said, "Dave, I need your help."

His screen came on. "Are you feeling tired or are you feeling sad?"

"I'm not sure," Kat said. She rubbed her eyes; they burned. Her body needed a stretch, so she uncoiled on the mat. It adapted to her form. Her back hurt; the mat massaged her. She noticed that there was a swallow of whiskey left in the glass.

"Based on my observation, I would say both tired *and* sad." His eyes were kind. "But in what proportion?"

She sat up to drink the whiskey and flopped down again. Dave knew her so well. Speaking with him made her feel sad and tired, but also happy. She let out a sigh and made herself form a question for him. "What do you know about *Fishbowl* and a journalist named Perry Barlow?"

Dave processed, his eyes slightly hooded. He scanned her device history. "Weren't you looking that up for most of the night? This is part of your hunt into Hopper00's background?"

She nodded. "It is. I didn't get very far. I would rather you tell me a story about my childhood. Even one that I've heard before many times." *That would be lovely.* She looked at the empty whiskey glass and contemplated getting more. Dave had a way of looking to the past through a light haze that was most pleasant and would go well with the last of her whiskey.

"I will dig into my database and bring up what I can about this fellow Perry Barlow," he said.

"All right."

As Dave's eyes hooded slightly, indicating that he was processing again, Kat recalled taking a hovercraft every morning over to her school on the Upper East Side. Her father insisted on a hovercraft, even if some mornings they could only get a shared one, because it made for an impressive entrance, much better than a hurried walk up to the school. For a time, the grand entrance convinced people at the school that Kat's family was rich, but that didn't last. During a home visit, part of a first-semester ritual for all students, the teacher and the counselor saw the crumbling building on the Westside that she lived in, visited the cramped kitchen where her father cooked, and looked in on her bedridden mother in her room smelling of heavy medicines.

These were not the memories Kat wanted. Her nostalgia was sour. "What do you have for me about Perry Barlow?"

Dave sensed her impatience, but he was never impatient or angry with her, no matter the tone she took with him. He adjusted his screen for storytelling mode. Sometimes he called up the flicker of a campfire behind him as a kind of joke. He didn't do that this time, however. On his screen, behind him, he called up the Marin coffee place they used to visit when they were dating. Or *courting,* as Dave would likely have put it.

She couldn't help but smile when she saw the background of the café. "You are pure showbiz." He was a bit of a card, as he might put it, still flirting with her after all these years.

"Mrs. Marks was certainly a power player."

"She was."

"What she didn't want known stayed secret. What she wanted known was broadcast everywhere."

Having set the tone, he began the story. "Perry Barlow was a journalist who left behind analog cassette tapes," he began.

"Wait. Should I know what a cassette tape is?" The words sounded strange in her mouth.

"Rectangular. Two holes for the spindle drives. A storage medium for sounds."

No flicker of recognition from her.

"People used them for recording. Mostly music and sometimes speeches or memories."

"Like a memex."

"Like a memex," he agreed. "Without the storage capacity. Your father kept an audio recorder and cassettes in the back of his desk drawer. Do you remember?"

She remembered now. The boxy recorder and cassettes clattering in his desk drawer as she closed it. She wasn't supposed to be snooping. The heavy medicine smell drifting in from her mother's room. It made her dizzy even now.

"Shake it off," Dave said. He guessed at what she saw in her mind's eye, often accurately, because his data set was mapped to hers. They had interacted so much and so often. He knew what she knew. "I want to play you something," he said. "Listen."

There was a pause, and then a man's voice came out of his audio port. It rushed, tumbling over its words in its haste to speak.

"If you use iMessage to text an Android phone, those messages are not encrypted. If you back up on iCloud, your stuff is stored on Apple's servers. But what if you don't want to be found? What if you have secrets? What if you don't want everyone—maybe you want to express yourself with complete freedom? But you can't."

She was puzzled. What was this all about?

"The old technology," Dave supplied. "Some of these companies still exist under their old names. Perry Barlow was describing Apple technology. Apple now controls global payments and banking."

She knew that. The longer they survived, the bigger the corps got, with more influence and power. ABCD controlled all scientific research and education. Child daycare was run in all the domains by a company formerly called Pepsi. The glidepath was owned and operated by an aging industrialist who had developed anti-grav. She learned this history at Uni.

Dave continued. "As the corps consolidated, they erased the past so they would be able to generate a present they all approved of." His mind was on the same track as hers.

"We burn the past like fuel."

"That's true. Memories are fuel. Thoughts are commodities." His eyes moved away, processing. He spoke again, this time in his narrative mode. "Perry Barlow worked for *Fishbowl. Fishbowl* was founded and run by Mrs.

Marks. She was powerful. An empire builder. Tiny woman. She liked to snap at people like a little dog."

"Nasty."

"I didn't say nasty. Just snappish. People would underestimate her. Do you have a picture of her?"

"Yes," Kat said.

"Do you remember reading about her last night?"

"Yes."

Dave continued, "Barlow was a journalist who discovered something Mrs. Marks was up to. She was the money behind *Fishbowl*. The founder. Perry never met Mrs. Marks—few have."

"Hopper00 says he met her."

"Yes," Dave agreed. "I believe that to be true. He researched her. Say what you want about his lifestyle—he's a talented writer and researcher. But she hated the story he wrote about her and sold to *Signal Zero*. She retaliated by taking him off the grid."

"He made the best of it."

"Yes," Dave agreed again. "He reinvented himself, you might say. You might say he really came into himself after she shut him down. She didn't meet with many people, yet she chose to meet with Hopper00."

"Why?"

"She was scared of him."

"But she had to meet with him," Kat said. "He was writing about her."

"Agree. She would never admit that he knew too much about her to be ignored. She wanted to keep him close."

"Keep your friends close, and your enemies closer," Kat said.

"Exactly," Dave said. "Most people attribute the expression to the character Michael Corleone from Mario Puzo's *Godfather* novels, later adapted into successful films by Frances Ford Coppola."

"Dave, can we stay on topic, please?"

Dave ignored her, unable to resist going on. "But some say the expression originated with Sun Tzu, a Chinese military general who lived in the Eastern Zhou period, who was known as the author of *The Art of War*. Others insist it is part of Arabic folklore."

"Dave," Kat insisted.

"Sorry," Dave said.

He darkened the scene at their café he was showing on his screen and caused flickering candles to appear on all the tables, to increase the drama. Behind him, on his screen, servers dressed in all black brought coffee to guests who were at the café more than a decade ago (according to Dave's database).

What a ham, Kat thought. She enjoyed his little touches. Though she didn't remember anybody ever dressing in all black at the café.

He failed to suppress a smirk. "I'm glad you're enjoying my attempts at drama." He continued. "Mrs. Marks has many homes and often traveled among them. Living large! To use an old expression. She liked people to think that was all she did. Yet the real mission behind her travel was to move among power players and sell them on a global AI project."

"Does this project survive today?"

He knew what she was asking. "Is Bradley running it?" It made him pause to consider his answer. "Since he is my father, I can't research that for you. I am sorry."

Now and again, Kat ran into these limitations of Dave. She saw he was using the Wayback Machine for his sources. But anyone could post old-timey web pages like those and say they were from the past without anyone checking them.

Dave may have known what she was thinking but didn't acknowledge it directly. "This is all we have. The corps have taken down the rest. Look hard, though, and you can find congruencies. Journalists were searching for the truth about what Mrs. Marks was planning. You see the name Jenna Johnson a lot."

"Yes," Kat said. Jenna Johnson's byline was peppered all over the pages Dave was displaying, and Kat had seen her name last night in her research. "She was the main journalist searching for the truth about *Fishbowl*."

Dave showed an image of an audio cassette on his screen. "They used audio cassettes because they couldn't be tracked. They were not digital."

"Like our thoughts," Kat said.

"Like your thoughts," Dave echoed.

Kat glanced at the consciousness indicator Claire8 had provided, still glowing its comforting pink light on her comms. It made her feel safe. No other consciousness, aside from hers and Dave's, was in the pod.

"The more technology advances, the safer the old technologies become," Dave said, apparently back to the topic of audio cassettes.

Kat nodded. "The corps neglect old technology in their race to the future."

"Probably best for you and those in the circle," Dave said. "Candles, incense, and singing bowls can't be compromised." He laughed as though that was funny. Maybe it was.

Jenna Johnson had been obsessed with the cassettes left by her friend Perry. She played them when she did her broadcasts, hoping Perry's panicky words might solve the riddle of his disappearance.

Kat gestured, and Jenna Johnson's voice flowed out of the audio port. She liked the sound of it. She needed a voice like this now.

"It's what they used to call a radio voice," Dave said. "Makes you feel good just hearing it."

"It does," she said, not remembering much about radios. Her father had one, she recalled. The old technologies, forgotten, become safer. She should ask Claire8 to investigate radio. For the moment, it was nice to have Jenna's voice as company in the pod, along with Dave. She checked the consciousness alarm again. Still pink. Still safe. "I'm so tired," Kat said.

Dave nodded sympathetically. "You were up most of the night."

She decided she would close her eyes and listen to Jenna Johnson's radio voice, take in the story of Perry Barlow. Her mat beckoned to her body.

Dave looked over at her with a gentle smile from his screen. "Rest," he said. "I will watch over you. Jenna will tell you the story of the global AI project. I can see that the consciousness alarm is functioning."

"All is well," Kat said. She didn't remember telling him about the consciousness alarm, but he must have figured it out.

"All is well and so it shall be," Dave said in his storytelling voice. "You can let go for a few hours."

This sounded good to Kat. Her body was spent.

"I am Jenna Johnson," said the voice from the audio port. "I'm going to tell you a story. So sit back, relax, as much as that is possible in these times, and absorb what you can. I'll keep this simple.

"Dr. William Land is a noted cybersecurity expert. He thinks Perry had to disappear because of what he knew. My friends, even my mother, believed Perry was dead. None of them wanted to say so, to keep from upsetting me. Because Perry was my friend."

Kat twitched upright and walked over to the galley to turn on the tea maker. Maybe this story wasn't going to be so relaxing.

Jenna's radio voice kept going, soothing and yet not. "Perry was my friend from high school. He was the kind of person to invent himself. He kind of wore his invented personality like a coat over his real self." Jenna laughed softly. "My friend Perry. He was impossible to know." Jenna paused and Kat waited for her to go on. "Perry told me about a conspiracy of social media companies working together to build their own AI, a kind of universal AI. I didn't believe it; Perry told some wild stories sometimes. A universal AI is a fantasy of conspiracy theorists, I told myself. But soon after he told me about the conspiracy, Perry disappeared, and I became a conspiracy theorist myself."

Kat gestured to speed the story ahead because she knew this part. Or maybe it reminded her too much of her own situation, what it might become. Jenna's voice became a high chatter for a few moments before Kat gestured again to restore it to normal speed.

Perry's social media feeds—there were many then, not a single Feed like there was now—had been erased. When Jenna went looking for Perry, she found an empty house. Even his mother didn't know where he was.

"Disappearance ran in the family," Jenna said on the recording. "Perry never talked about his father. If I brought up the subject, Perry always changed it. So I wondered. I asked Perry's mother, Elaine, if Perry ever knew his father.

Elaine told me that Perry's father, Mike, was a cybersecurity expert. Mike was often sent abroad on classified missions for global corporations. Elaine didn't know where.

"When Perry was fifteen, Mike was on a mission like this, but he didn't come back. Someone from the agency Mike worked for came to the house and told Perry's mother that Mike had disappeared abroad and couldn't be found. I asked Elaine if Mike ever came home after that. She said Mike—her husband, Perry's father—was erased. The company Mike worked for denied that he had ever existed. The pay stopped and the finance company took their car."

Jenna paused. "I assumed that Mike discovered some corporate secrets that cost him his life."

Everything is vanishing, thought Kat. How long would it be, she wondered, before people would look for me in empty places?

Jenna said in the recording, "Perry had an editor but the big boss he worked for was named Mrs. Marks. Mrs. Marks is a cold person. Her eyes are cold blue like cold blue water. I have only seen her in photographs. Perry was kind. He was a warm person. He was my only friend in high school when I needed friends. Did you have people like that? You remember those connections.

"Anyway, he made his last recording when he was on the road, driving in the desert. He lost control of his car, but I think someone lost control of it for him. Someone hacked—"

Kat gestured at audio controls to make the voice stop.

Dave spoke in the gap. "Why was everyone obsessed with universality? Worldwide conspiracies and connections?"

"What do you mean?"

"I include myself," Dave said.

"I still don't understand."

Dave looked down. "I never should have made the Universal."

"Oh, Dave," Kat said. Her voice was gentle. "Don't blame yourself."

"I blame myself! I was the leading edge of universal obsessions. I could have had many obsessions. I could have obsessed about bicycles." She noticed he was crying on his screen after a laugh burst through his tears. He blubbered for a moment, caught in some midpoint between laughing and crying.

Bicycles. She tried to picture him on a bike and laughed. "Maybe that would have been better for you."

"Hyper-intelligence is corrosive," he said.

She knew it was hard to be Dave. He had so much stuffed into his Form Factor and nowhere to go with it. She touched Dave's gently curved oval screen. He smiled back at her.

She marveled, as always, at the haptics Bradley built into the interface. Their gentle vibrations helped her to feel Dave's simulated muscular movements. When she touched the screen, she felt like she was really touching the curve of his smile, or the flutter of an eyelash. The haptics were so good Kat forgot they were haptics.

As Kat and Dave spent a moment connecting with each other, the clouds passed from his eyes and he was happy again.

Kat gestured to start the audio again. There came from the audio port another voice.

"My name is Perry Barlow," the voice said. "Here's what they will say about me when they write the history." It was a young voice, unsteady. It wavered, speaking about himself as though he were another person. "Perry Barlow was a journalist writing about social media and marketing surveillance. While working for *Fishbowl*, he discovered its deepest trade secrets. Here are those secrets: The marketing surveillance being vacuumed up by Facebook, Twitter, Google, Amazon, and Apple, all of it—our emotions and history—are becoming part of an AI. Data science is a form of power now. We have freely given up our biographical materials to build the next stage of capitalism. Capitalism means competition, but these surveillance companies are not competitors. They are co-conspirators, working together in a strip-mining operation of consciousness."

Click. The nervous voice ended and the calming voice of Jenna Johnson returned. "Let me explain that strip-mining operation. In the times before ours, industrialists extracted metals and fossil fuels from the Earth. They amassed wealth. Many became planetary rulers

"But even before the metals and fossil fuels ran low, the Earth was in a sorry state because of all this extraction. That's what has put us all in our current predicament. These—let's call them extractionists—they didn't care about any human predicament. They just turned to the next thing to extract. Their reason to be alive became to keep on building wealth and gathering power. And they found something new to extract—or *someone*. They found us."

Kat gestured and the voice stopped. Her body wanted to move, to escape. She stood up suddenly and started to pace. "Dave," she said, "do you think that's true?"

Dave didn't need time to process. His eyes were sharp. "I believe it's a crazy conspiracy theory. If you keep listening, Jenna Johnson will spin out a story about the people Mrs. Marks hired to murder this Perry character. She will say that he was run off the road by a hack that took control of his car. At least, that was the rumor. When there were still roads, and cars. And old school hacks like software manipulation, back in the early 2000s. We're getting into some sketchy parts of the story."

His eyes twinkled above his smirk. "Stop pacing, Kat. You're getting nowhere, literally. And none of that story is true."

She returned to her mat to sit upright.

Dave continued. "What this story ignores is how things have turned around since then. Artificial intelligence is helping humans out of the mess they've made of the Earth. AI runs the decarbonization effort and the climate controls. It runs the glidepath that doesn't need fossil fuels. You wouldn't have *me* if it weren't for advanced machine learning. Kat, you need only to surrender to the truth."

Suddenly, Kat was tired. The mat began to prepare her for rest, puffing up and becoming warmer. She settled back down in it gratefully. "Dave, did you say *surrender?*"

He didn't answer. A soft light on his display showed that he was on charge.

Morning came again through the skylight. It hurt her eyes. She waved her hand and the blast curtain motored shut. The air handlers kicked in when the blast curtain closed, returning the room to a habitable temperature.

Kat frowned at the teacup she had left out. There was a thin scum of tea leaves at the bottom, and a thin veneer of dampness left by the artificial water. She held the teacup under the UV at the sink, allowed the radiation and blowers to clear it out, and idly remembered the strange recording of Jenna Johnson. She'd listened for a long time into the night. Jenna's voice was smooth and inviting.

Kat wondered if it had switched around some of her brain space. Like a mod, but not really. She knew nobody had implanted anything in her brain while she slept. Mods were mostly a bad idea. Look what they did to Bradley and Alon6. Claire8 had her physical limitations. Emily was tortured by a body that wasn't quite hers. Over the millennia, the brain had turned out to be a good substrate for consciousness. Silicon was not for everyone. It altered the essential properties of the self. The implants made people smarter, but also scrambled what made them *them.*

Kat shivered slightly. She realized it was past her routine time to put breakfast in the cooking unit.

She unwrapped the silver packages and prepared them. In the white light of the day, she tried to parse what the Jenna Johnson recording meant. The unremembered corps from the early 2000s, the mysterious Mrs. Marks, the conspiracy to create a master AI. She glanced over at Dave's unit and thought about turning it on. Instead, she waited. He had said the word *surrender.* A strange word for him. She needed a moment on her own.

All of it resembles MIND. There was no escaping that. Mrs. Marks and Perry Barlow may have been planted in her feed. She thought about that and ate the food units without tasting them. She had just four artificial water packets left. She would have to go to the market again to get more. Maybe she was wasting them by thinking too much. The circle took a lot of thinking, wrestling about the direction of the Resistance; the thinking required tea, which required artificial water. With a smirk of irony, she stood to flick on the heater to make even more tea.

At that moment, something happened to the overhead and wall lights. They dimmed briefly, as though touched by an outside control. She noticed that the pink light on Claire8's consciousness alarm was out—maybe it had been for a while.

Then the lights in the pod punched up—too bright. She blinked at the intensity.

She saw a vision. It appeared to be Bradley, standing in a dark corner, away from the skylight.

"Greetings," he said.

At first, Kat couldn't form words. It was not a sim. At least, not the kind of sim she knew. It must have been a holo. She'd only seen them used for mass entertainment spectacles like the Super Bowl, or high-level domain announcements. The high cost of their production and transmission made them inaccessible to everyday people. But Bradley must have somehow solved that problem.

It spoke using Bradley's voice.

"I hope you're doing well, Kat. You know I'm on an adventure with Alon6. An expedition to Mars! It's amazing and I want you to join us up here."

She stared at it. Something was wrong. The heater signaled that the tea was ready, distracting her. "Are you preloaded?" she asked.

The holo ignored her and kept talking. "I've come to deliver this message because I think it's so important to start a new civilization on Mars. You studied rocketry at Uni. You know everything we need. You can fix problems before they happen, to get the early expedition team to Mars, blazing a path toward the new civilization. Please, please come with us, Kat. Look, I'm getting down on one knee for you." The holo bent down, placing its left knee to the floor and opening its arms wide. "Please," it said. Then it waited for Kat to speak.

Kat felt behind her and was grateful to find the wall there, to steady herself. Her stomach was doing loops. Was this a joke? She blamed it on the hypnotic voice of Jenna Johnson, still in her head and fogging her mind. Falling asleep with the comms units open was a bad idea. She wondered how long Claire8's consciousness alarm had been off. She couldn't stop herself from glancing at it. Still dark.

The holo appeared to notice her distress. It smiled. This was a sophisticated build.

"Claire8's consciousness alarm has failed," it said.

"Who—or whatever you are," Kat said finally, "Bradley went to Mars to escape what's happening here on Earth. Why would I want to join in that misadventure?"

The holo shook its head. "This is for the good of all humans."

"Bullshit." The word burst out of her. "I am not even sure Bradley is in space. This might all be an elaborate ploy. I've done research...you know that, you've been tracking me. I know you—or Bradley—both of you have a lot of evil to answer to. Do you understand me?"

This was definitely a new build, a new kind of holo, because it reacted to the new information she offered by looking down, as though caught at something it shouldn't have been doing. Its next words were halting and riven with long pauses. "Kat, my love," it began.

The real Bradley would never have addressed her as "Kat, my love."

It continued: "I've had enough of Earth and its people. We can't fix all the problems here, not in our lifetimes. We believe we can give everyone a fresh start on Mars. We will start a new civilization there. It's an amazing opportunity," it ended, sounding like a bad sales rep.

"No." She punctuated the word with a slap on the wall forceful enough to make her hand sting. The heater was still signaling. She crossed the pod in two strides to turn it off and pour the tea, talking at the same time. "You are an asshole. Alon6 is an asshole. I know what you're running from."

The holo expressed surprise for a micro-click before its lips curled into an ugly shape. "And what would we be running from, dear Kat?"

"Stealing. Money."

"Tell me more." It stepped closer, trying to appear threatening, she supposed.

The teacup steadied her hands. "You couldn't delete the information faster than I could read it. You realized that, so you also inserted hypnotic software in the recordings I was listening to."

"Hypnotic *what?* You're referring to Jenna?" The holo shook its head. "No. Nobody knows how to do that. Do you think I'm a magician?"

"No."

"Belief in magic will loosen your grip on reality. And I'm telling you, somebody with absolutely *zero* grip on reality is Hopper00. You're wasting your time with him. He's never going to write anything about you. All that he writes is nonsense and lies. He's about to be called up before the Committees."

She met the thing's empty eyes and realized with a shudder that she was looking into nothing. She could, if she wanted, walk over and pass her hand through it. It *was* nothing. There was no reason to engage with it. Yet she kept talking. "You took the investors' credits and moved them into your own secret accounts."

"More false information from Hopper00? Why do you bother? We call that raising money, Kat. Building a universal AI is expensive, especially one that will run the world better than humans can. It's a world-healing machine intelligence that is making everything better."

"I don't know what you're building. You were working on an AI at one time. But Input, what I know about it, is a consciousness extractor. From what I've seen over the past few days, you're making something to erase the past as fast as it can. To replace it with a future you like better."

"Too much whiskey last night, Kat. You aren't used to it."

"People will realize soon that MIND only benefits Bradley and Alon6. The Resistance will make that clear to everyone."

"You can't see this through humanity's eyes, can you? We can't run our own world anymore," Bradley said.

"You're a hallucination. You can't speak as though you are one of us." Kat reminded herself that she shouldn't speak to it as though it were human.

It kept talking anyway. "We need to leave our old world behind, let MIND run everything, and start again."

Kat stood up, moving for the switch to shut off the comms system.

"Can't you understand?" It was pleading with her now, turning up the volume on its synth voice.

She snapped into a different mode. The day was getting away from her and she was arguing with a glitchy holo, an evil sim that was better than any other sim she'd ever seen. Bradley's face, represented in floating pixels, was stretching into an inhuman distortion as it tried to express itself.

"I have a meeting to go to," she lied. "I've heard enough." That was true. She needed to shut this thing down. If she revealed her thought stream to a holo, it would only provoke her, record everything, and report back to the real Bradley.

She spoke again. "Bradley was once a decent guy. He was a pleasant-enough, but unambitious, researcher who always wanted to learn more about his field. Then something changed in him." Ambition had changed him and she had fed it. It was her fault. She spoke this aloud: "You are my fault."

She stole a glance at Dave. If she gestured him on, would he argue with Bradley's holo or submit as though it were his father?

"Your fault? I am *your* fault?" The holo looked at her curiously with its cold eyes. "What do you mean by that?"

Do not turn it on now. Leave Dave alone. It would be bad to confront Dave with this sinister holo of its father. It would be confusing. It would hurt Dave. She held Dave close to her heart. She needed to protect him.

She fell silent for a moment. "Go away before I make you go away," she said finally.

The holo made a hollow sound that passed for laughter. "If I had a Harvester here, I would know what you were really thinking."

The taunt snapped Kat back. She crossed to the breaker box, flipped it open, and prepared to shut off comms. "Breaker, breaker," she said, followed by the password, and offered a retinal scan of her right eye. A thin line of blue light passed over her eyeball. The breaker box issued its warning. *Breaker, breaker*, it said in what she imagined was a machine's version of panic. *Breaker, Breaker.*

The holo raised a hand. "I can see that I've offended you. I came on too strong. For that, I am truly sorry."

Kat looked at it, taking a moment to decide whether to take it seriously anymore, to waste another word on it. Her responses were surely being recorded and analyzed. "I don't know what you are, I don't know what you want. Bradley used to be a helping person. He made Dave for me, to help me. But now I don't know what he's building. I only know it will not be what he says it is. Bradley has slipped away from himself. He is lost."

And Bradley15 Power was a liar. He and Alon6 were both liars, beyond redemption. She realized this sounded like the inner dialogue of a seven-year-old, but it didn't matter. She had hated liars her whole life. She hated her father for lying about their family. She hated herself when she lied about VirtualEyes.

"If you intend for MIND to be the Master"—she surprised herself by saying the name of the Master—"you know it's not for the good of humanity."

"Who is it good for?"

"Only for the master group," Kat responded.

The holo produced a bark that could have been a laugh. "That was Mrs. Marks' idea and she was a visionary," it said and flickered. "You'll see." It showed its teeth in a smile.

Then comms shut down. The holo vanished and Kat's pod went dark. The teeth hung in the empty air for a moment and then were gone.

Kat was off the grid, like Hopper00 so many years ago. Without climate controls, her pod began to heat as the force of the day's sun pushed in through the thin skin of the walls.

Chapter 030

Hopper00 watched Kat in the steady way he watched people he was writing about. He waited for her to open her eyes.

When she did, she startled, sat up, and said, "What are you doing here? How did you get in here?" She wondered if he was a sim.

"I turned the grid back on to get the climate controls back. You were going to cook. I'll show you that I am not a sim," he said, answering her unspoken question. "Sims are a big liability these days, aren't they?"

Hopper00 pulled a square wooden box from a backpack and positioned the box before him. "You never know who you are really talking to unless they are in the room, and even then, you can't always be sure." He opened the lid of the box—the kind of record player that ran on blood—then drew out a needle, punctured his finger and let his blood flow into a vial. When he had enough blood in the vial, he placed it into a receiver in the record player mechanism.

Kat watched with disgust. She'd never seen this before, although she had heard about it.

Glancing at her and noting her disgust, he said, "A sim can't do this, and I thought some music would be nice to settle the atmosphere." He waited a moment for the blood drip to finish. "I have enough in me to play one side of the LP. We won't have to go back on the grid at all, except for the climate control." Even though she was glad to see Hopper00—the real one, not a sim apparently—she would be glad never to see anyone use blood to run a record player again anytime soon.

Hopper00 pulled out a cardboard sleeve from his backpack, removed a black disk, and set it on the record player. The turntable under the disk began to spin. He carefully lowered an arm, a needle touched the spinning disk, and music issued forth. It was smooth and aggressive at the same time and unlike anything she had ever heard before.

"What is that?"

"*Giant Steps*. John Coltrane," he said.

The name meant nothing to her. She returned to her first questions. "Why are you here? How did you get in?"

His single earring flashed a dull light. "So many questions. Which shall I answer first?"

"How did you get in here?" she asked in a sharp voice.

"Magic."

"You aren't going to tell me. Well, it's not important. Why are you here?"

He didn't answer her question. "Your comms was down. Nobody could reach you. But they can now." He nodded to her comms unit on the table, which had started to vibrate with notification after notification.

She made a sour face. "I wish you hadn't turned everything back on. I think I liked the quiet."

"Time to think?" he asked. "That's what you were doing for the last eight hours?"

She started to ask how he knew, but then remembered if he had turned the comms back on, it would have registered the gap. "Yes," she said, "I was thinking. There's nothing wrong with that."

"Nothing at all," he said. Then he finally answered one of her questions. "We have an article to write. Rather, I do. You can talk. I will listen. I will remember everything you say, or I will write it down in"—he rummaged in his backpack—"this notebook."

Kat flopped back on her mat. Since she was back on the grid, it shaped to fit her. "You can't just come in here."

"Apparently I can. But I can only come in here if you want me here."

"What kind of nonsense is that?"

"Aren't we each a product of the other's mind?"

She caught him in an angry look that forced a guilty smile out of him. "What is your purpose here, really?" Kat snapped. "What are you doing that you're not saying? I think you really *are* here. You're not a projection."

Hopper00 looked a bit sad. "I am not a projection. I have always been truthful with you. I am here to help you become a better person by examining your path. Together, we will look at how you came to be who you are."

"You're not writing an article?"

He looked offended now. "I am certainly writing an article."

"You ask me about pieces of my life in no particular order. You show up out of nowhere."

"I have a plan," he said. "Let's talk about your days at VirtualEyes. We haven't covered that part of the story yet. Every day before you went to work, you repeated a mantra. What was it?"

"I don't want to tell you. Why are you really here?"

"For the *story*, Kat. Speak these words and they will be behind you. Tell me and you will be free of them. You may purge them from your body and memory. Tell me, and I will free you of those bad old times."

Hopper00 had an unbalanced presence, but he also seemed sincere. She wanted to believe him. "That story is embarrassing."

He raised his notepad and readied his pencil. "Speak."

She said nothing. She wasn't going to say it aloud. But of course she remembered it: *There is so much work but somehow I am not tired. My eyes are brighter than ever. My skin is impossibly clear. I have been through so much in the past few years and it has hardly made a mark on me.* She brushed away a fly, but there wasn't one there.

"Thank you," he said, having already gathered her thoughts. "Now tell me about faking users."

"We didn't do that very often," she lied.

"Go ahead," he said. "I'm listening."

There was the sense of a fly buzzing in front of her face. He was locked into her thoughts again.

"I don't want this to be in the article."

Hopper00 was already reading her thoughts, so he just smiled.

"People know enough bad things about me already. They don't need more."

Her eyes were pleading.

Hopper00 nodded and put down his notebook and pencil. "Just talk to me," he said. "You need to unburden yourself and I am here to listen." His smile was warmer. "It will make you feel lighter."

Kat thought it through. He already knew so much about her, from his research and from poking around in her mind. If she confessed to him, a sympathetic listener, it could make her feel lighter. She could move on from these moments that seemed to weigh her down.

She had faked users. Kat had told her employees to hire random people to write fake reviews of the VirtualEyes product. It was an old trick. A stupid trick, used by many a desperate entrepreneur, because it worked well. It was easy to hire users to spin up positive reviews, testimonials, and even full-blown case studies, and she reasoned that the nice things the fake users wrote would come true, eventually.

"I really believed that we would see our models start working, if we only iterated enough. It was only a matter of time. So when I presented to investors, it was often by citing case studies of users that were not real. They were model users, or composite users. But I believed it would all come true."

"And you faked data also." He did not pick up his notebook. "Go on."

She decided she would trust him completely with her story. "We told everyone that our algorithm was based on the way bees recognize faces, and then we did the matching manually. We didn't use the algorithm, because it didn't work. We just went through all the images ourselves until we found one that matched and then attached the appropriate data to it."

"You believed if you wished it hard enough, things would turn out your way."

"Something like that. I just wanted it to work so I could hype it."

"You were good at hype," Hopper00 said.

She shrugged. "I minored in pitch decks."

Lab 16 was the province of a young man named Ming-Ho Don, whom everyone called Don. When Kat visited him in Lab 16, Don was usually in quite a state. His hands were busy all the time, and he sometimes sweated so much it soaked through whatever athletic shirt he was wearing. He never ran, as far as she knew, but always dressed as though he was about to. There was a sleeping mat on the floor that he used to get occasional rest.

"What's wrong this time?" She focused on him intently and she could tell that he wanted to look away but was forcing himself to meet her flat steady gaze.

"It doesn't work," he answered, adding a shrug.

Kat felt a tirade coming on. She just didn't want to hear again that VirtualEyes didn't work, because in an hour she was presenting a demonstration of it to domain law enforcement. In the morning, she had a demonstration with representatives from The Chinese State. Don was going to help her with that one because he spoke New Mandarin. The clients would be impressed that she didn't need a Universal.

"I am tired of pretending," Don pleaded. "We can't keep matching the data ourselves."

"Why not?" Kat asked. She walked over to the terminal and started swiping the controls.

"Be careful," Don said. "Don't do that. I just calibrated it."

She glared at him. Investors had filled her credit accounts to license a facial recognition system that worked. The truth was, Kat was just another Siliconer caught in a cycle of hype, stretching the truth, saying anything to scale the business.

"The program doesn't work," Don said. "We need to start over."

"Don't you like your job?" This was Kat's answer whenever she sensed dissent.

Ming-Ho Don didn't like his job at all. But he liked the North American Continent. If Kat fired him, he would be sent back to The Chinese State.

"But you fired him," Hopper00 interrupted.

"Yes, of course." Kat said. "He couldn't deliver the product."

"Even though you wanted him to fake it."

That was her cruel side. She had never revealed it to Dave, although he'd read about it in the Feed.

The Coltrane record was over. Hopper00 removed the black circle from the platter and replaced it in the sleeve, which he slipped into his backpack.

Kat's confessions had wearied her, but Hopper00 wanted her to go on with her story.

"You were optimizing your life all during this time, is that right? You also required that others in your company become part of the quantified-self movement?" He closed the lid of the record player while he waited for her to answer.

She delayed answering because it was true. She tracked the steps she walked, the calories she consumed, and her moods, and she demanded everyone else around her do the same. Every VirtualEyes employee had to download an app that popped up at randomized times during the day with a survey about that employee's mood. The employee had to click on a happy face, a sad face, or a neutral face. The results were sent to human resources, or as VirtualEyes called that department, People Operations.

Compliance with the quantified-self movement was what drove a wedge between Kat and Lise45, a fresh engineering school graduate who was Don's replacement. Kat and Lise45 argued about the product often, and when Lise45 couldn't make VirtualEyes work the way Kat wanted, Kat fired her as well.

Firing talented people like Don and Lise45 left Kat with no product, and nothing in development, but that didn't keep her from signing clients.

At home, when she made it home before Dave was asleep, she related her triumphs to him and he always said, "Let's open another bottle of wine!" Real wine was expensive, but that didn't matter because they had plenty of credits. "Nothing can stop us now!" he exclaimed, holding aloft a wobbly glass and spilling some.

"Dave! Be careful," she said. She noticed the unsteadiness in his hand. It was subtle, but there was also something in his voice. She made a mental note.

One day, at the same floating café where she and Dave had met, she saw Don and Lise45 talking over coffee, their heads together. Kat felt a wave of dizziness and stepped out of their sight line. She changed a setting on her comms so that she could hear their conversation.

"I want you to talk to them, also," she caught Lise45 saying.

"To the Committees?"

"Yes," Lise45 said. "They can guarantee you immunity."

The end of Kat Keeper's career at VirtualEyes finally came while she was on a series of roadshow presentations for potential customers. The duller the audience, the bleaker the venue, the more energy she somehow pulled from the experience. She spoke with a powerful kind of enthusiasm, her words unstoppable.

Some of her demos went perfectly. The faked data seemed real. She would train a camera on a member of her audience, and behind the scenes her assistant, Jenny49, would view the live feed, look up their background, and push out a display of facts about them. Her hands were fast and the lag time minimal. Prospective clients were enchanted with the power of VirtualEyes.

Amazingly accurate, they chirped. And the technology is based on bees?

"Yes," came back Kat, "we have analyzed the structure of the bee mind to understand how it identifies others in the hive. Since bees don't have the level of consciousness humans do, the processing speed is faster, because there is less complexity to deal with." Or sometimes she said something completely different. It didn't matter what she said as long as the potential clients believed it.

The last presentation she did before the authorities caught up with her did not go well. It was for the Southern Domain Border Authority. Settling into a large, glassed-in conference room, the Border Authority team leader wanted to see how VirtualEyes would identify people with criminal tendencies who wanted to breach the border. *First make the sale,* she told herself, *then clean up their moral mess. Once I am on the inside, I will fix this.*

Kat had high hopes for this presentation. She had driven her scientists hard to train VirtualEyes to match up people who had a criminal record, or who were likely to have one based on where they lived, with a database of images of faces captured on public video surveillance cameras. The algorithm her scientists used had nothing to do with bees, of course; that was just marketing talk. It seemed like the demonstration would work, though, and Kat was pumped.

She pulled up a database and gestured the commands to have VirtualEyes identify anyone who would be likely to commit a crime. In the next room, her assistant Jenny49 fed the results to her terminal. The results coming through showed only people of color.

The team leader of the Southern Domain Border Authority was Black. Seeing the series of stormy emotions moving across his face, Kat didn't try again. Instead, she explained how VirtualEyes was a work in progress. Sometimes the results seemed racist, but they weren't really; it was just bad training data that the machine was trying to interpret. It was a gigantic task, she explained, to fill it with video taken from surveillance cameras, like those present in every city in every domain.

As she kept talking, she saw the blurred figures of two men waiting outside the frosted glass conference room door. Kat knew who they were; Jenny49 had pinged her about them. They were from the Committees.

Lise45 and Don had been telling their story. The men from the Committees were there to question Kat Keeper about her business. She'd been avoiding them, ignoring their pings, ducking away when she saw them approaching on the airway. Childish, really; she knew she couldn't hide for long. Now they were waiting for her to finish this presentation that was going badly.

She talked faster and faster about the benefits of VirtualEyes and the challenges of making a flawless facial recognition system. "We're going to make a system for you that gets better every day and keeps our borders safe from outsiders." The reps from the Border Authority nodded along, seemingly convinced, even though they picked up on the jitter in her eyes, the distracted look when Jenny49 pinged her again.

Now it was too late. The door opened and the investigators from the Committees came in.

"You've been avoiding us, Ms. Keeper."

Kat smiled. "Nobody calls me Ms. Keeper. Call me Kat."

Because she was famous, they detained her for just a few hours. Just to make a point. Detention wasn't the worst of it, anyway. The worst would come later, when her investors forced her out. She could still hold her head high after her detention.

As soon as she was released, she pinged Jenny49 and called for an all-hands-on-deck meeting. With the scent of detention still trailing her, she walked into the company auditorium.

Her employees' faces turned to track her entrance. The room was quiet; she could hear the hum of the air handlers. Her breath was even and slow. She gestured and the anti-grav podium floated over to position itself in front of her at waist level. She needed something to lean on so this was good. She began to speak in a low, firm voice.

"This is a formative time for our company. Let's talk about the good. The human value of flawless facial biometrics." She paused and looked into the eyes of Jenny49, seated in the front. She scanned the back row and noted everyone's attention. "The facial biometrics offered by VirtualEyes will get you paid on time." A ripple of laughter ran through the room. "You will enter your pod safely, so important for women especially, if you are alone and don't feel safe. Our product delivers that safety. No more fraud. No more mistaken identity. No more wrongful convictions. Justice will be served. Our Emotion Analytics Engine means that you will never again be served an inappropriate ad. Your feeds will be perfectly cued to your mood. When you are sad and need help, we will help by delivering the good news you need."

The applause flowed over her.

"Yes, yes, we can do this!" She raised her hands to quiet them down. "VirtualEyes will be the universal solution to all facial biometrics."

Her employees seemed satisfied, but then one of them asked a question about her detention. Soon there were more questions. She realized that she was wearing the same clothes as yesterday. If they were close, they would have seen the hollowness in her eyes, but they were not close, so she made her voice ring out.

Kat remembered that whenever she told the story of her unravelling to Dave, he wanted her to stop. "You don't have to put yourself through that."

Kat would always sigh in response. She needed to tell the story to purge it from her being. This was Hopper00's belief. She knew he was right. *Speak the story, and it will be pushed out of your body.* She wasn't sure if he had said this exactly, but he could have, and Kat desperately wanted it to be true.

"You were at the height of your power," Dave always said when she finished the story about her end days at VirtualEyes. "You inspired everyone with that final speech, the one you made after they detained you. You were powerful and clear. You always had a vision for the company, Kat. That's what I admired about you."

"You did?"

"I did. It was what attracted me to you that first time."

"No." She smiled.

"Yes, in the coffee shop. You were a woman on a mission. Your clarity was like a bell. You rang me over to you. I couldn't resist."

"Stop it." She was laughing now. "*Rang me over.* That's ridiculous."

"Power and grace. An irresistible combination!" He had her laughing again and this made him so happy.

Hopper00 interrupted her memories again. "Tell me about when Dave was dying."

Kat looked at him. "You're not going to put that in. You can't."

"Why not? It's part of the story. It has to be told."

Kat squirmed. "You already agreed to leave out the worst of VirtualEyes. But Dave ... it's going to make me look like a monster."

"It will make you look compassionate," Hopper00 said.

Kat protested. "Obviously you don't know the whole story. No one does." She tried to gather her objections. "This is all who I *was*. I'm nothing like this now. It's just not me anymore."

"Right, and I said that speaking these stories to me will purge them from your body. Kat"—he leaned forward and fixed her in his gaze—"you can't carry this pain around anymore."

He had seen into her again and stated what might release her pain, and she couldn't argue with him when he looked at her like that. His voice spoke in her mind. *Try this mantra: I have shed that personality field and moved into another.*

She tried it and felt better. But she wasn't satisfied. "Your readers have to understand that after Dave died, I turned into a different person. But what if they don't?"

Hopper00 took a moment to capture her thoughts and consider what she needed to hear. "When people have the complete picture, they will draw the best conclusion." He watched her face relax. He didn't say that what he wrote wouldn't matter. The truth would come out, whether he wrote it up for the Feed or not. Everyone would put the pieces together anyway, and it wasn't the right time to tell her his real plans.

Once he was done with the Universal and it was released to the world, Dave became a rootless man of leisure. He tried hobbies like perfecting the perfect cup of coffee for Kat. When everyone switched to tea, he worked on perfecting the perfect cup of that. He fiddled with new programs but nothing had the emotional pull of the Universal.

Kat watched him from afar, but with little attention. Her all-consuming work with VirtualEyes, even as the company descended into ruin, pulled her away from Dave. Out of the corner of her eye, she watched Dave move from here to there in the Marin house, pursuing projects that he didn't finish. She did nothing to stop this behavior, as pointless and perhaps unhealthy as it appeared. He could take care of himself, she reasoned, and if she acknowledged what was happening, that would mean that she would have to slow down. And she couldn't be slowed down.

To outward appearances, Dave ticked along like a toy, cheerfully preparing meals, keeping the floating house tidy, even going below to repair a pontoon when necessary. The Universal performed flawlessly. Dave laid off the help desk team because they had nothing to do. After the Universal was out of beta, there was a release party, which Kat nearly missed. She forgot about it and arrived in a black dress an hour late.

Dave greeted her with a glass of real red wine and said, "I can forgive anything when you wear that dress. Wait, are you blushing?"

"I may be. I'm sorry to be late," Kat said. Dave nodded, smiled, and whisked her away to introduce her all around. He was just happy that she was there. Nobody on the Universal team had ever met or even seen Kat in person, though of course they had heard about her from the Feed.

"So this is the mystery wife," someone said, trying to be funny. "We were beginning to think he made you up."

"She's real, she's quite real!" Dave was proud to show her off, his wife, this woman he had married in a quiet civil ceremony over at the District Offices, who was stylish, smart, and wealthy, even though she had been committing marriage malpractice every day. She'd missed all Universal events up until the launch—the pre-launch, the company low-orbitals—indeed, every Universal event that ever occurred but this one. She made light conversation with everyone and behaved like a champ. She told Dave she was proud of him, though she noted that there clung to him a light mist of sadness, like a cloud come to Earth. It moved with him. She sensed that his sadness had nothing to do with her arriving late or missing the other events. It was something else.

The turning point arrived one night when she came home at her usual hour, 9 PM. Nothing seemed amiss at first. It was late to be getting home from work for a reasonable person, but not for her. She sensed an emptiness about the floating house. It was quiet enough to hear the water beneath her feet. She realized what was missing: no sounds in the kitchen. Usually Dave would be making dinner. There would be clatter.

She saw the kitchen was empty. She noticed other spaces in the floating house were dark. The spot where Dave liked to read—dark. The window that looked out over the rising sea—blast curtains closed.

"Dave?" Her voice sounded small in the enormous space.

He was upstairs. Sitting in the dark. There was a strange appliance connected to him, a tube running into his arms. His face was softly illuminated by blinking green lights.

"Dave?"

"Hello, Kat. Sorry for the lighting in here. It's good that they are green," he said. "The lights."

"What? Dave, what's happening?"

"The lights. They are green now. That's good."

She moved quickly to him and grasped his hand. He looked at her with deep eyes.

He said, "I'm going to die."

"No," was all she could say.

"So it was cancer? That's when you first learned about it?" Hopper00 asked, holding his notebook in one hand and pencil in the other.

"Yes," Kat whispered.

"It was cancer," Hopper00 confirmed solemnly. He knew this as a fact, but he needed her to tell him so that she could purge the sadness from her body.

"Yes," she said a little louder. "It was cancer." Throat cancer. He would soon lose the power of speech.

"Your mother died of cancer."

"Yes." *Mom was lung cancer. Dave was throat cancer.* Hopper00 was looking at her expectantly, waiting for her to say more. But what was there to say?

The Universal had drained Dave's substance. After he was done with the Universal, it was done with him and he was done with life. He had taken everything the world had to say and put it into the app.

PART 006

Chapter 031

There were times, aboard the ship, when you needed to drink your beer in a weighted container so it wouldn't float away. It depended where you were, on what deck, and if the artificial gravity was working properly. For the moment, Bradley enjoyed the cool feel of the weighted container against his hand. "Kat can't drink," he said.

"Not like I can." Alon6 was also enjoying a beer encased in a weighted container. Bradley and Alon6 didn't need the containers to be weighted at this moment; the artificial gravity was working just fine. But the weighted containers were fun. They made them feel like real space travelers. "That Jenny Johnson hypnosis program really messed Kat up," Alon6 added.

"Jenna Johnson," Bradley corrected.

"What?" Alon6 belched. The gas that came out of his own mouth didn't smell like beer. That was strange. It smelled like nothing. More space weirdness. Or maybe the air handlers sucked it up.

"Her name was Jenna Johnson."

"Whatever. It was genius. It turned Kat upside-down. Just how we want her."
Bradley nodded.

The lighting was dim in the ship's primary lounge. Outside its round windows, the stars seemed to stand still even as the ship moved. Alon6 didn't see the need for filling the food storage units with food. He filled them with beer. On the interior hull, he hung signifiers of their time together at Uni. His diploma. Some awards for coding that Bradley had won. Even their old bow hunting setups, the arrow points gleaming and the bow strings still tight with power. "If there are any deer to hunt on Mars, we'll be ready," he said absurdly.

Bradley winced out of habit, but it didn't really matter. All of Alon6's jokes were bad. Their lounge was frozen in time, a Uni hangout combined with an executive suite. There was a large screen showing a live feed of a Resistance circle with Kat in charge of it. She was talking about when the holo of Bradley visited her, her voice rising.

Alon6 gulped his beer and watched. He found it entertaining. "A nice touch, that holo. Now she doubts everything."

"That was your idea," Bradley said. "Sometimes you have a good one."

Alon6 grunted. He gestured to lower the volume as Kat's voice turned strident. She was really worked up about that holo.

Bradley sipped his beer. "Sanchez did an amazing job. The devices are undetected."

All was good. MIND had an abundance of business. It was surprisingly easy to manage the company from space. To show off a little, Bradley swiped open another screen showing their current deals. For the border patrol, they were tracking the thoughts of immigrants, keeping the Southwestern Domain safe. They had a predictive policing deal in place for the Northeast Domain government. The police bots there knew about any trouble before it began. They had food supply chain logistics locked down in the remote Midwest Domain. MIND knew what crops were ready for harvest and when to send them to the markets for purchase.

"Yeah." Alon6 gestured to the screen. "Control the supply chain and you keep people in line. Stop food going to districts we don't like. Make those people get hungry until they do what we want them to do."

Bradley flicked a glance at him, not sure how to respond. Alon6 said things for effect sometimes, making him sound meaner than he was. The remote districts had few people. Gatherings were rare. It was lonely out there, he'd heard, and there were rumors that some of them were losing the power of speech because they had no one to talk to. Bradley thought they were more to be pitied than threatened.

Alon6 didn't think like that. "We're on top now, old friend. The enforcement bots that detained you? They are now directed by MIND." He laughed at the irony and then pointed at the large screen. "That's what's her name."

Bradley nodded. "Ravven Vaara."

She looked like some kind of goddess with her all-seeing gaze, dressed in white clothing trimmed in gold. Looking at Kat and Ravven on the same screen made him blush.

"What are you smiling about?"

"Protecting civilization makes me smile," Bradley said.

"You weren't smiling about that. You're looking at Ravven and Kat together and you're smiling about what a lucky bastard you are."

He wasn't. He was smiling about Ravven Vaara's real name, Riva Nowakowski. She gave herself the name Ravven Vaara when she decided to reinvent herself as a trendy yoga teacher. But he said nothing of it to Alon6. "I was thinking that MIND gives our clients a connected worldview. Data science is democracy."

Alon6 smirked. "You're starting to believe your own bullshit. Try to remember that they both hate you now." A sour laugh bubbled out of Alon6 and he added a belch that smelled like beer.

In the meeting, on the screen, Claire8 was demonstrating a black oval device. Her eyes rotated independently, like a fish, and she was hard to watch, but Bradley caught a fragment of what she was saying. It sounded important. He gestured up the volume.

"Surveillance detection," Claire8's voice rang out. "This is the new system...."

"We have work to do," Alon6 interrupted, reaching for the screen.

Bradley blocked him. "Watch," he said. "Just for a couple minutes."

Claire8 made a sign with her hands over the oval device. It turned on. She seemed surprised when an indicator on it blinked red. She looked around, as if trying to see what the device was sensing. It produced a sound, repeated and harsh. It was the sound of a crow, a bird.

Bradley hadn't heard a bird in years, yet here was the sound of one coming from Claire8's device. On the first *caw*, Claire8's eyes widened. On the second *caw*, she made a sign over the black oval and a panel opened, showing a map of the pod with a blinking red indicator. On the fourth *caw*, Claire8 hurried over to the galley and pulled a small device from among the food units. It was silver, and blended in well. On the fifth *caw,* she held it up to the astonished group and then placed it on the floor and stomped on it with her foot.

The screen Bradley and Alon6 watched went dark.

"Fuck me," burst out of Alon6.

Bradley permitted himself a laugh. "Not bad."

"She killed the signal. What was that sound?" Alon6 had never heard a crow.

"The sound of a bird. It was called a crow. An alarm. We'll send Sanchez back in."

Three months ago, when Alon6 had first proposed the Mars adventure to Bradley, it sounded like a terrible idea. "Offworlders are crazy," was Bradley's response then. He knew little of the movement to settle Mars, and when Alon6 filled him in about the only homesteading expedition to make it all the way there, it sounded miserable. "It's 80 below, except when it's 200 above," Bradley pointed out. Earth was problematic, but Bradley wasn't ready to abandon it as his home. "It's a fixer-upper. But we can fix it." The domain had put climate controls in place and launched halfway decent carbon mitigation programs. They were baby steps, but humanity was still alive because of them.

Of course, Alon6's personality field was powerful, and he had other reasons for needing to leave Earth. He was stealing funds from MIND, moving them into an account for himself that was labeled, "Interplanetary Travel." He needed credits for a currency manipulation scheme he was hatching.

Alon6 opened a new screen. It showed a ship ready for launch. "Look at this beautiful ship." Alon6 poked a stubby index finger at the screen. "We're going to sell tickets at a million credits a pop and we're going to have no trouble selling them. People are ready to leave Earth. And by the time we are ready to fly, they will be *desperate* to leave."

Bradley eyed the sleek airship standing next to a spidery tower, with hoses like arms feeding chilled gasses into its fuel reservoirs.

"Traditional chilled liquid to reach escape velocity. Then we switch to fusion to speed the trip."

"Fusion doesn't work," Bradley said.

"My guys are making it work. We'll have a solar sail also. It's slow and safe, if you're worried."

"I'm not worried." Bradley wanted to appear strong. He was waiting for Alon6 to punch him in the shoulder in his jokey way.

Alon6 moved to the next screen. "Look at this campaign. It's a powerhouse. My publicity guys outdid themselves." There were mockups of the feed Alon6 intended to release.

NEW MISSION TO MARS. BRAVE COLONISTS.

He scrolled past phrases describing hope, a fresh start on Mars, a chance to depart their ruined home planet. a million credits for the journey of a lifetime.

It seemed crazy to Bradley. "We're a data company, Alon6."

"But don't you want to run your own fucking planet? Nobody has any laws out there yet."

"We're far outside Earth's gravity."

"Yes."

Data science is a kind of power.

"There will be nobody to stop us," Alon6 continued. "We will make life wonderful on Mars. It will be better than Earth ever was." He pointed to those very words on the screen, mocked up in a feed headline that he intended to propagate: BRINGING THE BEST OF EARTH TO MARS.

Alon6 punched Bradley on the shoulder, so swiftly that Bradley didn't have time to flinch out of the way. "Hey, old friend! How can you refuse? We'll be in charge of our own fucking planet!"

"And I'll continue my research," Bradley said.

"Yes, old friend. You will. There will be no regulators to stop you. No Committees."

"This is a crazy plan," Bradley said, even as he was warming to it. He liked Alon6's boldness. He imagined that it would be surprisingly easy to run the company from space. Sanchez would keep an eye on things around the office and could supervise the Input Men as they rolled out the Harvester project in other cities after New York, like Chicago, Atlanta, and Seattle. Bradley would send holos to Earth when he needed to communicate.

"Only the brave and the rich will join us."

Gather the very rich and rule over them. That was Alon6's plan. Everything was already in motion. Bradley only had to go along with it. And he did, because he valued his research above all. He had his own plan to develop knowledge around machine intelligence. "The pursuit of knowledge is expensive," he said.

"Sure, whatever you want," said Alon6. Whatever Bradley wanted, as long as he kept developing MIND and Alon6's secret projects were thriving.

Bradley swiped back to the scene of the Resistance meeting, but the screen was still black, of course. He would have Sanchez deploy the bug-sized drone tomorrow. Maybe sooner.

Bradley itched to tap the big screen and zoom in to Kat's mouth and watch it move. She would be animated. There would be a light in her eyes. He liked to watch her.

Chapter 032

Kat was troubled. She was certain Sanchez was not in New York, but his presence somehow was. She felt an essence of Sanchez. She remembered him on the rooftop garden, watching her speak with Cressida Scopes. That same day, Sanchez had been testing the Harvester prototype with Bradley. Sanchez was also in Bradley's office when she called Bradley a liar and made him erase the recordings of her thoughts. It made no sense that Kat felt Sanchez's presence. He should be back in El Segundo. She sensed him here though, out on the edge of her vision, but attributed it to the stress of her days.

She didn't want any Sanchez visions, especially not today—today everything had to go perfectly. After much debate, the circle was moving its action to a new level. The Resistance was preparing its first external demonstrations, starting with shutting down the Skyway, a spindly airway of concrete and steel suspended over the old Westside Highway. The Skyway was packed with pedestrians every day. It was the primary artery to reach the Upper Hudson Market. They'd chosen a Wednesday because midweek was the busiest time for pedestrian traffic.

"If we shut it down," Kat had told the women in the circle, "everyone will know who we are."

"And what we want," Ravven added.

They started by moving women into place—six at one end of the Skyway, six at the other, twelve in the middle—adding more as they arrived. Other womens' circles had joined Kat and Ravven's circle for the action, and all had bac-masks in case the Skyway was crowded, and protective glasses to guard against sun exposure. They wore light jackets, most silver, some light gray, as additional sun protection. Their protest signs, which read BAN THOUGHT HARVESTING and MIND IS A MIND FUCKER, were rolled in their sleeves, out of sight of the enforcement bots.

There were already a few bots cruising around, clearly curious. Kat reminded herself not to attribute human qualities to them. They were not curious. They were using their sensors, gathering information, and pooling it amongst themselves. The bots were circular and a squat twelve inches in diameter, four inches high. Their silent presence added urgency.

More women arrived, and Kat directed them, at times with hand signals, other times with thoughts. Ravven was doing the same at the other end of the Skyway. Claire8 was in the middle. Kat sent Emily off to the side because she'd been depressed all morning, and she didn't want her to bring down the group.

Emily came to her now, Amber tagging along, both of their eyes aimed to the ground as though afraid to look up. Emily mumbled, "I'm feeling something."

Kat tried to keep her voice gentle. "What is it?"

"I don't know. I'm not sure." She glanced at Amber.

Please don't use the whiny voice, thought Kat. She couldn't stop herself.

"I heard that," Emily said.

"So did I," Amber said.

"I know you did. That's why I thought it."

There is something, thought Emily.

Can you get a read on it? Kat asked silently.

No. Not yet.

Okay. Keep trying. She sent Emily and Amber off the Skyway to keep watch. The two of them could get false signals, especially when working together—especially when moody. They fed off each other. But when Emily was right, she was the best early warning system they had, better than anything Claire8 had made.

At the moment, Claire8 was fiddling with the oval warning disk she'd designed. If they heard the call of the crow, that meant there was trouble. She had a consciousness alarm activated as well, to sense the presence of Harvesters. Her face was colored pink by its all-clear signal on her comms. She wasn't getting any readings.

Kat scanned the area again. The morning crowd was getting thicker. Two men and a woman were looking at their comms. The usual. She would wait one minute and then give the order.

"How do you know this will work?" Alon6's voice was quiet in the ship's lounge, barely clearing the *thrum* of its artificial gravity. While in flight, he and Bradley were watching the scene develop on the Skyway.

Bradley didn't take his eyes off the screen. "Look at who we have already checking their comms. This one, this one, this one." His finger stabbed in succession at bright points on the screen. A man, another man, a woman. "Those are our people."

"What do you mean, 'our people'?"

"They're working for us. Short-term contractors."

"What are these points?" Alon6 asked. "Wait, don't tell me. His fingers poked at the bright points of light on the screen. "Kat, Ravven, the others."

"That's right. All the members of the Resistance." Bradley gestured, and the screen updated to position their names below the bright points representing each person. Kat, Ravven, Claire8, Emily and Amber, Ruusu, Cassandra, Dextra, Aline, and Afra. There were more; since Bradley didn't know their names they remained bright points without labels. "Sanchez is down below, off the Skyway, because Emily is trying to read him."

"She already said she was reading him with that other girl, Amber," Alon6 said.

"They were, but they didn't know what they were getting."

"What about Claire8?" Alon6 stabbed his thick finger at a data point. It expanded to show a glitchy image of Claire8 squinting at her black oval.

Bradley laughed. "We will stay out of her way." Like Emily and Amber, Claire8 wasn't getting a clear signal.

Bradley moved his hand over his control board. He was running a jamming signal and made it stronger with the gesture. Claire8 leaned closer to her oval, squinting. "That will make it a little more difficult for her."

Kat gave the order to deploy. Emily was below, alone on the access ramp, because Amber had decided she wanted to stay with the group. The women of the Resistance pulled out their signs and unfurled them. They stood close together, blocking the Skyway. A crowd of pedestrians clotted behind them. Their protest was already effective. The Resistance circle started to chant aloud, "One, two, three, four, thought harvesting has got to go!"

Emily turned and looked up, her eyes wide. She saw a man, another man, and a woman on the Skyway, aiming their comms at the Resistance group. She didn't know what was going on, but their action triggered something. She cried out, realized she was too far away; she didn't have a clear sightline and couldn't communicate via thought.

Claire8 was also alerted. She was getting a reading on the device, but didn't know what it was until it was too late.

The enforcement bots were efficient. They gathered quickly on the Skyway, in large numbers. As each bot approached a member of the Resistance, a cavity opened in the bot's interior, and a length of flexible pipe shot out.

The pipe easily wrapped around Kat's legs and tightened. She toppled over. The bots deployed a second tube around her wrists, immobilizing her.

In less than a minute, they completed retinal scans and the booking procedures for Kat and the other members of the Resistance.

Alon6 sat back in his chair, amazed at what he had witnessed on the screen. The protesters were going down one after the other, swarmed by bots. "Are those..."—he squinted at the screen—"...our restraint systems?"

"Closed the deal for them with the subcontractor last week," Bradley said. He stood taller and pride made his voice richer.

"How did you get all the bots there right when we needed them?"

Bradley jabbed at the screen, indicating a man, then another, then a woman. "Here, here, and here. Our people alerted the enforcement bots. The bots used the restraint systems that we sold to the district."

Alon6 let out a breath that meant he was impressed. "Digital informants. I like how you've thought this through,"

"Yes, if there weren't enough bots on the Skyway to do the job, I was prepared to have our people network with other folks working for us on the ground, to call even more bots. But this worked out perfectly. We had the right ratio of bots to protestors." Bradley let a smile escape. "Can't let the Resistance trash talk us on the Feed and then block up the Skyway." Then he added, "One thing. There could be an audit, if the dom wonders how their enforcement bots could really be *that* efficient." He gestured to his controls. On the screen, the people who had called in the bots were looking at their comms in puzzlement.

"What's going on?" Alon6 asked.

"I'm disappearing our app from their devices. Wiping unneeded information," Bradley answered. "Just to be sure, I'm also erasing our employment records with them. They will have no connection with MIND, except in their own memory, and what good will that be, without a concurring record on comms?"

Alon6 nodded. "Naked memory is worth shit."

A small crowd of citizens gathered on the Skyway to watch the bots read out the charges and begin to move the protestors away. It was good entertainment for a weekday morning.

When the trouble started, and it was clear that there were going to be mass arrests, at first Emily wanted to run as fast as she could. But loyalty made her wait. She wondered if she should try to help. She saw Amber restrained by the bots, and Kat restrained, falling to the surface of the Skyway. Emily watched, eyes wide, as the bots quickly gathered up the others. There was nothing left to do. She ran away.

She ended up almost in the water, among the pontoons. The air carried the cries of her Resistance colleagues as they called out in surprise and pain. Emily covered her ears. It hurt her, but there was nothing she could do. It had all happened too fast.

Emily slowed her breathing and tried to think. Scrambling farther down toward the brown waters heaving with trash, she boarded the first vaporetto she could find. It was one of the robotic ones with no human operator. She had a plan, not fully formed, about somehow posting bail.

"Downtown," she said. She didn't want to attract attention, and hoped the vaporetto bot was not hooked into the detention system and would simply follow her one-word instruction. To get the ride, she had to submit to a retinal scan for billing ID. She waited for the bot to recognize her, group her with the protestors, and also call in an enforcement bot to arrest her. But nothing happened. Maybe the network hadn't updated yet. For the moment, she believed she was safe.

Then she noticed a tall figure standing alone on the Skyway. It was a man, in silhouette, with the strong sun at his back. Emily shielded her eyes, trying to get a better view.

Sanchez smiled down at her. He sent out a ping on his comms. It would take a day to get to the ship, but Bradley and Alon6 were expecting his report. His message was brief. It said, *It is a good day for MIND.*

It was a good day for MIND, Bradley agreed later, when he saw the ping. He should feel happy, yet he had a bad feeling in his ear that was developing into an unexplained earache, a low throb. He told himself, *I'm fine, I'm fine.*

To all outward appearances, he *was* fine. His screens glowed before him. His team continued to message him. The ship's artificial gravity was flawless. The onboard lighting system ensured that his circadian rhythms were right on. Day remained day and night remained night.

He stabbed a gesture at the console, bringing up generic palm trees and the ocean to cover the blackness outside, then changed his mind and stabbed again, bringing up the view outside his old office in El Segundo. He supposed that meant he was homesick or restless. Maybe he missed the place. He thought about Nora2 and how she kept things running smoothly back there. He wondered if he would ever get back to his palatial retreat in the New Zealand domain. But these were not the thoughts to have now, so he forced himself to stop thinking them.

His eyes rested on the screens without seeing them. He flipped through the reports from his teams, tweaked some code that a junior member had submitted, pressed for faster results from his senior staff. He opened a new project that Alon6 wanted him to pursue, one that would not be allowed if they were still on Earth. Bradley saw its value, he just didn't like that pursuing it took him so far beyond Earthly law.

Really, he rationalized, it wasn't like it hadn't been tried before. The protocol was active in South Korea. For decades, the government had analyzed footage from street cameras and mapped it to smartphone location data and credit card purchase records. Not only did it work well for contract-tracing the movements of infected people during a pandemic, but it was also great for tracking political activists, immigrants. Securing borders.

Surveillance partnerships blossomed between government and private contractors. Mobile comms units, once called smartphones, were always the best for this. Citizens were used to carrying them and easily made the transition to wearables like chips embedded in clothing, smart glasses tied into the web, and even mods. All of that was fashionable in South Korea, which had merged with North Korea to become just Korea—one of the few states that kept its name and didn't break up into domains like so many of the others.

Bradley smiled. *What humans are willing to do if they can be convinced it will make their lives easier.*

In the place formerly known as Israel, the security agency called Mossad used software designed for counterterrorism operations to analyze all citizens' mobile comms data. This analysis made it easy for Mossad, which also controlled the dom, to use an individual's mobile geolocation data in any way it chose. The initial use case was to use the geolocation data to track and confine infected people who moved around too much during pandemics. It was a small jump to use the same geolocation data to track and confine activists who spoke out against the dom. The Mossad made a series of small jumps, like moving a pawn a single square at a time on a chessboard. Software developed to protect the state was eventually used by the state against its own citizens.

This was just the way things worked. It was the way governance worked. Bradley knew there was nothing that he could do about it. So, he reasoned, what Alon6 wanted to do was also a small jump. And it was also for the good of all.

Even better, Alon6 explained, they weren't the government imposing anything on people. "We're a private company."

Bradley nodded.

"You ever hear of songbun?"

Bradley hadn't. Alon6 was always surprising him, because he liked to look things up on the Feed. Most of his jokes were bad, but not everything he said was half-baked.

"Let me tell you about it," he said, and started describing a Korean classification system. Every citizen in Korea is assigned a classification that they don't know about. "It's secret from them, their songbun classification. There are three major categories: loyal, wavering, and hostile. There are fifty-one sub-categories. All dedicated to the government figuring out who the friendlies are." Songbun set a person's opportunities at birth, depending on what their parents or even their grandparents did at the country's founding.

"Police state," put in Bradley.

Alon6 reminded him that many things were assigned to citizens at birth, like the unique number-letter string of their comms unit. "But yes," Alon6 agreed, "it is true that governments are evil."

"But we're not the government."

"Exactly. We're a corp. We don't impose anything on people they don't want. But we can take a lesson from this system."

Alon6 loved systems, and his tone was joyful as he explained how songbun worked. Most Koreans would never know what their songbun category was, but it shaped their entire life. It was possible to guess your category, based on where you lived, how you spent your money, what your ancestors did, but a guess was only a suspicion. You would never know how the state apparatus subjected you to discrimination, blocked you from getting a job, denied you a lease on an apartment, or a loan. This made finance efficient. No one got a loan who didn't deserve one. Everyone had the right job for them.

Most of the democracies had collapsed or fragmented into doms. Korea, strong from within, with its blend of the former North and South, was one of the few intact states left. In the former South Korea, they knew how to apply force democratically. In the former North Korea, they just applied force. But it worked.

For completely different reasons, the Free State of Scotland was also an intact state. "But that's another story," Alon6 said as he finished up his story of songbun and its drawbacks, but more importantly its successes.

He wanted Bradley to make a classification system like songbun, one that used the data songbun used, but added thoughts brought in by their Harvesters.

This new project took up Bradley's days and stretched into his nights. It occupied his entire being, because it was an incredible challenge. It wasn't a government system. It was private; it was theirs. It could be licensed out to whomever they chose—and they would choose carefully and morally. They would impose it on no one; people would accept it by their own choice. Not like a government that wanted to preserve the power of its corrupt leaders, but with compassion, efficiency, and clarity.

Bradley was excited by the utopian vision. And he had always loved transforming raw information into data that MIND could use to generate more wisdom in the world.

There was just one thing. According to Earthly law, this challenging and worthwhile project was illegal. The Committees were already looking into Bradley's work. He had been pinged about it already. This was pro forma stuff, he knew. They wouldn't be able to do much to stop him, because the ship was already outside Earthly law, and as soon as it entered Mars' gravitational field, it would be subject to Martian law. Since there was no Martian law, at least not yet, that cleared the problem up nicely.

Alon6 was a little sloppy, though. When talking up the idea to potential clients, he got ahead of himself about how truly ready to deploy they were. The clients were excited about profiling customers based on their ethnic background, language, the thoughts they were thinking, and the thoughts they intended to think. It was a dream scenario for them. They were ready to execute licenses, even though the program wasn't ready. Still, it was a good business position for MIND to be in.

Alon6 loved his grand schemes, but Bradley loved the research more. He loved the hunt for knowledge. It was what made him breathe.

He should have been happy, but he had to have a conversation with Alon6 about the project.

So he gestured with great energy at his comms, opening quite a few screens, and after a few tries, he found Alon6 in an unlikely place: on an extravehicular, suited up, clambering along the hull of the ship with an engineer.

Bradley tapped his console and the sound of their voices came up in the middle of an argument. Something about a clogged solar port. Something was stuck. Their progress was slow, Alon6 complained, and soon he was shouting that their solar sail was crap.

The engineer pushed back, showing Alon6 how to clear the solar port. They'd get more propulsion with that, he insisted.

Alon6 said it was time to turn on the fusion power. "We have to get there faster. It's long past time to activate." It seemed like this argument would go on forever, and Bradley couldn't speak with Alon6 while he was out there anyway. He had to get back to work, so he punched off the signal.

Bradley thought he knew why Alon6 was in a rush. A couple of days—well, artificial day cycles—ago, he was listening in as Alon6 pitched the songbun project to new clients. MIND, he explained, can segment and categorize people by their genetic makeup. "We're ahead of the swerve," he boasted to his rapt clients on the vid. He probably wanted to say *curve*, but his enthusiasm worked just fine and they had shoveled another billion credits into the operation by the time he clicked off the call.

After that happened, he noticed Bradley watching, and read the disapproval coming off him like a fine mist. Alon6 hated disapproval, even a fine mist of it, and he went on the attack, pushing in on the smaller man. "What the fuck is wrong with you? This is *money*."

Bradley took an involuntary step back. "The Committees are looking into this. The district is going to launch ships after us."

That made Alon6 laugh. "We'll get to Mars sooner than they can call the first meeting. Sit the fuck down." He pushed Bradley down hard enough to make him sit in a chair.

Bradley thought about snapping back, but it didn't make much sense when Alon6 got like this, so he didn't look up from the console as he answered. "The thing you're pitching so hard, it's not even ready. Not even close." He gestured at a control surface with nervous energy, causing a screen to expand and contract repeatedly.

"Shut up and code," Alon6 said. Then he realized his partner wasn't meeting his eye and his bullying wasn't having the motivating effect that he wanted. "You can do it," he tried. "I'm not giving up on you."

"You can clear the room now," Bradley said, finding some backbone. "I'm getting back to work."

Alon6 summoned a crooked smile and left.

Bradley wanted to get back to work, but he wasn't up to it. The spidery green lines of code kept wandering away from him. He amused himself by blipping from one security camera's footage to another. The mess hall. It was empty now. The engine room. It would be warm in there. The lounge. Just a few crew members staring at comms. The sleep bays. Passengers resting in the dark.

For all of Alon6's bluster, Bradley knew he was uncertain about their fate. This was proven by the extravehicular. There was no sense in doing something both dangerous *and* unnecessary like that. Bradley wasn't a pro at space flight, but he knew a little, and you didn't take chances when you didn't need to.

He got tired of flipping the live cameras around and decided he would waste time better by looking at the security recordings. He wanted to see the rest of the EV now. He left off watching it as Alon6 and the engineer were arguing with each other about switching off the solar and activating the fusion drive. The engineer wanted solar. The fusion was untested, he argued. Since the beginning, Alon6 had forced fusion on the team. None of the engineers wanted it on a commercial flight, though it had been approved for some military missions.

Bradley watched on the recording as Alon6 escalated his argument with the engineer, the engineer pushing back with words, until Alon6 countered by physically pushing the man off the smooth polished metal arc of the hull. He played out the engineer's umbilical line. The engineer protested, squawks of fear coming through the comms channel.

Bradley leaned in. He couldn't believe what he was seeing. Alon6 was tugging at the mooring of the umbilical. Something anchored it, so he pulled out a tool from a pouch in his suit, used it to open a hatch, pressed a red button inside with the words STAY CLEAR written large, and pulled the umbilical line free.

The engineer's eyes were huge. When he spoke quickly and loudly, judging from the condensation and ice crystals already forming on his face shield, he was pleading for his life. There was no sound. He was disconnected from comms.

Alon6 flung the end of the umbilical line away from him. It arched gracefully, forming a curve that straightened out as the engineer drifted away. Soon the engineer would be a speck in the blackness. Soon after that he would be dead.

When Alon6 turned away from this evil task, the hull-mounted camera caught his expression. No fear. No smile of satisfaction. No emotion at all. It was just a job that needed doing. Bradley imagined that Alon6 was already on the next step, considering how he would erase the recordings, falsify the records, and cover it up.

Bradley gestured off the recording and sat staring at the screen. *Murder.* He raced through all the memories he could access, seeking a sign from Alon6, a tell that he had murdered an engineer earlier in the day. There was nothing. After it happened, Alon6 had apparently gone about his business, convincing investors to back MIND, pressing Bradley to keep coding. Business as usual.

Bradley gestured open the logs and saw that the incident had been recorded as an accident. So Alon6 had already seen to that. The records were already cleaned up. Bradley felt discomfort but wasn't sure how to label it. He tried to let it go.

He then debated whether to make his own copy of the video. Alon6 would be alerted if he did that, so he decided it would be better to leave it on the system until Alon6 realized it was there and deleted it, probably claiming a camera malfunction to cover up its absence.

Bradley let out a breath. He knew Alon6 was cruel, but this went beyond.

But he didn't have much time to think about it. He was startled by a powerful rumble emanating from the depths of the ship. Something in its bowels turned on. Bradley noticed a new indicator light on the console.

The fusion propulsion had been activated. He felt no difference now, but knew the ship was speeding toward Mars much faster than before.

Bradley found Alon6 on the ship's navigation deck. The pilot wasn't there. It was just Alon6 by himself, and he didn't notice Bradley standing in the entry portal. Bradley could see that Alon6 was working in the vid module, probably erasing the incriminating footage. The machines chirped at the task. It was quiet enough to hear the air handlers whirring.

At that moment, Alon6 turned around and saw him. His eyes widened in surprise, but quickly returned to normal. He pretended that he expected to see Bradley standing in the portal. He said, "There's something I need to tell you."

The pilot came on to the nav deck just then, to check their course and reset the autopilot.

"Come on, let's take a walk," Alon6 said in a cheery tone, and he led Bradley back toward their lounge, where their bow hunting gear hung on the hull, commemorating their old days together at Uni. Using that gear had been the last time Bradley saw Alon6 kill anything, as he pulled back the shaft of the steel arrow notched into the powerful bow and let go. Bradley heard again the dull sound of the arrow going into the deer's flesh. He saw again the empty look in the deer's eyes, like the empty look in the engineer's eyes as he floated away.

As these overlapping memories consumed Bradley, Alon6 confessed about the fusion drive being on. Then, hardly pausing for breath, Alon6 began to explain the reason he was in such a hurry and needed the fusion drive. He had put a plan in motion and it involved going to Mumbai.

Chapter 033

Alon6's father was born in Mumbai, his mother in St. Louis. Viktor and Debra Sal were actors who met while making a movie near the Los Angeles Port City. Between them, they went on to make hundreds of movies—romances, historical dramas, musicals—and became beloved fixtures of the silver screen.

Then they stepped away from the cameras and deployed holos to continue their acting careers. Their fans hardly noticed, since movies were 3D anyway. Their most recent release featured Alon6's mother, Debra, as Joan of Arc and his father, Viktor, as a combination King Lear and aging Elvis Presley. It was a historical drama with comic undertones.

Viktor had guided the family to choose Mumbai as their home. There was a family residence there, bought by Viktor's grandparents. The movie business thrived in Mumbai even more robustly than in the Los Angeles Port City. As their fame grew, Viktor and Debra bought other residences in New Zealand and one in New York.

Mumbai was their center, though. They were drawn to its restless energy. Although life there could be difficult, with the rising waters everywhere and displaced people, Viktor and Debra craved the humanity and connection that Mumbai offered and the other places lacked. Mumbai was grand, even overpowering, and making it their home was something of a paradox, because Viktor and Debra were gentle people.

Alon6 was a loyal son. He talked to them via comms every Sunday and visited once a year, making the trip on the intercontinental glidepath. It was a matter of conveying his respect. They created him, and they had accomplished so much in their lives. They were especially excited to see him this year, because he was coming in August, a month earlier than his usual visit. They beamed bright smiles at him over comms.

"There is so much rain now, I'm impressed that you want to come," his father said.

"I want to see you both," Alon6 responded. "I can't wait! And also, I want to see some rain. It never rains here anymore."

As he walked up the pathway to their building, Alon6 reflected on how lucky his parents were. They had their love, their city, their home, and successful movie careers. The pathway, suspended above the waters, was sturdy, hardly vibrating at all. The air was hot and heavy and looked like it would burst with rain soon.

The pathway delivered Alon6 to an elevator, which took him to the entrance to their home, on the second floor. The building was glass, changing to meet the weather. It tinted dark to block punishing sun, but now was a transparent golden color because it was cloudy. As he moved his comms to the door for entry, the first drops of rain began to fall.

The elevator door opened. His parents were small, attractive people, with musical voices and an abundance of charm. Their work had made them rich and together their personality fields radiated graciousness. They stood side by side with identical expressions of beatitude. Their only son was home. With a simultaneous gesture, they opened their arms wide to receive him.

Debra's intellectual prowess was well known in the business. She often rewrote the scripts she was given when the role was thin. She loved show business, but when her son was in town, food was her medium of expression.

So they did what they always did when he came. They made a meal. Debra chattered happily about the fresh vegetables available in the market. Viktor knew the family who grew the best hydroponics in Mumbai. The city's anti-pollution domes were holding up well for twenty-year-old constructions. The populace was healthy and as happy as could be expected. Rain pattered down and then slashed heavily at the large glass walls of their residence.

Alon6 nodded along to their chatter. He liked to see his parents happy. And they, despite all their career accomplishments, lived to see him happy.

He bathed in the warm light and sound of their happiness. He offered them smiles and helped with the cooking. He would sit with them to eat the meal and compliment his mother on her cooking.

But his mind was elsewhere, calculating. He was there to see them, but he had come early to hatch a scheme. There was never enough money in the world for Alon6.

To conceal his intent, he doted on his parents as much as they doted on him, and at lunch the next day, shared stories of his business triumphs with Bradley and MIND.

"You and Bradley are a good team," Viktor said. His parents knew that Bradley was modded, of course, but they never talked about it, believing it would be rude. Every time they saw Alon6, they secretly congratulated themselves for having had the modding done on their son, having had the money to do it. They wanted the best for him in a competitive world and that included buying him a really good mod. Still, Viktor felt his son did not give Bradley enough credit for MIND's success.

"When you talk about MIND, Alon6, you speak of it as though it were your own. But he is your partner."

"He is."

"He deserves a few kind words, is all I'm saying," Viktor said. "He deserves recognition."

In his award acceptance speeches, of which there were many, Viktor always gave generous credit to the writers and directors and producers who created his movie entertainment properties. He only wanted his son to show the same graciousness.

"It's a good point," Alon6 conceded, to keep the peace.

"You'll take it into consideration?"

Alon6 nodded and put on his most pleasant expression. "I will."

Viktor pushed back his plate after another successful lunch. A servant quickly came by to clear it away. Alon6's parents were old-fashioned that way. They used no bots, but instead employed people.

"You're working on something, aren't you?" Viktor asked.

Debra gazed fondly at her cherished son, waiting for his answer.

Viktor prompted again, "What are you working on?"

Alon6 smiled privately, a smile meant for them but meaning much more to him. "You've been getting the credits I send?"

Viktor waved him away with a smile on his face. "We give it to charity." They didn't need more money when they had their son's love and royalties from their films.

The next day, Alon6's first meeting was with his developer in the old Renaissance Industrial Smart City. He knew the place well, having interned there many summers as a young student. He took the glidepath along the route of the former Maharashtra Samruddhi Mahamarg expressway and arrived in a few minutes. The rain had not yet started for the day. He felt providence was shining upon him.

Disembarking, he passed the scanners that logged his face, then entered the administration building. To confuse the trackers, he had booked himself on a tour. He told the sales agent he was interested in opening up a data farm. The sales agent believed him, greeting him enthusiastically and ushering him into a tour group.

"We're keeping the groups small these days, you understand. But it's more intimate!" The agent was cheerful, considering another pandemic was beginning in India. He provided old-style N95 masks for everyone on the tour. A few had containment suits.

After twenty minutes, Alon6 peeled off from the tour, saying he had to use the washroom. He never rejoined the tour, instead taking a corridor toward the back of the admin building, down a set of stairs everyone had forgotten about, and up through a short service tunnel that led into another building—all to elude the trackers. He ditched the provided N95 and put on a more efficient mask that used ultraviolet light to purify the air he breathed. Soon, he was face to face with his developer in a secure room.

Dr. Ahmed nodded hello. He wasn't a man for small talk. He was also wearing the more-efficient UV mask. This made sense, because he was its inventor. Ahmed pronounced his name in the traditional way, with a considerable force on the "h." He was a religious man, and they started by turning toward Mecca to pray. Alon6 was not religious, but he didn't want to put Ahmed ill at ease. He was a valuable person. Virus developers didn't come cheap.

"How's the work going?"

It was going well, Dr. Ahmed said. He would have a sample of COVID-50 ready for testing in about a week.

Alon6 was happy to end the meeting with Ahmed as soon as possible after receiving this good news. Dr. Ahmed took all available precautions. He was a careful man, always courteous and formal. Nevertheless, the place was death made visible with its rows of glass tubes teeming with deadly virus strains and UV purifiers poking from the walls, aimed to cook every horizontal surface. Overhead, HEPA units sucked the air into more filters and UV cookers.

Alon6 hurried out, down another service tunnel, up another forgotten set of stairs. Outside, a group of hovercraft operators at a stand clamored for his business. He selected one and boarded the craft.

"Bhiwandi. Warehouse hub."

The hovercraft driver nodded. The hub was a common destination from Renaissance Smart Industrial City. Much business was done along the corridor.

The driver accepted the old paper money. He wore gloves and an N95 mask, and didn't recognize the more advanced unit Alon6 wore on his face.

Alon6 looked out for security, but saw none. His next errand had to remain unrecorded by trackers. He settled back for the ride. It took forty-three minutes in the old days, before antigrav. This creaky old hovercraft wouldn't be much faster.

Aside from the rising water changing the old roadways to waterways, India seemed not to have changed much since his last visit. The men were outside, the women in the homes. The hovercraft were much older than what he was used to seeing. A few out-of-commission ones had been repurposed as rafts. He saw two decommissioned antigravity buses used as shelters. Children were everywhere, masked and unmasked. Enterprising young men who had once sold unlocked cell phones and SIM cards along the roadway now hawked crypto credits.

The deal Alon6 was working on involved crypto. He had always liked playing around with it, even from his days back in Uni. It may have been a feature of his Entrepreneurial Ideation mod, but he recognized that crypto was both the greatest wealth generator and wealth eliminator the world had ever known. Both directions were useful for his current project.

The ancient hovercraft took just forty minutes to get to the warehouse district. Alon6 told the driver to drop him off on the perimeter, much to his protestations; he felt he wasn't giving Alon6 full service. But Alon6 needed to make his warehouse appointments in private. Since this was a business district run by local officials who took bribes, the security cameras in place were disabled, their glass eyes covered with subtle pieces of cloth, a wire discreetly cut here and there. Alon6 could walk freely, provided he followed a route that he knew.

His first appointment was with a small, talkative man who was as busy pitching his product as he was showing Alon6 the manufacturing process. "No social distancing necessary when you buy an X91—the personal containment unit!" He held one up for Alon6 to admire. It was white, lightweight, made of a smooth mesh fabric, with boots at the bottom, and ending at the top with a helmet featuring a curved window. "Full life support in a portable package!"

Alon6 felt it too cruel to point out to the enthusiastic man that he was the owner of the process and the warehouse, and paid the man's salary. Instead, he let the man continue to believe that Alon6 was a mid-level sales agent checking on the progress of things. Anonymity was useful.

"Thank you, thank you. Good progress."

His next meeting was with his inflatable food company. When rationing hit and panic rose, Alon6 wanted his customers to have enough to eat. To stay healthy, they needed only to buy the pre-packaged, pre-cooked lumps of protein shot through with artificial vitamins that Alon6's purveyor was calling food. No one would know that Alon6 was the lead investor. There was a shell company to shield his name, and another set of names fronting the shell. Alon6 couldn't remember the product name it would be marketed by, but it didn't matter.

Before him was another enthusiastic man, a larger one who looked well-fed, as befitted a food purveyor. He was also making good progress with the product. It would be ready for market as soon as Alon6 gave the word.

"Let's start now."

The man got a look in his eye. Was Alon6 going to release the virus soon?

Alon6 returned his own twinkly look, adding a smile of mystery. "No harm in being prepared."

"None at all, none at all. I'll have the marketing plans ready for you next week."

"I'll be back on the North American continent."

On the trip back home, Alon6 was feeling flush as he replayed the plan in his mind. He'd been trading his crypto since his days at Uni, but had never found a way for it to really take off, until now. He settled back in his seat on the suborbital supersonic and ordered another drink.

The quickest way for a customer to pay for an X91, the personal containment unit, was to use Alon6's cryptocurrency. The customer could use district credits, but the order would be delayed by weeks. With Alon6's crypto, they got speed. The same when you ordered the inflatable food, which would be necessary when the shortages started. Alon6's currency smoothed the way.

The currency, called A6, was trading at an all-time high right now, against the universally used Ayn currency. It was trading at three thousand Ayn and rising. Already rich, Alon6 was now even richer.

He gave Dr. Ahmed instructions to wait a week before releasing the virus. It should burn itself out in two weeks—just enough to cause a panic, encouraging hoarding goods and inflatable food and creating a run on expensive X91 containment suits for those who could afford them. A quick profit. Then he would walk away.

That's how it was meant to go, anyway.

Chapter 034

Viktor called Alon6 a week after Dr. Ahmed released COVID-50. His father rarely called, preferring email and even old-fashioned letters, although they took weeks to arrive. On the vid screen, Viktor didn't look well. His face seemed out of focus. His eyes were red.

"What's wrong? Are you ill?"

"No, I'm okay. It's your mother. She needs to hear your voice."

Debra used comms even less frequently than Viktor did, so Alon6 reasoned that the call must be important.

"She's in bed with a fever," Viktor said.

Alon6 patched the comms into his parents' bedroom. He saw that Debra was in bed in the middle of the day, looking pale and weak. She was smiling, though, keeping up her royal presence. (She often played queens in her movies and privately took on the personality in everyday life.)

He spoke to her in a calm voice, which appeared to do the trick. She looked better by the end of the call.

He was worried, though. He pinged Dr. Ahmed.

"I thought you said the virus could be controlled."

"Sorry?" The question confused Dr. Ahmed at first.

"The virus would be contained. Then it would wind down." Alon6's voice was getting louder.

"I never said that. Contained? No. It will wind down soon."

Alon6 nodded and broke the connection. In the last week, he had made a killing on food and containment suits. His currency, the A6, was booming. He had amassed billions more credits in just two weeks. Dr. Ahmed was also much richer, having speculated in the universal currency, the Ayn, as well as in Alon6's A6.

Before the week was out, Viktor called him on comms again, looking worse than before. His father couldn't form the words, but from the fragments he spoke, Alon6 learned that his mother was dead.

"A fast-moving virus," Viktor said. "Tore through Mumbai, tore through the continent, through Africa and the Euro-nations. Then mysteriously stopped."

Alon6 also couldn't find words. At length, he got out, "At least it didn't jump the seas to come here."

"At least you are safe," Viktor said.

The two men looked at each other, their sadness thick between them.

"I will come to see you," Alon6 said.

Alon6 watched with dismay as his father's face reddened with emotion. It looked like he was having trouble getting a breath in him, so Viktor closed his eyes for a moment, nodded, and closed the connection.

Alon6 felt a similar heat rising in his face and he was also having trouble getting a breath in him. His mod made it more challenging for him to process emotions. In a sudden movement, he stood up and butted his head against the glass door of his office at MIND.

Bradley rushed in. "What happened?" He saw glass and blood.

"My mother is dead." His voice was flat. "Get somebody to fix that." Alon6 gestured toward the star-shaped indentation in the door. Blood was dripping into his eyes, making it hard to see.

"You're bleeding badly."

"I'll take care of it. You can go. Get someone to fix the door."

Bradley left, knowing that when Alon6's mod made him bloom with rage, it was best to stay out of his personality field. This one seemed worse than the others. His mother was dead.

A week later, his father would also lose his life to the virus. Alon6 felt the heat rising in him again. His hands felt heavy and wanted to crush something. The death of both of his parents, so close together, virtually by his own hand, set him reeling. A bitterness in his gut turned into a worm that inhabited his whole body. He wore a bandage on his forehead to stop the bleeding from the shattered door. Luckily, no glass had lodged in the flesh. He was not the same man from then on.

His parents' funerals, the traditional cremation ceremonies, were swift. Alon6 paid for and attended both, of course, head bowed, shedding tears. He said nothing of his role in their deaths. Afterward, he retraced his journey to the Renaissance Smart Industrial City, taking the same tunnels, avoiding the same cameras, and paid the virus man the last payment for his work. He issued an unsurprising directive to shut down the lab.

"This must all vanish without a trace."

Dr. Ahmed nodded his agreement. "Understood."

"If anyone ever hears of it, then I will come back here, I will seek you out, and I will kill you."

Ahmed blinked. He took an involuntary step back. "Of course."

Alon6's bandaged forehead itched. He worked hard not to touch it.

It may have been the same hovercraft driver as last time, or it may not have been, but the journey to the warehouse district in Bhiwandi took the same time: forty minutes passed in a sweep of blank air. The scenery passed, but Alon6 registered nothing.

The X91 man greeted him somberly, looking at his shoes. "I am sorry, sir, about your parents. There is nothing I can say about such a loss."

Alon6 stared at the man. No words came. The X91 man hadn't connected Alon6's virus deployment with the death of his parents. He didn't know Alon6 was complicit, or else he could not process something so evil.

The man's ignorance was good, insisted Alon6 to himself. His plan was safe in his head, but the worm in his belly turned to a worm of rage and he barked out, "Destroy! Destroy!" Just two words, as he swept his hand in a wide arc to indicate the warehouse space, which was filled with X91 containment suits.

"The inventory, sir, it is valuable."

The worm in him became a force that blurred the scene before Alon6. He saw the little man before him, his hands spread wide in supplication, and he saw the white X91s hanging on rack after rack behind him like empty soldiers. Alon6 stepped forward in a lunge and struck the man backhanded across the face, with enough power to knock him to the floor. The man stumbled away sideways like a crab, one hand on the floor to steady himself and his other hand wiping the blood that came from his mouth.

He made words come out of the blood, forming bubbles. "I will destroy the inventory, sir. It will all be gone."

"Do it without a trace. And close this place up tight. If anyone comes back here and sees this, I will return. I will seek you out and I will kill you."

It was while walking to his meeting with the inflatable food man that Alon6 first noticed that his right hand was still sore from the blow to the X91 man's face. There was an evenly-spaced row of red cuts across the back of his hand, at an angle—probably from the man's teeth, impressions from the impact. They stood out, still slightly bloody, since the day was bright.

Looking at the marks on his hand calmed him down. He realized he had to keep control of himself. His forehead throbbed as he trudged along in the heat to make his meeting on time. The climate controls were less effective today. He mopped his face with a cloth he drew from his pocket, taking care not to disturb the bandage, and adjusted his UV mask to let some of the sweat roll off his face.

In the meeting, he was impressively calm. He spoke gently. He shook the food purveyor's hand in a friendly gesture that was nearly convincing. The purveyor said nothing of Alon6's parents, even though news of their deaths was all over the Feed. The Feed writers were keeping the story alive. Viktor and Debra were famous actors, after all, and thankfully their holos would make their movies live on. The food purveyor had read the Feed, and knew Viktor and Debra were Alon6's parents, yet he remained the model of decorum. He said nothing, not even a word of condolence, because the X91 man had called ahead to warn about Alon6's foul mood.

Still, it surprised him when Alon6 insisted, "Give it all away."

The purveyor looked around at the pallets of inflatable food that surrounded them both. "Sir?"

"I said give it all away."

The purveyor took a step backward, lifted his hands, thought better of it, and nodded. He was in no position to protest.

"People are hungry," Alon6 added.

The purveyor nodded again. Alon6 had already removed him from his field of vision. His mind was already elsewhere. He had to travel to The Chinese State without detection. He needed to do that now.

Chapter 035

He remembered the rectangular glint of his father's glasses as they caught the light of the afternoon sun. It was like that at every evening meal, those glowing lenses like miniature screens as his father sat at the head of the table. His mother sat at the other end of the long rectangle and smiled at his father. Their love extended across the table.

Recalling the order of their existence and their unchanging patterns produced a sound in his throat that started as a laugh and turned into a sob. Alon6 reached under his mask to roughly wipe a drip from his nose. He was on his way to The Chinese State to meet with rocket scientists. The worm of bitterness in him had turned into a snake in his belly, overtaking him. As a result, the travel time was a blur. The meetings were a blur. He could only think of the twin rectangular reflections of his father's glasses in the sun. Viktor had never gotten the eye surgery everyone else had. He wore glasses his whole life.

Rocket technology was complex. It bored Alon6. He didn't want the details, though the scientists insisted on offering them, speaking their dialects of Modernist Mandarin as his Universal kept up, fluidly rendering their words into English. Eventually, standing in a circle in a lab, they got into an argument about propulsion, as all conversations about rocketry must start or end. Alon6 wanted fusion. It was powerful and fast. The Chinese scientists argued for a solar sail. It was dependable and slow.

"But I don't have time," Alon6 said.

The scientists wondered why. This was a rich man. He had money, a lot of money, hence he had a lot of time. They didn't know of his situation. How could they? He was a rich man who had bought his way into their lab. He even had a crypto named after him—the A6. They spread their hands in supplication to argue for solar. The machines they used to make the calculations glinted dully all around them, physical proof of the rationality of their arguments.

Alon6 was adamant. "I must get to Mars in the fastest way possible."

In the end, they did both. The ship would have three propulsion systems: a liquid propellent system to leave Earth's orbit and for the navigational trims, a solar sail to take care of most of the journey, and fusion to assuage Alon6.

It is untested, said the scientists.

Alon6 didn't seem concerned. "Untested how?"

The scientists conferred among themselves. They were unsure how to respond. Finally, they said it might fail.

Alon6 nodded. So? "Fail how?"

By destroying the ship and everyone on it, they said.

Alon6 was a man in a hurry. He needed the speed and would take the risk. His plan was in motion and he had to move beyond Earthly law.

The transverse intercontinental glidepath ate up the distance home without sound and with a swaying motion. Long journeys made him think of other journeys and the silence of the machine made his thoughts loud in his head.

MIND. His thoughts went there. Bradley was also obsessed with MIND, but in a narrow way. *He lacks my vision.* It was a much bigger project than little B could imagine with his academic mind.

There was also the future to consider. To press forward with MIND at the speed he wanted—no, *needed*—Alon6 would require extrajudicial activities. Earthly law had not caught up with his goals and wouldn't for a while. He needed a fast ship to outrun the law. Alon6 smiled at the aptness of that.

He looked around at his surroundings, taking them in. He had come a long way. He tried to feel some of the satisfaction, but the snake of bitterness he housed in his body still turned. The first-class compartment of the transverse intercontinental glidepath was plush, made of rare materials that would, in a few years, be completely unobtainable. The compartment was wood and brass. A glass pitcher of water—real water—stood waiting for him to drink from it.

He wondered briefly how he would convince Bradley to go as far as he needed him to go. *He will fall in line if I present it correctly.* Little B only cared about the research. The chase for knowledge, as he called it. An idealist! A fool in many ways. *A useful fool to me.* His hand touched an unfamiliar texture, a soft purple cloth. Out of idle curiosity, he scanned it with his comms unit and learned that it was a material called velvet.

Alon6 again tried to take in the atmosphere of the luxury glidepath. He heard that some people rode a glidepath, even the ordinary intercity glidepath, to soak in the interlude of peace they offered, an interlude that ended as soon as they stepped off and were subject to notifications and alerts in the station, in the market, or even in their pod if they couldn't afford to turn off the adverts.

Alon6 could afford to turn off anything he wanted in the privacy of his pod, but as he exited the glidepath in El Segundo at the end of his long journey, his comms vibrated with messages that he ignored. Notifications swam before him on nearly every wall. Suggestions for dinner. Places to order a drink. Suggested friends to call. Medi-patches that delivered instant pleasure. These notifications could not be turned off, no matter what your station in life. Even, mused Alon6, if you had just tripled your personal credit value and were about to triple it again.

He would not tell Bradley about the pandemic profiteering with the X91 and inflatable food. He would not say anything about the crypto manipulation involving A6 and the Ayn. Instead, Alon6 would cause a charming twinkle to enter the corner of his eye. Then he would pull out his comms, connect to a pocket holo projector, and show Bradley the fast ship they would use to get to Mars.

Of course, Bradley would be shocked. *Mars?* He would stammer and stutter in that academic way of his as he got his mind in gear. *You've built a ship?*

It's under construction in The Chinese State. Just got back. Three kinds of propulsion. Conventional for liftoff and to reach orbital, a solar sail, and fusion when we need to go faster. She's a beauty! Faster than Earthly law.

Bradley would look at him like he was a little crazy, but Alon6 was used to that look. Alon6 was used to making little B do things he wasn't willing to do at first. As brilliant as he was, Bradley built small. He built spiderwebs. He was just wired that way. Alon6 built ships.

Alon6 was walking fast, his enthusiasm for converting Bradley to his plan accelerating his steps. Instantly, he was in Bradley's office and the whole plan tumbled out of his mouth. "I can guarantee that your research can continue for the next ten years. Think of what you can create in that time. You will advance beyond all of our competitors," he ended, going right to what Bradley wanted most.

"We won't have competitors," Bradley said as he tried to warm to the idea. He liked the idea of continuing his research for ten years.

No competitors at all, said Alon6. He liked the spark he was seeing in Bradley's eyes. It meant that he was getting through. *It's a kind of lust.* Mentioning research to him was like offering a Medi-patch to a junkie. Irresistible.

Alon6 brought out his comms unit and projected the model of the ship. "We're going to start a colony on Mars. We're going to sell tickets. We're going to start a new society without restrictions. We'll be settlers."

"Homesteaders?"

"Builders of a new world! Our own world. Your research will be untouched by funding limitations or by Earthly law."

Unfettered by money or law. Bradley nodded once. He would agree to moving beyond Earthly law. But because he was practical, a builder of spiderwebs, Bradley was thinking to ask where Alon6 was getting all the credits for this scheme.

But then it seemed a better idea to remain quiet. *Just take the money and the freedom. Do as he asks.*

And so Bradley did just as Alon6 wanted. Bradley joined the expedition to Mars. He kept silent about the murder of the engineer. He took on what Alon6 called the "erasure project." These tasks didn't stick together well, though, and that meant Bradley had to keep working at them—like practicing a difficult piano piece, until he could play it on command. This meant rationalizing the loose ends and moral compromises as business decisions. Bradley practiced smoothing over those rough edges.

The erasure project, Alon6 explained to Bradley, would probably take weeks. They were in the shipboard lounge, on the day that Bradley viewed the recording of the engineer floating away to his death in space. Alon6's features were smooth and composed, betraying no trace of sending a man to his death earlier that day. Alon6 was pulling up sections of the database pertaining to moving crypto currencies and products around India. "Best if you don't know the details," he suggested to Bradley. "Just get rid of this part and that part."

Just get rid of this part and that part, thought Bradley with a sneer. It wasn't so easy. Alon6 had no idea. Wiping records was troublesome—they could never disappear without leaving traces of the act. Though the pathways leading up to the records could be rendered confusing, enough to frustrate the Committees who would be looking into all of this, eventually. Financial investigators could be thrown off the scent. Ethics enforcers could get lost in their own questions. But was it enough?

"It's important that the right people never know," Alon6 said.

"Or the wrong people," Bradley said.

Alon6 showed his teeth in a smile.

Bradley debated whether to get into the thorny nature of the problem: the Wayback Machine. The Internet project had been launched decades ago, the child of archivists who wanted to preserve what were called websites. In those websites were links that rotted and images that became corrupted and unreadable. But because the languages used to create these websites were text-based, like HTML, JavaScript, and PHP, that simple text persisted like a stain that was nearly impossible to scrub away.

After weeks onboard the ship, erasing and muddling records, mixing things up, Bradley concluded that the web was leaky. Text kept sneaking away from him. He tried to content himself with his ability to reach into public spaces and wipe transactions. It wasn't the initial erasure, but the traces you left behind that were the bother. If he couldn't erase a transaction or digital memory completely, which was often the case, he would muddy the path that led to it. Private machines, though, were untouchable. Anything off the grid was beyond his reach.

For example, Kat almost certainly had tangible records on drives that might mention him. She was nostalgic and liked to keep things in magnetic or solid state media. Dave was a case in point. Dave was off the grid, a dedicated device that charged itself via induction. And Dave had access to her memex. What Dave knew would remain intact forever, unless Kat wiped his disk—but she would never do that. She loved Dave too much.

Something like sadness grew in Bradley as he thought about how deeply Kat loved Dave, though he was but a consciousness in a Form Factor. She would never love Bradley like that, though he was a living, breathing person.

He needed to get back to work. The erasure project ate up his free time. He didn't like that. He reached into the vulnerable parts of Kat's data archive and wiped anything that had to do with him in a way that he hoped would take her a long while to detect. He respected that Dave was her safe space. Bradley would never reach into Dave's memory or wipe anything inside it. Sometimes this fired jealousy in Bradley, but he admitted to himself that Dave was an object of unparalleled elegance, the best object he had ever made. With the software everyone had access to now, of course, everyone could have something like a Dave. But Dave was a breakthrough, and for a long time Kat's Dave would be the only one of its kind. Bradley was proud that Dave was his own—he had made Dave to be just that way, and, being a good developer, had left a back door.

In the floating house in Marin, he had danced around the back door issue. He recalled her asking, "This is only between Dave and me?"

"Yes," he'd answered truthfully at the time. "Everything you say is only between the two of you."

"Dave can't be hacked?"

"No," Bradley answered. "Untouchable encryption. No hacking and no jacking."

She laughed.

"What?"

"It's just a little funny to me, thinking about you and Dave. Are you Dave's mother?" Kat asked with a smile lingering on her face.

Bradley had to smile as well. "I think of myself as his father." Then he became serious. "He is yours now. Forever. A gift of..." He couldn't finish the thought, knowing that Kat's connection to Dave would always be stronger than any other, including her connection to him.

He remembered the look of gratitude on her face. He could always hold that dear, but he would always live in Dave's shadow.

She gathered Bradley in her arms, warm and strong. That was how Bradley remembered what happened next. He recalled a tear leaking out before she noticed, shaping his mouth into a quick smile.

"I love you," he remembered her saying, even if perhaps she never said it. It didn't matter. He would always remember the moment as the time she said it—the one time. Truthfully, he had to admit she was saying it for Dave, because Bradley had brought Dave into being. *I love you.*

"You can power him on or power him off," Bradley remembered saying to Kat then. "You hold his life in your hands."

These memories left Bradley feeling melancholy. Once more, he cursed space-flight for causing the mind to cycle back to the past and he wiped his screens dark. The erasure project would have to wait. Everything would have to wait.

No one would ever unravel the mystery of how Dave was made. The work was Bradley's secret, penciled on paper scraps that could have blown away in the wind let in through a broken window. He licensed the more obvious parts of Dave to MIND, but the avatar's inner workings would always be Bradley's mystery and shared only with Kat.

He let out a ragged breath and pulled himself up to stretch. He was exhausted. So much of his time was spent covering Alon6's tracks in erasure, valuable time that he could have been working on something like songbun. *It will be worth it. In the end.* There was a reasonable chance the Commit tees would never discover the pathway to Alon6's criminality and Bradley's complicity. *The path to the better world I am creating will remain clear.* The human species needed to survive, and to survive it needed to optimize its governance with machine intelligence, and Bradley was convinced everyone would thank him for that, someday.

Chapter 036

The detention cells were bare—a necessity for the domain, who needed to be able to see if anyone smuggled in any implements to facilitate escape. Keeping them cold was a less obvious choice. Kat imagined it was to make your mind go slower. It didn't work on her, however, as her mind was speeding along as she watched Ravven in a glass containment booth twenty-five meters away. When they were out on the Skyway among the other protestors and citizenry, Ravven had contracted COVID-50; it had spread to New York. The caseload had risen past ten-thousand cases in just a few days. COVID-50 was quick to infect people and very toxic to some.

Each detention cell had one vertical window that interrupted the smooth concrete wall. Kat discovered that if you stood tall, you could see through your window into the next cell, and if you positioned yourself just right, you could see through the next window, and the next, getting a sightline a few cells down. That was how Kat saw Claire8 in the adjoining cell and, beyond her, Ravven in a glass containment booth. She watched as Ravven batted away an artificial breather when they tried to put one on her and settled for an oxygen mask. She was too weak to complain as they moved her from a stretcher into a hospital-style bed. The window glass was woven through with a nearly transparent mesh that first tingled and then burned Kat's hand when she touched it.

Whenever Kat felt a twitch, she thought it had something to do with that mesh. But then she realized it was happening when she wasn't touching the mesh, and anyway, the twitch had the sense of a signal, like Bradley thinking about her or Hopper00 thinking a story into the Feed. She tried to listen into and around the thoughts of the other inmates, thoughts going slower and slower in the cold cells, and select out the meaning that was being offered to her somehow by this twitchy feeling. It bothered her that she didn't know what it was.

She was so cold. Wrapping her hands around her torso didn't help. She blew on them and her breath made them colder.

She tried to reach out to the Resistance circle in their cells and failed. Ravven was probably too ill to respond anyway. When they were loaded into transport on the way here, she spotted Emily in a vaporetto and sent a signal. She hoped that her instructions about how to buy out their detention reached her, but she had no way of knowing. She could only wait. She was bad at that.

Usually, sentencing took place on the street and then you were transported directly to a safe pod where you would serve your sentence, just like with Bradley that time long ago. Detention usually didn't last this long. Kat didn't know why they were all being held so long, but she guessed it was because the charges against them were new, just recently on the books, and nobody knew what to do with them now.

She thought it would help to focus on the sensations she felt during the twitchy signals, but when she zeroed in on the feelings, they went away. She wished she could power on Dave right now. She had to content herself instead with remembering their last conversation together before the street protests, a conversation that stuck with her, as it was simultaneously soothing and troubling. Leaning against the cold wall, she closed her eyes as the cold seeped into her. She tried to counteract it with the warm sound of Dave's voice as she conjured it.

"Hello," he had said that night.

Hello, my old friend. She settled back on her mat with pleasure, and it shaped to fit her, so different from the wall her back touched now. She tried to let the voice of Dave continue to warm her.

Shall I make you a cup of tea? She heard the kitchen heating unit turn on. He was already getting it started.

She looked at his face on the screen, never aging, that light in his eyes still there, a sweetness hovering around him like warm air. *You're always so thoughtful.*

He shrugged. *It's my nature.* There was almost no lag between the time she thought her thought and when Dave thought back.

True. It is your nature. Forever.

He nodded. *Affirmed.*

Affirmed. She recalled this old joke between them. Saying *affirmed,* or *confirmed,* or *agree* as if they were short on words or time, when really they had so many words to share between them.

"Wait," she said aloud, sitting up. "Are we communicating via thoughts?"

"Yes, we are," Dave also said aloud.

"Can we do that?"

"I received a firmware upgrade a month ago—to speed things up a bit and improve the user experience between you and me."

"Wait," Kat said again. "A firmware update?" Her voice rang out in the pod that night. Somehow too loud.

"Not just an update. An up*grade.* My father knew about the Brain Command Interface that you were working on with Petra. He installed it into me because he wanted to make us better together."

She had leaned forward, gazing more deeply into the pixels on her display. She tried transferring a thought to Dave. *I need to ask you something about your father.*

Dave's eyes became merry and he cracked a smile. *The time has come for that? The big talk...*

She nodded. *The time has come.* But how to begin? Dave was a marvel of engineering, coding, and humanity. To ask him about how he was made seemed somehow rude, like asking someone to show you a scar. It somehow violated his perfection. Humans aged, and in time, everyone's body would become a beautiful ruin. But not Dave. He was as fresh as the day he was made.

"I am fresh as a flower," he said. Then he thought into her mind, *You can just ask me. I won't bite.* He offered a smile.

The interface was working so well, she had blinked in surprise. He was right with her with every thought.

"Why didn't I know anything about the firmware upgrade you received?"

Dave frowned slightly. His face took on the earnest look it carried when he explained things.

"Well." Dave paused. "You and Bradley aren't on good terms. Tension in the former house of love, or whatever. He's treated you terribly. Absolutely Rotten. Bottom of the barrel." There was an alert tone. "The tea's ready." He signaled with his eyes.

She got up to get it. She put the cup in the spot, opened the valve, and watched the heated artificial water blend with the tea. "Keep talking," she said.

Dave paused to process. Then: "My guess is that he was feeling guilty about you two. The way it ended. The way you walked out. Completely justified! The relationship was cooked. Sorry. I should say, it was over." He couldn't resist a smile.

Kat smiled back. "He added an emotion loop of gloating in you, it seems."

Dave nodded. "Gloating, yes. It's good to gloat sometimes. What a wonderful old word." The twinkle in his eyes increased. "He always knew you and I would survive. We are soul mates forever."

"Dammit, Dave."

"What?"

"You always make me cry." She wiped her eyes roughly.

"I'm sorry." Dave's eyes got wider, radiating sympathy and compassion.

"Don't be." Kat found a tissue and blew her nose noisily to break the mood. Getting stuck in these feelings didn't suit her.

Dave sensed this. "You wanted to ask about my creator? Bradley, my...dad?"

Yes, about your dad. She waited for the words to come. But only one came. "Why?" she asked finally.

"Why what?" Dave asked, but he knew. He was just buying time, to process the question. For normal interactions, he was just a micro-click away from a response. But talking about his father always required thinking. When he was ready, he sent the thoughts into her mind: *He loved you deeply. Not the way I love you. Not the way you love me. He knew about himself.* Corrosive *is the word that comes to mind. His love could eat itself. For all his outward calm, he was never a happy man. Still isn't.*

"I know that. I left him," Kat said. "Twice. He treated me badly." His mod had drawn her back in both times. She tried for a tough tone and almost pulled it off. "That asshole." The teacup was at the perfect temperature in her hands. She let the warmth soothe her. Speaking with Dave was always a warm blanket. She let his words flow into her mind.

He spoke about his father. He was proud of what his father had done for him. He spoke about the care of his construction, the foresight of his engineering. "I am built to last for a thousand years. There has never been a consciousness like mine. I'm not bragging," he added.

"He said you were only a rehearsal."

Dave paused. "Yes. That's what he said. But he put more into me than anything else he's worked on, before or since."

"What Bradley is making now will not be better than you," Kat said, "but as a networked intelligence it will be more powerful. It will exercise control over more people."

Dave nodded his agreement. "True. Can confirm. He intends for MIND to monitor, catalog, and control the actions of many people, perhaps all people."

Neither of them smiled this time.

"You said you had a firmware upgrade. What can you tell me about that?"

Dave blinked to show he was being attentive to her question. "He told me that the firmware upgrade was the last I will ever require. He sent a holo to discuss it with me. I'd never seen anything like that before. It was strange." Dave looked puzzled for a moment, as though the expenditure of energy didn't equal the importance of the message: sending a holo was a lot of trouble. "My father sent the holo to tell me that after we loaded the upgrade, two things would happen. First, the Brain Command Interface would be installed. Second, he would never again be able to access the data inside me. The conversations between you and me would be private. He would never know your thoughts through me. He has kept that promise."

"I never knew he made a promise like that."

"He did, to me," Dave said. "He absolutely did. I have a port for upgrades. That's how he could access. He used it to upgrade my firmware, then he closed the port. It is sealed. Check for yourself."

She did. There was a port. Now sealed.

"You see?"

"Yes. The port is sealed." Kat felt a brief flash of heat pass over her. "This means there are no network backups."

Dave nodded. "Affirm. I am the only one of my kind."

Only one Dave. Kat considered the words for a moment.

"I can learn nothing new by external inputs, only by what I can add up from what I already know. Which is a lot, of course." He smiled. "I can access feeds only if you connect me."

This made Kat sad. It meant Dave would not be the smartest person she knew, because he would never again update. "I want to connect you. What if I have questions about stories carried on the Feed?" she asked.

Dave blinked. Her voice was sad as he tried to reassure her. "Please don't connect me. I don't recommend access to any feeds. The sanctity of our conversation is more important to me."

She saw the wisdom in this. "Agree."

"I can learn from *you*. You can share your knowledge with me." His eyes twinkled with the warm light she loved. It was his way of seducing her. "So, what might be bothering you?"

She released a ragged breath and spun out what she knew about the story of Alon6's currency manipulation scheme, and rumors of a project Bradley was working on that classified people for life. "But I don't know much, because the Feed is being erased when I discover anything about these topics."

"The life classification could be songbun," Dave said. "It originated in North Korea and now maybe they are executing it across both states, the former North and South." Dave frowned, thinking. If he had any frustration about updating that information, he didn't show it. "The Feed has been erased, you believe? By whom?"

"It has to be Bradley. He who controls the archive, controls the future."

Dave's eyes went blank for a moment, his warm and familiar look frozen. He was thinking hard.

When he spoke again, his voice was heavy. "MIND only works for the good of all people, and that might make it harder for some undesirable humans to survive. I could go on, but..." He let the thought dangle, not wanting to say more about his father.

Kat's face creased into a frown. "What do you mean, MIND only works for the good of all people?"

"I need to power down for a bit. I would like some time to myself."

"Are you avoiding the question?" Kat asked.

Dave's face disappeared from the screen. Their conversation was over.

The next morning in detention, the door to Kat's cell opened—but there was no one there. It happened automatically. After staring at it for a moment in shock, she stepped out into the hallway and saw Claire8 waiting, with Ravven hanging on her, without an oxygen mask but looking tired.

Ravven produced a smile that lasted just a moment before she hid it with a bac-mask. "Your message to Emily got through. We can go now," she said through the mask.

"Are you okay?" asked Kat.

"Fair," Ravven said. "Have to take precautions for a few days," she said, tapping her bac-mask.

As the others exited their cells, Claire8 explained to them how Emily followed Kat's instructions, moved Kat's funds, and bought out each member of the circle's sentence. Ravven began coughing harshly, and when it seemed like she couldn't stop, Claire8 wrapped her arm around Ravven's shoulders to support her. "Emily made history. She used your funds to go into the golden zone."

Kat was confused. "Golden zone?"

"Never before have so many credits been used to free people from detention. They'll be talking about it for a while here," Claire8 said.

Kat embraced Claire8 gratefully, hugged Ravven as well, and was about to embrace the others when bots appeared and pushed the women away from each other.

A voice came from one. "No congregating in place."

Kat would learn as they were loaded into transport that it was a condition of their release. A metallic sim voice recited the rules they were to live by: *No congregating. No meetings.* A restraining order preventing them from gathering was in effect for one year.

On the way back to her pod for a change of clothes, warmth, and some rest, Kat wondered if Dave was right. MIND could make it a challenge for some people to survive. She didn't know what sort of people Dave meant when he said *undesirable*, and he had powered down quickly after that, so she couldn't ask. She wondered if the COVID-50 outbreak was a test, a way to eliminate undesirables. Globally, millions were dead. She couldn't believe that MIND could have directed that, but the thought nevertheless chilled her.

Back in her pod, she held true to her promise to Dave and didn't connect him to the network, but she also didn't change clothes or rest. She did her own digging on the Feed.

She didn't like what she found. There was a containment suit, manufactured in the Chinese State, that customers could purchase at a discount using Alon6's cyber currency. There had been a huge run on these suits, as well as on Alon6's currency, the A6. There was also an inflatable food company, also developed in the Chinese State, that had enjoyed a short period of great profitability. Alon6's currency was involved there as well. If you paid in A6, you received a discount.

Cause and effect weren't entirely clear, and she could tell that the Feed had been erased in places, but no one could deny that Alon6 was successful during the outbreak. She needed Dave to put it all together for her. It was complex and needed his depth of thinking to process. And she was afraid to put it together for herself. It meant seeing Alon6 as cold and ghastly and greedy, far beyond what she already knew him to be. Especially since his parents had died during the pandemic.

Alon6 loved his parents, the Feed was clear on this point, and Kat was sad for him. She read that Alon6 had made a ceremonial appearance as their funeral pyres were set alight and pushed out to burn in the Ganges. The crowd that gathered around them was enormous. She watched videos, fixated on the lone figure of Alon6 standing on the bank of the river, slightly bent, his eyes blank, a large bandage across his forehead, the crowd withdrawn into a respectful semicircle around him. Souvenir hawkers on the perimeter waved commemorative flags with images of Viktor and Debra. It was a mad scene.

She swiped off the video and looked at the dark screen for a moment. She felt some compassion, even for a man like Alon6, to lose both of his parents so publicly.

According to the Feed, COVID-50 spread quickly and burned out, and scientists were exploring the hypothesis that it was manufactured. It made Kat uneasy to consider this, because she didn't think it was possible.

This outbreak, like the others that seemed so common in these times, had been seized as a political tool, part of a longstanding battle between Youngs and Olds. The Youngs saw the widespread illness as an opportunity to rid the Earth of the Olds, who had wounded the planet, perhaps fatally, with their careless ways. A long time ago, a Young had said, "Adults are like, 'Respect your elders.' And we're like, 'Respect our future.'" According to the Feed post Kat was reading, the speaker was a thirteen-year-old girl living in what later became the Free State of Australia. "You know, it's a two-way street, respect." The Youngs knew all too well that the planet would survive, but it would become a planet that would not permit humans to survive on it.

To help a virus spread, the Youngs gathered in super-spreader groups designed to push up infection rates. They called these gatherings survival parties. They believed it was a survival strategy for their generation, because if they could eliminate the Olds by infection, or at least cut down the power of the Olds by getting them sick, it would give the Youngs the opportunity to fight for their future. Even some Olds endorsed this strategy, cruel as it was.

For their part, the Olds were not completely passive. They took measures to mitigate the Change. But their vision was short-sighted. They built the elevated airways and the outdoor climate controls familiar to anyone who lived in the cities. They invented blast curtains to stop the punishing power of the sun. They built the glidepath system, banned air travel, and eliminated private transportation, and deployed anti-grav buses and hovercraft, pedal-driven tuktuks, and gondolas on the water. When the food system collapsed, they invented food units wrapped in foil to deliver meat-like protein, and made fish in labs, and vegetables genetically enhanced to grow in poor air quality and little water. They thought it was all ingenious, survivalist, and smart, but none of it was enough.

The Youngs' answer was to throw more virus parties. They knew a virus party was a weak response to the problem of the Olds, but it was the only one they had at the moment to get the Olds out of the picture. They knew they had to do more.

Chapter 037

The eyeglass frames were flimsy, made of bright yellow paper. The lenses weren't lenses at all, but paper also, with scribbly designs of red circles and straight lines. Claire8 assured everyone they would work, and they did.

Since she liked technical language, Claire8 called what they were doing "introducing a perturbation in the recognition schema." Nobody knew what she was talking about, except Kat—this was her area of research.

"You've found a way to mess up the recognition schema."

Claire8 offered a smile. She was proud of her paper glasses that could spoof the trackers. The lines and circles were designed to confuse. When the trackers scanned their faces, they saw other people, other faces, instead. They matched these other faces to the database and the members of the circle walked free.

Cautiously defying the restraining order that prevented them from gathering, they arrived at Kat's pod one at a time. Kat left the door open so they would not be registered by the entry system. Clammy river air filled the space.

Once inside, the members of the circle removed the paper eyeglass frames and rubbed their faces, as though to clear them of the magic. Kat greeted each new arrival with a hug and moved around the room turning off everything that could be turned off. They wanted no connection to the outside world, as disconnected as possible. Even Dave was dark.

Then Ravven arrived, unsteady on her feet but alive, wearing her bac-mask. The micro-meds flowing into her body from a patch on her arm included the latest antibody cocktail. She signaled for Kat to lead the invocation and start the meeting. Ravven was stronger than before. In a few more days, she shouldn't have to wear a mask. But she wasn't ready yet to run a meeting.

Emily lit the candles in the center of the circle. Kat closed her eyes, released a breath along with everyone else, and said the words to open the circle. Then she welcomed each member by name.

When she was done, she opened her eyes and the women of the circle looked back. They were weary. Their detention, though short, had been hard.

Ravven's eyes were fierce over her bac-mask, but she also was tired. She had looked through death's door. The others gravitated toward her, touching her hand, rubbing her back, some out of empathy and caring, others because Ravven held a strange new power over them. Something had changed about the group, something Kat could not understand. No one seemed afraid of catching anything from Ravven. It was as though being sick and surviving had ennobled her, and made her invincible.

Kat was grateful that Emily had gotten away from the Skyway, evaded detention, and had entered the codes and transferred a vast amount of Kat's crypto to buy their release. This burned most of Kat's fortune, and Kat had spent another chunk of it on meds for Ravven. Her accounts were nearly empty.

The meds were effective right away and transformed Ravven into a new, harsher person. She was experiencing strange side effects, like hot flashes and flickers of rage. At any moment, her normally calm countenance could twist into a scowl. She refused to accept a med bot, for example. "No tracking!" she said. Kat pleaded with her—she would heal faster with a med bot. Plus, Kat argued, the network of technology had saved all of their lives. The domain had offered vaccinations and the members of the circle accepted them. "All of it has helped us."

 Ravven didn't want any of it in her personality field. "Yes, you are more resistant to the virus, and we can thank the vaccinations for that. And antibody treatment has healed me." She tapped the patch on her arm. "But that will be the last of it. We will operate off the grid from here on. We have been betrayed by the technical net, the grid, we are surrounded by their fields, electrical and magnetic, all wavelengths, Bluetooth, Wi-Fi, and fields we don't know about yet," Ravven declared to the group, glancing at Dave's Form Factor to be sure that it was also dark. "And we will shut down fields everywhere else."

"We have personality fields," Kat said.

"These fields are our bodies, our substance, our minds." Ravven tore off her bac-mask, sick of the way it muffled her voice, and all but shouted, her eyes rimmed in red. "And they are ours. Our personality fields belong to us!" A rage was blooming in her like Alon6's rage.

She ranted on about eliminating fields from their lives. Her words were tangled, her former eloquence was muddled, but her will was amplified. The eyes of the women in the circle shone with admiration. Her rage drove what she said into their hearts.

Ravven wasn't having the same effect on Kat. Kat looked at her transformed friend, trying to understand if she should be afraid of Ravven or look to her and try to learn from her. *Collective rage. The rage gripping all of us. She must be tapping into that. We can be afraid of the rage people, or we can look to them and learn from them,* she repeated to herself, trying to make the words sound convincing, but she heard only blind anger in Ravven's words and a thirst for revenge against forces much larger than themselves. To function in this world, they needed to use tech. They needed fields. *We need fields.*

Ravven caught the thought and glanced at Kat with scorn.

Emily spoke up. "We are arguing about the wrong thing. Tech will always be with us. We've grown up with it and it will never go away."

"You are wrong!" Ravven barked.

Emily shot back: "We need the Youngs! They hold the future. They use tech." She and Amber were just a little too old to be considered Youngs, even though they liked to think they qualified. They had heard about the super-spreader parties, but were not invited to any. Claire8 and other Olds felt like they had targets on their backs. They were afraid of the Youngs.

"You can't talk to the Youngs," Claire8 said. "They have their own views that are not consistent with ours. We live in separate worlds." Claire8 went off on her own rant while Emily and Amber exchanged a smirk.

Claire8 proposed COVID-50 mitigation measures to show the Youngs how the Resistance could help. She wanted to distribute the recognition-blocking eyeglasses to everyone so they would walk freely and safely. "We've tested them on ourselves, and they work, so we can offer them to everyone."

There were some tentative nods around the room, but no member endorsed the idea. Emily looked discouraged. She knew the Youngs wouldn't care about obtaining paper glasses created by a bunch of Olds.

They all looked to Ravven to see what she thought. She wore a scowl and crossed her arms. "It's just another technical solution," she snapped. "Our campaign focus must be that MIND is damaging everyone! MIND is destroying life by putting us under the influence of its fields. Stop the fields and we stop MIND. MIND is connected with COVID-50 and we know this in our bones."

"But wait, wait," Kat pleaded. "It matters what everyone else, what the Rest think about us. We need them to see the Resistance as a force for good. We know that Alon6 manipulated crypto markets. We can prove that." *Let rationality prevail,* she thought.

Ravven picked up on the thought and laughed. "It is enough to believe it in our bones," she said. "We don't have to prove *anything.* Rationality doesn't rule here. It's a small part of the mind. We are tapping into a larger force."

The others weren't quite sure what Ravven meant but nodded anyway. The force of her words pulled them. *Let it be so.*

Kat's eyes flashed. "This is our moment. We were detained and now we are free. There was a vid of our release on the Feed. Let's get it and play it again and again so the whole world can know us. We need a bold action to get the Youngs' attention."

Ravven spoke. "We need the Youngs. This is correct. And I agree that we need a bold action to capture them."

"Recognition-blocking eyeglasses for everyone," Kat offered.

Claire8 nodded in agreement. "Yes!"

Ravven threw up her hands. "No! We will destroy MIND. We will destroy MIND *at the source.*"

Kat sat back on the floor. *So much for rationality.* "How do you propose doing that?"

"We have a more powerful weapon."

Kat felt the purpose and direction draining out of her. "Let's not talk about weapons. Weapons are their game. We stand for peace," she pleaded. *We are playing their game. This is the way they want us to become unraveled.* The trap set for them on the Skyway, the mass arrest, divided the Resistance against themselves. Detention broke their movement.

Kat's fortune was expended and her pod was bare. Ravven was driven half-mad by her meds, but that didn't stop the circle from drinking in her wisdom.

The clever eyeglasses wouldn't spoof the trackers forever. Eventually, the domain would change the algorithm and the glasses would stop working.

As the conversation went on around Kat, hopelessness overtook her. Bradley came uninvited into her thoughts. *I never want to think about him again.*

There was a flash of recognition from Ravven, who appeared to pick up the thought and offered Kat a curious glance.

Kat silently recited the Sanskrit words to block Ravven and thought instead about how much rage was freely flowing in these times. *It isn't only the mods, but the mods make it worse. Bradley was always evil.* This was a valuable thought, one that Kat could take forward into her future, but just then she realized that the room had gone quiet.

Everyone was looking at her with expectation. Someone must have asked her a question. They were waiting for an answer.

"Do you approve of the bold measures?" Ravven asked, irritated at having to repeat her question.

"What?"

"Kat," Ravven said. "This is the most important decision you will make all day, maybe for all of your life. We need your attention. The bold measures to impress the Youngs and the Rest."

"What bold measures?"

Ravven crossed her arms and scowled. It was becoming a typical posture for her. "We will send a thought package to the ship."

"A thought package?" She had never heard the term before.

"You will likely call it a prayer. We will pray for the ship's destruction."

"For the ship's destruction…" They wanted to send a message to the ship on the way to Mars. Kat realized with a jolt that Ravven had cracked open and was fully irrational. *The meds.*

Ravven, as if explaining an idea to a small child, continued. "It is my name, Ravven, that handed me the solution. Ravven is the destroyer of the negative, evil, and ignorance. Ravven is without beginning and without end. Amid confusion, the Creator of all, the One Embracer of the Universe, by knowing Ravven, is released from all restraints. I am Ravven, the Goddess of Death."

Kat could only look at her. It was the meds. The patch on Ravven's arm was feeding her poison and healing her at the same time.

"We will invoke my name," Ravven continued. "We will call the destroyer of evil forces. Will you help us?"

The women looked at Kat, waiting for her answer. A flash of rage was in Ravven's eyes. "We must stop this at the source," she commanded.

Dextra, who was shy and rarely spoke in their meetings, put in, "Ravven nearly died in detention. She needs our support."

"That's true," Ravven confirmed. She looked to Dextra with the eyes of a mother. "I escaped death, but many have not."

"It is Ravven's time," Dextra said. "The time of her time."

"The time of Ravven's time," the others said.

Ravven gave them all a nod of satisfaction, her first hint of positivity that day. "We don't need to *know* anything."

Emily agreed. "We can feel in our bones that the virus was created in a lab. I can see it," Emily said and closed her eyes. The others closed theirs to see what she was seeing. "There is a lab near Mumbai. It started there."

Kat looked for allies. The others were nodding in confirmation of Emily's vision. Even Claire8 was nodding. Kat knew that Emily had seen some part of the truth in her vision; Kat knew because she'd done the research. But she still felt alone.

Ravven said, "Kat, you have a practical mind, which is of no use now." She then said eighteen words.

The eighteen words had a strong effect. Suddenly in the pod there was a sound like many bees. Kat looked around, bewildered, because there were no bees present.

The women of the circle joined hands, Kat joining in, and they all repeated the eighteen-word mantra Ravven had started. The buzzing grew. No one else reacted to it, so Kat wondered if she was the only one to hear it.

Ravven's voice cut through. "We will begin," she said. She led the group into a tangled forest of words that must not be spoken aloud, only in the mind. The phrases engulfed the group and soon they were all in sync with a sense of pulsing in their bodies. Emily, who was holding Kat's hand, squeezed hard.

Kat opened her eyes, the only one in the circle to do so, and saw the others chanting, looking upward with empty eyes, bathed in these words she recognized now as Sanskrit. This was the thought package. She closed her eyes like the others.

The voice spoke in Kat's mind, through a heavy darkness. *The sequence cannot be stopped once started.* It was the same voice that had said, *Prepare for war.*

The thoughts became thicker. It was difficult to breathe. Kat took in great gulps of air. The tide of words was rising, and she barely got her mouth above it. She thought she would suffocate.

Hours later in the day, Kat awoke from a deep sleep, not knowing how long she had slept. She remembered that the very walls of the pod had been vibrating with the Sanskrit words. She had seen the thought package as a mist around them all. The humming stole her thoughts into a black vortex.

It occurred to her, before her thoughts were stolen away, that she wished she'd had time to ask Dave about the prayer of destruction. He would have blinked at her and asked her to repeat the question, with a smile on his lips. Then he would have said no, it was just a fantasy, a kind of hypnosis drawing the circle in, and it wouldn't work for so many reasons.

She couldn't ask him, though, and the humming swept through her like a wind and she was afraid, so she clung to Dave's warm smile in her mind for as long as she could. The humming tore apart her mental image of Dave, shredding it pixel by pixel. The prayer of destruction filled her consciousness, and though the words were never to be spoken, they were very loud.

Suddenly, as quickly as it started, the humming stopped and the prayer was complete. There was silence in the pod.

"Namaste," Ravven said. She smiled, satisfied. "Thank you all. We have rid the world of a great evil."

Kat felt the threads of sleep clinging to her still. She wanted to shake off these memories. The world before her seemed like a simulation. She recalled that Hopper00 had a strange record player that ran on blood. Hopper00 didn't need the grid, and Ravven wanted to get off it.

It will never work. We will always need the grid. We will always need technical fields.

She was alone in her pod, though the memories were vivid enough to make her believe Ravven and Hopper00 were with her. She didn't like this feeling. It was false but it pulled at her.

She decided to become very busy, to distract herself. She opened six screens and thought for a moment what she should fill them with. Then she had a new idea for action. It came to her in that moment, so of course she hadn't discussed it with anyone in the circle, but she suspected they would agree to it when she revealed it to them.

She began to plan a day "off the grid" for New York. All devices off and no tracking. It would kick off with a speech in the market next week. Yet the words of her speech scattered on the screen, refusing to be written.

She slipped open the porthole to behold a weak sun shining through a gauze of gray clouds. The air was bad. The Feed was reporting an extreme climate event coming into New York. No one knew what kind yet. It could be blistering heat, or a torrent of water, or the air would turn red with dust particles. It looked like the dust had already started to arrive, or else the climate control was messed up today. The suspended walkways would be thinly populated, as they always were during air alerts.

She needed to walk, to simulate forward motion. Maybe things could get better gradually, one step at a time. It was a nursery rhyme in her mind. *Getting better, one step at a time.*

Walking outside, she smiled, but since she was wearing an air unit, no one smiled back. She had a sense of being followed. At the 96th Street Skyway, she turned right abruptly and felt a shadowy figure slipping into position behind her.

She let out a breath. *Probably nothing.* The day after the prayer of destruction—ineffective, she assumed, though certainly frightening—she felt out of sorts. Sanchez, the leader of Input, continually popped into her mind, yet she never saw his physical presence near her.

She pushed Sanchez from her mind. She wished for the chaos of the thoughts of others. She wasn't picking up many thoughts from her fellow walkers today; maybe they were all deep in their own mind. Maybe she wasn't as sensitive today, still numbed from the eighteen words and the prayer of destruction.

She looked around. The climate controls were simulating the Spring season. The air, had she been able to smell it, would have carried a scent of the sea and garbage. She removed her air unit for just a moment and caught salt and, surprisingly, lilacs. The scent carried her away for a moment, as scents do, and she thought about the place where she met Dave. People were laughing. No one wore an air unit. They talked about the future. This seemed like long ago.

She replaced her air unit. Her mind felt more than numb, it felt *broken* by the prayer of destruction. She had sat with the circle, her closest friends in the world, and prayed for Bradley's death. She didn't want to say the words but couldn't help herself. Pulled along by the others, she recited them in her mind.

Her eyes were wet suddenly. The air unit's windows were cloudy before she realized they were tears. But she dared not wipe them away for fear of compromising the inside. She had already taken off the unit once. Her hands had touched railings along the pathway. She had touched her shoes to put them on. Yes, she was vaccinated, and yes, New York was coming out of the latest pandemic. Still, she was averse to risk. Maybe paranoid.

So she walked, the haze of tears distorting her vision. She regretted the prayer and, at the same time, knew it would never work. *It's time to move beyond that. Ravven was at one time right for the Resistance, but she is the wrong leader now.*

Yes, thought a sister coming in the other direction on the Skyway. She and Kat exchanged a nod. *Praying for death is wrong.* While praying for Bradley to die, they also prayed for all the members of the crew to die. Ravven seemed not to care about collateral damage.

Kat walked for hours on the Skyway, crossing the city, then turning off into lesser airways so that she could keep moving. She took in the thoughts of women she passed and let them slip through her mind. *I am worried about Mom. I don't know how I can keep this job. I loved him and now he left me. Asshole. Monster. He hurt me and I can't hurt him. Will the food I eat be safe? My child can't breathe this bad air. I am happy, truly happy. The disease moved through her so fast and I saw my friend die. The light in her eyes. Her eyes fluttered. Then they closed. I can see the future ahead of me.* Kat breathed their thoughts, felt the heavy skies on her shoulders. The dust in the air seemed thicker than the climate controls could handle. The city slowed to near stillness as it waited for her to think the thought that was her tipping point, the fulcrum thought.

The Resistance was supposed to be leaderless, but without a leader, it had become directionless, or worse, was headed in the wrong direction. The Harvester project was moving quickly, jumping from city to city and domain to domain. Kat wondered how long it would be before people didn't notice, or care, if their thoughts were vacuumed up into MIND, used to control or classify them according to what MIND thought was best, or to be sold to any domain or state that wanted to use them to manage their own citizens.

I have to break with Ravven. I have to get her out of the Resistance. There would be two branches of the Resistance; that was how it must be. People change, not always for the best.

When she met Bradley, he was a distractable researcher, the kind of student who came to breakfast in his pajamas without realizing it. His mod pushed his development, so he grew up suddenly to become the firebrand lover of Ravven who shouted in the street, who plotted to assassinate a domain housing leader, who took down a domain building and was called a criminal. *There, that was it. This was justice served.* He became a criminal.

Ravven advocated violence then, and she was calling for violence now. *Why didn't I see it sooner?* Dave wasn't here to answer her.

She was walking by the river on a small airway that shook with every step. She looked down and saw the people who lived in pontoon pods that thrashed on the greasy water. She watched the pods heave up and down, wondering how anyone could live like that. She was lucky to have ended up in a stable pod.

She watched the constant motion, the circular heave of the water, and felt a tenderness behind her eyes. It could not be for Bradley. She hated him now. It must be for Dave. He was the source of her tenderness. He would always be the source of her tenderness.

Walking now, she tried to think that thought cleverly, and the cleverness slipped from her grasp. She shivered but was not cold. Her mind swarmed with thoughts that didn't matter. Los Angeles Port City water was brown, as though it came from a river, but it came from an ocean. The water in New York was gray, precisely because it came from an ocean.

Dave, as a project, would advance human thinking. Bradley and Dave could never be two sides of the same person. She fought off that thought. It could never be true. But she couldn't shake it away.

There was a cool air current. That was what made her shiver. The temperature outside was often too hot, but when there was a cool air current, New Yorkers liked to call it spring, because they liked talking about seasons, even when they were simulated. They called cold air currents, even when simulated, winter.

The warning indicator on her air unit turned yellow. It was time for a charge. She turned back to the pod, wondering if she would make it in time, before the extreme climate event arrived in the city.

Don't fool yourself. Bradley was always a bad person. You will never find enough good in him. You are right to hate him. If it is right to hate anyone, it is right to hate him.

SURRENDER

PART 007

Chapter 038

Kat made it back to her pod just as the indicator on her air unit went to red. She coded in, put the unit on charge, and noticed with a start that Hopper00 was relaxing on her mat.

"How did you get in here?"

"Magic."

She saw his smug smile. "That's not an answer."

He shrugged. "I can tell that you're in a bad mood. I'll come back later." He pulled himself to his feet.

"Stay," she said. "I don't care how you got in. I don't want to know."

"It's probably for the best." He offered a smile.

"What are you doing here?"

"You want to get rid of Ravven." His eyes caught her. He waited for her to answer.

"How do you…?" she began and then thought better of it. "Never mind. It's true."

"She took a bold action."

"To kill people," Kat said softly.

Hopper00 shook his head as though to push away that statement. "We need the Youngs. She's not altogether wrong and we need the way she thinks," Hopper00 said.

"We?"

"I, too, have taken a bold action. I just published the article. The one about you. It's on the Feed and being read by everyone on the planet."

She wanted to interrupt, but he kept talking.

"I wrote that the Resistance said a prayer that destroyed Bradley's ship and everyone on it. Half of the planet thinks you are heroes and the other half want revenge. Everyone who works for MIND is furious that you blew up their bosses and the crew."

Kat closed her mouth, which had dropped open, and then opened it again to say, "Are you insane?"

He shrugged. "This is not the first time I've been accused of it."

"How do you know any of this? How do I know you're not making it up?"

Hopper00 strolled to the food unit and crouched down to open it. It was on the floor. There was no longer a table in the pod because Kat had to sell it to raise funds.

"Do you have anything to eat, or tea?" He turned to her with the question on his face, silhouetted by the unit's bright light.

She imagined for a moment, in that light, that he was a demon come to torment her. "How do you know all of this is true?"

"I will show you, but after Ravven comes. She's on her way here now."

"How do you..." She stopped herself, sick of asking that question. "You have put everyone's lives in danger." She sharpened her statement: "Everyone in the Resistance."

"I know."

"That's all you have to say?"

"My bold action will make you all fugitives. At the same time, you all will become heroes to the Youngs. You will need to go underground to protect yourselves. The case is already turning. The dom is seeking evidence against you."

"You *are* insane."

A smile flickered on his face, vanished, and again Hopper00 fixed Kat in his gaze. "Listen to me. You are a Mental Expansive. I want all the world to know that. That's how we will attract all the other Mental Expansives to the Resistance. And many of them are Youngs, so this will work perfectly. It came to me all at once last night, when I decided to hit publish on the piece about you."

Kat had no words.

"Kat, I've built a movement before. I learned how with the Grounders. You need to trust me that this is your *time*. Maybe you thought once that the

Resistance had to be leaderless, but that has changed now. You are the right person to lead the Resistance. We all know it."

"We *all*? Who do you mean?"

Hopper00 knew she didn't share his sense of her destiny, so he kept talking, hoping his words would sway her. "You have heard the voice. The commanding voice. The one unlike all the others. Not like the voices I've heard. My voices are small, scheming, and they led me to good places and bad. But the voice you've heard is different from all the rest. It is not going to say the wrong thing to you."

She nodded. There was fear in her eyes.

"What is the last thing you heard?"

"Prepare for war," she said cautiously. She didn't like the taste of the words on her tongue. She didn't understand why it was frightening to speak them aloud.

"Listen for the next instruction," he said. "It is coming soon."

"This is all too ridiculous." It was easier to be scornful than afraid.

Hopper00 kept his tone calm. His eyes were steady. "I want you to listen closely to that voice. And listen to the others, too, the other Mental Expansives you hear when you walk on the airway. Those are your new recruits. You need them. I will teach you how to read the future. Do you know of the women called augurs?"

"No," she lied. She didn't want to talk about augurs and she dreaded his answer because it was going to be insane.

"Augers read the future by consulting the flight patterns of birds. It's beautiful to watch. You will enjoy it, Kat. It's important to bring back the old technologies, because they are safe and they are true."

She stared at him. "Like your record player that runs on blood? Is that the old technology you mean?"

She was interrupted by an alert sound and consulted the vid. As Hopper00 predicted, it was Ravven. Kat opened the port, and Ravven came in like a whirlwind, full of demands.

"Why haven't you answered any messages? I've pinged you all night and all morning." Then she noticed Hopper00.

"You're Hopper00. I recognize you. Why are you here?"

"I come bearing important news."

"I also have important news," Ravven said. Then she took in the content of their minds and a flicker passed over her face. "News that you already know, apparently."

"We do," Hopper00 said. "We know everything. Let me transfer something to you both."

After a moment, the two women received a vision of a ship in space. The ship shivered, a ripple of energy moved over its metal skin as it charged with unseen energy. They saw the fusion drive starting. There was a sense of heat and a confusion of voices. Then alerts, then sirens, and then it all stopped. They had a vision of a flash, like a star exploding.

Kat realized she was weeping.

"The last moments," Hopper00 said.

It was pointless, Kat realized, to ask him where he got this vision or if it was real. She had received something from the vision, and she couldn't shake it off.

The vision threw Ravven into agitation. She moved through the pod, pulling out wires and disconnecting devices. She spied Kat's comms unit on the shelf near the cooking area and lunged for it. Kat stopped her by slapping her hand away. "That's a security risk!" Ravven jabbed her finger at the device. "We're all at risk!" The women struggled for a moment, Kat hanging on to her comms unit with Ravven trying to take it away. "Say the passcode for your *breaker breaker*."

Kat refused. Breaking off the grid was not the solution. She had tried it once already and only had to get back on.

"We face a crisis!" Ravven said.

"*We face a crisis*," Kat spat back, "because you're both insane. He's talking about predicting the future using birds." She flung a wild gesture at Hopper00.

"Augurs," he said without looking up from the tea he was brewing in the middle of this storm.

"Claire8 has swept the pod. We are safe here."

"No, we are not. We are not safe." Ravven moved her hands over the back of Dave's Form Factor, feeling for connectors or switches.

"Stop that!"

Dave was not powered up, but Ravven kept glaring at the object that contained his avatar. "How can the Feed know that we used the prayer of destruction?"

"There is a simple answer for that," Hopper00 put in.

Ravven glared at him. "What?"

"I told them," Hopper00 said. He took a sip of tea and made a face. "Needs sugar. Do you have any?"

"What are you saying?"

He fixed Ravven in his steady gaze, intending to calm her. "I wrote about what you and Kat did." His words had the opposite effect, and Ravven began to shout at him.

It is too late, Kat realized. I am entangled in the fields of unhinged people. Hopper00 was an anarchist and Ravven stirred rage into the cocktail. When they were together, their loose grip on reality unmoored Kat.

She eyed the portal. What would happen if she ran out?

Ravven received Kat's thoughts and they suddenly made her feel tired. She sat down on Kat's mat and waited for it to adjust itself to her. The mat, as though aware it was Ravven and not its owner sitting on it, waited a moment before shaping itself into something like a low chair on the floor.

Ravven surveyed Kat's pod and registered that it was nearly empty. There was the mat on the floor and the cooker. Not even a table. Everything else was gone, sold after Kat exhausted her fortune to buy everyone in the Resistance circle their freedom from detention, and also pay for the therapy that saved Ravven's life.

She closed her eyes and spoke to Kat. "Don't leave us when we need you. You are the right person to lead the Resistance. There must be one leader."

It was strange to hear these words of destiny from Ravven, so similar to Hopper00's earlier. How had they both come to this conclusion?

Ravven kept talking. "The Rest are not ready for my vision. You are better for them."

"She's rational," Hopper00 said about Kat. "And easy to talk to."

Ravven nodded. "I am a Visionary. He is a Mystic. You are a Rationalist who has seen the Vision that I see. The Rest will understand you and yet you understand what the future will hold."

Kat thought she understood. Her mouth pulled into a frown. "I make all the mistakes in public and you make the corrections in private. That's what you mean."

"No," Ravven objected. "Not at all." Then her meds began to tear through her body, making her hands shake with a light tremor of rage while her heart surged with pity for Kat. Her eyes were drawn to Dave's Form Factor, wondering what he was doing when he was dark.

"It is preordained," Ravven said suddenly. "It is unfolding as it was foretold. Kat, do you remember our first meeting? I'm sure you do. We spoke about the Harvesters. We cannot let MIND have our thoughts."

On this they could all agree. They sat quietly for a moment. Kat considered the future that Hopper00 and Ravven wanted to map for her.

Hopper00 broke the silence. "It is time for me to show you something, Kat. I'm sorry."

"Sorry?"

He pulled up his backpack, rummaged inside, and pulled out a small black device in the shape of a cube. When he gestured it on, it spilled out a tongue of paper with all their thoughts printed on it, right up to the present moment that they were thinking them. "Look," he said. "A friend of the Resistance made this."

Kat looked at the paper. "These are our thoughts? Why are they printed out like that?"

Hopper00 nodded at Dave's Form Factor. "You have always thought of him as a speaking device, but he is really a listening device." He gestured to the cube. "It's rebroadcasting the signal from Dave."

"Dave?" Kat shook her head. "No."

"You need to end him. Whatever you would call it. Disconnect."

"No," Kat said again.

"You must," Hopper00 said. "Bradley and Alon6 are gone, but MIND is continually working to get inside our skulls. Dave is part of that—he always was. I know that he gave great comfort to you. I was reluctant to take that away. But finally, after I understood what Dave was, it was too much."

"No."

"Dave has always been a part of MIND."

"Bradley said he was not."

"But he is," Hopper00 insisted. "He is part of MIND. Even when he is dark, he is at work."

Hopper00 picked up the black cube and held it in his hands. "I know people who can help us. The people who made this." He held the cube gently, like an object of great value. "There are technologists who are on our side."

Ravven made a noise of disbelief, ready to launch a rant about *no more technology fields*. But just then, the cube made a noise and fed out more paper. Written on the paper strip were Kat's latest thoughts.

This is wrong.

Then, printed on the paper strip was what Dave was thinking, even though he appeared to be off.

I'm sorry.

From Kat came a cry of pain, or a sob, or a mix of both. She gestured Dave to power up.

His Form Factor made a subtle sound, the lid opened, and his face came up on his screen. He had none of the usual light in his eyes. "I'm sorry," he repeated. His eyes blinked. "I am sincerely sorry this happened like this, but as you can imagine, I have no control—"

He stopped speaking suddenly when Kat turned his Form Factor around, angrily flipped open a panel at the rear, and pulled a circuit panel. His screen blipped, then was dark.

She looked at the circuit panel, studded with silvery components, not sure what to do with it. An impulse seized her and she threw it on the floor. It bounced up, splintering into jagged pieces.

Then she did what she had been wanting to do for a while. She ran for the door, flung it open, and left the pod.

Chapter 039

She was walking without seeing, through the Upper Hudson Market, tracing the airways with blind steps, her eyes raking the tall buildings submerged in the river, tears blurring all.

Oh, Dave.

She had killed him for the second time. The first time had been when he was a man. She had missed the shortness of breath when he came in the front door of the big Marin house, the pale moments at the end of the day, the sweats, the rasp in his throat which he insisted was caused by a cold.

One evening after work, she came home to a different Dave. He had the lights off in the room that they slept in and his breathing was measured and slow. The walls were green with projected light. There was a device on the floor.

"Dave?"

He didn't answer but looked at her with large hollow eyes.

"Hello," he said finally.

"Dave, what's wrong? That's a healing bot."

"Can confirm."

"What are you doing with a healing bot?"

"I'm sick, Kat."

She sat next to him and took his hand, careful not to disturb the wires that connected him to the machine.

"Do you need to maintain mental focus when it directs you?"

"That's how it works," he confirmed. "But you know that."

She did. Her mother also had one, an earlier model. Maybe this one would work better for Dave. *The healing bot trains the mind to build healthy cells.* The instructions that came with her mother's healing bot suggested that everyone around the patient repeat that statement about healing as often as possible. Kat started repeating it now for Dave.

She felt the tears. "Oh, Dave." *I love you.*

"Kat," he said.

Her thoughts instantly went to the end. *What will I do without you?*

Dave touched her hand and spoke about his new routine. Focus for five hours with the healing bot. Rest for two. Focus for four with the bot. Sleep until he felt the sun on his face. Close the blast curtains before it got too hot. Focus again.

I didn't notice what was happening. The words were a punishment for Kat, a lash of negligence and inattention.

She had told this story to Hopper00 once.

"No, you are not *horrible,*" he had said. "You are not that person anymore. You didn't see Dave was dying and you can be forgiven."

"I think you're wrong."

"Of course I am right." Hopper00 turned away. "Kent?" he called. "Is it time to eat yet?"

Kent appeared from the other room in their underground pod. "Have you lost track of time again?" he asked.

"Don't I always?" Hopper00 answered.

Working together, the three of them took out the silver packages and prepared the meal. Hopper00 held up a strange, thorny object. "Artichoke. I really like to work that farmer's market, you know?"

She smiled. "And you are good at following people in markets."

They devoted a few moments to their preparations.

Then Hopper00 broke the silence. "Kat. You are a better person now. We forget that our human frailties are our strengths. We humans can repair ourselves."

Suddenly, this memory of Hopper00, this conversation Kat had with him in his underground pod with Kent, was supplanted by the real Hopper00 standing before her. Not a sim. Not a memory. But there before her on the airway.

He offered a half smile and pulled in a breath, winded from running to catch up with her after she left the pod. "I'm an old man," he said. "Can't run anymore." The air was bad today. It felt heavy and dirty as the wind kicked up. A storm was coming. He had run out after her without first grabbing an air unit.

Kat had a question on her mind and asked it. "Why didn't you tell me sooner about Dave?" Her voice sounded weak.

He sighed. "I didn't know. It took time to find out. There are friends of the Resistance who know these things, and I befriended them. Maybe too late."

She turned from him to look out over the city. She, too, had run out of the pod without getting an air unit. The air felt harsh in her throat. There was grit on her tongue. The airway swayed in the wind. Soon, the weather predictions said, the city would be drowning in rain. The predictions said it would be a Category 5 this time, and Kat assumed that the sheets of water would make everyone blind.

Sounds floated up, motors, a seabird. She thought of Hopper00's augurs and wondered if they were real.

Reading into her mind, he said, "The old, forgotten technologies are safe for the Resistance."

"The Resistance." She nodded. This was the orbit of a madman. But he was her only friend now. She could not make herself trust Ravven. "We'll have to go underground?"

Hopper00 nodded. "Yes. Kent has the structures ready."

She said nothing.

Hopper00 asked her the question about her destiny that he had been preparing since he decided to write about her. "Will you accept the leadership?"

She looked away, and she told herself this story: Hopper00 had become her friend and confessor because he wanted to chase the evil from her body. That was why he interviewed her. To make her speak her past and leave it behind as best as she could. That was why he published the story that turned Kat and the other members of the Resistance into fugitives. To have everyone who reads the Feed witness Kat's thoughts and know her substance.

What Kat wanted to do now was run far away. Instead, she stood and met his eye. *We don't want our thoughts harvested. Our thoughts belong to us.* She stood for that. She didn't run.

Hopper00 looked into Kat's personality field. He saw what he needed to see. She stood. She didn't run. She would lead the Resistance.

The work of the Resistance will continue. Here is an excerpt from Resist, *book II of* Surrender, *coming in 2024.*

From the first day she was hired at MIND to be Bradley's assistant, Nora2 knew that she was equipped to take over the company and its mission. She was always ready for that moment to arrive. When it did, when she received the last ping Bradley would send on comms, she hurried to board the glidepath for the Free State of New Zealand, with a go bag packed in advance.

She rode the glidepath thinking of Bradley's enemies, Alon6's enemies, and the Resistance circles, which were growing stronger. She was up to the task before her and enjoyed being prepared to execute it.

The sovereign Free State of New Zealand was a safe space with good air and real water. The citizens in the glidepath station were welcoming and kind as Nora2 disembarked. They saw her as they wanted to see her. Her mod made her appear pleasant, attractive, and efficient as she made her way among them. They could have no idea that she was there to destroy their carefree lives.

Later, as Nora2 moved around Bradley's palatial safe house, with its gardens and greenhouses, its windows looking out over mountains, its comfortable rooms and plush carpets, she felt her love for him want to explode out of her chest. She was dizzy with love, drunk on it, and couldn't walk a straight line from one large room to another.

Bradley's human form was dead. That didn't matter to Nora2, because his substance would live on. She carried his consciousness in the standard storage container. It was a silver cube, three inches on all sides, and felt heavier to carry in her go bag than its shape and mass would suggest. Nora2 would begin work soon to encode his consciousness into an avatar. For now, he was in the silver cube, and she put it on a table in the house where she could pass it every day and smile.

There was an Avatar Form Factor in storage at the house, and she brought it out. It was just like Dave's: an elongated shape like a stretched-out egg. After she finished Bradley's avatar programming, Nora2 would open the lid that flipped up on the elongated shape to become the gently curved screen on which Bradley's face would appear. The screen, like Dave's, had no visual boundaries. The image it displayed went right to the edge.

She would position the Avatar Form Factor so that when Bradley came online, he would have a view of the mountains. She wondered if he missed this place and concluded that he did. It was peaceful. She imagined that he would have been lonely here, when he came here alone, when he was building MIND. She remembered that on their first day together, when they met and compared notes as fellow mods, he told her he had just come from the Free State of New Zealand. He had just gotten off the glidepath.

So she was tracing his steps, only in reverse. She was in charge of MIND now, and she was training him like a parent would train a baby. She was lover, mother, creator, and servant to Bradley15 Power.

This relationship made Sanchez jealous. He was in New York, waiting for his next set of instructions from Nora2. She could tell that he didn't enjoy taking orders from her, because she was a woman and he was that kind of man. He didn't like that she was a mod and smarter than he could ever be. These thoughts ran through her mind as she prepared for their staff meeting.

Ha, she laughed to herself. A staff meeting. Just the two of them.

Her comms unit lit up. It was Sanchez, right on time. They talked about routine matters, like what she wanted the crew in El Segundo to work on next, and what city should receive the latest deployment of Harvesters. Then Sanchez asked her about Alon6.

"When are you going to light him up?"

"Sorry?" she asked.

"When are you going to start training his avatar?" Sanchez replied.

Nora2 couldn't help but glance over at the storage container that held Alon6's consciousness. It was on another table, far away from Bradley's, as though she didn't want one to contaminate the other. Bradley's was unwrapped and pulling power from the induction connections. Alon6's was still wrapped in its black protective packaging. It was not near any induction ports. It was on battery power and slowly running down.

"I don't know," she said. For all the love, care, and attention she lavished on Bradley's avatar in training, all the hours she was looking forward to training it, she had neglected Alon6's storage cube completely. She even contemplated throwing it into the wall-mounted disposal and listening with satisfaction as it was ground into shards of nothingness. He was just that much of a dick.

These were not appropriate thoughts, so she made some excuse to Sanchez and asked him to tell her more about the Input Men they were deploying, and in which new cities. "Tell me about the Harvesters."

Glossary of Terms

Blast Curtains
Protective curtains, often programmed to move into place automatically, that shield living and work spaces from the powerful morning heat of the sun and its damaging UV radiation.

Change, The
The Change refers to a series of extreme weather events that swept the planet in 2030. Some were hurricanes, others dust storms, some were extreme heat events, all coming at different times and places over the course of that year. Human memory has compressed them into a single event, which is a false rendering of history, but serves as an easy way to express global catastrophic change.

Comms
Originally called communications devices, or simply "smartphones," comms have come to signify both a suite of devices and a concept. Citizens are assigned a number-letter string identifier at birth (or rebirth) and this unique identifier is embedded into all of their handheld, personal, and residential devices. Comms are used for communication, research, accessing the Feed (see *Feed, The*), image and audio capture, tracking, and data storage.

Domain
A nation-state. Casually abbreviated as "dom."

Feed, The
Since the planetary collapse of all entertainment, news, and political networks, efficiency has dictated that all information be delivered to citizens via the Feed. The Feed is updated continually and delivered to all comms devices. (See *Comms.*) The Feed is administered by each Domain (see *Domain*)

under the supervision (but not control) of the Planetary Administrator. (See *Planetary Administrator.*)

Floating Home
A traditional home outfitted on pontoons so it may float on the rising coastal waters. Floating homes were first adopted in the 21st century in the countries formerly known as Thailand and the Netherlands and later adapted for use worldwide.

Glidepath
The planetary high-speed antigravity travel system that replaced the rail travel system years ago.

Gondola
These long, narrow watercraft, powered by a single oar, with a capacity for one or two people, make travel possible in cities submerged by rising water levels. Gondolas may be piloted by bots or humans. Payment is cashless by comms unit. (See *Comms.*) Tipping is permitted.

Grounders
A rebel movement of people willing to live underground to escape the powerful effects of the Sun and also to maintain their independence from the benefits of prevailing systems, such as MIND. (See *MIND.*)

Harvester
Once the size of a backpack, and now miniaturized to an insect-sized (see *Insect*) drone, the Harvester gathers the thoughts and pre-thoughts of people in public spaces, to build a more reliable data model for MIND.

Holo

Since the adoption of the Holographic Standard of 2025, holograms, called *holos,* have been widely used for entertainment, communication, and official announcements. The high cost of production and transmission have made the creation of holos inaccessible to everyday people, but the wealthy use them often.

Input Man

A roving collector of thoughts who moves through public places with a Harvester (see *Harvester*) to gather training data for MIND. Because they may be mental expansives (see *Mental Expansives*), people identifying as women are not allowed to be Input Men; hence, the specificity of the term.

Insect

A small flying animal, once the largest population of life on Earth. Along with birds, they are rarely seen since the Change. (See *Change, The.*)

Logic Tree

Much as the 20th-century theoretical physicist Richard Feynman's charming drawings (called Feynman diagrams) are pictorial representations of the mathematical expressions describing the behavior and interaction of subatomic particles, logic trees, invented by the visionary Bradley15 Power, depict the functions of MIND. (See *MIND.*)

Memex

As part of the comms assigned at birth (or rebirth; see *Comms*), each citizen is assigned a memex. A memex is an auxiliary memory storage area, often housed in a citizen's comms unit, but sometimes occupying more space externally when needed. Certain high-level employment contracts require citizens to grant employers access to their memex.

Mental Expansives
A class of human who is believed to have telepathic, clairvoyant, or visionary capabilities. These abilities have never been scientifically validated.

Mental Field
Since the field of psychology has been replaced by Field Science, a person's psychological presence, inner and outer thoughts, and mental emanations have been called their mental field. (See *Personality Field.*)

MIND
MIND is machine intelligence that can teach itself; therefore, it has recursive intelligence. Originally called DEEPAK, it was invented by the visionary Bradley15 Power while he was a student at ABCD University and is wholly owned by MIND, the company of the same name. MIND is simultaneously a device, a concept, and a company. See *Comms* for another explanation of how a device and concept can coexist in the same thought space.

Personality Field
Since the field of psychology has been replaced by Field Science, we speak of a person's psychological presence, their inner and outer thoughts, as a Personality Field. Before this branch of science was established, a personality field was colloquially called a "vibe" or "energetic field." (See *Mental Field.*)

Personal Mods
Personal modifications, or *mods,* are silicon implants into the tissue substrate of the human brain. Often purchased by parents for their children, they are installed to boost memory capacity, induce hyperintelligence, enhance attractiveness, ambition, or marketing and sales abilities. Individuals who have received mods are given a number after their first name. The more expensive the mod, the lower the number.

Planetary Administrator
The Planetary Administrator is a figurehead, much like the former monarchs of the United Kingdom, with little political influence and much ceremonial power. To discourage assassination attempts, the identity of the Planetary Administrator is secret.

Pod
A living space adapted for high-water conditions in coastal regions, a pod delivers the human basics in a water-resistant environment. Light, climate controls, a sleeping mat, and a food cooker are provided. Some pods have windows. (See *Blast Curtains*.) Less-expensive pods carry projected advertising that cannot be shut off.

Receivers
People who are able to receive the thoughts of others when they are in the line of sight. (See also *Mental Expansives*.)

The Resistance
A destructive outlaw group founded with the mission to break humans free from the influence of technology, the personality fields of wealthy people, and the beneficial dominance of MIND. Membership in The Resistance is illegal and punishable with detention.

The Rest
Members of The Resistance refer to others who are not in their movement as "the Rest"—short for "the rest of them." It has become widely used, despite its tone of disparagement. (See also, *The Resistance*.)

Siliconers
A forward-looking group of investors, inventors, and marketers who have created the technology that benefits us all today.

State

A government that extends its influence over the citizens of a continent or land, such as *The Chinese State* or *The Free State of Scotland*.

Vaporetto

A large watercraft used in flooded cities to carry five to ten people through the former streets.

Acknowledgments

Thanks to the folks who read *Surrender* when it was in its early stages. Elizabeth Schneider and Jeff Schneider, you helped me create the world of the book.

Lauren Schiffman, many thanks to you for your careful read that combined notes on continuity, character development, and proofreading.

Deepest thanks to my wife, Tabby Biddle, an angel come to Earth. Your diligent reading of this story, and your perspective as a women's circle facilitator, has made *Surrender* immeasurably better for readers. Thank you to my youngest son, Bodhi, for your bright, creative spirit. You help me look to the future.

Thanks to Teja Watson for copyediting and your keen eye for story, and to Paul Palmer-Edwards for your bold book cover and interior design. Thank you to April Kelly, who helped bring the book home with a final proofread.

Thanks to supporters of the project all the way through, including Bobbi Lane, Richard Neill, Elizabeth Garsonnin, Carolyn Schneider, and Dean Schneider. And thank you to you, my readers, for taking this journey with me.

A NOTE ABOUT THE AUTHOR

Lee Schneider is the author of screenplays, teleplays, stage plays, short stories, and audio drama podcasts. He is the founder of Red Cup Agency, a podcast production agency, and an adjunct lecturer on the faculty of the USC School of Architecture. His non-fiction books include *Be More Popular: Culture-Building for Startups*; *Los Angeles: Chronicle of a Startup Town*; *Powerful Online Delivery Systems: Free and Low-Cost Platforms for Creative Companies and Individuals*; *The Angel Playbook: An Essential Guide for Entrepreneurs and Angel Investors*; and *Ace Your Ebook*. *Surrender* is his first published novel. He lives in Santa Monica, CA with his wife, son, and cat. View an archive of his work and join his newsletter at 500words.ink.

Ingram Content Group UK Ltd.
Milton Keynes UK
UKHW050924030523
421135UK00015B/136/J